FAREWELL INNOCENCE

PARTHIAN

LIBRARY OF WALES

William Glynne-Jones (1907–1977) was a novelist, children's writer, broadcaster and journalist. He was born and grew up in Llanelli and following school he worked at the Glanmor Foundry in the town. He left the foundry on medical grounds in 1943 and moved to London to pursue a career as a writer and journalist. During his time working in industry he developed his skills as a writer and observed and took part in much of the world he was later to use in his fiction. He wrote a number of novels of which *Farewell Innocence*, published in 1950, and followed by *Ride the White Stallion* in 1951, are semi-autobiographical accounts of the journey of Ieuan Morgan from foundry worker to man of letters.

FAREWELL INNOCENCE

WILLIAM GLYNNE-JONES

PARTHIAN

LIBRARY OF WALES

Parthian, Cardigan SA43 1ED
www.parthianbooks.com
The Library of Wales is a Welsh Government initiative which
highlights and celebrates Wales' literary heritage in the English language.
Published with the financial support of the Welsh Books Council.
www.thelibraryofwales.com
Series Editor: Dai Smith
First published in 1950
© William Glynne Jones
Library of Wales edition published 2016
Foreword © Huw Lawrence
ISBN: 978-1-910901-30-4
Cover Art: *April Morning, Wet Pavements* by John Bowen. With kind permission
of the estate of John Bowen and Carmarthenshire Museums Service Collection.
The painting is in the collection at the Parc Howard Museum and Art Gallery.
Typeset by Elaine Sharples
Printed and bound by Pulsio SARL

FOREWORD

I visited William Glynne-Jones, or Glyn as he was to all who knew him, at his modest, first floor flat in 10 Ossian Road in North London, in 1966. (The pen-name was to avoid confusion with his fellow novelist and friend, Glyn Jones). Maybe I arrived early, for there were plates on the table with kipper bones from breakfast. Glyn and his wife Doris both worked. Glyn had an exhibition of paintings showing in a local library. I'd had no idea he painted. I remember him from that visit as an unassuming but unexpectedly emotional man capable of sudden, vociferous bursts of humour. I was a hopeful practitioner of fiction, visiting a writer friend of my father's. My father and Glyn had worked for many years together as steel moulders in the Glanmôr Foundry, called Bevan's Foundry in Glyn's two autobiographical novels, *Farewell Innocence* and *Ride the White Stallion*. They were books that opened my eyes to my father's rarely mentioned early life.

Farewell Innocence takes you into every department of the foundry. We see the crusher crushing silica bricks to be milled in the compo shed for making cores in the core shop. We visit the smithy and the fitting shop and the canteen. We see the casting process. We get a feel of how everyone had his own little preserve to defend and how everyone knew what everyone else's job entailed. We see the slack, the ways the men eased off by sitting on the lavatory or hiding in sheds. We hear conversations, wise, ignorant, ironic. We see the apprentices amusing themselves, cruelly using living animals to make moulds of frogs or rats for casting in lead.

Glyn mixes up street names and juggles locations in the town he calls Abermôr, but it is unmistakeably Llanelli, full of Llanelli-like nicknames for characters whose speech often makes for an odd kind of English, being direct translation and a reminder that the language of the Glanmôr Foundry and of Llanelli was Welsh. It was not the language of the 'County School', which became the 'Grammar School' I attended. The town in Glyn's books is certainly the one I grew up in, greatly changed though it is now. Tony Marasiano's shop was Bracchi's, and I recognise the Park Surgery with its row of bells and emblems bearing the doctors' names. The park is People's Park. The 'Monkey Parade' was still going strong in my day, the walk around Stepney Street and Broadway (now demolished) where teenage boys and girls gazed at each other and sometimes talked or even made a date. I remember, too, the Llanelli acknowledgement when you passed someone on the street, 'a quick, sideways toss of the head'. I remember the status accorded the front room, or 'parlour'. The class system, too: "Like one of them boys from the cold rolls you are. No manners, no respect and no brains." In my day the girls who worked in 'The Stamping' — the tin-stamping works referred to in the book — were called 'common'. Their appearance was very much as described by Glyn. They were the salt of the earth.

I remember the hooters. The tin-workers' 'crys bach' was worn by my grandfather. I would walk as a young child past the Old Lodge and the still operating Marshfield tinworks on my way to my grandmother's in Glanmôr Road, in what Glyn calls "the dingy houses grouped outside the boundary wall of the foundry." My father had no more than a few yards to travel for his first day at work, at fourteen. Nor did my grandmother have very far to go just nine years earlier when, as I was told, she 'picked up her skirts' and ran with other women to the station gates to see if her husband had been shot. Six men died in 1911, in the so-called 'Llanelli Riots', two of them shot. My father was five and Glyn eight months younger when five thousand men came out in support of five hundred rail workers, who worked a seventy-two hour week for less than £1. It was not an isolated event. From 1910 to 1914 troops and police were used by government in massive and combative confrontations with industrial workers across Great Britain. 'The Great Unrest', fuelled by deprivation, hunger and injustice, was only halted by the Great War of 1914 to 1918.

Glyn wrote about the period that followed on: the inter-war era when industrial managers again took to seeking more work for less pay, just as if The Great Unrest had never happened. Some of that pre-war momentum reared up again in the form of the 1926 General Strike. Glyn and my father were nineteen, obviously involved. Real improvements in working class lives would only come after the Second World War ended in 1945. In *Farewell Innocence* an old foundry worker tells Glyn's protagonist, Ieuan Morgan, how improved things are since his youth. Yet, covering the years 1923-1925, *Farewell Innocence* describes a part of town where rat-infested houses flood and the furniture is made of tea chests, though the rents paid to chapel-going landlords were still high. He describes a wretched young couple making their way towards the workhouse, their paltry possessions piled in a pram. While this clearly happened in my home town, I find it hard to believe that only one generation separates me from what Glyn records. Did I reflect when I was young how lucky my generation was that a new socialist government had emerged to gift us the NHS, the Welfare State and the education denied to Glyn and my father? No, we all took it for granted! Looking back, I see this to be the main difference between me and that friend of my father's whom I visited in his small flat in 10 Ossian Road.

In *Farewell Innocence,* Ieuan is an adolescent, observing, thinking and learning. "The conceptions and theories of socialism were still vague to him." In the sequel, *Ride the White Stallion*, he is an agitator, worrying his wife by publishing inflammatory letters in the local newspaper, as Glyn himself did. And, after a day's work in the foundry, he was writing stories, and attracting wider attention. His talent did not go unnoticed. His creed, though, was already formed. There is one piece of outside evidence as to Glyn's politics, a letter of introduction in 1944 to the influential public figure Thomas Jones (TJ), president of the university at Aberystwyth at the time. It was written by an education inspector in Cardiff named W.J. Williams. The letter states: "... I think that this is eminently a case where we ought to try to do something if we can. The young man is certainly, decidedly 'left', if not communist, in his make-up, but he is none the worse for that." (William Glynne-Jones Papers, National Library of Wales).

Like other Welsh working class novelists of his generation writing in English in this period, Glyn was mainly self-taught, and the inappropriate model available to them was the English middle-class novel, which focused on individual relationships rather than community. Yet our novelists produced biting political indictments of a Britain in which close-knit, Welsh working-class communities were repressed by ignorance and poverty. Rather than dwell on stylistic imperfections we should celebrate the few voices in our literature who managed to express the humanity they saw in the grinding work and domestic penury around them. Work, in pit, tin works and foundry, was life-giver and death-bringer in that almost forgotten Wales, which we should not forget but forever remember. Many books have been written about coal mining, but the only author I know of who gives a detailed, intimate picture of a steel foundry — no less essential a part of our history than coal — is William Glynne-Jones.

A children's book by Glyn, presented to my father in 1949, has an inscription indicating that my father shared Glyn's feelings about the foundry, and I know he did. But I suspect these feelings were stronger in Glyn, mocked as he was for a hare lip and speech impediment. His fictional protagonist stutters under pressure and Ieuan's account is unrelentingly joyless and bleak, until near the end of the book when he falls in love, and even that emotional release is portrayed as a threat to the matriculation he hopes to achieve through private study. We read of the remorseless pranks and bullying suffered by new apprentices, and of Ieuan's relationship with the domineering mother who took him out of the 'County School' two weeks before his matriculation exams. Rarely in literature do we encounter such hatred from a son towards his mother. *Farewell Innocence* is the bitterest 'coming-of-age novel' you will ever read. Yet, even so, the causes are finally presented as social, not personal. The bullying stems from the bullies' resentment of their own wasted lives, and Ieuan understands that having to fulfil her domestic responsibilities with never enough money is what has changed his mother into a hard-hearted nag. Neither Ieuan nor his author matriculated, but Glyn did escape the foundry, as did my father, via a teachers' training course when he was forty.

Glyn himself was not in fact plucked out of school, like Ieuan Morgan, just two weeks before his matriculation exams. According to a booklet written by his son, Dennis, Glyn left school at fifteen to work as a tea-boy in a chemical factory. So, we ask, what is the relationship between 'fiction' and 'truth' in an autobiographical novel? Glyn uses poetic licence to bring Ieuan very close to a different future from the one he (like Glyn) is fated to live through at the foundry. It is in fiction only, though, that this future is lost by a margin of just two weeks. In so heightening the drama, the connection between self-improvement and education is underlined. A young worker says to Ieuan in the foundry: "If I'd had the chance of a County School education I wouldn't be in this dump pushing a barrow." The point is that virtually no one who was working class had any real chance. Workers were kept in their place by being denied an education. The 'fictional' message was more important, Glyn knew, than the autobiographical 'truth'.

The same question arises in relation to the horrific accident described in the book. The 'true' event was dramatic enough, but Glyn's description is downright stomach-turning. In reality, the victim was a newly married young man who was doing my father's job, having asked for his overtime. He was 'splashed' with molten steel according to my father, who visited him in hospital where the man screamed with his hands tied down to prevent him tearing at his bandages. Glyn's version is even more dramatic and horrible, underlining what the Glanmôr Foundry could do to a worker.

Glyn made it to London in 1943, where he met and made friends with now well-known Welsh writers, and built a better life. When I met him twenty-three years later he still spoke with a Welsh accent and revealed cherished childhood memories of Llanelli. Looking back, I don't think he fully resolved the life he'd found with the life he'd left behind. His transplanting was perhaps less understood by him than by the generation that followed — my own. We encountered *en masse* (courtesy of the 1944 Education Act) both the benefits and uncertainties of this transition. For, effectively, it was a change of class and culture. That is why, for my generation, books like Glyn's help preserve our integrity. They underline the values embodied in the communities that have produced us and remind us, and those who will come after us, who we are and how we belong the one to the other.

Huw Lawrence

FAREWELL INNOCENCE

CHAPTER ONE

THE boy climbed slowly up the linoleumed stairway, his fingers lightly drumming on the polished banister rail.

A childish voice called: "Ieuan, is that you?"

He paused on the landing.

"Yes," he answered softly. "What d'you want?"

"Come in for a little while, please. Only just a while."

"Not tonight, Phyl. I'm tired. Tomorrow night, perhaps."

He crossed the landing to his own room.

"Ieuan!"

This time it was his elder sister's voice he heard.

"Oh heck, what's the matter, Gweneira?" he asked, impatiently.

"Little Phyllis wants a story. Aw, come in for a couple of minutes."

The tone was so pleading that it brought a smile to his face. These sisters of his — could he ever resist them? He tip-toed into the little bedroom they shared.

"Why don't you go to sleep?" he breathed urgently. "It's nearly half past nine, you know, and if mam hears you there'll be ructions. You don't want her to start shouting again, do you?"

Phyllis, a dark-haired child of six, sat up in bed. "Please tell us a story, Ieuan. Only a little one." She drew her plaits under her chin. "You told us one every night, haven't you?" she challenged.

Before he could reply, Gweneira leaned forward and caught him by the sleeve.

"Why didn't you come up earlier?" she whispered. "We've been expecting you a long time ago, and I'd have gone to sleep but for Phyllis. You know she won't close her eyes till you've told her a story."

"I'm starting work tomorrow," he said gravely.

"Yes, there's nice," Phyllis piped, "an' you'll have long trousers like Idris Jenkins's got."

"Ay, and a tweed cap with a big peak, and a pair of dungarees, too. A swank you'll be, won't you?"

Ieuan was silent. The prospect of starting work worried him. Sadness, fear and apprehension — he had been inflicted with each emotion ever since his mother had pleaded with Mr. Bevan, the foundry manager, to give him an opportunity to learn a trade.

Without discussing the matter with dad, she had immediately gone to one of the cheapest clothing shops in town and bought a dungaree suit, a workman's peaked cap, navy blue flannel shirt, and a pair of heavy, hobnailed boots.

"You start in Bevan's foundry on Monday," she said, with finality. "I'll write a note for you to take to Griffiths Headmaster in the morning. You've been in school long enough, and I see no sense in keeping you there much longer. Nearly sixteen, you are, and plenty of schooling you've had to last a lifetime. There's five bellies to feed in this house, and what money I get from your father goes like water. Poor as church mice we are, indeed."

Her attitude had startled him. He had expected to go to work some day. All his pals were employed in the tinplate mills and factories scattered about the town and the surrounding districts.

But to have so short a notice! The Junior Examination was to be held in a fortnight's time, and Mr. Griffiths had confidently predicted that he would pass with honours. The headmaster had impressed upon him the importance of this exam., for on its result would depend his matriculating. Success would establish a secure foundation on which his future career might be built.

The work he had in mind had no connection with the steel foundry or any other form of hard, manual labour.

His tastes ran to art and literature, and in one of these spheres he had often dreamt of finding a place for himself. He realized that it would mean years of study, but he was ready and eager to apply himself to the task so that he might achieve his ambition.

To dad he had confessed this, and was encouraged by the

8

advice given him. But when mam came back from the interview with Mr. Bevan and told him what had been arranged, dad had said nothing — just sat in his chair, staring at the fire, while she kept on stressing what a difference the twelve and threepence a week was going to make.

"Story ...."

Ieuan sat down on the edge of the bed. A small white hand plucked at his sleeve.

"Which one are you going to say tonight?"

"Oh, for goodness' sake tell her a story or I'll never go to sleep," Gweneira urged.

Ieuan lay back across the bed and rested his shoulder against the wall. He could sense their childish expectancy as they waited patiently in the darkness.

"Sorry," he said after a while, "but I can't tell you a story tonight, Phyl. I'm too tired, honest I am."

"Aw, don't be daft." Gweneira was peeved. "You haven't had no homework nor nothing, so how can you be tired?"

"But I am," he protested. "I just can't think .... Tell you what, though — I'll recite a piece of poetry. Will that be all right?"

Phyllis clapped her hands. "Oh, yes. Lovely."

"Then you promise to be quiet? No interruptions, and no questions, mind."

"No, I shan't ask nothing, and I shan't int'rupt. I'll be quiet like a little mouse, strike me down dead if I don't."

"And you, Gweneira. You promise, too?"

"Won't say a word. Cross my heart, spit three times, look-up-to-God-look-down-to-Jesus."

Ieuan slipped off the bed and stepped to the window. He looked down at the street corner, his nose flattened against the pane. Under the pale yellow circle of light from the lamp-post a shawled woman stood, her arms akimbo.

Davie Dan Daniel's mother. There was no mistaking the bunched shoulders, the long, aquiline nose, the buttoned boots, and the untidy ends of hair straggling from beneath the cap she wore.

He drew a hand across the window where his breath had clouded the glass. The woman pulled the shawl vigorously around her thin shoulders, and bending forward from the waist, inhaled deeply.

"Da-a-a-vie Dan-i-i-iel !" she sang, in a high, shrill soprano. "Da-a-a-vie Dan-i-i-iel !"

She called again and again, stamping her foot on the pavement as if to emphasize the urgency of her call, her anger and impatience. A passing tomcat, startled by the noise, arched its back and hissed, then scuttled into the shadows.

Presently, a tall, thin, bespectacled boy in a tattered raincoat fastened at the neck with a safety pin, and wearing boots many sizes too large for him, emerged from the darkness.

"Come here, you good-for-nothing. Why didn't you answer me when I called your name first time? Leavin' me to shout till my insides are wore out," Mrs. Daniel screeched. An arm flashed out and struck the boy across the cheek. "Where's your father, the waster?" she demanded. "Still boozing, is it?"

The boy hung his head.

"Been — been telling him to come home, I have, Mam," he whined. "He says for you to get his supper ready." The arm shot out again, and the boy ducked. Mrs. Daniel pointed up the street.

"Go home," she rasped, "an' to bed with you. I'll fetch the old pig myself. Get his supper ready indeed," she shouted to the deserted street. "Him and his Workmen's Club an' his beer! It's Sunday night. All decent people've been to chapel. But Aarfon Daniel must go to the club, if you please. No chapel for him — oh, no. The loafer — I'll show him!"

Gripping the shawl firmly about her throat, Mrs. Daniel marched away from the lamp-post. The boy, whimpering, shuffled homewards, his shapeless boots slapping against the pavement.

"The poetry, Ieuan. When you going to tell it?"

Ieuan turned from the window. A beam of light from a passing car penetrated into the room and fell across the pillows. He could see the ragged white ribbons Phyllis wore in her plaited hair, and as he stooped to pat her head she whispered: "Gee, there's a long time you are tonight. What's the matter?"

"Nothing, nothing at all." He ruffled her hair. "I was just puzzling which poem to recite."

"Not 'Abou Ben Adhem,'" said Gweneira. "We get that at school."

"Nor 'Twinkle, Twinkle, Little Star' and 'Dickory Dock.' I know them off by heart."

Ieuan glanced at the window once more. He wondered what Mrs. Daniel was doing at that moment. Was she on her way to the Workmen's Club, there to wait for her husband to come corkscrewing out into the street? Maybe she would push past Dai James, the doorkeeper, drag Aarfon by his ear from the bar and shout at him all the way home like she often did on a Sunday night?

And what of Davie Dan — poor Davie Dan, who was not very bright? Who had never heard of Arthur and his famous sword, Excalibur.

"Excalibur!" The word came out involuntarily.

"What's that? What did you say, Ieuan?"

He smiled. "I was only thinking — just thinking."

Excalibur. What a wonderful sword to own! And what adventurous days were those to live in! A world of beauty and chivalry. King Arthur and his knights of the Table Round. Sir Geraint, Kay, Lancelot, Bedivere, Tristram, Lionel, Ector, Gawaine, the flower of chivalrous knight-hood. Uwaine, Perceval of the Long Lance, Acolon, Agravaine, Dodynas the Savage, Sagramore — resplendent in silver-crested armour, bearing shining lance, and girded with the sword of honour. Riding on snowy steeds through rich, green meadowland and shady woods, their lances tilted at the foes of virtue. Sir Modred the Traitor. Lanval of the Fairy Lance, Sir Galahad, whose strength was as the strength of ten. Galahad, who....

"Listen, Phyl — I'll recite about Sir Galahad, and how he went to far-away lands to find the Holy Grail. It's a lovely story."

11

"Oooh, yes. That is lovely," she emphasized. She wriggled under the bedclothes and lay still.

"Light the candle, Ieuan."

"What for?" Gweneira asked.

"'Cos it will be like the Holy Grail," came the muffled reply. "I know mam won't be willing, but I promise not to tell her if you promise the same."

Ieuan smiled. "Close your eyes, Phyl," he coaxed, "and just picture that the Holy Grail is shining up there on the ceiling, like a big star made from all the gold and silver and diamonds in the world. There's no need for a candle. Just you close your eyes, good girl."

He sat down gently on the bed. The room grew still. Only his sisters' quiet breathing intruded on the silence. With eyes closed, he cleared his throat and softly began to recite.

"My good blade carves the casques of men,
My tough lance thrusteth sure,
My strength is as the strength of ten,
Because my heart is pure.
The shattering trumpet shrilleth high,
The hard brands shiver on the steel,
The splinter'd spear-shafts crack and fly,
The horse and rider reel;
They reel, they roll in clanging lists,
And when the tide of combat stands,
Perfume and flowers fall in showers,
That lightly rain from ladies' hands.
"When on my goodly charger borne —"

Ieuan felt a cold hand touch his.

"Hey, you made a mistake," Gweneira breathed. "That's not the second verse."

He pressed a finger to her lips. "Sh-h-h!" he warned, then whispered in her ear. "It'll take too long to say it all. I'll recite two more verses, and perhaps by then Phyllis'll be asleep. She's dead tired, poor little thing."

Leaning back over the bed, he closed his eyes once more and continued in a lilting tone:

"When on my goodly charger borne
Thro' dreaming towns I go,
The cock crows ere the Christmas morn,
The streets are dumb with snow.
The tempest —"

"Ieuan!"

"Yes?"

"She — she's asleep."

"Good — that's good." He moved off the bed. "Now, let me tuck you up, and off to sleep with you, too. See?" He straightened the pillow, then patted her affectionately. "There you are, nice and tidy. Good night, Gweneira."

"Good night."

He stepped quietly to the door.

"Ieuan!" Her voice brought him back to the side of the bed. "Thank you for the poetry, it was beautiful. Such a nice sad story it was, and it makes me want to cry. I — I'll have a lovely dream tonight, I know, and..." She paused. "Good luck to you tomorrow. I — I hope you'll like it in the foundry."

Ieuan said nothing. He stood there in the darkness, suddenly feeling alone and frightened. Tomorrow the foundry, a new life, lay before him and he dreaded to think of it.

"Are you still there?" Gweneira called softly.

"Yes, yes, I'm here."

"I'm sorry you have to go to the old foundry, truly I am." Her voice was heavy with sadness. "It'd be better if mam let me go to work. You're a good scholar, Ieuan, and you should stay in school to pass your exams. When the doctor says my lungs are strong enough I'll go look for a job myself. I'm nearly thirteen now, so it won't be long. Then p'raps you could go back to school again? Or to college?"

13

The question remained unanswered.

"You don't say nothing, Ieuan. P'raps you want to go to the foundry after all? A bit deep you are sometimes, and don't say what you're thinking about. If I was a scholar like you I wouldn't let mam put me in a foundry — that's the truth."

Ieuan leaned over the bed and groped for her hand. He squeezed it gently. "Don't you worry about me, Gweneira. I'll be all right. I'm getting to be a big boy now, and it's time I should be doing something to help mam. I can't expect to be in school all the time, can I?"

"But I can earn money when I'm stronger. We don't go without food or nothing, do we? Mam could wait till I'm ready to go to work. I could get a job anywhere. The tinstamping wants girls, and in the tinworks, too, there's plenty of chances. I could have fifteen shillings a week.

That's more'n you get in the foundry... Ieuan, why don't you ask dad to let you stay in school?"

"Oh, it's no good," he sighed. "Dad won't say anything. Mam's made up her mind to put me into the foundry. Everything's been arranged, and it's too late to draw back now. Besides, Mr. Bevan wouldn't like to be made a fool of. He's given his word to let me start."

"But you don't really want to go there, Ieuan? Do you?"

"No. I — I'm frightened of it. Oh, I don't know what to think, Gweneira. Sometimes I'm sorry I'm leaving school, and then sometimes I'm glad to think that I'll be earning money to help mam and dad. 'T'isn't fair to expect them to keep me in school all the time. Other boys, good scholars like Danny Derrick, Hugh Phillips and Elwyn Price, have been working in the tinworks since they were fourteen, and I'm almost sixteen."

Gweneira sat up. She clasped her hands around her knees.

"Gee, why don't you coax mam, and see if she'll change her mind?" she suggested after an interval of thought.

He shook his head.

"Don't you worry your little head about it," he murmured.

14

"Go to sleep, there's a good girl. Maybe I'll find that I'll like the foundry. Then we'd feel silly, wouldn't we?" He kissed her cheek. "Well, I'm off to bed now. Good night, *cariad*."

"Good night, Ieuan. Sleep tight."

"Mind the bugs won't bite," he sang with an unconvincing show of lightheartedness.

Closing the door quietly behind him, he crossed the landing to his room. He fumbled for a box of matches and lit the stump of candle stuck in the cracked saucer on the small bedside table.

He shivered as a gust of wind blew into the room. The candle flame flickered, and he hastened to close the window, the brass rings screeching as he drew the curtains together.

He began to undress. The wavering candlelight cast weird shadows over the room and played across the marble-topped washstand with its large, flowered jug and bowl, china soap dish, and candlesticks that were never used.

The brass bedrail shone in the yellow light, reflecting itself in the glass-covered, embroidered texts on either side of the room, and in the cracked wardrobe mirror near the window.

A picture of an angel, lily-bedecked, leading a golden-haired child along a precipitous mountain path, looked down from the wall at the head of the bed. In the corner nearest the door stood a small bookcase fashioned from an orange-box, its rough, unplaned shelves sagging from the weight of the many books they bore.

Here were Ieuan's favourites: *Quentin Durward, Treasure Island, Swiss Family Robinson, Gulliver's Travels, Tales from the Mabinogion, Westward Ho!, Ben Hur,* Palgrave's *Golden Treasury, Morte d'Arthur, Idylls of the King*.

On top of the orange-box, flanked by two bronze bookrests in the form of sleeping lions, were other volumes presented to him on school prize days and for good attendance at the Sunday School classes: *Midshipman Easy, Last of the Mohicans, Tom Brown's Schooldays, Pickwick Papers,* a gold-leafed Bible and three Common Prayer books.

The room was small, its faded blue wallpaper patterned with climbing roses. Above the window a wide strip of paper, green with mildew, curled down from the frieze and draped itself over the drab-coloured curtains. The floor was bare of linoleum, and two square pieces of frayed coconut matting hardly covered the space on either side of the bed. An open firegrate curved out from the wall opposite the door. It had never held the warmth of a fire, and the space between the bars had been stuffed with newspapers yellow with age.

Ieuan stepped out of his short trousers and looped the braces over the ornamental brass knob at the foot of the bed. Woollen jersey and socks followed and were folded neatly over the bedrail. He rubbed the chill from his feet, then climbed in under the blankets. The flannel shirt he wore next to his skin made him itch. He twisted and turned, and finally lay on his side, knees drawn up to chin, his hands wrapped in the folds of his shirt.

The candle flame fluttered agitatedly as a draught from the space between door and lintel swept into the room. Outside, the November wind rose. Now and then it came like a giant nightbird beating its wings against the curtained windows, and rattling the loose framework.

Ieuan slipped an arm out of the bedclothes. He nipped the candle wick between thumb and forefinger, and shivering, pulled the rough woollen blanket over his chin.

The wind sighed through the bare branches of the trees in the garden, and as he listened it sounded to him like the faraway, confused voices of children laughing and shouting at their play; an echo, reminding him of the past when he was but a little boy playing in the streets, the back lanes and the fields with the childhood friends he knew.

He thought back to those early days, striving to retain the impressions that crowded into his mind. He saw, as though on a shadowy canvas, the front parlour of the old house where he was born before the family came to live in Pleasant Row.

But why should he think only of that specific parlour in a

house which had five other rooms? What significance did it hold for him?

Was it not into that room they brought his father news of the son born to him? And had it not been told that his father had wept? And when a man cries, especially a father, it is something important, something big in a boy's life — something one can never forget. For a man is not supposed to weep. Tears are for women and little girls. Men never cry.

But his father wept, and he had wept in the parlour, the best room in the house. Ieuan remembered that parlour, with its aspidistra and heavy, gilt-edged Bible resting on the stand before the lace-skirted window. A parlour of horsehair sofas, and sleek, shining, ice-cold chairs on which one sat as though in chapel.

A parlour of glass-wreathed, imitation flowers, fretwork-framed photographs of moustached and bearded men; of ladies in voluminous gowns from under which no trace of ankle peeped. Photographs of little boys in velvet suits, white lace collars and cuffs; of little girls with plaited hair, beribboned, in starched frocks with waists satin-sashed.

A parlour in a mean street of mean houses, above which the black smoke of factories curled. Houses, each identical with its neighbour, brick for brick, slate for slate, chimney pot for chimney pot, room for room, rent for rent.

A parlour where people laid their dead in silver-handled coffins; where the corpse candles burned in tall, brass-based holders. A room where the neighbours trooped in solemn procession to view with curious dread the waxen faces of the white-satin-dressed dead. The best room in the house; the showroom of death.

This vision gave way to another which time had made clea rer, and he saw before him the red-tiled roof of the infants' school where proudly perched the golden weathercock with arrogant head, flamboyant tail. The grey stone walls, and the pointed bell tower where the iron bell swung its rounded tones out over and across the town to call: "Little children, little children, come to school." And the asphalt playground which resounded to the music of tiny, toddling feet; and the rusty gate that groaned with agony.

In those early days it was, "Touch your caps, little soap-scrubbed, shining boys. Curtsey, little girls — for here comes Miss Mallory, headmistress, queen, goddess." He smiled as he saw her coming into view from the black, winding lane behind the school, her corkscrew curls askew beneath the flowerbed hat. Tall, skinny Miss Mallory of the red lollipop nose, prominent teeth like Jason the Waggoner's horse, thin, blue-ridged hands that seemed frozen both in summer and winter. And oh, so sedate, with the black-tasselled umbrella under her arm, her sparrow-like gait, hoppety-hop, hoppety-hop, and the smile of assumed benevolence.

In her wake would come Miss Williams, Miss Lee, Miss Mackintosh, Miss Thompson. "Good morning! Good morning! Good morning! Good morning! Brush the floor with your caps, little boys. Curtsey till your spotless, linen-covered bottoms touch the heel behind you, little girls, for the teachers have arrived. The queen and her ladies in waiting have passed through the rusty, groaning gate."

He saw the children seated at their desks, tracing what childish imaginings they might in shallow trays of gritty, mouse-coloured sand. He felt again the soft, sweet-smelling modelling clay of many colours, appetizing in appearance as Miss Mallory's lollipop nose.

High above him was the small, round, swing chair suspended from the ceiling, and in front of the class stood Rosy-posy, the little curly-curly girl in her white pinafore, tucked and frilled.

Rosy, who cried so long and loud that Miss Mackintosh put her in the swing chair and rock-a-byed her into the air until she laughed, and cried again when Miss Mackintosh rock-a-byed her too high.

He had wished then that he could cry, so that he could be swung to the giddily high white ceiling and feel the cold wind racing from his toes to the nape of his midget's neck. But, try as he would, the tears never came, and he yearned in vain.

Sometimes Miss Lee would take charge of the babies' class. Miss Lee, bow-legged, her false teeth champing, patting her hair into place every minute of the long, long day; her eagle's eyes searching the pupils' timid faces, her twitching hands ever eager to reach for the dreaded jinny-cane.

Miss Lee, Miss Williams, Miss Mackintosh, Miss Thompson, Miss Mallory.... Why did the good Lord suffer little children to gaze up on such unprepossessing beauties in the world of their innocence? They were dragons in shirtwaists, witches clad in black satin frills and starched, milk-white cuffs-creatures fearsome and terrible.

But playtime came, and the children forgot their fears, their lessons in discipline, as they laughed and sang and danced in the springtime of life. They slid heroically on iron-studded boots along the sun-drenched, asphalt play-ground, sensing speed and power in themselves, who were so new to a world so old.

Then came the awakening of the intellect, and Ieuan stood on the threshold of knowledge. The eyes saw, the ears heard. He smelled and tasted and knew what was good and what was bad. He was at the beginning of the journey to completeness. Infancy blossomed into boyhood, and gone were the days when he was but an infant in that sleeping, eating, playing world of his.

Eating and tasting the tongue-cleaving, green-bladed grass; the bitter, white milk juice of dandelion stalk; the sweet, sweet honey; the sour, acrid ivy that entwined the bitterness of the rough bark of oak; and the melting, soothing sweetness of sugar.

Playing in the white-walled lanes in the sunlight and the shadows. Lanes sometimes like a fairy world agleam with sunshine of a bright summer; a summer which was brightest of all times. But summer would fade, and autumn, with' leaves flying like gulls in windy skies, scattered her crisp leafy carpet upon the lanes.

Autumn, when life slowly died around those who were about to live. And after she had gone, winter stalked into the children's world like a monstrous, raging beast.

With winds howling and sneering, from around the corner at the end of the lane he came dancing, this mighty monster, his icy whip slashing through the naked branches, snapping, snarling, twisting.

But on the children played in dark, dismal days when silver, untrodden snow blanketed the long lanes; when gleaming icicles stretched their talons into the whiteness of everything, and the wild winds thundered and moaned.

And with the passing of each season they were a step farther from the womb. It was farewell infancy, farewell baby world. Now to pastures new we embark.

Goodbye, Miss Mallory, Miss Lee, Miss Thompson, Miss Mackintosh. Not good morning, but goodbye. Goodbye, too, Rosy curly-curly. Goodbye, swing chair. Goodbye ... Goodbye.

There were no regrets, no sorrows, for memories were yet to be born.

* * *

He felt an ache around his heart. His throat was parched and dry as he recalled these moments. He lingered over each happy memory or association which the passing of time had made mellow and sad.

Never again would he race across the sloping, hawthornlined field, a red-and-green striped jersey on his back, the ball tucked firmly under his arm, and the tumultuous cheers of a thousand schoolboys to spur him on towards the goal.

"School! Go on, School!"

They pushed and jostled over the sawdust touchline, caps waving, red-and-green scarves fluttering in the wind.

"Three cheers for good old Ieuan Morgan!"

They carried him shoulder high from the sloping field. And Harry Britton, the head prefect, clapped him on the back.

"Well done, Tich. You played a rattler."

Those were happy moments. When, in summertime, the field,

no longer bared by winter winds and rain, was rich and green, the hawthorn trees bright with berries, and the fragrance of hedge flowers heavy in the air. A blue sky, golden sun. White-clad boys, cool in the summer heat.

The red leather ball gleamed as it curved from the bowler's swinging arm. The batsman drove between the covers.

"Oh, well played, sir. Well played."

Schoolboys crowded the circled outfield, some lying on their stomachs, caps pulled down over perspiring foreheads, shading their eyes from the sunshine which made them frown involuntarily; others seeking the cooler shadow of the green pavilion which fell across the field to touch the heel of cover-point.

Came yet another memory of a summer day as he stared into the darkness of his bedroom. He saw himself on People's Park, the town team's football ground, captain of the cricket side chosen to play the Old Boys in the most important match of the season. And he had carried his bat for a good, solid fifty-one, which gave his team the win it never anticipated.

It was the hottest day of a memorable summer. So fierce was the sun that it caused a hurt at the back of one's head. Eyes blinked, foreheads creased. People moved with indolence. Handkerchiefs were pressed to perspiring faces. The heat mist danced in waves over the wilting grass, and the air was suffocating. There was no coolness anywhere. The very water one drank to quench the universal thirst, was warm.

Tony Marasiano, the ice-cream man, stood within the humid shade of a weary, sun-blistered oak, his little pony with head bowed, listless and sleepy-eyed. Parched schoolboys, their red-and-green caps rolled into pockets, climbed on to the hubs of the scorched yellow wheels and tendered their pennies for Tony's pyramids of sweetness.

The little river that bordered the football ground flowed wearily along a channel of arid brown soil. Flowers drooped, the sap drained from rooted stems. Between the innings, elderly relatives and friends who had come to see the match, lay on their backs on the grass, handkerchiefs and newspapers spread over their faces, while the young girls in flowery summer dresses paraded round the field in company with flannelled heroes.

The white marquee, guy ropes taut as banjo strings, was crowded with visitors. They clustered round the long, refreshment-laden counters. Mineral-water bottles popped. The contents were swallowed at a gulp, but even then the great thirst was unquenched.

To the west of the playing field, under the glaring eye of the laughing sun, lay Dinas Wood. Not a leaf stirred, and the tall trees seemed to lose their dignity in the searching heat.

It was too hot to play, to sit, to talk, to sing; too hot even to think. But he had carried his bat for fifty-one. That was the thing to remember!

Those happy days, so full of life and laughter, were gone, no more to be recaptured save in the fleeting glimpse of recollection. He remembered the friends he had made: Stinky, Flick, 'Appy, Colin Beynon, Benji, Rhubarb Leyshon — stalwart boys in striped jerseys or white flannels, who could run a hundred yards in thirteen seconds and kick a goal from the half-way line.

The masters, too, he regarded as his friends, for they had patiently taught him what he eagerly wanted to learn: Dee-Gee, of the suntanned face and beetled brows; Doldrums, the geography master; Pappy, the benign, doe-eyed philosopher; Edmunds, the poetical, whimsical Welsh master who commanded his scholars to lay their heads on the desks to listen to the grass growing; Dai Tot, tall as the tallest beanstalk; Bowen Bach, whose diminutiveness belied his capacity for knowledge; Monsieur, the French master, whose voice was like the wind among the reeds, and whose eyes ever twinkled with laughter; and Shon, the quiet, dignified literary scholar.

The pattern he weaved dissolved into another design as he took up the threads of memory. He saw himself in the years before he gained a scholarship to the county school, trudging up a rock-strewn hill to the grey school building which overlooked the town and the muddy estuary beyond, a heavy satchel slung over his shoulder, and his friends walking by his side: Jamesie, of the corn-coloured hair, Alcwyn, Trefor, Elwyn, Danny, Ezra the Haulier's son, Harry Cabbage, Shunshy Bevan.

They were the gang. Together, they shared every boyhood adventure. Fishing for silkcoats, tadpoles, newts and brown-backed lizards in the old quarry pool; climbing the scarred rock face; shooting down Hill 60 on toboggans of corrugated sheets. And how they enjoyed the minutes and the hours of those days that seemed without end!

In springtime they would race to the fields behind Dafydd Prosser's farm to gather vetch peas and sour leaves, and dandelions for old Elen Davies's home-brewed ginger beer. Then, in the summer evenings the gang would meet on the street corner near St. David's Mission Church. There they'd discuss what games to play. Cat and Dog, One and Over, Tol, Strong Horses, All Over Again ... which should it be? And where should they play? In the fields or in the back lanes?

And in winter, when the street lamps were lit early, they'd consider and choose from the variety of amusements to while away the hours before watchful parents summoned them to bed. Tally Ho, Jack o' Lantern, or, if the mood was apparent and the spirit willing, a game of soccer in Maesyrafon Road with a ball made of rags or newspapers tied with string, the goals two lamp-posts at the end of the street.

On these occasions, trouble in its guise of Richards Weights and Measures would assail them. Richards was a bachelor, and lived in a big, bay-windowed house at the top of Maesyrafon Road, with two pianos and five cats to keep him company.

Out he would come, grizzled head sunk into his shoulders, his fists menacing the air.

"Away with you, you ragamuffins! Go somewhere else to play your games, not disturb decent people who want a quiet evening after working hard all day."

Sometimes he would confiscate the ball, and in revenge, the gang would collect pieces of paper from the gutter and stuff them into the rainpipe that ran down from trough to pavement. The papers were set alight. An ominous rumbling was heard as the draught drew yellow tongues of flame up the pipe, and columns of black smoke raced into the night sky.

Stick in hand, Richards would dart out of the doorway and give chase, threatening to knock the skin off the backside of the first boy he caught. Through streets and back lanes the pursuit continued, and ended only when Richards's lack of wind triumphed over his desire to administer punishment.

Ieuan smiled at the recollection. It was a sad smile. Within him he felt a deep ache, a nostalgic longing for the past. The wind rattled the window pane. It whistled through the lilac tree in the garden, and the bare branches of the apple tree next door creaked and shivered as though in protestation against the wind's unceasing vigour.

Two trees. One a lilac, bereft now of leaf and blossom, in whose shady fork he used to sit and read his books in the long days of summer; the other, bearing ripe red fruit in its season.

He recalled how the apple tree thrust her fruit-laden arms over the broken fence in their garden, and how he and Gweneira had gazed longingly at the tempting juicy redness that shone before their eyes. And in the want and innocence of childhood they had reached out and plucked from the tree the fruit which God had planted there.

His fruit was theirs, they reasoned. The tree that grew in the garden next door was *their* tree, and the broken boundary of fence mattered not. No one could tell them it was wrong to take the fruit. Fruit was for all, for everyone, else God would not have given the tree strength to bear it.

They ate, and tasted the wine of the red fruit, and marvelled that such things were possible, for in winter when the snow lay thick upon the naked and miserable branches there was nothing, no bud, no leaf; but with the coming of the warmness of sun and

24

earth, the spring winds and rain, the tree bore leaves, and blossoms sprang into life from a thing which had been dead.

The fruit grew green, then reddened into ripeness, the ripeness of which they had tasted, Gweneira and he.

And Lewis-next-door, a mean, grubby little man who owned the apple tree, cursed them and sent them trembling into the shelter of the house. Old Lewis, a miser who, in the darkness of his parlour at night, would play with his hoard of golden sovereigns.

A million pounds he was worth, so people said. A miser whose money fell into the hands of a drunken, profligate son.

Ieuan remembered him well, this tall, lean son with burning eyes; a wild and fierce creature whose madness drove him to the grave. In drunken delirium he had tried to kill himself one night, but Ieuan's father had taken from his hand the knife poised for destruction, and calmed him down.

The next morning an ambulance came to Robin's house. The neighbours had seen it, and they talked. At ten o'clock it came, with two policemen and three men in white uniforms. They tied Robin into a coat with long sleeves which fastened behind him. His arms were crossed over his breast. He made gurgling noises in his throat, and his mouth was all frothy like a horse's.

Up to the asylum, the neighbours said he was going. To the big stone building on the hill in Pontmorlais, where men and women screamed and made awful faces. A padded cell he would be put into. A room with soft walls so that Robin couldn't hurt himself. And he would be kept there for a long, long time, like Martha Probert, who threw her baby under a train. Men like Robin must be locked up until they got better; but to get better they would have to stay for years in the asylum. Perhaps he would die there, and be buried with his feet towards the gravestone, like they did to people who committed suicide.

Ieuan had listened open-mouthed to this strange talk. If Robin was dangerous, then all the more credit to dad, who had faced him without fear. It was difficult, hard to reason why dad was not afraid of a raving madman, and yet was cowed down by mam. Always when they had an argument he would give in to her, and she never failed to get the last word.

That was what mam wanted. He had often heard her say to dad whenever they disagreed: "I'll get the last word, Dick Morgan, even if you keep on talking all night. There's no man going to keep me under his thumb."

Yes, dad was hard to understand. Fearless he was in some things, and a coward in others. When Evan Jones, the rollerman, tried to cut his own throat, and his wife came screaming out into the road, it was he who went with her to the house and took the bloody razor from Evan's hand.

And when Captain Jim Llewellyn came home on leave and threatened to shoot the neighbours with the heavy, black revolver he carried at his waist, it was he again who stepped in and pacified the drunken captain.

But why hadn't he said anything to mam? Ieuan reflected bitterly. Why was he afraid of her? Was it right for a man to be frightened of a woman? It was all so strange, so mixed up.

And yet everybody was afraid of something or other. Jenkins the Coal was scared of the dark, and wouldn't go out into it by himself. Rocyn Bowen, who used to fight in the boxing booths every time the fair came to town, was afraid of dogs. If one happened to get in his path he would stop, terrified. His eyes would bulge.

"Good dog, good dog," he'd say breathlessly, and, with body slewed, he'd shuffle away from the creature as though he were walking along a narrow ledge overlooking a precipice.

Elen Davies, the ginger-beer woman, covered her face every time she heard thunder. Screaming loudly, she'd run into the pantry, lock the door and refuse to come out until the storm had passed.

Paddy Rourke, whose father raced greyhounds in Dafydd Prosser's fields on a Sunday morning, would catch a live rat with his bare hands, but if he saw a worm he'd scream with terror and his face would become white as a sheet.

26

But why think of Jenkins the Coal, Rocyn, old Elen and Paddy Rourke? Wasn't he himself afraid — afraid of the foundry? Did the thought of starting work really scare him, or did he look forward to it as something new and adventurous, like Jamesie, who was too excited to sleep the night before he took on his first job as a greaser in the Meadowland tinworks?

"Am going to work tomorrow, Ieu," he had said when they met on the street corner after chapel one Sunday night. "Christmas Moses! Won't it be grand? No more stinking homework, and worrying about geography and history and counting up sums all the time. It'll be sloshing, Ieuan."

And Jamesie enthused over the prospect of having his first pay in a fortnight's time.

"A quid for the old woman, and five bob spending money for me. Then look out! They'll be seeing Jamesie Harries cutting a dash in town. Grey suit I'll have. A double breaster. And brown shoes — them ones with pointy toes, you know? Slouch hat, too. An' I'll join in with the rest of the boys at the billiard hall in Station Square. Have a game of billiards, black pool, skittle pool, or snooker — losers to pay. Then watch out for me on Sundays, Ieu. Up to the Monkey Parade in my posh suit, with one of them scenty handkerchiefs sticking out of my breast pocket. By crikey, I'll click with some smart jane. Plenty to choose from in the Monkey Parade. Remember how we used to see 'em when we were kids?"

There were enough girls — pretty ones, too — for Jamesie to pick up if he wanted company. Up the main street, from the Town Hall to Brady's Emporium and back again, they strolled every night.

"To and fro like monkeys in a cage," a minister had denounced from the pulpit, and the High Street became known as the Monkey Parade. On Sunday evenings it was so crowded with young people that the traffic was forced to crawl along the road, and the police were kept busy dispersing the groups that gathered in the shop doorways and on the pavement.

Laughing and singing, the boys and girls would ogle one another. A handkerchief snatched from a breast pocket would result in a wild chase through the noisy throng until the offender was caught and "points" made for some night in the week.

To filch a handkerchief was only one of the many ways in which to "click." Another method was to walk behind a girl and pretend to cough. When she looked round, the boy would touch his hat and smile.

"May I see you home, miss?"

The same question was asked by every boy, and the girls had come to expect it. They had their answer ready, pat.

"I beg your parsnips?"

The introduction made, the boys would start showing off, and behave like the sleek, polished, vaselined ladykillers they had seen on the films, and in the end they and the girls would arrange to meet again.

The girls of the Monkey Parade were very attractive. Most of them were employed in the tinworks and tinstamping factory.

It was easy to find out whether a girl worked in a shop, or was a clerk, or a servant in a middle-class home. One had only to hear her speak.

The shopgirls, clerks and domestic servants spoke in quiet tones, but the voices of the tinworks' girls were harsh and strident.

That was really nothing to be ashamed of, and no one could blame the tinworks' girls for having such coarse voices. After all, what could one expect from them when they were forced to shout to be heard above the clatter and roar of the mills every day?

Ay, Jamesie'd have plenty to choose from if he wanted a girl of his own. All painted up and smelling like flowers, with slender legs in silk stockings that shimmered below the hems of their short, swinging skirts. Once a boy started working he just had to find a girl, it was the first outward sign of approaching youth and manhood. And so, every boy who brought home a pay packet at the end of the week had a "jane" with whom he could walk up

Lovers' lane on a Sunday night and lean against the hedge, or take to the pictures on Saturdays and Tuesdays.

To Jamesie work meant money and everything that five shillings pocket money would buy: playing billiards, losers to pay, clicking with the girls. Then later he'd be allowed to smoke in front of his father, and swank about the streets like Alf Parry, a cigarette behind one ear and another dangling from the corner of his mouth. And perhaps call in at a public house on a Saturday night and order a glass of shandy-gaff.

Would the foundry do this to him? Ieuan wondered. As he grew older and had money in his pocket, would he wish to spend his leisure in the billiard hall or on the Monkey Parade?

No, he'd study every night, or attend evening classes at the Technical School. Then he'd try his matriculation and maybe he'd win a scholarship to the university. He would save his money and give it all to mam. She'd be pleased if he saved all his pocket money for a year, or perhaps two years, and then she might be willing for him to go to college.

The thought was exciting. Rapidly, he began to count how much he could accumulate in a year. Out of twelve and threepence he would be allowed at least two shillings pocket money. That would mean a hundred and four shillings a year. Five pounds four.

Five pounds four! The total sum disheartened him, and the excitement subsided. Once more he felt frightened and lonely: if only dad had said something, done something to keep him at school. Why—

Suddenly, he heard the sound of voices raised in argument. He listened, tensed. His mother's voice shrilled up the stairway. Throwing back the blanket, he climbed slowly out of bed and opened the door.

The mother's voice grew louder. He heard his name mentioned.

"Oh, God, please, dear God, don't let them quarrel again," he prayed. "Please let them be happy, dear God and sweet Jesus, my Saviour."

29

He crept on to the landing and crouched against the banister, his heart beating loudly.

The kitchen door was open. He saw his mother facing his father as he sat down to supper. Her eyes were blazing.

"Go on" he heard her shout. "Call me a nincompoop. Say I'm not fit to be a mother to the children. Say it. Go on, say it!"

His father pushed aside the plate of cold meat, and looked up.

"Be reasonable, Millie," he said softly. "Why not let the boy stop in school? Griffiths was telling me the other day that there was a brilliant future for the lad. Then, Lewis Thomas, the bank manager mentioned him to me. Seems Lewis's boy is in the same class as Ieuan, and he said how clever —"

The mother tossed her head impatiently.

"Let him stop in school, indeed! What's got into you?" she stormed. "He's almost sixteen, and it's time he should be put into a job and do something useful. We can't afford to keep him on our hands much longer. Phyllis is growing fast, and there's Gweneira to think of. Doctor's bills have to be paid, you know. And there's clothes to be bought, and food, and rent to pay. His wages'll be a great help to me, I can tell you."

"But, Millie, you don't realize what's in front of the boy. Hard work for little money, which will bring you no benefit in the long run. Believe me, it's far wiser to let him remain at school. Education is a fine thing, Millie. It'll lead him into a better job than the foundry. God knows, I don't want him to fall into a job like mine using a shovel and pushing a barrow around. Give the boy a chance. Why, even now it's not too late. You could see Bevan in the morning and explain to him that we've changed our minds."

The mother frowned.

"*We've* changed our minds! I like that," she retorted. "I'm telling Mr. Bevan no such thing. Ieuan goes into the foundry tomorrow. That's settled. Rubbish to all this silly twaddle about his future, is what I say. I know what Ieuan's good for and I'm sure I can manage my family's affairs without any interference from outsiders.

We've got to live, and you know very well we can't afford to keep Ieuan in school all this time. It's quite all right for the likes of Griffiths, the headmaster, to spout about a brilliant future for him. What does *he* know of my pinching and scraping to make ends meet every week? Does *he* have to count his ha'pennies and wonder where he's going to get a few extra shillings for to buy a pair of shoes for his daughter, Myfanwy? And that wife of his, traipsing around in her fur coat and fancy hats!

"No, Dick Morgan — we've got no money to go spending on Ieuan just to keep him at the County. Even if he passes this examination you're so fond of talking about, we'd never find enough money to pay for the new books he'd be wanting. And there's them sports fees he has to pay every quarter. Paying hard-earned money just for to play football and cricket and such nonsense. What next, I wonder?"

"Listen here, Millie. I understand how hard it is for you, but education is so important," the father attempted to reason.

"Bah! Education, indeed. What has it done for you, I'd like to know? You're supposed to have a good brain. A good scholar you were, too. Oh ay! 'A smart one is Dick Morgan,' I hear people say. 'Very clever head he's got.' Yes indeed, a smart one you are, right enough — but where has it got you? Look at yourself — a labourer in a boxworks. That's what your schooling's done for you, isn't it?"

The father tried to remonstrate, but she cut him short. "Don't look at me like that. I know you could ha' been a teacher if I hadn't come along. But it happened that you got married sooner'n you expected, eh? And you had to earn quickly so that you could make a decent woman out o' me. Student teacher! Sounds grand, Dick Morgan. But no time for swanking had we in them days. Money we wanted, not swank. Education, my eye! Who's going to pay for Ieuan's books, his clothes, and them sports fees? And where's the money to come from? Ay, it's time enough, and Ieuan's old enough to be doing a job of work. Look at Danny Derrick, young Elwyn Price and the Arthur boys — they had good educations, too, but they are working. My boy's no different to them. If you're so keen on keeping him in school with his head between a book, then you pay for his —"

"Don't go off the deep end, girl. Face the facts," the father said, half-heartedly. "Danny Derrick and Elwyn Price — yes, I'll look at them, now and in twenty years' time if I'm alive. What are they doing, I ask you? Greasing in the cold rolls. Muck and sweat, all for a measly twenty-five shillings a week. What future have they? What prospects? Years of education thrown away, and all because their parents didn't have the savvy to let the lads stay in school."

Mrs. Morgan winced. She brought her hands sharply to her hips.

"Savvy! So I've got no savvy now, is it? You — you, Dick Morgan, got all the brains in this family, eh?" she shouted. "Well, don't you go flattering yourself. You can have all the old brains you want. They don't help to bring food into the house, and they don't pay the bills, oh no! I suppose the tinworks' cold rolls is not good enough for our Ieuan? If I was a hard woman, p'raps I'd have put him there same as the other boys. But I put him into a foundry. Into a foundry, d'you hear? It's extra privilege for to have him learn a trade. That ought to please you, and we should be considering ourselves lucky that he's found a job as a tradesman's apprentice, and not have to start his working life as an ordinary labourer. But there, no thanks do I get for doing my best, only a lot of sneers and sly dabs.

"You can stare at me as much as you like, Dick Morgan," she went on spitefully. She slid the plate of cold meat towards him. "You'd better eat that," she snapped.

The father rose from the table and, without saying a word, took off his jacket and hung it behind the kitchen door. He loosened his collar and tie, then stooped to untie his boot laces.

"So, you got nothing to say now, have you?" the mother challenged. "Just like a dummy, eh? Thinking that you'll get the better of me, eh? Well, let me tell you — you're not putting one over on me. Oh, no. No man's going to have any ideas in his head about putting me in my place. You and your talk about education. Just a waste of breath, that's what it is. P'raps you think I'd like my boy to be a teacher or a minister, just for the swank of it. For you to go about, saying to people: 'Our Ieuan? Oh yes, he's a teacher at the grammar school,' or 'My boy's getting on splendid, minister of a big chapel in Cardiff he is.' If other folks want to brag about their children and the good jobs they've landed, well, let them."

She paused, then, with the same fierce contempt, continued: "I'm not a one for swank. Look at Mrs. Matthews Bay Window! How would you like a woman same as her for a wife? She's got her two boys in the college, and there she is walking about like a queen with her airs and graces. I remember the time when she was working in the Meadowland tinworks, opening stickers. But now, of course, she don't wish to think of those days. Forgotten herself completely, she has. And there's another fine beauty — that Sarah Excursions! A son a bank manager in Porthcawl, and two daughters in a school for gentlewomen in 'Arrogate. School for gentlewomen, indeed! The other day they were running about the back lanes with nothing on their feet. A proper swanker is their mother, what with her grand piano, and her putting a cooked turkey or chicken in the parlour window for everyone to see how well she's got on since her husband was left a bit of money after his uncle in America. And those trips she used to make to London every fortnight for her shopping. A proper gallivanting sort is she. How would you like to have married her? She's put her children on the way to good jobs, hasn't she? And that's what you want me to do, isn't it?"

Ieuan crouched on the landing. He saw his father's fists clench. He felt a thrill of excitement as he watched him. "Now he'll tell mam off," he thought. "Now he'll be mad with her."

He waited anxiously. But the father said nothing. The clenched fists opened. Ieuan sat down dejectedly on the stairway and drew his shirt over his cold knees.

33

Nothing, not a word had dad said in answer to mam's furious tirade, but just listened to it like a little boy being scolded. Why didn't he say something, to show her he wasn't frightened of her? A husband was always supposed to be the master in his own house, so people said. Then why didn't he assert himself? Did he want to be labelled as a man who was tied to his wife's apron strings? A henpecked husband?

Ieuan felt ashamed of his father. The shame gave way to anger and resentment. Dad was too lenient, too soft with mam. If he were dad, he would — yes, he would slap her across the face. It wasn't right for her to talk to h.m the way she did. He was so tender and patient. Everybody loved him. Yet in his own home there was hatred and distrust on mam's part. It was all so strange, this relationship between them. How was it that dad was not afraid of Robin in his madness, and could still be so docile and quiet in front of mam when she had her tantrums?

Perhaps, like every other decent man, he wanted peace and love in his home? Perhaps he was thinking of the children, Gweneira, Phyllis and him? It was wrong to quarrel in the children's presence, he had often heard him reason with mam. It did things to them, made them nervous and frightened. And in the end they would have no respect for their parents.

But his words were wasted. Mam just wouldn't listen.

Maybe he had been daunted trying to reason with her, and that was why he seldom said anything in answer to her abuse? But it was wrong of him to behave like that. It made him appear as though he was scared of mam, and no man should be afraid of a woman, or he would be called a weakling and would not be respected, not even by his own children.

A blast of cold wind swept up the stairway. Ieuan shivered convulsively. He rubbed his numbed legs and returned slowly to his room. Heavy-hearted and fearful, he clambered wearily into bed. A pain gripped his throat. His eyes filled with tears.

When mam and dad quarrelled, the world to him became suddenly dark like night, and gone was all joy and happiness, all the laughter and singing. He would feel lost, a stranger in a world where there was nothing but deep, horrible darkness and desolation. A stranger searching for love and comfort. A hand to take his. A word of cheer.

The argument downstairs continued. The mother's voice, now muffled, could be heard above the wind that sighed against the window, and Ieuan, his head buried beneath the blanket, began to weep silently. He thought of the wretched and miserable life his parents shared. Long ago it seemed that sometimes a little happiness would shine in their world of quarrels and misunderstandings. But it was only for a short while. A spasm of joy. There had been days when the house was filled with laughter; but the memories of such days were all too few.

Saturdays, when they went to town and brought back a basket laden with goods, and then, as a special treat, Gweneira and he would have a *Comic Cuts* and a *Rainbow* and half an egg each for tea. And often in the evening dad would sit mam on his knee and swing her up and down, and they'd both laugh. Then he would say something in her ear which made her blush, and she would point to Gweneira and him, and whisper back secretly.

And there were memories of Sunday afternoons when they would go to bed for a rest. Everything seemed so lovely, for when mam came downstairs her cheeks would be flushed, her eyes sparkling, and all the day she'd be happy and singing. She was very beautiful in those days.

She had been more than beautiful once, as the picture showed on the sideboard in the parlour. Slender, with long hair the colour of gold. Eyes that were large and round, with a tender look in them like a little girl's.

He remembered how he had asked dad if she was just as beautiful when he first met her, and his answer was full of pride: "She was the handsomest woman in town, my boy. Every young man was wishing to marry her, and doing his best to be courting her. Ay, she was a real beauty, was your mother. And I was a very lucky young man to have married her."

Now, the beauty that once was hers had changed into a brassy hardness. The slender waist had gone. The rich, yellow hair was straggling and unkempt. Her eyes were cold and cruel, and the rich, full lips were thin and bloodless.

Since Phyllis's birth she had become moody and irritable. Always nagging, nagging all the time. Dad never swung her on his knee any more, and they never went to bed for a rest on Sunday afternoons. The *Comic Cuts* and the *Rainbow* and the half an egg each he and Gweneira looked forward to were only a memory.

If only — oh, if only they all could be happy like they were in the old days. When the house echoed to the laughter and song. When his mother's beauty glowed, and all was well with the world.

Outside the wind gently sighed. The trees in the garden stirred. Then all became still, and Ieuan slept, his face still wet with tears.

CHAPTER TWO

"IEU ... AN!"

The mother's voice rose in a piercing cadence.

He opened his eyes and blinked sleepily. The room was still in darkness.

"Ieu ... an!"

There was a shrill note of anger in this second call. He felt for the box of matches on the table. The glare blinded him momentarily as he reached over to light the stub of candle. He rubbed his eyes and, reluctantly throwing back the warm blanket, sat heavily down on the edge of the bed.

His eyelids drooped. His thighs ached as though they had been constricted in steel bands. Once more he rubbed his eyes, but he found it difficult to keep them open. His head sank on to his breast.

"Ieu ... an!" the voice persisted. "Come, boy, or you'll be late."

He got up from the bed. The icy coldness of the bare floor stabbed into his feet. He shivered and, hopping painfully on his toes, took his trousers from the brass knob. Leaning against the bedrail, he began to dress.

He stepped awkwardly into his trousers, then pulled on his socks. He drew back the curtains. A shaft of bright moonlight cut into the room as he glanced out of the window. It had been raining during the night, and the rooftops glistened grey in the distance.

Wisps of blue smoke swayed from neighbouring chimneys. Somewhere a door slammed. A voice called: "So-long, Jim," and the metallic dip-clop of clogged feet on the roadway told of the tinworker on his way for the morning shift.

Ieuan tucked the flannel shirt into his waist, and flicking away a stray, downy feather, stood before the cracked mirror.

He had not grown much since he left the elementary school. Still the same narrow shoulders above a body which, though lacking in strength, was sturdy enough.

And the same straight limbs, and small, delicately formed hands; a thoughtful face with high nose, full, decided, well-opened, quick grey eyes, and wide forehead with well-shaped ears.

"Ieuan! Ieuan! This is the last time I'm calling. If you're not down soon I'll come up and get you myself."

The threat in her voice made him hurry. He snapped the braces over his shoulders and blew out the candle.

"I'm coming, Mam." With jersey bundled under his arm, he thudded downstairs.

Mrs. Morgan, a long, shapeless overcoat covering her nightdress, her hair hanging in two straggling plaits, leaned against the table in the gas-lit middle-room, a loaf of bread held into the pit of her stomach.

She began to cut the loaf, placing each slice on a large plate at her elbow. A pile of corned-beef sandwiches lay beside it. Two squares of greaseproof paper were neatly folded at the table edge.

"What's the matter with you this morning?" she snapped, without looking up. "Taking a long time, aren't you? If it was a Sunday School trip or one of them football excursions to Swansea with your father you'd be up soon enough, I suppose. Come on, have a wash, and get into your things. They're over there."

She pointed to a pair of canvas dungarees and dark flannel shirt folded over the armchair.

"And hurry. It's nearly twenty past six. Tidy if you're late on your first day. Not a very good impression you'd make on Mr. Bevan after my telling him what a punctual boy you are."

She placed a kettle on the gas stove in the kitchen and prepared to rake out the dead ashes from the grate. The kitchen was the biggest room in the house, and the orderliness which prevailed there showed that whatever faults the mother possessed she was undeniably an industrious woman.

The oak dresser, with its rows of plain and willow-patterned plates and jugs of many shapes and colours, shone so brightly that every aspect of the room could be viewed in it. No less polished was the wooden, highbacked settle, and the tall, mahogany armchair. A long, rectangular brass sheet hung from the mantelpiece, and directly beneath it a wire clothes line.

Fronting the black-leaded grate was a burnished fender and complement of heavy, ornamental tongs and fireshovel. They glistened like silver, and were the most cherished articles in the kitchen. A sheet of newspaper was spread over the fender, and on it rested two pairs of stout, hobnailed boots.

The mantelpiece, painted in streaks of black and white to represent imitation marble, rivalled the dresser in its display of polished ware.

On either side of the cheap alarm clock stood a slender brass candlestick. Two black-and-white china dogs squatted on their tails and stared lugubriously into space. Next to each was a proudly prancing, long-maned brass horse, flanked by two upright, cardboard calendars, one dated 1923, and the other for the prevailing year, 1924.

The father's watch hung from a small hook screwed into the edge of the mantelpiece. It ticked in hurried duet with its larger companion above. Four kitchen chairs, an oilcloth-covered table, a high stool, and clothes cupboard made up the rest of the furniture. The walls were distempered a pale cream, and two sepia pictures in carved walnut frames, "The Battle of Jutland" and "The Soldier's Return," hung above the settle. A multicoloured rag mat stretched across the red-and-blue tiled floor, and on the doorstep facing the kitchen close a folded sugar sack had been placed.

Ieuan knelt beside the settle and drew out a pair of tattered sandshoes. Slipping his feet into them, he rolled up his sleeves and hurried to the water tap outside.

In the meantime, his father had come down into the kitchen.

"Bit too cold even for a cat's lick, eh, Ieuan?" he greeted on his return. "Come on over here and have a warm."

Ieuan blew into his cupped hands and held them over the steaming kettle. He looked at his father.

"Why are you up so early this morning, Dad? You don't start till eight."

"Well, this is an important day for you, my boy." The father smiled. "I can see that before long you'll be boss in this house, especially when you bring home your first pay."

Poor dad, trying to be cheerful, and making light of what had happened the night before, Ieuan thought. If he only knew that every word of the conversation had been overheard. He was completely dominated by mam and just wouldn't face up to it. He didn't really mean what he said — about this being an important day. He was just pretending to be jovial and happy — anything for peace and quiet.

Ieuan took the smaller pair of boots from the fender and drew them on. They were heavy and uncomfortable, and when he stood up he felt as though his feet did not belong to him. They seemed out of proportion, big and clumsy.

He stepped timidly across the floor, supporting himself against the table.

His mother surveyed him.

"Well, how do they fit? I asked for fives. Should be plenty big enough for you."

"Champion, Millie. Looks fine in them, doesn't he?" the father commented. "Good, strong pair."

"And so they should be-for eleven and sixpence," she said drily. She took the kettle off the gas ring. "Draw up your chairs, both of you, and come and have this cup of tea while it's hot."

They drank their tea in silence. Ten minutes later the mother looked at the clock.

"Good heavens, boy, look at the time. Come, hurry. Get your shirt and dungarees on. You've only half an hour."

Ieuan took them from the armchair and sat down on the settle. He drew the shirt over his head, then stepped into the dungarees. They were coarse, and stiff with starch, and rustled loudly with every movement. He glanced self-consciously at his father.

"Dad —"

"You look fine, Ieuan. Indeed you do. Listen to your mother now, son, and get ready. It wouldn't be nice for you to be late on your first day. You'll be all right, my boy. Just don't worry about anything. Then, when I come home tonight we'll have a good old chat together. See?" He smiled, and pulled out the table drawer. "I've got something for you, Ieuan. A little present to remember the first day you started work. Here you are." From the drawer he took a broad leather belt with a nickel-plated buckle.

"Strap it round your waist, my boy. And here — something else to help you. It's a moulder's trowel. A good one, too. I bought it in Jones's on Saturday night. Thought it'd be a very useful little present for you."

"Yes, that's what we do for you," the mother thrust in. "Not many boys would be so well looked after, I can tell you. New shirt, new boots, new dungarees, a belt and a trowel. How many boys would have those on their first day, I'd like to know. Ay, a very lucky boy you are, you take it from me. Well, there's no time to waste. Put the trowel in your belt, and fetch your overcoat."

She handed Ieuan the packet of sandwiches. "Here's your breakfast, and this," she took a small, oval tin from the mantelpiece, "this is your tea and sugar box. You can borrow your father's tankard to drink from. I'll buy you a new one when you get your first pay."

Ieuan pulled on his coat and placed the sandwiches and small tin in one pocket. Into the other he forced the black-stained tankard.

"There! You're all right at last," said the mother. "Off you go. And be careful of those dungarees, mind. I can't afford to buy you another pair. Be home early for dinner," she instructed. "Don't loll about the streets with the other boys.... Oh, and here's your new handkerchief." She stuffed a large red-and-

41

white spotted handkerchief into his trousers pocket. "Don't lose it."

Buttoning up his overcoat, Ieuan stood in a state of nervous indecision, his hand on the door leading to the passageway. His father smiled encouragingly.

"I know how you feel, my boy. Little bit scared, aren't you?"

"Yes, Dad." He glanced apprehensively around. "Am — am I bound to go, Mam?"

"What's that I hear you say?" She eyed him sternly. "Bound to go, indeed! I should think so. You're a big boy, Ieuan, not a child. Come now, be off with you, or the hooters'll start blowing." As an afterthought, she added: "Good gracious me, no one's going to eat you at the foundry. There are plenty of other boys the same age as you working there, and you'll soon make friends, just like you did at school."

"Yes, you'll be all right, Ieuan," the father reassured. He put a hand on his shoulder and patted him affectionately. "I'll come to the door and see you off," he whispered. "Don't be frightened, boy. It won't be as bad as you think and, believe me, when you come home tonight you'll be laughing at the nervous little chap who put on his dungarees this morning for the first time. Come on, son, let me hear those new boots of yours marching down the street."

His voice assumed a cheery tone. "Got your trowel safe? That's good. Now, when you get to the foundry don't let anyone take it from you. Boys are always apt to be mischievous, so keep your eye on it. Some day next week I'll have your name written on the blade. One of my mates at the boxworks does a bit of engraving for a hobby. He just rubs on a little soap, scratches out the name with a needle, then pours a couple of drops of nitric acid over it. If —"

"Hey, you two," the mother interrupted. "Are you having a conference, or what? Dick, let the boy go, or he'll be as late as can be."

Ieuan walked along the passageway with his father. He opened the front door and stepped out on to the pavement.

42

"Remember what I told you, son. Don't let anything or anyone frighten you. We all had to start work some day, and it's not quite the terrible thing you imagine it to be."

Ieuan nodded. "Yes, Dad. And...."

"Yes, my boy?"

"Thank you for the belt and the trowel."

"That's all right. So-long, good boy. Best of luck to you."

"So-long, Dad."

The door slammed. Ieuan gritted his teeth. He wanted to cry. Again that feeling of terrifying loneliness descended on him. He waited on the edge of the pavement, tortured with indecision. He felt compelled to run back into the house and tell them — shout out aloud that he wasn't going to the foundry. He would stay at school. And if they refused to listen to him he'd run away. Then they'd worry and grieve over him, and beg him to come back. There'd be a notice in all the papers telling of his disappearance. The police would be searching for him. His mother would be really ill with worry. She'd feel sorry for the way she had treated him, and promise to give him anything he wanted. She'd let him stay in school until he'd passed his exams. And perhaps she would promise to be kind to dad. No more quarrels. No more shouting at him. And she and dad would smile and sing again. Everything would then be grand. They'd all be happy, and people would envy them.

The melancholy blast of a tinworks' hooter shook him from his reverie, and the daydream vanished. Almost unconsciously, he began to run through the cold, damp air, down a street where the black shadows were turned to grey.

He drew up his coat collar; then, slowing down to a walking pace, crossed into the narrow lane bordering the old brewery building at the bottom of the street.

Before him, in the distance at the other end of the lane, he could see the lights of the crowded tramcars as they swayed down the main street to the terminus at Station Square. The wet road lay like a winding river of silver in the moonlight. The shops and houses were vague and indistinct; shadowy, like a dimmed memory; reminiscent of another world — a world of fantasy.

The roof of the brewery building shone bluish-white, the colour of snow at dawn. A black tomcat scurried surefootedly along the boundary wall. When it saw him it stopped, and waited, motionless, until he had passed.

He continued along the dark lane, but as he came out into Maliphant Street he found the moonlight so bright that he could plainly read the inscription on the lucky French coin he kept in his overcoat pocket.

He crossed over to the other side. Two tinworkers came walking tiredly towards him. They had just come off the night shift. Their cloth caps were pushed back from their foreheads. Sweat towels hung limply round their throats. The long, white canvas aprons, which had been crisp and clean the night before, were now scorched and soiled.

They dragged their clogged feet along the pavement, and stopped to talk every few yards. Their *cryseu bach,* or small, sleeveless flannel shirts they had worn during the night shift, were rolled into neat bundles and tucked under their arms. Empty ginger-beer bottles slewed out from jacket pockets.

The millmen halted as he drew near, and heatedly began to discuss their work. He could hear them clearly. The taller of the two, a broad-shouldered man with a flat nose and cauliflower ear, whom he recognized as Jack Matthews, a neighbour, was declaiming in a loud, sonorous voice:

"I tell you, Tommy, them cross orders are a damn nuisance. Fifteen times me and Evan, the second helper, pushed a sheet through the rolls."

He shook a fist as if to emphasize each word.

"Fifteen times. No bloody sense in it." He scowled. "What sort of pay am I going to take home to the old woman on Friday? Them cross orders mean more work for less bloody pay, and if I don't give the old gel a big wage packet this weekend, then she won't stop gabbing for a month."

The tinworkers passed on. Their voices faded down the street. Ieuan turned the corner near the council yard. A crowd of workmen hurried singly and in twos and threes through the wide gateway. Some hailed him in the Welsh fashion — a quick, sideways toss of the head.

He returned the unspoken greeting and continued into the road named after the prosperous Mr. Bevan, which led towards Station Square and the foundry.

Bevan's Road was thronged with workers hurrying along in the same direction. Young girls from the tinstamping factory mingled with others who were making their way to the various tinworks.

The tinworks' girls, the majority of whom were employed in opening "stickers," were conspicuous in their clogs, sack aprons and rubber hand shields.

Each one was lavishly made up, as if she were bound for a party or a dance. Permed heads, hatless, and of all shades, varying from deep, dyed auburn to peroxide platinum; cheeks smeared with rouge; lips shaped into Cupid's bows or exaggerated out of all proportion; shapely legs in cheap silk stockings.

They clattered along in pairs, or in groups of four or more, arms linked, talking loudly with a show of excessive vitality. The tinstamping girls were not so incongruously dressed, and but for the coloured aprons or flowered smocks they wore under their coats, a stranger would find it difficult to distinguish them from their more sedate and supercilious sisters, the shop assistants and lady clerks.

French heels, Cuban heels, Spanish heels; high-heeled court shoes, tarnished evening slippers, elegant walking shoes and thick-soled brogues. No cumbersome clogs for these girls. And they walked with a livelier grace than their companions of the tinworks.

Men and boys strove to catch up with them, or hurried by, some pausing to crack a joke or cast a coarse, ribald remark over their shoulders.

Halfway up the street Ieuan saw Elwyn Price and Danny Derrick. He increased his pace, and finally caught up with them.

45

Danny was small, round-shouldered, while Elwyn, a head taller, was thin and anaemic. Both had pallid complexions and looked considerably older than their sixteen years. They had been in the cold rolls since they left elementary school at fourteen. And two years in the cold rolls, with its steam and fug, was guaranteed to put something into a boy's face that never existed there before. They gave him that strange look one sees in the face of a midget — a half-man, half-boy appearance.

The two boys turned their heads slightly as Ieuan slipped in between.

"Hallo, Ieuan. How b'ist?" Elwyn eyed him casually. "Where you off to?"

"Starting work today," Ieuan answered.

"Where?"

"Bevan's Foundry."

Elwyn made a wry face. "What! That bloody hole."

He swore with the self-assurance of a veteran tinworker. He bent forward and spoke to his partner on Ieuan's left.

"Hear that, Danny boy? Ieuan's going to work in old Bevan's place."

The other shrugged. "Not much of a cop. Rather be where I am than in that dump," he announced.

They walked on a little way in silence. When they came to Crooked Row, a semicircular, sloping street of low-roofed houses that led directly into Station Square, Danny knelt to tie his clog laces. He looked up.

"Bit of a la-di-da, aren't you?" he said, adjudging Ieuan's new boots and dungarees. "What you goin' in for?"

"Steel moulder."

"Moulder, by heck!"

"Oh, Christ! you're not going to be a moulder?" Elwyn asked with surprise. "Sand rats — that's what they call moulders."

Danny got up.

"Rather be in the cold rolls any day," he repeated sullenly, "or have a job as a mason."

46

"But why did you ask for a job in Bevan's?" Elwyn went on.

"I didn't," Ieuan confessed, his air of unselfconsciousness slowly deflating. "Mam spoke to him."

"Why the hell didn't she let you work in the boxworks with your father? Better than the foundry. Much cleaner, too."

"An' better money," Danny added. "Fifteen and eight Jori Rees is getting, only for boiling tea. You don't get much to start with in the foundry, do you?"

"Twelve and three," said Ieuan.

"Crikey! that's all? Not enough to pay for your salt."

"But I'll be learning a trade."

Danny snorted. "Bit of a dasher, aren't you?" He became aggressive. "Chaps who have a trade think they're high and mighty. Think they're better than us because we have to wear sack aprons and clogs. Swank, I call it — same as them chaps in the shops. Because they go to work in clean collars and shirts they think they're it. But you wait a couple of years, Elwyn an' me'll be behinders. Then we'll have the laugh over 'em. Won't we, El?"

His companion nodded. "More than five pounds a week. And some weeks we'll only be working five days. Two-to-ten shift, you know. No work on Saturdays."

Ieuan kept silent. He knew the fierce antagonism that existed between the boys of the cold rolls and others who were apprenticed to various trades. A tinworks' boy was bitterly resentful of the higher status in which the apprentice was placed and jealous of the greater respect paid to him.

The cold roll department was looked upon as the last resort when a parent failed to place his son into a trade or a profession. It was regarded as a section of industry fit only for dullards and failures, for lads who had more muscle than brain, and whose main ambition was to leave school as soon as they reached the age of fourteen.

A mother, harassed by an unruly son, would not find a more effective insult than to shout at him: "Like one of them boys from the cold rolls, you are. No manners, no respect and no brains." Or a threat would be sternly issued: "I'll send you to work in the cold rolls — that's what I'll do, you ruffian."

* * *

The boys continued down the lower end of Crooked Row. Back-lane doors opened and shadowy figures, clutching food packets or tin dixies in their hands, merged into the stream of workers. A hooter sounded a plaintive note.

"D'you hear that?" said Danny, anxiously. "Ten to seven!"

He pulled Elwyn forward into a trot. "Come on, we'll have to put a spurt into it. Ieuan hasn't far to go, but we've got a good step before us."

The wooden soles of their clogs made a hollow clatter that echoed loudly along the street. Ieuan fell in with his partners.

"Aw, no need for you to run," Danny advised. "You've got bags of time."

"It's all right. I'm just keeping company with you till we come to Station Square."

They sped past the corner where Crooked Row joined the main street, and wheeled into the Square. The sky had grown cloud-ridden and dark. Heavy drops of rain splattered on to the roadway.

"Here it comes!" Elwyn groaned. "Let's go and hide." Hardly had he spoken than the rain came hissing down in a torrential shower. The wind rose, and in short, sharp gusts, blew the heavy drops into a fine, showery spray that whirled about in the damp air. And as the rain increased in intensity, the wind changed its direction.

Suddenly, it seemed to split up into many winds of varying force and blew into the Square from every angle. It drove the wildly beating rain into a pattern of crisscrosses, smacking it against the shop windows. Powerless to resist this onslaught, the rain swept in all directions. It stung into the faces of the scurrying passers-by, and rushed in a wide curve along the sheen-like surface of the road.

48

Men and women, boys and girls, darted into the dark doorways to seek shelter. Tramcars, filled to capacity, clanged noisily towards the terminus, the drivers crouched forward over their gears while they dragged on their heavy service mackintoshes and sou'westers.

The rain lashed down the camber of the road, and the gutters filled with black, murky streams that raced madly along to disappear with a loud gurgle into the drains. Street lights, eclipsed previously by the brilliance of the moon, dazzled across the rain-swept road. Puddles quickly formed on the uneven surface, and the rain peppered them with a myriad rings and splashes.

The hidden moon slid out from cover. It lighted up the gloom for a brief moment. The shadows raced across the slippery road and climbed the walls on the other side, only to be swallowed up once more in semi-darkness as the moon sought the shelter of another black cloud.

But in that fraction of time and space, beauty had her sway. The windows of the houses and shops shone with a pearl-grey lustre. Tears of rain shimmered on the glass panes, and the wet, gleaming road quivered with light and shade.

Voices issued from doorways. A workman cursed the rain for delaying him. A girl laughed. Someone began to sing in a wheezy tenor:

"Oh, it ain't goin' to rain no more, no more,

It ain't goin' to rain no more ...."

Two tinworks' boys, dwarfed in the cold, melancholy light, darted out on to the pavement, sack aprons thrown over their heads, and hurried down the street.

Danny grew restless. "Shall we risk it?" he ventured.

"No, wait a bit," Elwyn replied. "It's only a shower."

"Shower-all-day," grumbled the other. "If we're late, the foreman'll put someone else on instead of us. Come on, let's go."

"Not me," said Elwyn decisively. "I don't want a soaking."

"Soaking, by damn. I'd rather have a wet shirt than lose a day's pay."

"But I tell you, it's only a shower. Wait a couple of minutes. We'll get to the works in plenty of time."

"No we won't."

"'Course we will."

"Aw, put a sock in it, El. How ...."

While they argued, the rain stopped. Gradually, the wind died away. The shelterers ventured out from the doorways and soon the road was black with surging humanity. When they reached the middle of the Square they were joined by other workers who poured in from the three converging sides.

Tramcars jerked to a vicious halt that threw the occupants forward in their seats. Gear levers were unscrewed, and the drivers crossed to the opposite end of the trams to prepare for the reverse journey. The passengers scrambled out on to the road to make room for returning night-shift workers who had waited under the canopy of the station entrance.

A local train steamed in from the valleys and expelled its cosmopolitan horde of men and women. The Square resembled a gigantic ant colony. Everyone was in a hurry — girls and boys, little more than children in years and appearance; old men whose shoulders were bowed by years of labour; young women, sprightly and vivacious; fathers, mothers, brothers, sisters; old, young; handsome, ugly. The deaf and the dumb; the lame and the sure-limbed; the weak and the strong; the wise and the foolish — they were all here. A seething mass of people pressing forward, turning to the right, to the left, pushing, jostling, swaying, side-stepping. Cursing, laughing, singing, shouting. But each and every one in the great, desperate rush to be on time.

The majority joined the long black column which made its way down Jerusalem Street, past the bleakfronted chapel of that name, to the estuary and the docks, where a number of tinworks sprawled. Others turned left into Maesyrhaf Road and the chemical factory, while the remainder crossed the Square into Heol Morfa, swarming past the railway station towards the tinstamping factory, the foundry and the Goliath Tinworks.

Ieuan stopped on the corner. Here, he and his companions would have to part. He was about to say, "Solong," when someone called.

Elwyn and Danny looked around.

"Christmas!" the latter blurted. "Dai Screws, the loafer!" He nudged his pal. "Let's beat it, El. Once Dai starts talking he'll keep us here all day."

A short, thick-set, elderly man, with a stubbly growth of beard on his chin, ambled towards them. He was dressed in a blue reefer coat tied with string in place of buttons, and a grey woollen sweater. A master mariner's cap perched at a rakish angle on his head. He seemed partial to string. The patches on his coat were sewn with it. A yard or so, knotted round his waist, served as a belt. Even his boots were laced with string.

"'Allo, Elwyn; 'allo, Danny," he greeted.

They were anxious to be off, but the old man commandeered them.

"Bit of a storm that, boys. Reminds me of the day when I sailed out from Marseilles nearly forty years ago. Bound for the Honduras we was, and, by golly, did we run into a storm! Why — "Suddenly, he caught sight of Ieuan. "'Allo good boy."

He turned to Elwyn. "Who's this little chap?"

"Ieuan Morgan," said Elwyn.

"Oh ay. What part does he come from?"

"Pleasant Row."

"His father works in the boxworks," Danny thrust in sharply. He began to move away. "Listen, Mr. Willi Elwyn and me's got to be off. Ten to seven's gone already."

"Tut-tut." Dai waved a hand airily. "Don't worry about the time. An' plenty of time you'll have to vex about the time — if you see what I mean?"

Danny was nonplussed, but in no mood to listen to the old man. "We're late," he said. "We've got to go."

"So his father works in the boxworks, eh? An' the little chap's from Pleasant Row," Dai went on. "Ieuan Morgan. Hm!" He

51

scraped his hedgehog's chin. "Funny that I don't know him." He addressed Danny once more. "Sure he's from Pleasant Row?"

"Yes, Mr. Williams, and we're in a hurry."

"All right, all right. If you want to wear out your little legs, go-run down the street as fast as you like. Don't worry about me. Go on, be off with you."

Thankful for the opportunity, Danny and Elwyn said a hasty goodbye.

"Half a tick, boys." Dai called them back. "Say, have you got a bit of a stump on you?" he asked persuasively.

Danny fumbled in his pockets. He drew out a crumpled Woodbine packet, and handed it to the old man. "You can have one o' these," he said.

Dai extracted a cigarette. He straightened it between thumb and fore finger. "Thank you, Danny. Thank you very much. Now, have you got such a thing as a match?"

Danny searched again in his pocket. A dirty matchstick was proffered.

"Thank you. Thank you very much. Indeed, a tobacconist you ought to be." Dai placed the cigarette behind his ear and, manoeuvring his fingers under a loop of string, meticulously dropped the match into a waistcoat pocket.

Before he could offer further thanks or have an opportunity to cadge anything else, the two boys had gone. He now turned his attention to Ieuan.

"Well, good boy. Up bright and early you are this morning, indeed. What is your name?" he asked.

"Ieuan Morgan," Ieuan replied, wondering why the old man had forgotten so soon.

"Oh, Morgan, is it? Not John Morgan's son? You know — John Morgan, clerk to the county council."

"No, my father's name is Richard Morgan — Dick Morgan."

"H'm!" Dai pursed his lips. "Don't seem to know him. Was he on sea some time?"

Ieuan shook his head.

"And where are you working, good boy?"

"Bevan's Foundry."

"How long you been there?"

"Starting today."

Dai's grizzled eyebrows contracted. "Too bad, too bad," he said in a whisper meant only for his own ears. "No sense in it. No sense in it at all, letting little boys go to work so early in the morning. Where does it get them in the end? Ay, where does it get them in the end?" he repeated, completely unaware of Ieuan's existence. "Work! What a thing for a man to have on his shoulders. Same as marriage it is. An' both don't agree with me, no indeed. So long as a man has got something to eat, a bit of a suit on his back, an' a roof over his head, what more does he want? Will work bring these things quick to him? Not that I know of. Fifty years ago I did say to myself: 'No more ships, no more sea, and no more work for you, Dai Williams. Some people can live without working, so why can't you?'"

The old man turned an inquiring eye on his audience.

"And who's to blame me, I ask you? Who's to blame me?"

Ieuan shuffled uneasily. "Mr. Williams, I've got to hurry," he said, "or I'll be late."

Dai did not seem to hear. "Funny thing this business of going to work every day," he continued. "Why should a man spend his time and strength doing this and that for somebody else who's going to get a profit out of it? Yes, that's the question you want to answer, Dai Williams. In fact, you have answered it, fifty years ago. Another thing, why should — ?"

Ieuan did not wait to hear any more of the old man's philosophizing.

"So-long, Mr. Williams," he cried, and ran up Heol Goffa.

* * *

The boundary walls of the station curved into Llandafen Road. On the corner stood Tony Marasiano's shop. It was open, and

53

Tony and his buxom, dark-haired daughter were busy serving cigarettes and matches to the customers who had broken their journey to the works to call in for their daily packet of fags.

As Ieuan drew near the shop, the crossing gates swung out. The crowd was galvanized into swift action. The younger people sprinted through the narrowing space left as the four wire-meshed gates closed against them. One boy was too late, and found himself shut in on the railway track. He stepped back, then, measuring his distance, leapt upwards, his hands gripping the top of the gate. Agile as a monkey, he pulled himself over into the roadway on the other side.

The rest of the crowd surged forward to the gates and waited impatiently for the oncoming train to pass. Cyclists drew up, brakes screeching, and sat with one foot on the ground, the other on the pedal. They crouched over their handlebars, posed as if for the start of a cycle race. Ieuan crossed to Tony's shop and leaned against the window ledge. Two men near him were discussing the previous Saturday's football match on Potter' s Park.

"Brilliant try, that one of Billy Bassett's, wasn't it, Fred?"

"Ay, indeed, but not so good as the one I saw Elfet Bowen score at St. Helen's last season. Right between the posts. From his own twenty-five, too. Must have beaten eight men, then gave a beautiful dummy to Joe Rees, full back. Best try of the season it was. Earned him his cap."

A huddle of girls were talking animatedly of the latest films.

"He's a handsome ma-a-hn, mind you."

"Ricardo Cortez? Ye-e-es," grudgingly, "but give me Milton Sills every time."

"Huh! He's no oil painting."

"A good actor, though."

"Was that his wife with him in the picture? I mean, his real wife?"

"Yes."

"Lovely clothes she had on, didn't she?"

54

A boy cyclist leaned over and said to his partner, loud enough for the girls to overhear: "Pictures on the brain."

One of the girls spun round, eyes flaming. "You shut up," she snapped, "and mind your own bloody business, Tommy Tucker." She was a pretty girl, with plucked eyebrows, vivid red lips, and bobbed hair with a fringe across her forehead — the fashionable "donkey-crop."

Ieuan stared at her. Gee, she was a pretty girl. Her coat was open. He could see the bright sheen of her yellow satin blouse and how it curved over her young breasts. She wore a pleated skirt, silk stockings, and white, high-heeled shoes with large black bows across the insteps. "A real smasher," as Jamesie would say.

Just the kind of girl he would like to take to pictures, he thought. When he had money in his pocket, of course. Every boy had to have a girl when he started working. It was nice to brag about. You felt grown up. And on Saturday nights you could take her to the picturedrome; ninepennies, back row, where the aisle was curtained off, and no lights on.

You could put your arm around her waist and steal a kiss. "Spooning," the boys called it. But what it had to do with spoons, he could never make out. He couldn't ask dad what it all meant. One never spoke about girls to one's father. Not when one was only sixteen.

A goods train rumbled by. Ieuan drew up with a start, his eyes still intent on the girl with the yellow blouse. What a joke! To think that he would like to take a girl to the pictures. How could he afford to buy two ninepenny tickets? Where was the money to come from? Besides, he had planned to save his allowance. Two shillings a week for a whole year. A hundred and four shillings. And he would give it to his mother so that he could go to college some day. All at once he became conscious of having given thought to all this last night, and it had made him sad and miserable. And now, as he stood in the light from Tony Marasiano's window, the very same thing was happening. He was beginning to feel wretched and miserable again. In five minutes' time he would be in the foundry. Five minutes — and then his name would be written down in the office ledgers. "Ieuan Morgan. Apprentice steel moulder. Commenced, November 14, 1924. Age, 15 years 7 months."

He would be given a number like a soldier in the Army, or a convict in jail. A number, so that the clerks could do their work easier. He had no number at school nor did he have to punch a clock to show that he had arrived in the morning.

It was like selling one's body; giving it out on hire, as his father had said. So much an hour for the use of his muscles and brain. Twelve and threepence a week for forty-seven hours.

He made a rapid calculation. Three and six fortysevenths of a penny an hour! In five years he would earn the district rate of three pounds seven and sixpence a week — one and fivepence ha'penny an hour.

There would be no pension, even if he worked at Bevan's all his life. Wasn't it better for mam to have kept him in school? Didn't she — couldn't she realize what she was losing by putting him into a foundry? In five years he would earn only three pounds seven and six!

The signalman leaned out of his box and motioned the crowd forward. He pulled back a lever. The steel blocks holding the gates in position slid below the road surface, and the four gates closed.

A thin, bespectacled boy in a long, shabby raincoat staggered across from the other side. He carried a heavy sack of cinders on his back and was bent almost double under the weight. Ieuan greeted him friendlily.

"Hallo, Davie Dan."

The boy blinked. He drew a glistening sleeve across his nose. "'Lo, Ieuan. Heck, this load's heavy. What time is it?"

"Five to seven."

"Is it? Crumbs, I'll have to hurry. Got to fetch another sackful from the Goliath before the policeman comes back."

Davie gripped the sack and swung it over his shoulder. "This is for our mam," he explained. "Fetching the next one for Mrs. Delaney Top House, I am. She promised to give me threepence-fo'pence if there's any coal lumps in it." He shifted the sack from one shoulder to the other, stumbling forward under the weight.

"You started work?" he asked, his head lowered.

"Yes. Bevan's Foundry. Starting this morning," Ieuan replied slowly.

"Heck, wish I had a job there. Think I'll have a chance when I leave school? Be fourteen next Feb'ry."

Davie winced as the sharp cinders dug into his back. "Sack's heavy," he mumbled. "See you 'gain, Ieuan, sometime. So-long!"

"So-long, Davie Dan."

Ieuan followed the crowd over the crossing. To the right, along the muddy lane, lay the foundry, the tall framework of the water condenser gaunt against the lowering clouds. A maze of sidings, bounded on one side by an iron fence, led out from the main gateway, ran parallel to the main line for a distance of a hundred yards and disappeared behind the station outbuildings.

A row of stationary trucks loomed in the darkness, the buffers gleaming faintly in a beam of yellow light which slanted down from the signal box. Here the crowds broke up once more. Some carried on down Llandafen Road; others followed the line of trucks into the lane. Both the lane and road led to the tinstamping and the Goliath works, but the former, though dimly lit, was a short cut, and was taken advantage of by the younger boys and girls.

The silhouetted twin roofs of the steel and iron foundries, the rounded tower of the cupola, and the shrouded office buildings reared above him as Ieuan approached. An arc lamp swung gently above the main gate and shone into a dark pool directly underneath. On the right was a small, red-bricked office with a door at each end.

The men in front of him carefully skirted the pool and entered the door nearest the gate. Soon a queue had formed, and with each loud ring of the "pegging clock" it moved slowly forward.

CHAPTER THREE

"HELLO, nipper!"

Ieuan felt someone touch him on the shoulder. He glanced round. A young man in a red scarf and battered trilby greeted him pleasantly.

"Haven't seen you round this way before, laddie? New here, aren't you?"

"Yes," Ieuan replied nervously. "This is my first day."

"What job?"

"Apprentice moulder."

The young man grinned. "Oh, a young sand rat, eh? Where you bound for? Iron or steel?"

"Steel foundry."

"Good! Then you'll see plenty of me. My name's Frank — Frank Jones." He paused. "Seen the timey yet?" He smiled at Ieuan's confusion. "Timekeeper. He'll give you a pegging number. Listen, don't stand in the queue. Walk into the office and wait there for me. Shan't be long. I'll talk to Timey about you."

Ieuan stepped out of the line and squeezed past the crowd in the doorway.

"Damn cheek these youngsters got," a man grumbled. He scowled. "Get hack into the queue there," he shouted.

"Keep your hair on, Bill," Frank returned. "He's a new recruit, doesn't know the ropes yet. He's waiting for me."

The queue pushed on. Ieuan watched each man swing the slender arm of the clock to a certain number and punch it into its corresponding hole. Clong! Clong! Clong! The bell rang continuously, and the procession moved out into the darkness of the yard.

Perched on a high stool in a small ante-room was an elderly

man. His back was towards the clock and, pen in hand, he crouched over a big ledger on the desk before him. To his right, a small fire burned, and now and then he turned and held his hands out over the a blaze.

Some of the workers greeted him with: "How goes, Pritchard?" as they entered the time office. He answered each by name, though he never as much as glanced over his shoulder.

At last, Frank came into the office. He winked at Ieuan, who stood nervously in the corner by the clock. "Be with you in half a tick." He punched his number, then slipped out of the queue.

"Pritchard!"

The timekeeper swivelled round on his stool.

"Yes, Frankie?"

"Got a new youngster for you. He's to be one of us. Dish out a number for him, will you?" Frank turned to Ieuan. "By the way, what's your name, son?"

"Ieuan Morgan."

"Same family as the bold, bad Captain Harry Morgan?" Frank asked, smiling.

The timekeeper, tall, blear-eyed, with a face wrinkled like dried leather, adjudged Ieuan. "Step over here, good boy."

Ieuan stood before him. "Yes, sir," he said nervously.

"Hey, hey, don't call him 'sir,'" Frank said with mock gravity. "He's only the timey."

Pritchard frowned. "What did you say your name was, good boy?" he queried. Then, to Frank: "You'd better get a move on. The hooter's on the blow — and be a bit more respectful next time."

"Yes ... sir," Frank grinned. He tossed his head towards Ieuan. "What about showing the youngster the way to the foundry?"

"I'll see to that," the timekeeper answered gruffly. "I've got some questions to ask him first."

"Righto! So-long, Pritchard. Be good. And keep your feet dry."

Frank hurried out into the yard to the accompaniment of a loud, shrill blast from the work's siren.

"Well, good boy, what's your name?" the timekeeper repeated.

"Ieuan Morgan."

He wrote it down in the ledger in a large, round hand. "How old are you?"

"Fifteen years and seven months!"

"No, no, good boy. I mean, when were you born?"

"April the fifth, nineteen nought nine."

"And where do you live?"

"Number three, Pleasant Row."

"Number three ... Pleasant ... Row." The timekeeper placed his pen in a groove on the desk and carefully pressed a sheet of blotting paper on the wet page.

"Now, my boy, let's see what department you're to go to." He took a sheaf of papers from a drawer in the desk and scanned through them. "Ah, here we are." He held a pink time sheet in his hand. "Ieuan Morgan, apprentice moulder, steel foundry," he read. "That means you're to work under Lu Davies. Well, now that's settled I'll give you your number."

He drew a bony finger down a long column of names. "Forty-seven, forty-eight, forty-nine. Forty-nine, there we are! Forty-nine's your number, my boy. You remember that, won't you? Now, come over here with me." The old man led him to the clock. He brought the pointer round to Ieuan's number. "You swing it round like this, see? Then push it into the little hole that has your number over it. Do it every morning when you come in, and at five o'clock when you've finished for the day. Don't forget, mind, because if you do, then there'll be no pay. If you forget to peg in I'll have to mark you absent in my book. Understand now, good boy?"

"Yes, thank you very much, Mr. Pritchard."

"That's the spirit." The timekeeper patted him on the head and hobbled back to his fire. He held his hands above the flames.

Ieuan waited.

"Well, what are you waiting for?"

"The foundry. I — I don't know my way."

"Oh yes, of course, of course." Pritchard shuffled to the door and peered into the yard. "H'm! Bit too dark for me to take you," he mumbled. He rubbed his hands, and shivered. "Wait a little while. The late ones'll be rushing in to peg in a minute; I'll have one of them to show you the way."

Presently the door on the far side flew open and banged against the wall.

"Steady on there! Steady on!" the timekeeper shouted angrily. He scowled at the young boy in a belted mackintosh who bustled in to the office. "Humph!" he grunted. "Thomas Hughes, you it is again, eh? Late as usual, of course. What's the matter with you in the mornings? A young fellow like you ought to be ashamed of himself, indeed he should. I'm losing patience with you, and if there's any more of this nonsense I'll be reporting you to Mr. Bevan."

The boy took no notice of the threat. He punched the clock savagely, and made for the exit.

"Just a minute!"

Thomas spun round. "What've I done now?" he asked, aggrieved.

"Nothing," the timekeeper retorted sharply. "Come here, and don't be so cheeky." He introduced him to Ieuan. "This little lad is starting in the steel foundry. Take him up the yard and show him into the coreshop. Abraham knows he's supposed to start today, so he'll be expecting him."

Thomas jerked his head towards the door. "Come on." Ieuan followed him into the yard.

"Keep this side of the railway, or you'll get your boots all splashed."

They walked along a narrow black path which zigzagged past the main office buildings. Ieuan's eyes soon grew accustomed to the gloom. The outline of the tall water condenser resolved into stout, tarred timbers and iron stay rods, and the winding railway glimmered as doors of the various departments opened to throw out a sudden flood of light.

The yard was deserted. Thomas slowed down and waited until Ieuan drew abreast with him.

"What was your name?" he asked. "I didn't catch it just now. I was mad with old Timey — that's why."

"Ieuan — Ieuan Morgan."

"Been working anywhere before?"

"No, this is my first job."

"My name's Thomas Hughes and I work in the coreshop. That's where you'll be, I suppose."

"I don't know," said Ieuan.

"But Timey told me to take you to Abraham. You heard him, didn't you?"

"Yes, that's right."

"Well, Abraham's charge-hand in the coreshop. Seeing as you're an apprentice moulder you won't be put into the foundry just yet. Nobody's sent into the foundry — not first go off. All apprentices got to spend a year in the coreshop. If they're O.K., they get shifted into the steel shop — that's what we call the foundry. But if they're slow learning they get stuck in the coreshop for another year. Just like it was in school — if you're a dunce you stay in the same class until next year. See what I mean?"

They walked a few yards in silence.

"What's the coreshop like?" Ieuan ventured. "Is it a lot different from the foundry?"

"It's where they make cores for the moulds. You'll see when you get there," Thomas replied. He stopped. "Say, what d'you think of Timey?"

"Mr. Pritchard?"

"Yes, old Pritch. What d'you feel about him?"

"He seemed a nice old man, I think." Ieuan was on the defensive.

"Bosh! Don't you believe it." Thomas held his nose. "He stinks. Listen here...." He became confidential: "Don't you trust him. He's a sly one, is old Pritch. Know what happened the other day?"

62

Ieuan's silence gave him an incentive to continue.

"I'll tell you what happened, and then you'll see what a nice old chap he is. Morris Bugs — he's one of the improvers in the steel shop — had a message to say his mother was very sick. Dangerously ill she was, and going to be taken to the hospital. Morry had to rush home. He asked Lu for time off, and Lu said all right, although Morry was working on a breakdown job. When he got to the gate Pritch stopped him and asked what was up. Morry told him his mother was being rushed to hospital and that he had to go home, and that Lu had given him time off. Old Pritch was very sad about it. 'You go, Morris,' he said, 'as quick as you can. And when you come back let me know how the poor soul is.'

"Morry goes home, and the ambulance is there. He rides up to the hospital with his mother to keep her company, and after she's put to bed for an operation, he comes back right away to the foundry. Pritch stops him again and asks if everything went off well. Morry said yes, but his mother was to have a major operation. Proper worried, he was. Then Pritch puts a hand on his shoulder, friendly like. 'Dop't you worry, Morris,' he said, 'everything'll come out right. Don't you worry.'" Thomas spat to the ground. "Yes, that's what he said.

"And know what happened next week? I'll tell you. When Morry went for his pay packet he found Pritch had cropped him an hour — the time he'd taken off to see his mother to hospital. Now, what d'you think of that? There's old Pritch for you! There's your nice man — the waster! The stinking waster! Nice talk he's got. Butter-won't-melt-in-my-mouth, if you see what I mean. I wouldn't trust him farther'n I could spit. Take a tip from me, Ieuan — don't have nothing to do with him. He's a master's man, from his bloody boots up."

Ieuan said nothing. The story seemed improbable, and he couldn't bring himself to believe that such a quiet-spoken old man could behave in the callous manner Thomas had described. He gave it no further thought, for he was too concerned with his own state of mind. Each step he took made him more apprehensive of the future. What lay behind that grim, dark building? How would the men greet him? Would he be able to adapt himself to these new surroundings, and would his fears vanish with the passing of each day?

From within the smithy came the loud, persistent throb of dynamos as the compressed-air valves were opened to kindle the forges, and above it the heavy thud of the steam hammer, and the sharp, metallic ring of the blacksmiths' tools striking against the anvils.

The adjacent fitting shop resounded to a low, muffled hum that gradually increased into a roar. It seemed as though a colossal machine had been set in motion, with hundreds of wheels spinning around, gathering momentum from each revolution.

A door opened, and Ieuan caught a glimpse of dark, overalled figures bending over the whirling lathes. Men shouted to one another across the steel-plated floor. Lathe belts slapped viciously against the racing pulley wheels. Overhead, the forty-ton crane quivered and groaned as it jolted along the girders.

Huge steel castings, flaked with rust, and held in position by thick wire cables, moved slowly under the sharp edge of the planing machine. Inch-wide strips of steel curled up from the rusty surfaces, leaving a silvered trail in the wake of the cutting-tool blade. Under each lathe lay a pyramid of steel, brass and copper bearings which were shovelled into iron barrows and wheeled out into the yard.

A splay-footed workman passed by with a barrow load.

"How be you, Thomas?" he shouted with a grin. "See somebody slept on your shirt this morning again, eh?" He took a quick glance at Ieuan. "New boy, aren't you?"

"Yes," Thomas cut in, annoyed by the man's reference to his unpunctuality, "if it's any business of yours, Jack Shanty."

"That's enough. None o' your impudence, or I'll give you a lander," the man threatened. He dropped the barrow. "And call me by my proper name, you cheeky little runt."

"You give me a lander?" Thomas returned. "W'ho's going to help you? Gertcha!" he sneered. "You couldn't hit an elephant in a passage." Dodging the blow aimed at him, he darted along the yard, with Ieuan at his heels. Presently they drew up before a large door.

"Here we are." Thomas paused awhile to regain his breath. He grinned at his partner. "Nervous?"

Ieuan shook his head.

"Good ! " Thomas pushed a finger through a small hole in the door and raised the wooden latch.

"H'm! Quiet this morning. Doesn't look as if they've started yet. Lu must be late. Hope he doesn't show up till nine," he added, wishfully, "though if old Abraham's here, he'll see we do a bit of work. Come on, hop in."

Ieuan found himself in a dark, narrow alleyway. The walls were covered with a layer of soot and grey silica dust. Wrought-iron rings of various thicknesses hung from staples driven deep into the joints between the bricks. In the corner near the door through which they had just entered stood a triangular wooden bench, an iron vice and a small anvil.

A deep water bosh protruded from the wall, its sides smeared with grey moulding paint. The tap fixed above it dripped steadily on to the black, greasy surface of the water. Cropped ends of wrought-iron rods, and snake-like coils of rusty wire littered the floor. A naked bulb dangling on a length of flex from the rafters provided the only illumination, which failed to penetrate the farthest corners of the coreshop — a building no more than twelve yards square.

"Listen," Thomas looked closely at Ieuan, "if any of the chaps try to be funny with you, don't get your monkey up. Just don't take any notice of them," he advised. "They like to be cocky with somebody new. Remember now — keep your hair on, and say nothing to start a quarrel. See?"

From the other side of the wall came a murmur of voices.

"That you, Thomas?" a man's voice called.

"Yes."

"Who's that with you?"

"The new apprentice."

"Then bring him in and let's have a look at him. What the hell're you hiding for?" another loud and insinuating voice shouted.

"That's Bull Jackson," Thomas said under his breath. "He's the oldest apprentice. A big bully, too — so keep clear of him."

* * *

Six pairs of eyes watched Ieuan as he stepped into the coreshop. On a plank resting on two upturned bricks, three men and three youths in dungarees sat with their backs against the door of a core-drying stove.

The eldest of the men, bearded, benevolent-looking, smiled at Ieuan. "So you're the new little boy? Well, come on over here and sit down." He moved to make room for him, and Ieuan sat down timidly.

"What's your name, good boy? — Ieuan Morgan, is it? H'm! Nice name, indeed. Now, let me introduce you to the other lads who'll be working with you." He turned to a powerfully built youth who sat next to him. "This is Jimmy Jackson, and — "

"Aw, keep quiet, Isey." The youth scowled. "One'd think we're in a bloody Sunday School." He thrust his face close to Ieuan's. "I'm Bull — Bull Jackson." He pointed to the old man who had just spoken. "He's Isaiah Charles, call him 'Deacon' if you like, I shan't mind. The feller with whiskers is Abraham, chief-sir-hand in this dump, and next to him's Dicky."

"And what about me?" a youth who sat at the end of the plank inquired. He rose and, with a flourish, bowed to Ieuan.

"Name's Reginald Bowen," he mimicked in falsetto. He held out his hand delicately. "Now that we have all become so bloody polite, may I say, 'How do you do, Mr. Morgan?'"

Bull grunted. "Put a sock in it, Reg." He pulled the other back to his seat. "Reg Bowen," he said to Ieuan. "Works in the steel shop. And this," he jerked his head towards a pallid-faced,

66

ungainly boy, dressed in ragged dungarees, "this shrimp is Tight-arse, messenger boy and tea-boiler for the whole caboose."

The latter leaned forward.

"Titus — till you know me better," he said aggressively.

"Okay, Tight-arse," Bull sneered. "Keep your shirt on, and speak when you're spoken to next time." He thumbed to the wall on the far side where a number of coats hung. "Shove your coat over there," he commanded Ieuan. He paused. "What did you say your name was?"

"Ieuan Morgan."

"Ok! From now on you're 'Iron.' We all got names here. You heard mine, didn't you? Bull Jackson's the name. But when you say it, don't try and be bloody clever. See?"

Ieuan crossed over to the other side of the shop and hung his coat on a nail.

"Hey, what's the idea?"

Reg Bowen, round-shouldered and mean-eyed, darted after him. He took the coat off the nail and flung it to the floor. "That's my peg. Get another one."

Thomas stepped up to the improver. "Lay off, Reg. Let him have yours for today." He looked at him suspiciously. "Where's your coat?" he asked.

"In the steel shop. Why?"

"Then what're you claiming this peg for? How many pegs d'you want?"

"Mind your own business. Why the hell don't you put his coat on your peg?"

"Suits me." Thomas shook the dust from the coat and hung it under his own mackintosh on the wall.

Abraham, a short, sharp-featured man with a tumbling grey moustache, got up from the seat. Dicky, his deputy, followed him meekly to the wooden bench built against the wall, and on which lay a series of wooden coreboxes.

This was the signal to start. Dicky, whose right hand was withered, did not say a word to Ieuan, but just nodded casually

67

as he proceeded to damp the heap of sand mixture on the bench. The old man, Isaiah, rose slowly and brushed the dust from the seat of his trousers, while Reg and Titus made their way towards the sliding door which opened out into the steel shop.

Bull stood in the middle of the floor, glaring at Abraham.

"What's up?" he grumbled. "Starting early, aren't you? Lu's not in yet, so for Christ's sake take a spell." He walked to the bench and sat down, arms folded. "I'm not making a move until he comes in, and not a bloody minute before."

A door slammed. The heavy crunch of footsteps approached, and a tall man in a dark overcoat, with an umbrella over the crook of his arm, peered into the coreshop. His sharp eyes glinted.

"You'd better make a start right now," he said to Bull, "or take a walk out through the gate."

"Lu!" Bull sprang to his feet and bustled blindly around in his excitement.

"There's plenty to do on the bench," the foreman rasped. "What about those cores for Tregonning's, have you done them?"

"No, sir. I — I'll do them right away."

Bull picked up a corebox at random. Throwing in a handful of sand, he began to ram it quickly with a thin steel rod.

Titus and Reg, on seeing the foreman, had darted into the foundry to warn the men that he had arrived. Soon, the cranes were heard rumbling along the girders. The automatic rammers barked, and the big "bumper" was switched on, wheezing, groaning and thumping like a giant with a sore throat.

Lu noticed Ieuan standing near the stove. "You're Morgan, the new apprentice Pritchard was telling me about, I suppose?" he said sharply. "Well, you can start here in the coreshop. Take orders from Abraham, and do what you're told. Remember, this is a place of work, not a convalescent home. Do your best, and I'll see you're all right. Play about, and — well, you heard me warn that boy just now, didn't you?"

"Yes, Mr. — Mr. Davies."

The foreman passed on and entered the steel shop. Bull turned round and spat viciously to the floor. "Swine!" he muttered. He called to Thomas. "Ram the Tregonning cones, will you? And show Iron what's what. I haven't time. Got to go down the lav'."

"Half a mo', Bull." Abraham caught him by the hem of his coat as he prepared to leave the coreshop. "You'll give us a hand to get the bogie out first. And not so many trips down to the lavat'ry today, d'you hear?"

"To hell with you," Bull retorted, shaking himself free. 'I'm going down, and you nor nobody else's going to stop me. It comes to something when a chap can't go to the lav. They got time for that, even in jail."

"Hush, hush! Careful with your language, boy," Isaiah remonstrated. "There's no need to talk like that."

"Hark to the deacon," Bull scorned. "Thinks he's in Sunday School again." He thrust his hands into his pockets and, rocking on his heels, began to sing:

"Roll the ol' chariot along,
Roll the ol' chariot along,
If the deacon's in the way, roll right over,
An' you must hang on behind..."

He stopped short. "That's for you Isey, so dry up." Wheeling round, he stamped out into the yard.

Abraham slid back the steel door of the drying stove. "Let's have the bogie out, boys," he said quietly, apparently tired of the many attempts he had made to check the unruly Bull during the latter's apprenticeship. He drew out a thick rope from under the bench and knotted it through a link in front of the bogie.

"Now, all together!"

Isaiah, Dicky and Thomas gripped the rope. Abraham summoned Ieuan. "Take hold of the end, good boy, and pull as hard as you can."

Digging their heels into the floor, they strained at the rope. The bogie, loaded with heavy cores, screeched over the rails leading from the interior of the stove. The cores rested on thin, circular iron plates. Baked to a lightbrown colour, they were too hot to touch with bare hands.

Abraham took a small hand-brush from his tool cupboard and brushed away the particles of soot that clung to them. Ieuan stood aside and, perspiring, watched the others get ready for the tarring. They dipped longhandled, hempen swabs into a tar bosh fixed below the bench and, standing well back, rubbed them briskly over the hot cores.

The tar crackled and boiled. Greenish-grey fumes hissed to the roof, and the small building was soon enveloped in a thick fog. The men coughed and retched. Ieuan clapped a hand to his mouth and, holding his breath, rushed out through the doorway into the yard. The others followed him, their eyes watering, their hands and faces covered with minute splashes of tar.

"Good — good stuff for the whooping cough," Thomas spluttered. He wiped his forehead with the back of his sleeve. "See what you're in for every morning, Ieuan? Crikey-better if you'd taken on a job in the gasworks."

After a short rest they returned to the shop. The fumes had cleared, and the tar on the cores was already dry. Abraham took a shallow box from a shelf above the bench.

"Here, Thomas, make twelve cores for the job Frank's working on. Let the new lad help you."

Thomas showed Ieuan to a corner of the bench. He scraped off the dry sand with his trowel.

"We'll have to get some fresh compo before we start," he remarked, placing the corebox on a smooth, square steel plate. "Hand me the quarter riddle. Over there by the wall."

Ieuan picked up a quarter-inch meshed sieve and waited while Thomas took a shovel from a tall cupboard near the tar bosh.

"Got a trowel, I s'pose ?"

Ieuan proudly exhibited the shining tool.

"Gee, it's a beauty. Guess you'd better leave it on the bench till we come back from the compo shed, or you might lose it."

"Will — will anybody steal it?"

"No, not while Abraham and the others are here. Bull's the only one who'd try any games like that, but we'll be back before him."

Just then, Bull swaggered into the shop. Making a pretence of buttoning his trousers, he cast a sidelong glance at the bogie.

"Have a good look," Thomas grunted. "The work's done. Funny how you always get caught short when there's tarring jobs to do."

Bull waited until Abraham's back was turned. He tapped his head significantly. "Up here you want it," he sniggered, "and that's just where you haven't got it. You ought to go to night school, Tommy." He strode to the bench and pushed the steel plate aside. 'I'm working here," he announced, "so go look for another place." His eyes fell on the new trowel. "H'm! Nice job this."

Ieuan watched him apprehensively. "That's mine," he blurted.

"Did I say it wasn't?" Bull tossed the trowel to a corner of the bench. "Better keep an eye on it, else it'll walk. Know what I mean?"

"You keep your paws off it, Bull Jackson," Thomas snapped. He nudged Ieuan. "Come on, let's get the compo so's we can make a start."

They were about to move off when the steel shop door slid noisily open. A youth, about nineteen years old, with small, beady eyes set in a square-jowled face, marched towards them.

"I hear there's a new customer hanging around, Thomas," he grinned. "Where is he?"

"Here, Charlie." Bull gave Ieuan a forceful push which sent him stumbling over the sieve. "Name's Iron."

"Scrap or cast?" Charlie asked facetiously.

"His name's Ieuan — I-e-u-a-n," Thomas interposed. "Don't try and be a comic, you just don't come off."

Charlie brought back his hand as if to strike the apprentice.

"Shut your trap, you!" He eyed Ieuan from top to toe.

"Ah, new boots I see." He bent down to examine them, and

71

winked at Bull, who, anticipating a joke, threw him a tar swab. Suddenly, he whipped the swab over Ieuan's boots.

"There, that's better. Gives 'em a real spot of polish, what d'you think?" He stood up and looked Ieuan up and down once more. "So your name's I-am?" he began.

"Ieuan," Thomas corrected.

"The great I-am," Charlie continued. He called to the smirking Bull. "Say, tell me — does it speak?" With the same sly grin on his face, he turned to Ieuan.

"Any sisters?" he asked.

No reply came.

"Come on, open up. Any sisters?"

"Yes, two," Ieuan replied softly.

"Two? Lucky boy! Tell me," Charlie pinched his arm until he winced, "are they hot stuff?" He winked suggestively. "You know what I mean."

Thomas linked his arm in Ieuan's. "Come on, Ieuan, don't take any notice of him," he said. "He should have his mouth washed out — with bloody rat poison."

"What's that?" Charlie spun round. He reached over the bench and grabbed a handful of damp sand. "I'll rub this down the back of your neck, you cheeky little bastard," he shouted.

Isaiah overheard him. The old man looked up from his job. "Now then, that's enough of it. You'd better be going back to the steel shop where you belong," he said sternly. "And be quick about it, or I'll get Lu in to have a talk with you."

"Lu, by damn! Think I'm scared of him?" Charlie boasted.

Bull's eyes twinkled. He looked furtively over his shoulder. "Look out, Charlie," he breathed. "He's here!"

The improver did not wait to give a further opinion. His self-assurance and arrogance vanished. With six rapid strides he was out through the coreshop door into the yard.

Bull smacked his thighs and laughed uproariously. "Oh, Christ! Oh, Christ! Did — did you ever see a rabbit run so — so bloody quickly? Couldn't see his arse for dust."

72

Abraham approached him and tapped him on the shoulder. "Get on with your work," he said angrily. "I've just about a bellyful of you. By heavens, won't I be glad to see you sent into the steel foundry where Lu can keep an eye on you."

Bull turned his back on him. Unperturbed, he pretended to carry on with his work. As he leaned over the bench to scoop a handful of sand into his core box, he brushed against the new trowel. Glancing swiftly around while Ieuan and Thomas were on their way to the compo shed, he quickly daubed a swab of tar under the handle.

"Hey, Iron! " he called, holding the trowel by the blade. "Take this thing with you. If you leave it here somebody might take a fancy to it."

Ieuan reached for the tool. "Thanks." His fingers closed over the handle. Bull smirked at the look of bewilderment on his victim's face.

"Just a trade mark," he laughed. "Something to remember me by."

Ieuan placed the trowel gingerly on the bench. A glutinous mess of tar stuck to his fingers. He looked beseechingly at the grinning Bull. "Why — why did you do it?" he asked. "I've done nothing to you, have I?"

Bull shrugged. "All in the day's work, Iron. You'll get more'n that before you're through."

Thomas dropped the shovel and advanced towards the bully, his fists clenched. "Leave him alone, Bull, you bloody big coward," he shouted, "and pick on someone your own size for a change." He shot out his arm and caught the older boy a glancing blow on the chest. Bull lifted his foot and attempted to trip him to the floor. A heavy hand gripped him by the shoulder, and he was jerked round to face the angry deacon.

"Daro! I am a man of peace and quiet, but indeed, it's a good thrashing I'll give you if you don't behave properly," old Isaiah panted, trembling with rage. "Indeed I will," he repeated.

Abraham stepped between them. "All right, Isaiah, leave him

73

to me." He caught Bull by the collar. "The next time you take advantage of that boy you'll get thrown out of here on your neck," he warned. "You heard what Lu said to the youngster. You're paid to do a job of work. If you don't feel like doing it, then get out, d'you hear? Get out!"

"You ought to report him to Lu," Dicky ventured timidly. "He's always causing trouble in here. He ought to be put to work in the steel shop."

Bull's lips curled into a sneer. He shook himself loose and straightened his coat collar.

"Hark who's talking — Bloody Dicky-one-hand! He's a fine one to tell me to go into the steel shop. He couldn't do a day's work if he tried. Always riding on some other poor beggar's back."

"Keep quiet!" Abraham shouted. "You've enough to do to pass remarks about yourself, you big lout. Now, get on with those cores before I really lose my temper. Big as you are, I'll soon put you on your back, have no fear of that." He brushed his hands in a gesture signifying his contempt for the bully, and called Thomas.

"Take the boy to the stores and wash his hands in paraffin," he advised. "You can leave his trowel with me till he comes back. I'll clean it."

'I'm glad you didn't lose your temper with Bull," Thomas said, as they retraced their steps to the main office. "You'd have had the worst end of it. He's a strong chap, and he might hurt you a lot. Another thing — if Lu caught you fighting on your first day he'd send you packing. Lu's got no patience with anybody who ups with his fists. So take a tip from me, Ieuan — don't let Bull and the others rattle you. Remember what I told you before?"

"Yes. Thanks — Thomas."

Lewis, the storeman, was weighing a number of small brass castings when the boys appeared in the doorway.

"What can I do for you?" he asked, without looking up from his task.

74

"We've come down to — Thomas began.

The storeman pushed his spectacles back on to his forehead. "Oh, you it is, Thomas. Well, what do you want? Don't tell me it's core gum again — you chaps seem to be eating the stuff."

"Not this time," said Thomas. "Abraham sent me to get some paraffin to wash the tar off Ieuan's hands."

Lewis was annoyed. "How many times do you fellows from the foundry have to come here bothering me? Getting to be a nuisance, this tar and paraffin business. You know I'm not supposed to give you anything from the stores, not even a nail, unless I get a chit from your foreman. I expect you haven't one, as usual?"

"No," Thomas admitted.

The storeman clicked his tongue. "I thought not. Ah well, let's see those hands of yours, boy." He raised the lid of a large drum of paraffin and dipped a wad of cotton-waste into it.

Ieuan held out his hand. Lewis rubbed the tar-stained fingers clean, then tossed him a piece of dry waste. "Here you are. Wipe your hands, and remember," he said firmly, "no more trips into these stores unless you have a chit. I'm not paid to be nursemaid to you apprentice chaps."

"Righto, Lewis." Thomas walked to the door. "And thanks."

The storeman dried his hands. He studied Ieuan through half-closed eyes. "You're new here?"

Ieuan nodded.

"Thought so. First trip is always down here to see me. And always for paraffin. Tar on fingers, tar on trowels, tar on faces, tar on backsides. Never seen anything like it. The fellers who play these tricks on you young 'uns ought to be made to eat tar. Maybe it'd cure 'em." He turned sharply to Thomas. "Bull Jackson, I suppose?"

Thomas shook his head. "Accident, Lewis. Ieuan slipped over the bogie, and —"

"Yes, yes, I know, I know. I've heard that story before." Lewis adjusted the glasses over his nose. "All right. Be off with you. I've got work to do."

Abraham and Isaiah were trundling a heavy cast-iron core box to the middle of the floor when the boys returned. The space had been swept clean by Dicky, who now leaned on his broom and watched them. Bull was busy at the bench.

"Not so young as I was, Abraham," Isaiah sighed. He straightened himself and rubbed the small of his back. "Think the lads'll give me a hand to get a barrow-load of compo?"

"You bet we will," Thomas volunteered, anxious to please. "Only too glad to do you a favour. Ieuan and me'll go right away."

The compo shed was a dark, dismal building. Along the walls, compartments of different sand mixtures had been partitioned off. A grinding mill rumbled, the two perpendicular wheels travelling in reverse to the horizontal dish into which the mixtures were shovelled.

Two men were employed in throwing in the pile of silica stone, china clay, red sandstone, yellow loam and the various ingredients of which the moulding sands were composed. On the other side of the mill a third man scooped out the powdered mixture and tossed it to the floor, where it was shovelled into a barrow by another labourer and wheeled to the bins.

Thomas claimed an empty barrow. Grasping a shovel, he dug into the bank of sand and spread it out over the floor, watering it carefully.

"What're you working on?" the man on the far side of the mill called to him.

"Cores for Frank's job."

"Christ! you don't want a barrowful for them things."

"O.K., keep your hair on. I'm getting some for Isaiah as well."

"Oh."

Ieuan stood by with sieve in hand, poised over the barrow ready to riddle the damp mixture. "That's Brin Compo," Thomas whispered under his breath. "Boss, of this place. Looks on compo as if it was gold. Watches you like a cat. Could think he wants to hoard the stuff. The other two chaps shovelling in are Sammy Compo and John Henry Compo. They all get the name 'Compo' because they work here."

Soon the barrow was filled. Ieuan gripped the shaft. The weight pulled at his arms. They felt as though they would be wrenched from the sockets.

"Sure you can manage it?" Thomas eyed him doubtfully. "I'll wheel it if you like."

"No, it's — it's all right, thanks."

"O.K."

With shoulders bent, Ieuan lifted the barrow and pushed it along a slight gradient into the coreshop. His knees shook. He felt a sharp ache in his joints. His feet scraped against the floor. Determined not to show himself a weakling, he set his teeth and pushed forward.

The barrow wobbled round the corner by the water bosh.

Bull watched him with cunning amusement. "Half a mo', Iron. Lemme give you a hand." He ran to meet him, and leaned over the wheel, gripping both sides of the barrow.

"Steady on, Iron. Pull up. Hell, watch out!" Stumbling sideways deliberately, he pulled the barrow over. The load of sand slid across the dusty floor.

"Oh, hell! Sorry, Iron, but accidents will happen."

Thomas rushed at the bully. "Accident on purpose, wasn't it?" he challenged. "You're a stinking rotter. A bloody pest. A —"

"Shut your trap." Bull lunged at him.

"Now then, now then, that's enough," old Isaiah warned, stepping forward hurriedly. Bull dropped his hand. The Deacon helped Ieuan to right the barrow. Together they refilled it, taking care not to shovel in any of the dust.

The old man frowned. "Never mind, boys. Go back to the bench, and don't take any notice of that big good-for-nothing."

They took their share of compo and began to work on the core boxes Abraham handed to them. Ieuan showed an eager interest

77

in the job. He was anxious to learn, but Bull's presence made him nervous and awkward.

"You want to take some tonic tablets, my lad. You've got the shivers," Bull grinned. He leaned against the bench and lit a cigarette. He offered a soiled packet of Woodbines. "Smoke, Iron? Good for the nerves."

"No, thanks."

Bull shrugged. "O.K., if that's how you feel." He blew a cloud of smoke through his nostrils. "Look here," he said presently, "I'm sorry about that accident. Honest to God, I am." The cigarette end was nipped, and the butt placed behind his ear. "What about me taking you round the place, introduce you to the lads? Just to show there's no bad feeling. I'd like to make up for what happened with the barrow. Cripes, I wouldn't do a thing like that on purpose."

Ieuan looked at Thomas. He felt embarrassed at this new approach.

"Do what you like," said the latter, sharply. "You know what I've told you."

Bull scowled. "What did you tell him?" he grunted.

"A pack of bloody lies about me, I bet."

The question was ignored.

"Well, coming?" Bull crossed to the sliding door. Ieuan followed, still hesitant. "It's all right — I mean, I can leave my job?"

"Oh hell, stop worrying, Iron. You're not in jail. 'Course you can leave your job. Lu won't say nothing to you. Look at me, when I want to walk out, I walk out — see? Come on, don't be bloody windy."

Inside the steel foundry the atmosphere was gloomy and oppressive. Below the high-saddled roof a row of twenty globes was strung. A pale, greenish-white light shone down on the men, transforming them into strange, unearthly creatures, green-faced gnomes dwarfed by the towering steel girders and massive moulding boxes.

A world of green: a new and weird world of grim, dark shadows and frenzied activity; of conflicting sounds varying from the roar and thunder of overhead gantries, the sharp, shrill staccato beat of automatic hammers, to the echoing ring of steel upon steel, and the hollow wheezing and thumping of the hydraulic moulding machines.

The windows in the high wall were covered with a thick layer of soot. Two heavy cranes tracked along the steel girders, the cranemen crouching low over their gears, vague and indistinct. With each jolt, the girders shook and a fine shower of black snow drifted gently down on the workers below.

"Nice and cosy, eh? Plenty of fresh air."

Bull's words drew Ieuan out of his reverie. He looked around, fascinated with the scene. At the top end of the shop stood a long line of small moulding boxes, where the improvers worked.

"Hey, there!"

Ieuan turned. He saw the improver, Reg Bowen, in the distance. The latter dicked his heels and saluted. "Come on over and meet the boys."

He still stood at attention when Ieuan and Bull approached. "Welcome to our humble home, Cast Iron. We salute you, comrade."

His neighbour was on his knees, dressing the mould of a small pulley wheel. Reg tapped him on the rump with a long steel rammer.

"Bonzo, meet the latest recruit to the nut-house."

The other stood up and straightened his back. He regarded Ieuan dubiously, then stepped back a pace. "Looks a bit skinny to me." He felt the boy's biceps. "H'm! Ha! You'll do. Guess we can fatten you up on a bit of compo and core-gum now and again." He turned to Reg. "The usual question. Has he got any sisters?"

Reg grinned and held up two fingers. "Don't get ideas, Bonzo," he smirked as the latter whistled through his teeth. "They're young tits."

"Oh, tiddley bits, eh? No oomph, and no can do?"

79

Ieuan flushed. "Don't talk like that about my sisters. It's not decent," he said hotly.

"Oh, hell, hark at him," Bonzo laughed. "He's gone la-di-da all of a sudden. D'you hear him, Reg? Our little ninny don't like us to talk about his sisters."

Bull winked. "Leave the kid alone," he said. "You, too, Reg." He caught Ieuan's hand. "Take no bloody notice of 'em, nor any of these improver chaps. They're just trying to get your goat. Come over here with me, I'll show you how the big moulds are dried."

He crossed the floor to a drying stove flanked by two rows of smaller moulding boxes similar to those on which the improvers were working.

"Here's No. 1 stove," he explained. "Feel it. There's a hell of a heat."

Ieuan advanced with hand outstretched. Bull, seizing the opportunity, dodged smartly behind him and signalled to Reg. Suddenly, a ball of dry sand crashed high above the door. A cloud of soot and particles of gritty silica showered down on the boy. His dungarees were smothered with black smuts. The sand trickled down the back of his neck.

Bull chuckled. Ieuan wheeled round, his fists clenched. He looked wildly about him.

"Keep your rag in," Bull grinned. "Accidents will happen — I've told you that before."

"Is — is this why you brought me here?" Ieuan was almost in tears.

"Oh, hell, don't start blubbing," Bull grimaced. "You'll get used to accidents as the day goes on. Here, let me brush that muck off you. Bend down so's I can get the sand out of the back of your neck."

Ieuan bent, and as he did so a second ball of sand caught him on the shoulder and sent him stumbling against the iron door. Again he spun round, his small fists clenched, but once more he saw no sign of his assailant.

"Jesus, this is too much." Bull was enjoying the joke. "Come on, Iron — let's skedaddle before someone tries to bury you."

At that moment the foreman came striding up from the casting bay. Bull grew excited. "Hurry, Iron. Quickly! Here's Lu. If he finds me away from the bench he'll play merry hell."

Scared by the foreman's approach, he bolted through into the compo shed, leaving Ieuan to follow despondently and still near tears. But presently, when Ieuan entered the compo shed he was lounging against a bin, a cigarette butt stuck between his lips. Bull greeted him coolly, as though nothing had happened to stir him into the wild activity of a few minutes ago.

At his side an elderly labourer sat on the shafts of a barrow. The latter nodded to Ieuan. "This the new chappie?"

"Yes," said Bull, manoeuvring a pin into a stained cigarette end and drawing a whiff through puckered lips. "That's the bloke. Mammy's blue-eyed baby."

"Think he'll do me a favour?" the old man asked.

"'Course he will. Anything to oblige, that's his motto." The labourer creaked to his feet. "Do me a little kindness, my boy," he said persuasively. "Bit of rheumatics I've got, and this barrow load's too heavy for an old fellow like me."

He sighed. "By jingo, there's nice it is to be young. No need to ask favours then, no indeed. But look at me — can't push a barrow only when it's empty, and here I am, come to a full stop. Fancy sending me out to the yard with a load of compo. No sense in it, no sense at all — an old fellow like me."

Ieuan brightened. 'I'll help you," he volunteered.

The labourer smiled. "Good! And let me tell you that old Dafydd Richiets won't be forgetting your kindness. No indeed. Here you are, my boy. Just as far as the coreshop do I want your help, that's all. I'll manage after that."

Ieuan slipped between the shafts and lifted the barrow. Bull and the old man watched him, their eyes unblinking. Suddenly, they both guffawed loudly. Ieuan's hands felt wet and sticky. He loosed his hold and looked down apprehensively. They were

81

covered with thick tar. Unable to restrain himself any longer he burst into tears.

Dafydd disappeared into the coreshop, and Bull, blowing a smoke ring into the air, sauntered after him.

"What's the matter, boy?"

Ieuan looked up. A pair of earnest eyes regarded him. It was Frank, the young moulder who had spoken kindly to him on his way in to the foundry.

"What's the matter, lad?" he repeated. He pursed his lips when he saw the tar-smudged hands. "Who did it?"

Ieuan did not reply.

"Tell me, boy — who's been messing about with you?"

Brin Compo, who had witnessed the occurrence, came forward, shovel in hand. "Old Dafydd Richiets and that Bull chap — them's the fellers, Frank. A bloody bright pair, if you ask me."

Frank shrugged. He patted Ieuan on the shoulder. "Never mind, lad, we'll soon fix those hands of yours. You mustn't pay any attention to Dafydd, the old bloke's in his second childhood. Look here," he rolled back the boy's sleeves, "go down to Lewis, the storeman. He'll give you some stuff to clean up the mess. Know where the stores are?"

Ieuan nodded.

"Good! Tell him you slipped into the tar bosh. There's no need to mention Dafydd's name, the old bloke will only get into trouble with Lu. As for Bull — leave him to me. I'll settle his hash."

"No, please don't say anything," Ieuan pleaded. "I mean, about Bull. It was only a joke."

Frank smiled. "O.K. You can tell Lewis it was an accident. He'll be all right."

Ieuan hesitated. "I — I've been to the stores once," he stammered.

"What?" Frank looked hard at him. "You've been down once before this morning? Is this the second time you've been tarred?"

"Yes."

82

"Not Dafydd again?"

"No."

"Then who did it?"

"I — I'd rather not say.

"All right — I've got a good guess all the same. Bull Jackson, no doubt. Never mind, I don't want you to tell me if that's how you feel. Well, if you've been to the stores once, I reckon it's no good going down the second time. Lewis won't like it. The old boy's always grumbling, not that I blame him. Anyway, I know where I can fix you up. But listen, if Bull or anyone else tries to get one over on you again, let me know. I don't mind a joke, but there's a limit to this sort of thing. Remember now, let me know, and I'll put a stop to it."

Frank called Brin Compo's attention. "If Lu asks after me, tell him I've gone to the bughouse. Be back in a shake."

Motioning Ieuan in front of him, he stepped through a small door at the side of the mill and walked along a narrow path which ran parallel to the drying stoves and the steel furnaces. He had gone a distance of about a hundred yards when he drew up before a dilapidated lean-to.

"In you go, Ieuan. I'll soon fix up the mess."

He looked around. Hanging on the wall was a hurricane lamp. Frank took it down and shook it. "We're lucky, my boy. There's still a drop of paraffin left. Now, let's have a look at those hands."

Ieuan extended his fingers. The lamp base was unscrewed. Frank whipped a dirty rag from his pocket. He tilted the lamp and soaked the rag with the oil that remained.

"There! that's got you clean at last. Now, when you go back keep your eyes open. This tarring business is an old stunt. It's got whiskers on it, so it's up to you to be careful. O.K. ?"

Darkness was slowly lifting when they returned across the yard. The main office was open, and the charwomen at work, dusting the tall desks and placing the various ledgers and papers in neat order.

Frank skipped over the rails and ducked under a row of trucks, beckoning Ieuan to follow. Oil-encrusted pools glistened in the faint light. Buildings, hitherto indefinable, changed into grey stone walls, zinc-sheeted roofs, and iron-barred windows blacked out with a coating of creosote.

Man and boy skirted the tall mound of rusty, rain-soaked scrap iron and steel that lay between the furnaces and the pattern shop. A moulder hurried by, casting a quick glance over his shoulder.

"That you, Frank?" he called. "Any idea of the time?"

Frank drew out a cheap watch from his waistcoat pocket.

"Another four minutes, and she'll be on the blow," he replied. He nudged Ieuan. "You'll have to make a dash for it, lad. I suppose Abraham told you about the teaboiling? That's an apprentice's first job, and a very important one, too. You'd better go back to the coreshop and see young Titus. He'll show you the ropes. The canteen's just over there, round the pine end of the pattern shop. You can have your breakfast with the men — that is, if you're not going home for a meal. Anyway, you'd better hurry along. I'll have to leave you — got to grab my coat and buzz off home for grub."

* * *

Thomas stood outside the coreshop. "Where've you been, Ieuan?" he demanded. "Titus's waiting for you. He's got the cans ready since quarter past eight."

"I've just been with Frank to clean my hands," Ieuan replied.

"Your hands!" Thomas paused. "Hell! you haven't been tarred again?"

Ieuan felt uneasy. "Yes," he admitted.

"Jumping Moses!"

Isaiah's head jerked up. "What was that, Thomas?"

"Nothing — I was just telling Ieuan about the tea-boiling."

"Oh, yes, of course, of course." The old man walked to the bench. Six tankards stood on it. He picked up a black enamelled

84

one. "This can's mine, good boy. Only half full I want it, you remember that. You watch Titus, he'll tell you what to do."

Abraham and Dicky were discussing the work to be done after breakfast, while Bull, who had said nothing since Ieuan's return, cleared a space at the foot of the stove and made a rough seat with the plank and two bricks.

Thomas gathered the tankards. "It's getting late. Think I'd better come with you, Ieuan. Got your own can and tea ready?"

"Hey there! Half a bloomin' mo'." Titus came dashing into the coreshop. He scowled at Ieuan. "Where the devil've you been, Iron? D'you think I got time to go chasing after you? From now on this tea-boiling job's yours, so don't try and dodge it. See? Nobody's going to come the old soldier on me."

"Aw, cheese it, Titus. Take Ieuan along with you, and don't be such a fuss-pot." Thomas handed him the cans.

"Yeah, take him and leave him," Bull shouted after them, "and tell him to be careful he don't burn the water when he boils it. A nit-wit is our little Iron. Goes to cry when you look twice at him."

Titus bundled the cans under his arm. "Have a look in my pockets," he said to Ieuan. "You'll find the tea packets there — half a dozen of 'em. And mind you don't spill any. Come on!"

A constant stream of men and boys passed in and out of the canteen, steaming tankards in hand. It was a small, red-bricked building, in appearance very much like an ordinary dwelling-house, with two front windows and a brick chimney.

"Keep your eyes skinned for Ephraim," Titus warned. "He looks after the canteen, and he's a proper old woman. Spill a drop of tea on the floor, and he'll play holy smoke. He's crackers, if you ask me. Ephraim-bloody-half-wise, I call him. One'd think he's caretaker o' Buckingham Palace, not an arsehole of a dump like this. If he was working in the tinstamping I wouldn't say nothing. Now, there's a canteen for you, the one in the tinstamping. They got proper cups and saucers, and sell pastries. Here, you can't buy a bloomin' biscuit. Lousy joint, that's what this is." Titus spat into a pile of silica bricks that lay in their path, and strode into the canteen.

Inside, the building was spotlessly clean. Whitewashed walls reflected the light that poured in from the open windows. The floor was covered with clean sawdust. Two long tables scrubbed to a shining whiteness occupied each half of the room, and were separated by a circular iron stove. Drawn up against them were four wooden benches.

A shelf fixed along the wall above the windows held the men's food boxes and tin dixies. At the far end of the room stood a stone-topped table fitted with three gas rings and a burnished copper urn.

Two youths, their dungarees smeared with oil and grease, leaned against a small washbasin in the corner. One held a length of looped wire in his hand and was timing a cast-iron saucepan full of eggs which boiled on the gas ring.

"Hallo, Titus," he greeted. "Late, aren't you?"

"Got a new boy — showing him the job," Titus replied. Ieuan placed the packets of tea and sugar on the stone table.

"What's your name, kid?" the youth with the length of wire queried.

"Ieuan Morgan."

"Sand rat?" his companion asked.

"Apprentice moulder."

"Same thing. Say, why didn't you try for a job in the fitting shop with us? Better than being a dirty sand rat. Today you started?"

"Yes." Ieuan felt uncomfortable.

"You'll be sorry before the day's out. The moulders aren't bloody civilized."

Titus placed the cans on the scrubbed table. "Don't be so bloody high and mighty," he sneered, making a face at the two fitting-shop apprentices. "Because you had to pay a premium for a job you think you own the blasted works."

"Well, we're better off than you are, anyway. Ours is a skilled trade," came the rejoinder.

"What's moulding, then?" Titus showed defiance. "Just a game, is it?"

"No, playing with mud pies. Building castles on the sands, like kids do."

Titus emptied a packet of tea into one of the cans. A few grains fell on to the table.

"Drat you, boy Roberts!"

Titus looked round. A wizened old man in dungaree coat and moleskin trousers sat on the bench near the stove.

"Boy Roberts, wipe that mess up," he shouted. He got up from the bench and tottered across the floor. "Wipe that mess up," he repeated, shaking his fist, "and take them cans away. What d'you think this is — a stable?"

"Go and chase yourself twice round the gasworks," Titus said with derision. "You're always on the grunt."

The caretaker waved his puny fists. His wrinkled face was red with anger. "On the grunt, eh? I'll give you what for, you impudent little ragamuffin. On your backside I'll put you, in two shakes." He struck the apprentice a blow on the chest which hurt him more than it did Titus.

The latter stepped back and regarded the old man with malice.

"Oh, Christ; go and sit down in your corner, Ephraim. You couldn't bust a balloon."

The old man was trembling with frustrated anger. "Wipe that table!" he screeched. "A place fit for food this is, I tell you, not a pigsty for the likes of you."

"O.K., O.K., don't work yourself up." Titus pulled off his cap and flicked the tea leaves on the floor.

The two fitting-shop apprentices laughed. Ieuan waited, not knowing what to say or do.

Ephraim pointed a trembling finger to the urn. "Fill your cans and get out," he shouted, "before I fetch Lu after you. He's the one to settle young blackguards who got no respect for a man old enough to be their grandfather. Fifty years I've been working here, and no man did dare raise his hand against me. Lucky for me I got control over my temper, or out on your head you'd be."

"You couldn't control an elephant in a passage."

Ieuan heard the remark, but old Ephraim was too preoccupied in picking up each single tea leaf from the floor. Titus turned the small brass tap at the base of the urn and held a tankard under it.

"Oh, blast the thing. It's empty," he cursed as a trickle of water fell into the can. He scowled at Ieuan. "It's all your fault. Why the hell didn't you stop in the coreshop when you was supposed to? If there's no water here for Bull's tea you'd better go and hide yourself." He snatched Ieuan's cap and, gripping the edge of the urn with it, pulled forward.

A stream of boiling water poured out.

"Put the tea and sugar in the other cans."

Ieuan did as he was told.

"Now fill 'em up. Here's your bonnet." Titus threw the cap on to the table. The six cans were filled.

"Got your own can filled?" Titus asked.

"Yes."

"Where you having breakfast — in here, or with Bull and me?"

"Here," said Ieuan, without hesitation.

"Windy, eh?" Titus waved a hand airily: "It's O.K. by me. You can eat your grub with the old fogies if you want to. But first of all, you take two of them cans back to the coreshop. One's for Bull, the other's Charlie's. And don't drop anything on the sawdust. Ephraim's got his monkey up, and he don't like to have his parlour messed up."

The old caretaker bustled Titus out of the canteen.

"Clear off, you — you cheeky beggar, and don't come back here again with your flaming cheek, or I'll break the bone of your back."

"You couldn't break the skin off a rice pudding," Titus shouted. He leapt nimbly through the doorway as Ephraim lunged at him with his boot. Turning, he extended his fingers and held a thumb to his nose. "Next time you try that, take some Kruschen salts," he mocked. "Then maybe Aston Villa'd sign you on."

Ieuan self-consciously walked out after him, a steaming tankard in each hand. When he got to the coreshop he glanced round the wall. The seat by the stove had been fixed, but Bull was not to be seen. He placed the tankard on the plank. Thomas watched him.

"Where're you having breakfast, Ieuan?" he asked.

"In the canteen."

"Then wait for me, I'll join you."

Abraham, Isaiah and Dicky gathered their food boxes and waited near the stove. Titus went into the steel shop. Presently the half-past-eight hooter blew. Men streamed out from the compo shed, throwing their jackets over their shoulders.

"Righto, boys, let's go." Abraham led the way to the canteen. "A bit of 'chaff the old horses are needing."

"No work between meals, that's what I say," Thomas remarked.

CHAPTER FOUR

NOW that the hooter had blown to announce the first half-hour break in the day, the workmen appeared to be invested with a new vitality. From all quarters of the yard they hurried; from behind crudely built barricades of zinc sheets where they had been lying in wait for the hooter's warning; out of the pattern shop, fitting shop, smithy, fettling department and foundry.

The yard labourers untied their sack aprons and tossed them into empty trucks or on to the piles of scrap iron. The crowd headed for the main gate. The majority lived in the dingy houses grouped outside the boundary wall of the foundry, but some had a long distance to walk. There was no time to spare for any of them.

The moulders and labourers who utilized the canteen queued behind one another and made their way leisurely along the narrow passage between the two low stone walls leading into it.

Bull, Reg, Charlie and Titus sat down on the plank near the coreshop stove, food tins and tankards beside them on the floor. In the compo shed Brin and his fellow workers formed a semicircle facing a brazier. They drew up empty barrows and sat on the shafts, their food balanced in their laps. Brin roasted a kipper on a shovel held over the flames. A young sandy-haired moulder who ate his meals in the compo shed balanced a piece of slate on the edge of the brazier. He took a spotted handkerchief from his pocket, opened it, and shook a dozen mussels to the floor. Placing each mussel on the slate, he sat on his heels and waited for them to cook.

Ieuan, his packet of sandwiches under his arm and tea can in hand, kept close to Thomas and entered the canteen with trepidation. Now that the men were seated together they would have more time to notice him, he mused. They would question him. What was his name? When did he start? Did he like the job? What made him come to the foundry when he could have made better use of the education he'd received? Were his parents alive? Where was his father working? Any brothers or sisters?

Nervous, he took a seat next to Thomas on the bench nearest the stove. Isaiah sat on the farther table with Abraham and Dicky and five other men whom Ieuan did not recognize. On the bench he and Thomas occupied were six moulders, all well over middle-age, whilst on the, opposite side sat two white-haired men who were identical as blades of grass.

"Joseph Matthews and his brother Owen," Thomas whispered out of the side of his mouth as he noticed Ieuan staring at them. "Twins, they are. Always trying to get one over on the other. You watch 'em. They'll start arguing the toss over something before breakfast is finished."

Old Ephraim crouched on a stool in front of the stove. He nibbled like a mouse at a small piece of bread and cheese, his eyes alive to every movement of the men around him. From time to time he craned his neck, watching for the careless crumb-dropper or spiller of tea.

Food boxes clicked open. Tea gurgled into tankard lids. Benches dragged against the sawdust-covered floor. Feet scraped. Mouths opened and closed. Jaws moved, incessantly up and down. The breakfast had begun.

Ieuan watched one man with amazement. He thrust his food savagely into his mouth and rammed it down his throat with his fingers. Another attacked a cold, greasy sausage with penknife and fork as though he held a grudge against it. Someone made a loud sucking noise as he drained his tea, and belched without apology.

As soon as the first pangs of hunger were satisfied, the men began to talk to one another. To Ieuan it seemed as though they all conversed simultaneously. The noise was akin to a corner of a fairground.

91

He carefully unwrapped his sandwiches and rolled the greaseproof paper into a ball. So far no one had asked him any questions. The relief he felt was accompanied with a certain tenseness. They would surely cross-examine him before long, he thought. The best thing to do would be to avoid encouraging them to ask questions. He lowered his eyes and concentrated them on the sandwiches.

He pecked at his food, self-conscious of each movement he made. Once he looked up to find Ephraim's eyes on him. They burned into his. The greaseproof paper was still clutched in his hand. He jammed it into his pocket and made a pretence of eating.

But the old man was ever watchful. Ieuan found it difficult to swallow, and after eating half a sandwich he took out the greaseproof paper and covered what was left of his meal.

His hand shook as he raised the tankard to his lips. A drop of tea fell on to the table. Hastily, he placed his elbow over it and his heart almost stopped beating.

The caretaker had not seen the incident. His rheumy eyes, watering from the intensity of his stare, turned elsewhere, and Ieuan gulped. He folded the paper over his sandwiches, and sat, tensed. Conversation came to him in bits and pieces.

A high-pitched voice spoke from the other side of the table.

"Nice council houses they're building on the old Morfa tump. What d'you think on them, Owen?"

"Humph! Nothing much," came the disgruntled reply.

"Bit small they are, if you ask me. A chap'd have to cock one leg out of the bedroom window for to put his trousers on in the morning."

Ieuan looked up. The twins were talking. Thomas nudged him. "Here they go — Damn and Blast, the terrible twins."

"Tryin' to be clever, is it, Owen?" the first twin was speaking. "Well, let me tell you, they may be a bit small but they're all right for us workers. A nice little parlour they got."

"A parlour, indeed! Is that important, then?"

"I should blinking well say so," the other brother returned. "Every house ought to have a parlour where a feller can go to enjoy a smoke on a Sunday afternoon. Why, man, a house without a parlour is like a pub without no dominoes."

"Humph! Only advantage I see in having a parlour is that it's useful for to keep a coffin in. We Welsh blokes — too much fuss we make over parlours. Places for coffins and courting couples — that's all they are. And a piano, of course, which nobody plays."

"Clever, aren't you?"

"Ditto to you." The twins relapsed into silence, glaring vindictively at one another. Other voices spoke, and Ieuan listened, surprised, and at times amused, by the strangeness of the talk. Here was humour, wisdom, irony and ignorance.

"Owen's talking about pianos reminds me of Dan the Socialist. I was on the Town Hall Square one night when Dan was spouting. Know what he said?" The speaker did not wait for an answer. "He said about some chaps he once met in a pub. Talking about 'Our Empire' they were. And after three half-pints they were giving colonies away. There's a joke for you."

"I don't see any jokes, Amos."

"Nor me. An' what's it got to do with pianos, anyway?"

"Well, Dan was saying, 'Fancy them chaps giving colonies away when they couldn't afford a piano unless they paid instalments for sixty years.'"

"Instalments! Sooner you die, sooner you're out of debt, eh?"

"That's right — same as old Cheap-Jack Harry used to say on Thursday market when he couldn't sell his watches."

"Say what you like, chaps, but that Dan is a clever boyo."

"He's no mug."

"Like the chap who invented interest."

"What about the chap who invented interest? Who was he?"

"Didn't say I knew him. But he was no mug, see?"

Ieuan's confidence returned. No one had taken the slightest interest in him. It was as though they had already accepted him

93

as a member of their company. Presently, he looked around, reassured and smiling.

The twins, who had been silent for a long while, addressed each other again. The one named Owen said: "Pity for old Shenkin Jones's daughter-in-law. She's having a rotten time with that infinite paralysis, a rotten time."

His brother scowled. "Talk proper English, man," he snorted. "Infinite paralysis, my foot! You're as bad as Tommy Dunce. He had no schoolin', but, by crumpets, he can speak better'n you."

"What! That old numbskull who's got one foot in the grave and the other on a banana skin? What are you talking about, you blockhead? Why, every time he goes on a trip he has to ask for a ticket back and front. Don't even know how to ask for a return ticket, he don't."

"Humph! You are just as awkward. If you had to go away on an excursion I'd have to pin a label on your coat for to let the porter know where to send you back to. Man alive, you are just as daft as Lewsin Fag Ends who saved up his money for to go on a holiday to Heligoland when the war was on."

Once more the brothers became dumb, and resumed their scowling. They regaled each other across the table with fierce eyes, then took out their pipes and began to smoke, puffing angrily, and spitting to the floor, impervious to Ephraim's hysterical: "Pigs! Pigs! I'll have you thrown out on your backsides, the blinkin' pair of you!"

It took much tact and diplomacy to quieten the caretaker. One of the men hurriedly scattered a shovelful of fresh sawdust over the offending brown stars of tobacco juice.

The breakfast finished. Tankards were swilled in the sink. Food boxes were closed. Then the men relaxed and the conversation became more subdued. But it's tone remained the same.

An elderly moulder in the far corner called across to another who sat next to the twins.

"Dai, I heard Mary White Lion was married last week."

"Which one? The widow or the barmaid?"

94

"The barmaid — you know, the one who got in trouble with Jack Pensarn Insurance."

"*Iesu*! I didn't know she was in the family way agen."

Ieuan blushed. The conversation continued across the room. Everyone was interested, even Thomas.

"Well, Alfie — the chuckerout — was telling me the wedding came off just in the wee nick o' time. He thought the kid would ha' dropped during the service. Never seen such a bump on a woman, so he said. Like as if she had swallowed a plum pudding whole, basin an' all."

The company chuckled. Suddenly Isaiah stood up. He glowered at the elderly moulder.

"You'll please to remember we've young lads here, Mostyn," he said sternly. "There's a time and a place for everything, you know. And this is no time and no place for such talk. More fitting it is for a public house."

The man named Mostyn grinned, showing a row of black-stained teeth. "Hold your horses, Isaiah," he said. "This is no place for sermons, either. As for them youngsters, they'll live and learn."

The Deacon sat down. "You've lived, Mostyn," he retorted, "but seems to me you haven't learned much. One should show a bit of respect to these young boys."

"O.K., O.K., Isaiah, I'll dry up. Maybe I ought to talk Sunday School instead. *Arglwydd!* It comes to something when a feller's got to pipe down all on account of a couple o' kids. When I was an apprentice I knew all the answers. No flies on Mostyn Phillips, I can tell you. These youngsters nowadays — proper sissies they are, if you ask me."

An awkward silence fell over the room. Then someone began to discuss Welsh nicknames and their origin. Why was Idris Great Thoughts so called, and Lias Shakespeare? Who gave the name "Three-eights" to Enoch Price, the yard labourer, and "Elastic-belly" to Tom Evans, landlord of the Barley Mow? Why call P.C. Harry Thomas, Harry Chew-tobacco, when he had never been known to chew tobacco? And why Gomer Determination, and Johnny Preacher?

"I'll tell you the story of Gomer Determination," one volunteered. The others waited, settling themselves comfortably in their seats.

"A one for his beer, was Gomer. Couldn't pass a pub without calling in to wet his whistle. But he was a hell of a tanker, as you know." The speaker rested his elbows on the table. His eyes sparkled, and he obviously enjoyed the role of story teller. "His old woman, Mary Jane Straight — she was called 'Straight' not because she was honest, or anything like that, but because she was as stiff as a plank — well, she was always on to Gomer to give up the booze. 'Don't call in at the pubs on your way home, Gomer,' she used to say to him every night, regular as the clock. 'Give up the old beer stuff, mun.'

"Well, Gomer thought as much of his Mary Jane as he did of the beer. A real toss up it was between them. So one night he made up his mind to chuck the beer, and chuck it for good. 'Determination, that's what you need, Gomer,' Mary Jane had told him. And Gomer remembered what the old woman had said. He was walking home with my brother one night from the Dulais tinworks, after the two-till-ten shift. They passed the Crown and Anchor, the first pub on the road just outside the works, Gomer saying to my brother: 'Determination, that's what I need, Edgar, my boy. Determination — not beer.'

"Now, Edgar had been listening so long to Gomer with all his talk about determination that he had forgotten about the Crown and Anchor, but as soon as Gomer mentioned beer my brother looked round and saw what a mistake he'd made. Edgar made tracks for the pub. He said to Gomer: 'Coming in to have one, for old time's sake like?'

"'No, indeed, thank you all the same,' said Gomer, and he was nearly crying with the effort he made to get the words out. On went the old boy. But ten minutes later, just when Edgar was chucking down his third pint, into the bar comes Gomer, his tongue hanging out. He taps my brother on the shoulder. 'Edgar,' he says, 'a quarter of a mile I walked down the road, thinking of my Mary Jane all the time. By damn, there's determination for you!'"

The joke brought a roar of laughter from the men. Someone applauded. Ephraim grunted and sat motionless near the stove, staring into the grate.

A little later Thomas got up. "Let's go outside, Ieuan," he suggested. "We've got ten minutes before the buzzer sounds. Do us good to have a bit of fresh air."

They took their tankards back to the coreshop. Bull and his satellites were sitting on their heels around the stoke-hole of the miniature furnace which heated the drying stove. The furnace had been built into the pine end of the coreshop, and out in the open.

The furnace door was ajar, and the group huddled close to the fire, their hands arched over the flames. Bull glanced over his shoulder.

"Coming across, after?" he called to Thomas.

"Where?"

"To watch the janes, of course. Where the hell d'you think?"

A purple haze smudged with heavy, dark grey clouds hung over the foundry like a painted back cloth on a stage. Water dripped from the troughs, and the yard surface was thick with mud.

A cold, piercing wind blew. Seagulls wheeled overhead, tossed here and there like scraps of paper, strangely white against the sombre background of leaden roof and pregnant sky. They screeched desolately in discordant symphony as they swooped down on to the canteen roof and the scrap dumps in search of food denied them in the howling estuary from which they had been driven.

The group around the furnace stood up. Bull swung out his arms and beat them vigorously across his chest. He stamped his feet.

"Let's go and see the janes, boys."

They skipped over a mound of ashes and walked to the crusher, a mechanical monster which was used to grind the silica bricks into fragments before they were wheeled into the compo shed mill. A lean-to had been built over it to protect the pulley belts and machinery from the elements.

Bull climbed on to the galvanized iron roof. Charlie, Reg and Titus scrambled up after him.

"Hey, Thomas, come on up. Bring Iron with you to see the sights."

The two boys got on to the roof. It sloped upwards. The apex overlooked a street twenty feet below. A wooden footbridge spanned the main railway line at the northern end of the street, and over it came a crowd of women and girls on their way back from breakfast to the tinstamping works.

They pushed slowly forward, battling against the strong wind, heads down, their hands occupied in holding their skirts as the wind strove to embarrass them.

In pairs, or groups of three or more they came, conscious of the gang on the roof. The older women passed by with a show of unconcern, but the younger ones looked up, laughing and giggling at the remarks shouted to them from the rooftop.

Bull and Charlie lay full length, their heads jutting over the edge. Red and Titus sat down, legs swinging into space. Two attractive girls, one blonde, the other auburn-haired, hurried along the pavement directly underneath. They made no attempt to hold down their skirts, and shrieked shrilly as a gust of wind exposed their silk-stockinged thighs.

Bull grinned. "Hey, there!" he shouted down. "Play the game, girls. That's how Nelson lost his eye."

The blonde threw back her head. Her red lips pouted in pretended annoyance.

"Always the funny wonder, aren't you, Bull-bull?"

"Come up here," Bull called, "and I'll show you what a wonder I am. And not so funny, either."

"Yeah — and bring Ginger with you," Reg added. He whistled through his teeth. "You, Ginger — how d'you feel?"

"With my hands," the auburn-haired girl laughed.

"Izzat so, izzat so!" Reg returned. He began to sing:

> "Ginger, you're barmy,
> Fit for the Army .... "

Then, with a sly grin, he shouted: "Fit for me, too. Come up here and let's see what you're made of."

The two girls walked on, and the audience on the roof turned its attention to a party of six who followed a few yards behind.

Charlie turned round. Thomas was sitting with his back to the road, and Ieuan, shivering, crouched on the lower edge of the roof.

"Jumping Jeez, what's the matter with you two?" he bawled. "What the hell're you freezing there for? Slide up here and have a decko at the damsels."

"Seen plenty," said Thomas, gruffly.

"Then why the flaming heck did you come up? To have a sunbathe?"

"Anything to pass away the time." Thomas crawled to the top of the roof. "Well — what's what?" he asked.

"Nothing's what. Just have a look at the janes." Charlie pointed to Ieuan. "Isn't he interested?"

Ieuan overheard the remark. He had no wish to look at the girls, and could not find anything to say.

"Here, you!" Charlie slid down towards him and dragged him to the rooftop. "There's a filly just your size coming down the road. Wait till you see her, she's a wow!"

"You bet," Titus agreed. He winked. "And hotter'n mustard she is, too."

Bull guffawed. "Oh, hell, hark at him, boys. Tightarse, the Romeo of the back lanes, who's never walked a tart home in his life."

"That's what you think, Bull Jackson." Titus was annoyed.

"But let me tell you, I had points with Ruby last Sunday night, and I took her up Lovers' Lane. You ask her."

The six girls passed below the roof.

"Ruby-O!" Bull called.

A small, round-faced girl of about sixteen glanced up.

"What do you want?" she cried. Her voice was carried away by the wind.

"Nothing now, something later." Bull laughed at his own joke. "Say — listen, Ruby." He crooked a hand over his mouth. "Did you go sparking with Titus last Sunday?"

"Who is he?" The girl stopped. One of her friends, a stout, red-faced girl, pulled her forward.

"Don't take any notice of that rough lot," she said, loud enough for Bull to hear. "They're not civilized."

Reg prodded Bull. "That's what I call a telling-off, Bull boy. We're not civilized. Bloody monkeys, see? So put that in your barrel and roll it home. Now, let me talk to her. You've got no romance in you."

He lowered his head. "You meet me next Sunday night, Bessie, an' little Reggie-peggie'll show you who's civilized and who ain't. And if your little girl friend, Ruby, wants to learn a bit of homework I've got a nice chappie here who'll oblige. Name's Iron. New to the foundry, new to life, and new to love. Most obliging, and anxious to help any little girl who wants to know the facts of life."

"Aw, shut your smutty mouth, Reg Bowen. You ought to be ashamed of yourself. I don't know what your mother'd say if she heard you. You're a dirty-minded beast."

The girls walked on.

"Same to you," Reg called after them. "But do you know something?" The girls paid no attention.

"Hey, Bessie, I'm talking to you."

Bessie looked up. "Yes?"

"Next time you're passing this way blow your horn," Reg sniggered. "You're getting to look more like a bus every day."

Ieuan felt ashamed of his associates and the lewdness of their talk. It brought back to mind the conversation of the older boys in the district where he lived. How they whispered furtively on street corners, boasting of their knowledge of the word love, and what it implied. They giggled like girls when they mentioned "spooning" and "courting," showing off to the wide-eyed, blushing little boys who had gathered around them in hero worship.

They professed to know how babies were made and how they were born. Sometimes they would relate of strange happenings they had seen in the shadow of the hedges and in the sheltered hollows of the quarry where young courting couples went in the summer evenings.

These whisperings of things unmentionable had caused a strange stirring in his blood. He had felt a warm tingling within him, as though a flame were burning in the pit of his stomach. His limbs had filled with a vigour they had never known. And the curiosity aroused in him became something which had to be satiated.

The Bible, which had been to him a source of beauty, became something vile, for it gave word to that which created this peculiar quickening of the blood, this new awakening he felt in his loins.

"And ... went in unto his wife, and she conceived." On the street corners he had been told of the great mystery. It was something to be spoken of in whispers. Something sordid, base, unworthy and unclean. Yet here, in the holy book, it stared at him in cold black letters, making him confused and ashamed.

And the same boys, on the same street corners, had spoken with fevered, burning eyes, of the story of Susannah and the Elders, of Onan, and the Songs of Solomon, changing beauty into ugliness, virtue into vice, and he had been sickened.

Then later he had been prompted to read Shakespeare's *Venus and Adonis* — prompted by an incentive born of the street-corner whisperings. And in that secret moment of revelation; the greatest of all English poets became a man of whom he was ashamed. The poetic imagery dissolved, and all that remained was a terrible picture of a man and woman doing things which parents and elders never mentioned or even hinted at.

And now, on the rooftop on a bitter November morning, with the wind screaming along the foundry yard and the dismal streets, came the same strange pulsating of the blood. The lewd talk, the sight of the silk-stockinged girls with pouting lips and flashing eyes — these combined to make him feel once more ashamed and wretched.

"Look out, boys, here she comes — Bill Taylor's daughter. The real goods."

Charlie jumped to his feet and balanced himself on the slippery roof. He quickly drew two oranges out of his pockets and stuffed them into the breast of his dungaree coat. Mincing along the edge of the roof, his chest thrown out, he whistled down at a tall, attractive brunette in a tightly belted mackintosh who, the last to step down the bridge, came trotting in high-heeled shoes along the pavement.

The girl glanced upwards, then averted her eyes.

"Yoo-hoo, Sandra! Yoo-hoo!"

Reg, Bull and Titus waved their hands and shrieked in high falsetto, but the girl hurried on.

"By God, she's got a pair on her," Charlie breathed. He pressed his hands over the two oranges under his jacket. "What I wouldn't give for a night out with her."

"She's a nice girl, much too good and decent for your sort."

The voice was subdued.

Charlie looked down. "Thomas, the goody-goody, eh? Mamma's little lovely boy, eh?" He lunged at the apprentice. Suddenly he lost his balance and began to slide headlong down the slope. The oranges slipped out and rolled down after him.

With a loud yell of fear, he leapt from the roof to the foundry yard, and stumbled into a yellow pile of sharp, jagged silica bricks.

Bull and his gang laughed unrestrainedly. Ieuan watched Thomas and trembled for his friend's safety. There would be a fight, of that he was sure, and Thomas would get the worst of it. Already Charlie had picked himself up and stood, with fists clenched, waiting for Thomas to descend.

The younger boy was not perturbed.

"You don't put the wind up me," he shouted. He swung himself down on to the ground and strode up to the irate Charlie. "Go on!" he challenged. "Hit me! Go on!"

The other jammed his hands into his pockets. "Aw, dry up. And clear off," he muttered. Then, turning on his heels, he disappeared into the coreshop.

"Well, well, well." Bull clicked his tongue. He jumped from the roof and landed ankle deep in the ash heap. "Our Thomas is up with his fists again. Brave little Tommy," he said sarcastically. He stepped out of the ash heap and flicked the dust from his trousers. "Come and cool off by the fire."

He made a grab at Thomas's coat.

"Oh, no you don't." Thomas pushed the bully aside.

He walked across to the crusher and helped Ieuan down.

"That's right," Bull sneered. "Watch your palsy-walsy doesn't hurt himself. By Christopher! I never seen such a pair o' bloody pansies."

Reg and Titus laughed, and the three cronies passed through the coreshop door. After they had gone Thomas and Ieuan crossed to the stoke-hole. Thomas pulled out a long-handled shovel embedded in a bunker of small coal. He threw it to the ground and invited Ieuan to sit down beside him on the handle. They stared into the flames, both silent and miserable.

The workers who had gone home for breakfast were now returning up the yard. The canteen door opened. A man appeared in the doorway, tankard in hand. He took off the lid and swished the remnants of his tea over the muddy yard. He said something to the men inside. The benches dragged over the floor.

"Back to war we go again, boys."

Ieuan recognized the high-pitched voice of Joseph Matthews, one of the elderly twins. He turned his head and watched the

103

streams of men pass out from the canteen. They walked as leisurely as when they entered half an hour ago, chatting amicably to one another.

Old Ephraim, broom in hand, stood in the doorway. When the last man had left the building, the caretaker began to sweep the sawdust out on to the narrow path between the walls.

A row of seagulls perched on the foundry roof swept downwards in anticipation. They hovered low in the air, screeching, their frail legs like sticks of red coral hanging limply. Some of the men threw scraps of food to the ground, and the birds swooped hungrily down, fighting and squabbling amongst themselves for possession.

When the last note of the nine o'clock hooter faded, all the men were back on their jobs. The silent foundry awakened again. From within came the growling of the cranes. Stove doors were raised, and the bogies groaned over the dust-covered rails.

Moulders who had been waiting for the use of the cranes shouted to the cranemen, each claiming priority over the other. The crusher was started. It snorted and grunted, wheezed and choked, loudly and asthmatically. The frightened seagulls circled above the canteen, then flew farther inland through the purple haze.

Inside the coreshop, Abraham superintended the unloading of the bogie. The heavy cores were lowered on to a bed of wood shavings, and the charge-hand marked the order number on each with a piece of chalk: S 246, P 509, P 806, P 807.

Thomas was sent to the fettling department to salvage lengths of steel rods and core-irons used in previous cores. He left Ieuan at the bench, promising to return soon. Bull, with a show of energy which did not impress Abraham, scraped the dry compo from his corner of the bench and prepared to ram up some more cores.

"Like to give me a hand, Iron? I'll be bucked as hell if you fetched me a sieveful o' compo."

Anxious to please, Ieuan took a sieve from the bench. "Are you coming with me?" he asked Bull. "I don't know how to mix it properly yet."

Bull had a look to see if Abraham and the other two men were busy.

"Listen, Iron," he said. "I've changed my mind. I'll see to the compo, but there's a favour I'd like you to do for me." His eyes were on Abraham. "Will you do it?"

Ieuan promptly agreed. He was glad to be able to help. Anything to keep the peace and establish good terms.

"After I've finished these cores," Bull went on, "I'll be pushed on to a special job, and I'll have to have some blast to mix with the compo."

Ieuan's face clouded. "Blast?" he asked loudly.

Bull brought a finger to his lips. "Hssh!" He took the sieve from Ieuan's hand and walked across to the water bosh. "Come here!"

He whispered into the boy's ear. "Don't let Abie know anything about this. He's got his knife into me this morning. Look you now — he became confiding — blast is expensive as hell. Two quid a pound, and old Abie's scared of using the stuff. But I've got to have it, see? I used two barrowfuls last week, and the old man'd throw a blue fit if he was to see me getting some more. So you fetch it for me, will you, Iron?"

"Right-ho." Ieuan held out his hand. "Shall I take the sieve with me?"

Bull plucked at his lower lip. "No," he said after some deliberation, "better take a bucket. It'll hold more."

"And where do I go for it — the blast?"

"To the blacksmiths' shop. Know where it is?"

"Yes, on the way to the stores."

"Good! Well, when you get there ask for Ben Bassett. Tell him that Bull wants half a bucket o' shot blast — the best, mind, tell him. Then on your way back go into the pattern shop. Hal Jenkins, he's the oldest apprentice there — ask him to give a dollar's worth of the number one stuff. It's for Bull, say. I'll hurry up and get the compo. O.K.?"

"Yes, I'll get the blast for you. Shall I ask Abraham for a ticket?"

"Oh, Christ, no!" Bull blurted. "Don't say a word to Abie or he'll conk out. There's no need for a docket. Me and Ben and Hal's got everything taped off, see? Wait here half a mo', and I'll get you a bucket." He went into the steel foundry and returned with a bucket under his arm. "This is Charlie's," he said, "so look after it. If anything happens to it he'll be sweating blood. Off you go, I'll meet you outside the compo shed in a quarter of an hour."

When Ieuan walked into the smithy the men instinctively turned to look at him. The blacksmith tending the forge nearest the door called him forward.

"Don't seem to remember your face," he said. "Where you from?"

"Coreshop," Ieuan replied. "I started this morning."

He anticipated the next question. "My name's Ieuan Morgan."

The blacksmith nodded. His "striker," a muscular young man with sallow features, noticed the bucket.

"What's that for?" he queried.

"I've come on a message," said Ieuan. "Bull Jackson sent me down to ...." "His words were drowned in the noise from the hydraulic hammer which two men were using. He watched it, fascinated, as the heavy steel arm rose and fell in rapid motion, shaping a square block of red-hot steel which a blacksmith gripped with a tongs and twisted dexterously.

The ear-splitting thud-thud of the hammer and the continuous roar of the forges deafened him. When the men spoke to one another they had to shout to be heard above the din.

The striker again turned his attention to him. "What were you saying about Bull Jackson?"

Ieuan raised his voice. "He sent me to ask Ben Bassett for some blast. Shot blast, he said — the best."

"Oh-h!" Ieuan was glad that the striker understood. "Yes, of course, of course. Well, let's see what we can do about it. There!"

he pointed across to the other side of the smithy, "that's Ben — the fellow using the sledge."

Ieuan looked at the leather-apron-clad, perspiring man on the other side.

"Tell him to give you some," the striker said. He whistled to Bassett. "Ben! Blast for Bull Jackson. This lad's come down for it."

Bassett tossed the sledgehammer aside. He spat on his hands and wiped them on the apron. "Gimme the bucket, boy," he said when Ieuan crossed the floor to him. "How much does Bull want?" he asked. "I can't spare much, you know." He scratched his chin. "What kind does he want?"

"Shot blast — the best," Ieuan replied. "Only half a bucketful."

"That's all he'll get, too." The blacksmith looked around. "Hey, you — Dan!" he called. "Pop over here a minute, will you?"

The man he addressed, a strong-armed giant with scorched face and beetling brows, strolled up to Bassett.

"This boy wants some shot blast," said the blacksmith. "Got any to spare?"

"Who's it for?" asked Dan.

"Bull Jackson, the coreshop wallah."

"H'm. Don't know if I ought to give him any."

Ieuan was perturbed. "He asked me to get it," he said urgently. "It's very important, he's working on a special job."

"I know, I know." Dan took the bucket from Bassett. "The trouble with Bull is, he don't appreciate us chaps when we help him out of a spot. I s'pose Abraham knows nothing about this, eh?"

Ieuan shook his head.

"H'm. Thought so. Well, I'll give you some this time, but tell Bull there's no more favours coming from this place until he sends back that left-handed spanner and sky-hook he borrowed last week."

Dan walked to the far end of the smithy where a rack of long-handled tongs had been built into the wall. He bent down. Ieuan

107

saw him lift a square block of iron from the floor and drop it into the bucket. He covered it with a thick wad of cotton-waste daubed with black grease.

"Here, boy!"

Ieuan looked at him wonderingly. "That — that's not blast?"

The blacksmith was offended. "What the hell is it then, I'd like to know. You tell Bull that this is the only bit I can spare him. By the way, shot blast you asked for, wasn't it?"

"Y-yes," Ieuan answered timidly. "But he — he can't mix that with compo?"

"He can do what the devil he likes with it," the blacksmith snapped impatiently. "Tell him to play about with it till he loses it. Now, watch out!" He gripped a tongs and snatched a red-hot coal from a forge. He tossed the burning lump into the bucket. Blue flames raced up. The grease crackled, then burst into flames.

"There — that's shot!" Dan waited until the flames died down. He wrapped a dirty piece of newspaper around the bucket handle. "O.K., boy, here's your shot blast. Off you trot, back to where you came from. And don't forget to remember to tell Bull about the left-handed spanner and the sky-hook."

Ieuan crooked the handle over his arm and swung the bucket across his hip. Staggering under the weight, he swayed out of the smithy. When he got to the pattern shop his arms ached, and he was out of breath. He pushed the door open with his foot. Hall, the apprentice pattern maker, was more than willing to oblige him with the "number one stuff" Bull had asked for. He filled the bucket with a mixture of wood shaving and sawdust, and as Ieuan struggled up the yard to the coreshop, he ran after him.

"Gee, I almost forgot," Hal panted. He struck a match, shielded the flame in his hands and applied it to the shavings. A gust of wind scattered the flaming shavings into the air. Ieuan clenched his teeth and began to trot as best he could over the remaining distance, squelching through the thick mud.

To his chagrin, Bull, Charlie and Reg were leaning against the wall outside the coreshop. They watched him coming, and burst

108

out into wild laughter, slapping their thighs and pushing one another about.

All at once he realized that Bull had deliberately sent him on a fool's errand. He dropped the bucket to the muddy floor. It toppled over on its side, and a thick mess of grease and sawdust trickled over the handle.

Charlie stopped laughing. "You clumsy little bastard!" he shouted, "what d'you think you're playing at? That's my bucket. Pick it up, or I'll give you one on the snot and two on the kisser."

Ieuan made no attempt to pick up the bucket. "You be careful with your language, and don't call me a bastard," he said hotly. "You don't know what you're saying."

'I'll call you what I like, you little runt," Charlie shouted. "Bastard, backstud, bachelor's son — anything I fancy. Who the hell d'you think you are, Lord Muck? I s'pose because you've been to the County we're not good enough for you, eh? And our language is a bit too rough, eh? County School, my Aunt Fanny. I know what they do there. Peep over the lavat'ry walls to look at the girls in the one on the other side — that's what they do. County School, my eye!"

The improver rushed forward. He shot out a hand and pushed Ieuan back forcibly. "Pick that bucket up!" he bawled.

Ieuan staggered against the pile of silica bricks and fell awkwardly. He scraped his hands on the sharp stones. Jumping to his feet, his eyes brimming with tears, he lashed out at his adversary.

Charlie brushed the blows aside. He thrust out his right leg and tripped Ieuan to the ground. "Don't come that game on me," he hissed, "or I'll bash the daylights out o' you. Get up!" He jerked the boy to his knees and grabbed him by the nape of the neck. His fingers squeezed into the pale flesh.

"Let go, let go! You're hurting me!"

The appeal was useless. The strong fingers increased their pressure. Ieuan squirmed with pain. His body doubled.

"That's the stuff, Charlie. Make the little runt do what he's

109

told," Bull encouraged from the doorway. "Give him the old Nelson twist. That'll show him that us chaps aren't to be trifled with."

Ieuan's cries grew louder, and brought Abraham out into the yard. The charge-hand dashed forward and smote Charlie hard across the head.

"Leave the boy alone," he shouted. "Damn you, you lout!"

Charlie wheeled round with fists upraised. The sight of the inflamed moulder scared him. He dropped his hands and, mumbling under his breath, shambled back through the doorway. Bull and Reg sniggered at him as he went by.

Abraham was rattled. "Back to your work, the pair of you," he barked. "I've had just about enough of your nonsense." He pointed to the coreshop. "And you, young Morgan, get on with your job. I'm getting sick and tired of this shenanagin. I've got my hands full as it is. What's all the bother about this time, tell me?"

Ieuan adjusted his coat collar and scraped the mud from his trousers. He put out a hand to pick up the bucket.

"I asked you what was the matter?" Abraham said crossly. He waited for a reply but there was not one forthcoming. "All right, if you want to be a dummy, it suits me." Annoyed with Ieuan's silence, he pushed the bucket out of his hand. "Leave that where it is," he commanded, "and go back to the bench. It's time you should do a bit of work now, not play the goat with these ruffians. If you don't feel like learning your trade, then go home."

Subdued and humiliated, Ieuan returned to the bench. Thomas waited until Abraham went on with his job. He saw the scratches on Ieuan's hands.

"Been in the wars again, eh?" he hinted. "Jumping crackers — why the blazes did you listen to Bull? He told me he'd sent you down for a bucket of blast. Haven't you got savvy enough to see that he's just rigging you — making you look a fool?"

Bull, who was working at the far end of the bench, strained his ears to listen to the conversation. He cast a malevolent glance in their direction, and while Abraham and Isaiah were discussing the next job to be done, he took a handful of compo, squeezed it into a hard ball and tossed it high above the heads of the apprentices.

The missile fell on Ieuan's cap. He ducked instinctively. The particles of sand clung to the hair at the back of his neck and rolled down under his collar. The expression of alarm on his face changed to one of utter dismay. He looked so comically pathetic that Thomas could not resist from laughing at his plight.

"I — I can't help it, Ieuan," he choked, "but you — you look so bloody sorry for yourself."

Ieuan gritted his teeth. The only apprentice who had shown kindness to him was now laughing at his predicament, laughing just as Bull and the others had done. He wanted to close his fists and slam them hard into Thomas's face — into the grinning Bull's face — into the smirking faces of all his tormentors. What kindliness and friendship could one expect from these fellows? They seemed to delight in seeing others suffer who were weaker than they.

What had he done to deserve this persecution? Was he expected to suffer it without retaliating in some way? Did they think he was just a butt for their jokes? He felt his blood surge within him. The colour rose to his temples.

Thomas, Bull, Charlie, Reg, Titus — yes, and even Abraham — they were all of the same breed. Cowards, the lot of them. Cowards and fools! Ignorant fools!

He ran to the bosh. Stooping over the tap he washed the back of his neck. The sliding door of the steel shop opened. A brick curled through the air and fell with a loud splash into the bosh.

The bib of his dungaree was drenched, and the black, turgid, foul-smelling water smacked into his face. It trickled, cold as ice, down his throat and under his vest.

Groping blindly away from the bosh, his eyes closed, mouth open, he knocked against a shelf of cores. He heard Abraham shout a loud warning, but he stumbled forward. The cores toppled to the floor and disintegrated.

"You clumsy idiot!" The charge-hand brushed him violently aside. "Why don't you open your eyes and look where you're going!"

Ieuan drew a hand over his wet face. Streaks of black grease stained his cheeks. He opened his eyes. Thomas and Bull were laughing at him, and Abraham's eyes were blazing.

Isaiah caught the charge-hand by the arm. "Steady now, Abraham, it was an accident," he said quietly. "The boy couldn't help it. Someone threw a brick into the bosh, and —"

Abraham would not listen. "I've had more trouble with this boy than with anyone who's been apprenticed here," he stormed. "Where does he think he is? In a circus, or what? I'm telling you, Isaiah, I'm not putting up with this state of affairs much longer. Any more trouble and I'm going to report him to Lu. Why, man alive, if I allow this sort of thing to happen there'll be nothing done in here — nothing. Look at these cores — ten hours' work wasted, and all on account of that boy. Disgraceful, shameful, that's what it is."

"But the boy's not to blame, Abraham," Isaiah protested. "You saw what happened, didn't you?"

Abraham made a wry face. "What did he want near the bosh? There was no need for him to go there. He's just asking for trouble, I tell you. Just asking for it."

Ieuan stared at the floor. All the courage had been knocked out of him. He could not find words with which to defend himself, nor did he wish to offer any excuse. A feeling of sadness gripped him. His throat was dry, and it hurt. Again the tears were not far off, but he resisted them.

He left the two men to carry on with their argument and, ignoring the apprentices' laughter, walked slowly into the yard.

Outside, he paused to wipe his face. The wind stung his cheeks, and his hands were red and frozen. He drew open the furnace door and, heavy-hearted, crouched before the fire, the damp handkerchief held to the flames.

Presently he heard someone hurry from the coreshop. When he

looked up he found Abraham standing beside him. The charge-hand's face was creased with anger.

"What's the idea of staying out here?" he demanded. "Your job's inside with the others." Abraham snorted with impatience. "How much more trouble am I to expect from you? The sooner the better Lu gets to know of this rigmarole. I've tried to put my foot down, but it's useless — useless! Come on, get back to your work."

Isaiah regarded Ieuan solemnly as he walked back in front of the irate charge-hand.

"Look here, Abraham," the old coremaker said, "if you was to tell Lu to give a good talking to those young ruffians he's got in the foundry you'd be doing the new lad a kindness. Every new apprentice goes through this sort of bullying. There's no sense in it — "

Abraham turned on him angrily. "What's biting you?" he asked.

"All right, all right, Abraham — don't go losing your patience with me. Get a hold on yourself, man. I was just giving you a bit of advice."

"I've got enough worries on my mind," Abraham countered, "and I don't want your advice, nor nobody else's." He ushered Ieuan to the bench. "Not a stroke of work have you done today." To Isaiah, he added, with a faint note of apology: "I know the boy hasn't had much peace, but that's the lot of every apprentice, I suppose. Sometimes I wish I had a nice, quiet job like sweeping the roads or something. Peace of mind, that's what a fellow needs — peace of mind."

Isaiah silently agreed. Sweeping the roads was a nice, peaceful job. Indeed, it was. But Abraham was boss of the coreshop. That was his job, now. And he should see that young lads under his care were not subjected to such bullying and browbeating. An age of civilization we were living in today. Not back in the old days, when little chaps were looked upon and treated as slaves. Kindness and tolerance — that's what was wanted to put the world in proper shape. Love, friendship and Christianity — those were the things that should be encouraged. An abomination in the sight of the Lord were the wicked and the sinful. Did not the Iesu say...?

The old man shrugged. He shook his head slowly, and returned to his work.

* * *

Bull, who had watched the proceedings with relish, grinned slyly and winked at Thomas. The latter, however, appeared contrite. He shook hands with Ieuan and apologized for his conduct of a little while ago. Anxious to be friendly, he opened his cupboard which rested on a shelf above the bench, and began to show him his selection of moulding tools.

Humiliated, but determined to make amends for the trouble caused to Abraham, Ieuan worked assiduously at the bench, listening carefully to Thomas's instructions as the apprentice showed him how to ram and part a corebox. Within the next half-hour he had completed six small, rectangular cores when Reg and Charlie appeared.

Hands in pockets, a cigarette dangling from the corner of his mouth, Reg saluted Bull with a toss of the shoulder. The two cronies sat down on the edge of the bench. Abraham frowned at their approach, but said nothing.

"How's the kid shaping, Bull?" Charlie surveyed the six cores which had been placed carefully on a steel plate ready for drying in the stove. He picked one up and pressed it hard between his fingers.

"Should ram 'em harder, Iron," he remarked as the core crumbled into dust. "Like iron, Iron. See what I mean? Bit more elbow grease on the job, that's what you need." He took a second core and ground it between his fingers. "No, no son. Must ram 'em harder."

Ieuan stepped to the plate and pushed Charlie vigorously when the improver attempted to break another core.

"Cheeky little backstud!" Reg called from his seat on the bench.

"What's the game?" He leapt forward, pretending to make a grab at the plate, and simultaneously nipped his cigarette end into Ieuan's dungaree pocket.

There was a smell of burning cloth.

"Pooh, what a stink!" Reg held his nose. "Who's smoking old rope?"

"Not me," Bull grinned.

"Nor me."

Thomas had seen the occurrence.

"Look out, Ieuan, your pocket's burning," he warned.

Ieuan whipped a hand to his side. A neat, round hole appeared in his jacket pocket, and the lighted cigarette end dropped to the floor.

Charlie laughed. "Funny, I thought I smelt something burning. Instinct — that's what I call it. Instinct, and a sensitive snot."

Goaded into a temper, Ieuan picked up a core and suddenly aimed it at the improver's head. Charlie ducked smartly. The smile disappeared. His eyes narrowed, and he flung himself at the boy. With a quick movement he knocked his cap from his head and, as Ieuan stooped to retrieve it, Bull and Reg snatched a fistful of compo and threw it down his neck.

Abraham, hearing the scuffling, glanced around. He saw Bull hurriedly wipe his hands. Then he noticed Ieuan's plight. A bucket of water stood at his side. The charge-hand grabbed it by the handle, and swung it back.

"Get out!" he shouted at the top of his voice. "Get out, the three of you, before I drown you! Go! D'you hear me?" He was livid.

The three backed towards the compo shed. Then, as they reached it, the door of the steel shop was dragged open and Lu, the foreman, stood framed in the doorway.

CHAPTER FIVE

"WHAT'S going on here?" Lu demanded wrathfully. "Abraham!"

The charge-hand lowered the bucket. Ieuan, petrified with fear, hung his head, not daring to look up into the foreman's angry face. Bull had swiftly returned to the bench and was working more energetically than ever.

"I asked a question. What's this racket?" Lu strode up to Charlie and Reg who, self-concious and ill at ease, stooped down to examine the heavy cores that had recently been unloaded from the bogie.

"Nothing's wrong, Lu," Reg flustered. "We — we're just getting some cores."

"I didn't ask what you were doing," the foreman rasped. "Now," he jerked a thumb over his shoulder, "hop it back into the foundry, the two of you. As soon as my back's turned you're off somewhere or other. I'll put an end to this game. One of these fine days you'll be asking me to put in a word for you at the office when you're ready to claim for the rate, but let me warn you here and now — if you don't stay on your jobs I'll pack the pair of you out through the gates, bag and baggage. And the only things you'll get from the office will be your cards."

Lu's eyes focused on the broken cores. He swept them aside with his boot. "Who's responsible for this?" he asked. "Bull!"

Bull paused, rammer in hand. "Y-yes, sir?"

"These cores — did you break them?"

"Why, no, sir. I've been busy here all morning, sir."

"Humph, that's a good one," the foreman said sarcastically. "It's the first time I've heard you've been busy."

He addressed Abraham: "I'd like to know just what's been happening here, Abraham. And what's up with the new lad,

116

there? Has anyone been throwing compo again? And these cores — how come they're smashed?"

Abraham exhaled loudly. "You'd better ask Bowen and his mate. They were here when it happened."

"Please, Mr. Davies — " Ieuan trembled.

"Yes, what have you to say for yourself?" The foreman stared hard at him.

"It was an accident. I—I kicked against the plate and they — they tipped over."

"And I suppose they fell down your neck, eh? What's that stuff all over your collar?"

"No, Reg Bowen threw — I mean, Reg Bowen.... It was an accident, Mr. Davies."

"That's enough!" Lu spun round to the two improvers who were crossing the floor towards the foundry door. "If I hear that either of you has been up to his tricks again, there'll be trouble. I'll get rid of the pair of you, I'm telling you straight. This lad is paid to learn a trade, not to be pestered by hoodlums."

The improvers slunk through the doorway. Ieuan watched them as they slid the door to. They waited until the foreman's back was turned, then Reg held up his fist.

"We'll get you for this," he mouthed silently.

Lu lectured Abraham on the inadvisability of letting the improvers enter the coreshop unless they were on essential business. He gave him strict instructions that no horseplay was to be indulged in. To Isaiah and Dicky, who stood silently by, he gave the same warning. After he had left, Abraham gave vent to his spleen.

"You!" he shouted to Ieuan. "How much more trouble are you going to give me! This is the sorriest day for me, I can tell you. Nothing but upsets from the very minute you put your head in here. In future I'll not care a rap what happens to you. I'm not sticking up for you any more, nor for anyone else. It's I get the kicks around here. Like a dog I am, to be shouted at by Lu. I'm not putting up with it, not another minute. Enough I've got on my plate as it is."

117

He turned his attention to Isaiah and Dicky. "Fine pair you are," he grumbled. "Like sallies in the fair, deaf and dumb whenever Lu pokes his nose in here. Why didn't you speak up for me? You saw what happened. It wasn't my fault. Two hands I've got, and two eyes, and it takes me all my time to use them on the job. Lu had no right to talk to me like he did. After all, I've been charge-hand in this place for twenty-five years. He ought to respect me a bit more, considering how conscientiously I've done my work. But there, the more a man does, the less thanks he gets. More kicks than ha'pence — that's my lot ever since I've been in this place. Far less worries I'd have if I were just an ordinary moulder. The worst thing I ever did was to take on the responsibility of this place. Drive a man daft; it does. Fair daft."

Isaiah tried to pacify the disgruntled charge-hand. "Don't vex yourself over nothing, man," he said with irritation. "No blame is there on you, and nobody says so. Lu was only acting in his rights. What could Dicky and me say to him, and what'd be the use of it? Come, come, Abraham — making yourself ill with worry, you are. The old coreshop will carry on long after you are dead. More important things there are in life to worry about than a foreman's temper."

Ieuan felt choked. The feeling of utter loneliness he had so often experienced crept over him again. A kind of self-pity overwhelmed him. His bowels moved. Embarrassed, he asked Thomas where he could go.

He ran blindly out of the coreshop and down the yard. Once more he did his utmost to fight against the tears that burned his eyes. He brushed them away as they formed, and, head lowered, turned the corner at the rear of the pattern shop where Thomas had directed him.

The cold air freshened him, and the sight of men passing up and down the yard, the sound of their voices, made him less susceptible to the loneliness he felt.

He hurried into the latrine, a narrow, rectangular brick building with sloping, zinc-sheeted roof which jutted out from the pine end of the pattern shop.

The place was drab and unclean, primitive in the extreme, and a foul smell seeped into his nostrils as he entered. Walls, once bright with whitewash, were now a dirty yellow. The whitewash had peeled away in many places, leaving patches of green mildew and fungus. The lower half of the outside wall was a solid structure, but in the top half the bricks were interspersed for ventilating purposes.

An opening cut into the wall served as an entrance. There was no door. The cubicles were open, separated one from the other by a wooden partition. Privacy was not possible, and the men were exposed to all who passed along inside or outside the latrine.

The cement floor was covered with an inch of water. A narrow gutter which ran from end to end was littered with dirty newspapers, empty cigarette packets, cigarette ends and used matchsticks. The flushing system acted automatically and the rush of water from the cistern swept along the one channel and down a drain at the extreme end of the latrine.

A number of men were seated in the cubicles. Quite unselfconscious, they read newspapers, smoked, or chatted with one another. Ieuan stepped cautiously over the flooded floor to the far end. He found a cubicle with a door to it. He raised the latch and pushed. The door remained closed. He tried again.

"Hold hard a bit, boyo! What're you trying to do?" A head appeared out of a neighbouring cubicle, and the young man who had spoken looked at Ieuan curiously.

"You can't go in there," he said. "That's a special closet. For privileged people only — foremen and old Seth Hughes, the lavat'ry sweeper. Got to keep up the class distinction, you know, even when coming down to a perfectly natural job like this."

Ieuan took his hand away from the latch. "Sorry," he faltered.

"That's O.K., boyo." The young man called him over. "Sit down there — in between Bill and Emlyn." He nodded to an empty cubicle. "Bit new to this place, aren't you?" he asked.

119

"H'm I thought so, else you wouldn't have tried to trespass on protected property. What's your name?"

"Ieuan Morgan."

"Where you working?"

"Coreshop."

"Cripes, what a hole! How long you been there?"

"This is my first day."

The young man sounded friendly, but he was talkative.

"What school were you in?" He saw Ieuan look round nervously. "Sit down, boyo," he said casually. "Unbutton yourself. Nobody'll bite you. This place isn't like home sweet home, but the bosses think it's good enough for the likes of us. Go on, boy, sit down, and don't be bashful. I know how you feel. I was just the same when I first came to look for this place. But you'll get used to it. Familiarity breeds contempt, you know the old saying. Why, now I come down just for a spell. And, believe you me, I'm not the only one. The only good thing about a works' lavat'ry is that it's a bloody good hide-out from the foreman."

Ieuan sat down.

"What school were you at?" the young man repeated.

"County," Ieuan replied.

"County! That's a damn fine school. What the devil made you come to a foundry, of all places? Couldn't you get something better? I mean, there's good openings for boys with your education."

Ieuan left the question unanswered.

"Ah well, boyo, it's your funeral, not mine," the young man went on. "If you don't want to answer, then it's O.K. by me. But if I had had the chance of a County School education I wouldn't be in this dump pushing a barrow around." He took a tattered magazine from his jacket, which hung on a nail above his head, and began to read.

The two men in the cubicles on either side of Ieuan had listened to the conversation without making any comment. They now resumed their talk which had been interrupted by the young man's questioning.

120

"Did you have a go at the coupons last Saturday, Bill?" asked the one on Ieuan's left.

Bill grunted. "Ay, I had a go all right."

"What did you do — eight homes?"

"No, three draws."

"Did the shot come off?"

"No, but I had a good run for my money, though. Like this it was, Emlyn. You know them chickens I got in the back?"

"Yes, I know them chickens."

"Well, last Thursday night I was getting 'em into the coop. Been out in the garden all day, they had. But three of the little beggars went stubborn on me; couldn't get 'em in at all."

Emlyn interrupted. "What's the hell's chickens got to do with football?"

Bill raised his voice. "Shut up, mun, let me finish my story — that is, if you want to hear it."

"'Course I want to hear it, but don't be so bloody longwinded. Trouble with you, Bill, is that when you spin a yarn you go round the Cape of Good Hope and up to Alaska."

"Cape of Good Hope, by damn. What d'you mean?"

"Never mind, I'll tell you some other time. Carry on with the chickens."

"Well," Bill continued, "after working myself up into a 'ell of a temper, I got them three birds in. Then I goes into the house for a bit of supper, and starts marking out my football coupon.

"What shall it be this week, Annie?' I asks the missus. She goes half-shares with me every week, you know. The old girl doesn't mind speculating a tanner when there's a chance o' winning something.

"'Three draws was a big price last week,' she say. 'Why not try them?' 'Good enough,' I says, 'three draws it'll be.' I starts thinking. Then, all of a sudden-like I saw them three chickens, and me chasing 'em all over the garden. Three hens they were, Emlyn. Three hens — three Ns, see?"

Emlyn couldn't see. "Three hens?" he queried. "Three hens?

Look here, Bill, you're all right? I mean, you haven't come over sick, or something?"

Bill grew annoyed with the other's facetiousness.

"Three Ns, mun. Not hens," he said sharply. "Ns — letter Ns."

"Oh, ay." Emlyn's reply was not very convincing.

"That was a sign for me, Emlyn," Bill's annoyance had changed to enthusiasm, "and so I looked for all the teams beginning with an N. There was Newport County, Newcastle, Northampton, Notts County, Notts Forest and New Brighton. I plonked for Newport, Notts County and the Forest."

"And the shot went down?"

Bill sighed. "Ay, down the drain. Newport County put me in the cart proper. Lost two-one. Some youngster, Brown, from a local team was playing his first game and missed a sitter." He began to curse the team, the manager and the individual players in turn, retaining most of his invective for the young Brown who had missed the "sitter."

"It's no good letting a local youngster like Brown play for the County's first team before having a trial with the reserves. He got no experience for the Third Division. Six hundred and eighty to one the dividends were last week. Thirty-four quid for a bob! And all gone down the blasted drain because of Brown. There's no sense in playing youngsters before they've had experience. I remember when I was a young feller of twenty, I had a chance of a try-out with Loughor Rangers. They were champions of the Carmarthenshire League, and I — "

"Oh, *Arglwydd!*" Emlyn groaned, "you're not going to tell me that story again? It's got whiskers on it."

"All right, all right," Bill was aggrieved. "I'll keep it under my hat. But fancy now — thirty-four quid for a bob! A small fortune, ay indeed."

"You said it, Bill. Thirty-four quid — one thousand three hundred an' sixty pints! Crikey enough to float a battleship."

Emlyn uttered a long-drawn-out "Whew!" He got up and

hitched his braces. "What'd you do, Bill, if you was to scoop a pool and win a couple o' thousand quid?"

Bill reflected for a while.

"Chuck up this job," he began. He paused. "Then I'd buy a little bungalow over on the Gower Coast, facing the sea. On a little hill with green, green grass and tons of flowers. I'd get some chickens — prize ones. White Leghorns, Wyandottes, and maybe — yes, a couple o' Silver Campines." His voice became dreamy. He spoke softly. "Annie and me'd have a quiet time of it. No more getting up in the mornings at six. No more dirty dungarees and corned-beef sandwiches, and worrying over next week's bills. I'd have a motor car, p'raps, and a boat — a speedboat. There's just me and Annie. I'd see that she'd have a lady's life for a change. Her hands'd be white as a lily, and I'd dress her like them women on the films. A good gel is Annie, and nothing's too good for her. I could run her into Swansea on Saturday afternoons for to do the shopping. And on Sundays we could drive into the country, and come back when we liked without having to think of getting up to go to the foundry on Monday morning. Then, maybe, I'd buy a — "

Emlyn laughed. "A couple o' thousand, I said, Bill — not a million."

"I don't want a million," Bill replied seriously. "Too much money isn't good for a chap. A couple o' thousand'd see me happy for the rest of my natural. You wait, Emlyn boy, my luck'll turn one o' these days." He tossed his head and smiled. "Oh hell, what's the use of dreaming? You going, Emlyn? Arf a mo' — be with you in a jiffy."

The buddies walked out. Ieuan followed them with his eyes as they passed along the yard.

"Thirty-four quid for a bob. Eighteen weeks' wages," he heard Bill contemplate sadly, and Emlyn's sympathetic comment: "Bloody hard cheese!"

Pity for Bill, he reflected. Pity for all men who were tied down to the foundries, the factories, the mines and the steelworks. Pity

123

for the workers everywhere. Why shouldn't Bill have a couple of thousand pounds? Why shouldn't every working man have a couple of thousands? They worked hard every day, and at the end of their life's labour they were no better off than when they started.

Without them, the world would stop. Nothing would be made. And yet the people who did nothing had the best time. Why shouldn't the workers have enough money to get the things they wanted in life? For Bill — the cottage, the chickens and the motor car. Why not? Why not?

Pity for Bill and his dreams. Like that poem of Robbie Burns — how did it go?

> "The best laid plans o' mice and men
> Gang aft agley ...."

Bill had his dreams, ay, as every man. They were but dreams and nothing more. There would be no bungalow on the Gower Coast, no little hill with green, green grass and flowers. No chickens, no motor car. They existed only in his mind.

Ieuan moved slowly out from the latrine, his mind charged with a bitter, desperate hatred of the foundry.

> "The best laid plans o' mice and men .... "

The phrase recurred. His plans, too, had failed. His dreams were unfulfilled. The foundry! Was he to be tied there for the rest of his life? Would he become like Bill and the countless others like him, building up hopes that were never to be realized? Living in the hope that some day his luck would change, and he would find himself suddenly blessed with a fortune?

The thought depressed him more than ever. They — Bull, Jackson, Charlie, Reg — persecuted him for no reason. But there must be a reason for it, there must! Surely they wouldn't hurt him without cause? He had tried to forget their inhumanity, but failed. They humiliated him at every opportunity. But why? Why?

He trudged up the yard, shoulders hunched, his hands sunk into his pockets. The wind bit through his clothes, and he shivered violently. A little distance away he saw an old man standing by a heavy iron barrow filled with steel borings. The old man's gnarled hands were protected by strips of red rubber tubing. He coughed wheezingly, and tapped his chest.

Sighing, he grasped the curved handles of the barrow and strove to push it forward, but the load was too much for him. He grumbled to himself and, pausing, sighed once more and let the barrow drop. The sack apron he wore dangled to his ankles, and hindered his progress. He undid it and threw it around his shoulders. Then, tying the strings of the apron round his throat, he adjusted the buttons of his faded dungaree jacket and fumbled in his pockets.

For a moment, a look of bewilderment crossed his face. His right hand strayed to his forehead. He drew it across to his right ear. He smiled as his fingers closed over a cigarette stub. Flicking the burnt end, he placed the butt in his mouth. He searched in his waistcoat pockets and withdrew a blackened matchstick. This he struck on the barrow handle, and bent low over the cupped flame. With knees crossed he sat on the handle and inhaled deeply, blowing out the smoke with a sigh of satisfaction.

Ieuan greeted him as he went by.

The old man's face creased into a warm smile.

"Hallo, boy," he hailed. "Come over by here for a minute."

Ieuan drew his jacket tightly about him, approached.

"Good morning, boy *bach,* a new face you are around this way, aren't you? When did you start? This morning, eh? Well, well, what a place to come to, indeed. Wiser you would have been if you'd stayed in school, my boy."

The old man took another puff at his cigarette. "That's what I tell all the boys who come here," he continued, "but they don't seem to care. But there! P'raps I shouldn't say such daft things. There's no money to be earned at school, and I'm thinking you're anxious to get a little bit for to take home to your mam and dad, eh? All the same, this is no place for a slight little feller like you — though you might be a lot better off than I was when I was your age. In them days things was terrible hard, ay indeed."

The old man uncrossed his legs. "When I was a nipper, we were so poor that my dad couldn't afford to have my boots mended. Had to be carried to work when it was raining, that's a fact for you. However, times have changed a bit, thank goodness. It is better now than in them days, indeed it is. Indeed it is."

The speaker shivered. "Blinkin' cold, isn't it?" He breathed into his hands. "But tell me, boy, why did you come here? Awful place it is, and nothing but hard work every day. Hard work for small pay. And what do we get after spending our lives here, I ask you? No pension, not a ha'penny. A gold watch, p'raps. A gold watch for fifty years' service. What good is that, tell me? A man who got no job and no pension don't want a watch, even if it is a gold one. He couldn't eat it if he was starving, could he?"

Ieuan stood as though in a spell. The old man's eyes held him, and he could not drag himself away. Suddenly, as if from nowhere, a bowler-hatted man in a belted raincoat appeared before them. They had been so engrossed, the one talking, the other listening, that they had not noticed the newcomer's silent approach. He was youngish looking, with a neat, well-trimmed moustache. His eyes were mean and narrow.

"What's the meaning of this, Robert? Is this what we pay you for?" he demanded, staring at the old man. "You've been sitting here for the last ten minutes. I've been watching you from the pattern shop."

Startled, old Robert got up from the barrow handle; in his confusion he dropped the cigarette butt into the mud. "I—I—" he stammered.

"The less you talk, the better for everybody concerned, including yourself," the other thrust in sharply. "The trouble with you is you talk too much. What if I, as the manager, sat down and did nothing? Where would the company find itself? In a fine mess, I warrant you."

126

"I—I'm sorry, Mr. Beynon. I was just having a bit of a spell."

"Spell, indeed! You've been talking to this lad for ten minutes. I don't want to hear your excuses, Robert. All I can say is you're lucky it's I caught you out, not Mr. Bevan. Now, get on with your work."

"Yes, Mr. Beynon. Thank you indeed, sir." The old man strained once more at the barrow handles, and moved laboriously in the direction of the steel furnaces.

The manager turned to Ieuan, who had been too frightened to move while he remonstrated with old Robert. "And what are you supposed to be doing?"

"I'm working in the coreshop, sir."

"Well, get back there, and stay there. We don't pay you for standing idle."

Ieuan's feelings revolted at the manager's tone. He felt a fierce resentment against the manner in which he had spoken to old Robert. What right had he to shout at a man old enough to be his father? A man who had worked in the foundry all his life and helped to build it into the huge concern it was.

"Give a man a uniform, and he ceases to be a man," someone had once said. How right it was. This man had no uniform, but he had been given authority over everyone in the foundry, which was the same thing. And because he had been given this, he thought he had the right to speak disrespectfully to old men like Robert.

"Well, what are you waiting for?"

The manager's voice broke in on Ieuan's thoughts. He turned and began to walk away. But once again his mind dwelt on the old labourer who had spoken in such a friendly way.

Poor old Robert! Once he had been young and full of life and energy, but the foundry had sapped all his vitality. Pity for Robert .... Pity for Bill .... Pity for Robert.... Pity for Robert.

Ieuan walked into the coreshop, his eyes focused on the ground.

"Here's the young cock-sparrow, boys. Now's our chance to tame him."

He looked up sharply.

"Where's Abraham and the others?" he asked, his breath catching in his throat.

Reg and Charlie watched him balefully.

"The whole tribe's gone down to the pattern shop, Mister Lord Muck," Charlie jibed, "and we're going to pay you back for what you did just now, see? You bloody little tell-tale-tit. Bull! Grab him."

Bull darted behind Ieuan, and the other two lunged forward. They pinioned his arms to his side.

"Now then, lads, all together!"

Ieuan was powerless in their grasp. They rushed him off his feet and carried him into the compo shed. He tried to cry out. Reg stuffed a dirty handkerchief into his mouth and screwed a fist into his ears until they ached and burned.

"Dump him in here," Charlie gasped.

They threw him on to a pile of damp compo. Before he had a chance to resist, the two improvers pinned him down.

"Get the stuff, Bull! Hurry!"

Bull clattered back to the coreshop, emitting a loud war-whoop. Ieuan lashed out at his opponents, but they were too strong for him. His efforts grew weaker, and soon he exhausted himself.

"We've got the little stool-pigeon just where we want him now," Reg panted. "Hold him, Charlie, while I do the job. Where the hell's Bull?"

"Here I am." Bull came forward. In his hand he held a sheet of brown paper and a small brush. He gave them to Reg.

"Okay, Charlie, let's have him." He bent down and gripped Ieuan's trousers by the waist. Once again the boy began to struggle desperately.

"For Christ's sake, hold him!" Reg shouted. "Hey, Bull, gimme a hand before someone comes."

Brin Compo, attracted by the noise, came nosing up to them. "What's going on here?" he asked.

"Mind your flaming business," Charlie snapped. "This is our affair. We're paying him back what we owe, that's all."

Brin looked on coolly, and made no attempt to interfere.

128

Reg unbuttoned Ieuan's trousers while Bull tore at the dungaree straps.

"That's got him!" Reg tugged downwards. The boy's trousers were drawn down over his knees, his naked thighs exposed.

"Hand it over, Bull — quickly!"

The brush, wet with clay and core gum, was rubbed over Ieuan's thighs and along his abdomen. He began to sob, pleading to be let free.

"Go on, cry as much as you like. There's not a bloody soul going to hear you." Reg rubbed the brush vigorously into the glutinous mess and once more dabbed it between the boy's thighs.

"That'll teach you not to split on us again. Let it be a lesson to you, d'you hear?"

Brin Compo's ears pricked. "Tone down, you noisy idiots," he warned. "Listen ... someone's coming!"

From the coreshop came the sound of voices.

"Jesus, it's Lu! Watch out!"

"Hell's bells!" Reg and his accomplices leapt up and scattered across to the door leading into the foundry. They scrambled through it on top of one another just as the foreman entered the compo shed.

Ieuan picked himself up slowly. Mortified, he dragged at his trousers. His body trembled all over. Losing what control he possessed he burst into a spasm of weeping.

Lu approached. He surveyed him with sympathy, and without saying a word, led him back to the coreshop.

Abraham and his co-workers had returned. They looked at the foreman, then at Ieuan. No one ventured to say anything. Then Lu spoke.

"Hand me a bit of waste, Abraham."

He wiped the clay stains and thrust the waste into Ieuan's hands. "Dress yourself, boy," he said kindly. "I'll find out who's responsible for this outrage, and then," his voice grew cold, "God help them!" Casting a vindictive glance in Abraham's direction, he went on his way.

Ieuan dressed. Shamefacedly, he returned to the bench, conscious that the charge-hand was furious with him. A hush fell over the coreshop, a strained silence which was felt by everyone there.

Presently the foundry door opened, and the young moulder, Frank Jones, white-faced and angry, strode in.

"Who's to blame for ragging that boy?" He pointed a quivering finger. No one answered. "Who was it?" he demanded again. He glared at Abraham. "Come on, speak up!"

Abraham turned his back to him.

"Right-ho — if that's how you feel. I'll damn well make it my business to find out. There's a limit to everything, and this persecution's got to stop before something really serious happens." Frank stalked out of the shop, his fists clenched, and as soon as he had gone, Abraham spun round.

"See the trouble you're causing me," he complained. "Not a minute has gone by without you being in some scrape. Haven't I told you often enough to leave those ruffians in there alone? Sick and tired, I am, fed up to the teeth with all this hotch-potch."

Thomas jumped to Ieuan's defence.

"Aw, shut up, Abraham. Shut your trap. You're too bloomin' windy to do anything. You know who's responsible. Every apprentice goes through the same thing, and you don't do nothing to stop it. All you do is complain and grumble like an old woman. And that's what you are — a proper old granny."

Abraham almost danced in his temper. "Don't you dare talk to me like that," he stormed. "There's no new boy given me all this trouble, and well you know it. Ever since he put his foot in here there's been one fandangle after another. He should use his sense, and keep away from them fellows in the steel shop. And as for you, my lad, you'd better control that tongue of yours. The impudence of you! Talking to me as if I was a bit of dirt or something. You want to learn respect, and if I was your father I'd —"

The argument developed, and soon the charge-hand and apprentice were shouting at one another across the floor, while

Isaiah did his best to mediate.

The quarrel was at its height when the foundry door slid open again, and Frank appeared with Reg at his heels.

"Ieuan!"

Ieuan raised his eyes.

"Listen, boy, I want you to tell me the truth. Was this fellow one of the gang who messed you up just now?"

Reg pursed his lips. He stared at Ieuan, his eyes wild and threatening. "Did I do anything to you?" he challenged. "Go on — tell him if I did."

"Was he one of the gang?" Frank was adamant. "Don't be afraid to tell me, Ieuan. Come on, boy, speak up."

Ieuan gazed at him dumbly.

"Speak up, boy. Don't be scared."

Ieuan hesitated. "I—I don't want to say anything," he said at last. "I—I'd rather forget what happened."

"All right, if that's how you feel." Frank shrugged. He strode to the door. "But if you change your mind, let me know."

* * *

Dinner time came. The yard was deserted. The workmen who were going home for dinner had left the foundry, and those who remained were already seated in the canteen and in their accustomed places in the compo shed, fitting shop and elsewhere.

It had begun to rain again, and the wind was still high. Ieuan drew his coat about him, while Thomas, head sunk into shoulders, trudged heavily alongside. They came to the main gate. Outside, in the shelter of a railway truck, stood a woman clad in a long Burberry and a widebrimmed hat decorated with faded cloth flowers. She held an umbrella over her head. A second, and smaller one, rested on the crook of her arm.

Ieuan drew up with a jerk. "I—I'll see you later, Thomas." He glanced over his shoulder. Bull was approaching a few yards behind.

131

Thomas looked at him, mystified. "What's up?" he asked.

As he spoke the woman drew near. She extended the smaller umbrella. "Take this, Ieuan. I thought it would be raining, so I dropped everything and came to meet you."

Ieuan wavered. "It's all right, Mam," he said nervously. "I—I shan't get wet."

"Shan't get wet, indeed! What new nonsense is this? Soaked to the skin you'll be," she rapped. She jerked the umbrella open, and at that moment Bull passed by, smirking.

Ieuan bit his lip. It was his sister's umbrella, a flowered, summer one. He felt a hot blush spread across his face as Bull laughed and threw a meaning look at him.

Thomas, who stood a few paces away, did his utmost to conceal a smile, for the situation was comical.

"So—long, Ieuan," he grinned. "See you this afternoon."

"Well?" Mrs. Morgan snapped. "What have I done wrong now?"

"You—you shouldn't have come to meet me, Mam," Ieuan protested feebly. "I could come home by myself."

"Indeed, now! And is that all the thanks I get for thinking of you? Cooked a nice dinner for you, I have. Been out shopping for to get a piece of steak special for it, and rushed off my feet proper for to be here by one o'clock. Got your interest at heart, I have. Not many mothers would rush out in the rain for to meet their sons, I can tell you."

They walked over the railway crossing in silence. Ieuan closed the gaudy umbrella, and as if in defiance of his action, the rain increased. It showered from the leaden sky with the spiteful hiss of angry snakes and spattered on the roadway.

So violent was its force that the slanting rods of rain bounced as they touched the ground, and from the gleaming road surface transparent, needle-pointed blades of grass seemed to sprout interminably.

Ieuan clenched his teeth. The cold rain slashed across his face, and the wind howled mournfully around him. It blew in under the hem of his coat and lifted it high above his waist. It held his arms rigid at his side, whistled shrilly through his ears, and bit into the lobes with sharp, invisible teeth of ice.

His mother struggled forward, the umbrella held low in front of her face. She panted loudly, one minute straining against the antic wind, the next, scuttling forward in a jog trot as it whirled behind her.

"Come under here with me," she gasped. She pulled Ieuan to her side. "You and your silly nonsense! This is the first and last time I'll ever come to meet you. Thankless you are, with not a thought for your mother. If I had known, I wouldn't have put a foot outside the house, but let you walk through the rain to get your clothes all wet and your feet soaking."

"I didn't want you to come, Mam," Ieuan said, in a voice almost inaudible.

"And your why not? Are you too proud to be seen walking with your mother? Ashamed of me are you, or what?"

"'Tisn't that, Ma. But I'm grown up now. The boys'll only make fun of me."

"Fun, ach! Tommy-rot to all that nonsense. Too sensitive you are, Ieuan, like your father — and full of silly ideas. Stubborn, too, just like him."

Ieuan lapsed into a deep silence. It was useless trying to explain how he felt. His mother would not understand; she would not try to understand. Better by far if he had said nothing. It only made her angry and impatient.

But the mischief had been done. Bull had seen him, and when he got back to the foundry there would be no peace for him. They would mock him, strive to make him appear ridiculous, and the hours would be as intolerable as those already gone.

If only he had refused to go to the foundry! If dad had only spoken up and insisted on his remaining at school, how different things would be. But it was too late now. Too late!

"Have you lost your tongue all of a sudden?" His mother's voice rasped in his ears, and the chain of thought snapped. Irritated by her presence, he hurried onward, and his moody silence prevailed.

133

They crossed into Station Square, the rain drumming incessantly on the open umbrella. The wind suddenly seemed to withdraw from them, as if tired of its efforts to check their progress. It raced under a cluster of mud stained, brown leaves in the gutter and chased them into the air where they sailed erratically like wounded birds in flight. Then, seeking another diversion, it swooped into the sky, caught the columns of smoke from the distant tinworks' chimneys and made them curl and sway like huge, black reptiles across the darkening, oppressive clouds.

"What a day! Not fit for a dog to be out," Ieuan heard his mother grumble. "And to think that I came to meet you, with not a word of thanks for it. Ungrateful, that's what I have to say about you."

The miserable journey brought them to the house.

Gweneira and Phyllis were sitting at the table. They ran to meet their brother as he entered the kitchen, and the younger girl threw her arms around his waist. She looked up into his face, her eyes beaming, and a happy smile on her lips.

"Gee, Ieuan, there's nice you look in your dungarees. Like a proper man you are, all grown-up. Isn't he, Gweneira?"

"He is indeed," Gweneira laughed.

They led him to the table, while their mother slipped off her wet coat and hat.

"Take off your old coat, Ieuan, and come and tell us all about the foundry. Did you like it? Was it nice there? Did the time go quick? And did you see anybody you knew?"

Ieuan forced a smile. "Let me have dinner, girls, then I'll answer all your questions, one by one," he promised.

His mother poured out a cup of tea for him and brought a plate of steak and chips from the hot oven.

"You've lost a quarter of an hour," she reminded him sharply, "so hurry up and eat your dinner. You can talk to the girls tonight when you have more time."

To her daughters she said: "You, too, children — eat your food, and no talking at the table, please."

Ieuan ate without relish. His sisters watched him across the table, their eyes eager with unasked questions. They waited their opportunity, patient to the last fragment of their meal. Then, when dinner was over, they unburdened themselves.

"How was it, Ieuan?"

"Are you sorry you went — same as last night?"

"Yes, I am sorry. I—I hate it," Ieuan blurted. He rose from the table. "I hate it like — like nothing I know, and I don't ever want to go back there."

Gweneira gulped. She threw an anxious glance at her mother. "I knew you wouldn't like it, Ieuan," she began, "I — "

"Quiet — all of you!" Mrs. Morgan rapped the table. "How dare you to speak like that, Gweneira. Ieuan likes the foundry. Strange to it he is, that's all. He's a big boy now, not a child. Of course he likes his work, so say nothing more to put ideas into his head."

"I hate the foundry," Ieuan cried. He stared vindictively at his mother. "And I don't want to go back there."

"Ach, boy, you don't know what you're saying. Come, now," Mrs. Morgan became persuasive, "a bit upset you are. It's only fair to expect you to behave like this on your first day. Strange and new everything is to you. But you'll get over it, my boy. Just a little bit of patience, that's all you want. P'raps I did shame you, bringing that old umbrella with me. Indeed, that is what has made you upset like this, is it?"

Phyllis and Gweneira left the table. They sat together on the wooden settle, and waited apprehensively.

"Whatever is the matter, boy?" Mrs. Morgan's tone softened. "Surely you ought to be glad to be bringing a bit of money into the house. A big help you are to your father and me now, and it's proud you should be. There's nothing gone wrong today, has there?"

Ieuan shook his head. "No," he replied wearily. "No, nothing's gone wrong."

"The boys there — p'raps they've been rough with you or

135

something? You know how boys are, but they don't mean to be cruel. Just pulling your leg they are, like they do to every new boy."

Ieuan picked up his coat. "After today I'm staying home, Mam," he said slowly. "I shall see Mr. Griffiths tomorrow and ask him to take me back to school. I hate the foundry. I—I hate all the boys there .... I'm sorry I listened to you."

His mother clutched at her breast. Her eyes were like fire.

"You ungrateful boy!" she shouted, all semblance of patience and kindliness gone. "Selfish, you are. Not a fig do you care for anybody but yourself. Let me scrape and pinch, you would, for to bring you and your sisters up decent, while you sit on your behind in school for the rest of your life. You wait till your father hears of this, my fine boy. He'll be letting you know one or two things. Just you wait till he comes home tonight."

Ieuan rushed up the passage and flung on his coat. He slammed the door loudly behind him. Choked with tears and frustrated rage, he ran blindly down the dreary street. He hated his mother. Hated her, even as he hated the foundry. Let her tell his father. He didn't care. He would let his father know the truth, and then perhaps he need never go back to the foundry.

He hastened on down the road, the keen wind stinging the tears on his frozen cheeks. Let mam wait — he'd show her. He'd make her understand that he was never going to stick the foundry after this day. She knew nothing of what had happened there. She didn't understand. She never would understand. And she had called him selfish! It was she who was selfish and cruel. Why couldn't she have left him at school where he was happy with his studies?

Some day he would get a degree, and then she would benefit much more — she and dad, and Gweneira and Phyllis. There was so much he could do for them all, but she couldn't see it. All she was concerned with was the twelve shillings he would bring in from the foundry. Twelve shillings! And she had sacrificed his schooling for that much!

Distressed and overwrought, his mind assailed with the dread

136

of the foundry and the afternoon that was yet to come, he walked on like a person to whom sense of direction was lost. The stream of workers passed him by at the entrance of the works. He was oblivious to them, his mind tormented with doubts and fears.

"Well, well, well, Ieuan. We meet again, and on the same old spot. What a coincidence, ay indeed!" a cheerful voice sounded.

Startled out of his despondency, he looked up to see Frank Jones at his elbow.

"How you feeling now?" Frank asked solicitously. "Better?"

Ieuan walked by his side, not knowing what to say in answer. He felt sick at heart, and each step that brought him nearer to the coreshop made him shudder inwardly.

Frank slowed down. "Listen, Ieuan. I know what you've been through this morning, lad." His voice was low, and filled with sincerity. "And I realize, only too well, how you feel. I know your attitude towards the foundry and the fellows who work there. You hate it — despise it more than anything, don't you? But, believe me, I can sympathize with you. I went through almost the same kind of torture, and I dreaded every minute of the first days I spent in the coreshop."

He took Ieuan's arm as they passed the open door of the smithy. Presently, they drew up under the protecting girders of the yard crane. Frank turned his back to the wind. The workers slouched by, and to some of them he nodded in greeting.

He was deeply concerned over Ieuan. He placed his hands on the boy's shoulders and looked closely into his face.

"There's so much I could tell you, Ieuan — so much. that would help you to try and understand," he said earnestly. "Bull Jackson, Charlie Rees, Reg Bowen — they are the three who've pestered you most. And they've done so, not because they hate you as a boy, but purely because you've had a better education than they. They've realized, in their own ignorant fashion, that you are more refined than they are, more sensitive to things, and for that reason they want to hurt you — to bring you down to their level. They don't want to be working in the foundry any more than you do. They'd like to have decent jobs, with a decent rate of pay, and be able to hold up their heads proudly. They are aware of their ignorance, Ieuan, and it hurts them, although they don't show it outwardly. To be truthful, my boy, they would be the last to confess their weakness. And there are other things, too: frustration, that longing for something which is denied one — a good home, decent surroundings, clean-minded, honest and sincere friends. Oh, so many things that one strives for and never gets! And the failure, the frustration, makes one bitter, cruel and cynical."

Frank shook his head and shrugged. He patted Ieuan gently. "Strange that I should preach to you like this," he went on, "but I've been very worried about you, Ieuan. Maybe you think I'm just a bag of wind and don't mean half what I say. But, believe me, my boy, I'm telling you the truth. Sometimes, like this morning for instance, I lose my temper, and the bullying and ragging gets me into such a state of mind that I could cheerfully thrash those who made you suffer. That's wrong of me, Ieuan, to lose my temper. But it's so easy to talk, isn't it? After all, a man is only human, and often patience and understanding go overboard."

A gust of wind whirled up the yard. Frank shivered and blew into his hands. He turned up his coat collar.

"This place does things to one," he continued, rubbing his hands vigorously. "I know the cause of Bull's and the other fellows' hooliganism. I've explained it all to you. And yet, at the moment when I should realize it most, I forget. A man works hard, and there is little rest. What leisure we get is no real leisure at all, for even in the hours after work is finished we know that the next day we have to return to the treadmill again. And there's sickness, unemployment, the worry of making ends meet. Jesus God! No wonder a man becomes bitter, Ieuan. Naturally, someone must work in the foundries, the mines, the steelworks, the tinplate mills and all the other places in industry, but conditions in these places must be changed. Industry should be made more attractive.

Men should work less hours and get better pay. Then, and then only, will they change. Look at me, boy. Do you think I wanted to be a moulder? And young Thomas — he was a grand little scholar, so I've been told. He would have gone to the County, just like you, and it's probable that he would have made good progress there. But — well, I've told you all I can, Ieuan. Whenever you feel that your little world has tumbled down before your eyes, just throw your mind back to this moment, and remember what I've told you."

Frank puffed. He tapped his chest and grinned. "Whew! That certainly was a long speech, Ieuan. Crikey! It's a Member of Parliament I ought to be. I'd do well in the gasworks, wouldn't I?"

He chuckled to himself. "Reminds me of that M.P. from Pantyrheol. We used to call him the 'silent Member.' He sat in the Commons for ten years, and the only words he ever spoke in the House were: 'Please shut the windows. There's a draught.' Well, come along, Ieuan. Let's go, or the men'll think we've planted our roots here."

CHAPTER SIX

THE two o'clock hooter shrilled, its dying wail more desolate than the cry of the lone white seagull wheeling in slow motion above the foundry.

The dark clouds lowered, and the wind lashed out with a new and greater fury. It swept the workers forward as if impatient with their seeming indifference to be at their jobs. It tore along the roofs of the foundry and pattern shop, snarling and whistling, and burrowed beneath the damp crust covering the ash heap near the crusher. The dry dust was blown hither and thither, and the men buried their faces in their arms as they passed.

The zinc sheets enclosing the rear part of the furnace landing rattled. A yellow poster, tacked loosely on the pattern shop door, was snatched from its fastenings and ballooned into the air to disappear over the rooftop.

"God help the sailors on a day like this," a workman muttered, one hand shielding his face, the other fastened grimly to his cap.

"You said it, George. Proper November weather, isn't it?" another answered, battling his way through the wind.

Frank stepped out from the shelter of the girder.

"Guess I'll have to leave you now, Ieuan," he said. He tucked the collar of his overcoat tighter around his throat. "I'll be working in the casting bay this afternoon, so I'll pop in under the furnace arch and hang up my coat to dry. We're casting at three; take a walk down and have a look at us if you feel like it. And don't forget what I told you — the long speech, you know."

"I won't, Frank. So-long."

Ieuan pushed on up the yard. He had reached the coreshop door when he heard someone whistle. Glancing over his shoulder he saw Thomas standing under the lean-to which covered the crusher.

"Dash over here a minute, Ieuan. I got something to tell you."

Ieuan skipped over the ash heap that lay between them. "It's gone two, Thomas. We're late," he began.

"Oh, what odds! There won't be much work done this afternoon. Up-ladle's at three."

"Up-ladle?"

"Casting — that's what we mean when we say up-ladle. All of us in the coreshop take things easy then. Take your coat in, and come with me to the watchman's shanty for a sit down. I'll wait here for you. O.K. ?"

Not wishing to appear nervous, Ieuan fell in with the idea and hurried into the coreshop with his overcoat. He did not wait to hear what Bull had to say, and took no notice of Abraham and the two men.

Thomas took him along a narrow path between the coreshop and the boundary wall. Sheltered from the wind, they came presently to a small brick building near a wide door facing the side street down which the girls from the tinstamping works had gone earlier in the day.

The door of the building was in two halves, similar to a stable door. Thomas rapped on it, and the top half swung outwards.

"Room for two small ones?" he asked as a puckered face appeared over the edge.

"Yes, come on in — but be quiet."

The bottom half of the door opened and the two boys stepped inside. The shanty was no more than eight feet long and six wide. A wooden bench rested against one wall, and on this five men huddled close together. Facing it was a crude wooden table, and, above the table, a window across which a sack curtain had been drawn, leaving a narrow gap through which a look-out could be kept. A small fire burned in the grate built into the wall opposite the door, and looking down at it from the mantelpiece was a coloured painting of Christ walking on Galilee. To the right of the fireplace was a fretwork pipe rack, and hanging from a nail was the watchman's dungaree jacket.

"You can sit by here and have a warm for a few minutes. Old Jonah, the watchman, has gone down to the main office," one of the men invited. He nudged his neighbour, and the five moved up towards the door, turning their knees to allow the boys to pass.

"Thanks, Dai." Thomas sat down uncomfortably close to the fire. He held his hands over the grate. "Been here long?"

"About five minutes," said Dai. "But don't talk a lot, just be quiet and relax while the going's good."

All at once, almost before Ieuan had time to seat himself, the man nearest the door jumped up in alarm.

"Lu!" he exclaimed. He pushed the door open an inch and peered into the yard. "Dammo, he's heading this way. Watch out, lads."

Pandemonium followed the warning. Without hesitation they ducked under the table, pushing and scrambling on their knees. There was hardly room for one man to hide himself in the small space afforded, and consequently their posteriors bulged out.

The sight was so ludicrous that even Ieuan, in spite of his nervousness, was compelled to smile. Thomas, however, was in no mood to feel amused.

"Sit tight, Ieuan," he breathed urgently. "If Lu catches us we're for the high jump."

No one said a word. It seemed as though the very act of breathing had been suspended. From the coat on the wall came the ticking of a watch. It sounded so loud and ominous that one of the men turned his head and stared at the coat with fear, cursing the watch under his breath.

The foreman drew near. Ieuan gripped the seat, and held himself rigid. Thomas clapped a forefinger across his nose and suppressed a sneeze. He peered through the slit in the curtains. A loud sigh, and then he relaxed. He patted a posterior. "O.K., boys. All clear."

The foreman had by-passed the shanty and gone down the yard.

"Crikey, that was a near go."

142

"Ay, by damn. We'd better get back on the job, boys. Lu's missed us, no doubt, otherwise he wouldn't be on the prowl."

"*Iechyd!* It comes to something when a chap can't take a spell for five minutes. Lu's got eyes like a bloomin' hawk. Somebody ought to give him a dose of jalap. That'd keep him away from the foundry for a bit."

Grumbling, the men trailed out of the shanty and shuffled unwillingly to whatever tasks awaited them in the foundry.

The storm had subsided, but the clouds still hung dark and heavy. A shower of fine rain had begun to fall, and the damp, grey mist descended lower over the foundry buildings.

The two boys hurried down the narrow path and were met by Abraham, who waited at the entrance to the coreshop, a deep frown on his face.

"And what time d'you two intend to make a start this afternoon?" he said gruffly.

They did not choose to answer, but sidled past him into the shop.

"Suits me, if you want to stay dumb — " they heard him say as he followed them. "But you won't be quite so tongue-tied when Lu comes looking for you. But p'raps you'll feel inclined to do a bit of work when I tell you that he's been on the warpath again? Yes, Lu's been tearing around like a cat on hot bricks. Up-ladle's at three, and not half the cores are ready."

Abraham sighed loudly. "What made me take on this job, I don't know. Must have been half-daft. All the responsibility of this place falls on my shoulders, and what do I get out of it? Nothing but trouble and worry — nothing ...."

* * *

The afternoon passed without the complications Abraham had feared would arise. Lu did not put in an appearance, being too occupied with the cast. Practically every moulder and improver in the steel shop was equally busy. There were moulds to be closed and arranged in the casting bay, ready for the waiting ladle brimful of molten steel. And even after the cast there was much to be done. The smaller and more delicate castings had to be stripped to allow for contraction, and the larger ones had to undergo the same process some hours later.

For the first time that day Ieuan was left in peace. But the torment was not ended. Towards the end of the day's shift came further molestation.

Just before five o'clock, Thomas put away his tools. He took Ieuan's coat from the hook in the wall. "Here y'are, hooter's on the blow." He extended the coat, when suddenly Bull made a quick grab at it.

"Leggo!" Thomas tried to swing the coat away. "Don't play the fool."

Bull jerked the garment from the other's hands, and whipped it behind his back. "Dry up, Tom-tit. I just want a bit of fun to finish the day off."

Ieuan rushed up to him. "Give me my coat," he cried, angrily. He looked round to appeal to Abraham and the other men, but they had already made their way down into the yard to wait for the hooter's blow.

Bull side-stepped, and darted to the steel shop door. He cupped a hand over his mouth and shouted into the foundry. "Gang-O! Come on, boys. Who wants a game o' rugby?"

The invitation was hardly extended when Reg, Charlie, Bingo and a crowd of improvers came running to the coreshop.

"What's up, Bull? What's all the excitement about?"

Bull held out the coat. "This. Thought you'd like a game."

"Whose is it?"

"Little Iron's."

"Then we don't mind if we do." Charlie stepped back, the others crowding round him. "Come on, Bull, out with the ball."

Bull thrust out his arm ready to swing the coat. Thomas jumped forward and attempted to wrest it from him. The older apprentice gave him a forceful push that sent him stumbling against the wall.

"Hand that coat over, Bull Jackson," Thomas shouted, reaching for a hammer. "Hand it over, I say, or I'll brain you with this." He gripped the hammer threateningly. "Come on, give it me. Ieuan's had enough for today, so don't start any monkey business again."

"Aw, put a sock in it," Bull sneered, "and put that hammer down before you hurt yourself. Christ! You're like a kid on the breast. I shan't hurt Iron's ragbag. Just want to show it to the boys. I'll give it back, honest I will."

"What a bloody hope!" Thomas snatched at the coat. "Come on, give over."

The elder apprentice brushed his hand away and before either of the boys could prevent him, he darted into the steel shop. They ran after him, but the bully was protected by a ring of improvers.

"Chuck it here, Bull." Reg held out his hands. The coat was tossed to him. The improver withdrew his hands and as the coat dropped to the dusty floor he lunged at it with his boot.

"How's that for a drop goal?" he cried. He broke through the ring and prepared to take another kick, when, with a cry of frustrated rage, Ieuan sprang on his back and hit him hard on the cheekbone.

"Swine!" Ieuan struck him again. "Bloody, bloody ...."

In his frenzy he searched for a word to express his outraged feelings. "Bastard — bloody bastard!"

The onlookers crowded in on the struggling pair. Charlie shouldered Thomas aside as the boy attempted to go to Ieuan's aid. "Keep out of this, Tom-tit," he warned, "or you'll get the worst of it."

Thomas ignored the threat. Once again he tried to barge his way through, but the excited improvers linked arms and held him back. Meanwhile, Reg had thrown Ieuan to the floor. He hurled himself on the boy and struck him fiercely, blow after blow falling on his unprotected face.

Ieuan winced from the savage assault. He threw his arms

145

around his aggressor's shoulders and struggled to pull himself off the floor. His feet slid from under him. A fist smashed against his nose. He felt the warm blood trickle over his mouth. His nose swelled. Tears blinded him. He was powerless to retaliate. Crying bitterly, he loosed his hold and fell heavily back into the dust.

Reg staggered up and rubbed his aching cheek.

"Hot-headed little runt," he growled. He swung round and took a flying kick at the coat. "Take your bloody ragbag. Shove it where the monkey shoved his nuts. By Christ! I'd have murdered you if you'd hit me again." He rolled up his sleeves. "Now, get up, and beat it while you're all in one piece."

Ieuan stumbled to the door, a hand held over his bleeding nose. He groped for the water bosh.

Presently, he found himself alone. With the shrieking of the hooter the workers poured out from the steel shop. The mill in the compo shed grated to a standstill. There was a frenzied rush to be away from the foundry. It seemed as though the men were prisoners suddenly granted an amnesty. Cheery "So-longs" betokened their relief, and they hurried into the yard with a vigour unknown to them during the working day.

Ieuan washed his face under the tap. Breathing heavily, his face bruised and swollen, he limped into the deserted steel shop. The coat lay in the dust where the improver had kicked it. Ieuan gathered it up and made his way slowly down the foundry.

A fettler wished him good night as he passed through the sack-covered entrance into the yard. Darkness had begun to fall. The swinging lamps shone down on the oil-encrusted pools, and the glistening rails and the furrows in the sludge were touched with gold.

A long queue weaved in through the time-office door.

The pegging clock bell rang incessantly, and the workers, black ghosts in the darkening light, trudged out of the main gateway.

Ieuan made no effort to join the queue. He stood behind an empty coal truck, and waited until the time office emptied. The men who were the last to leave their jobs passed within a few

146

yards, but none noticed him hidden in the deeper shadows of the truck.

He did not feel like mingling with the crowd, for he had nothing to say — nothing. And yet he yearned for someone in whom he could confide. Someone to whom he could speak of the terror he felt, the humiliation he had suffered; of the hatreds that had been born to him this day. Someone who would listen sympathetically. But there was no one. No one to whom he could turn.

He drew up the collar of his coat and pressed his fingers gently against his swollen cheek. An overwhelming pity filled him. He felt alone and unwanted, in a world devoid of hope, of love. Even in his own home he would find no sympathy, tolerance, or understanding, and the knowledge drove him into an abyss of black despair.

While he stood there, tortured by his thoughts, a familiar figure passed down the yard. He withdrew farther into the shadows. But the figure had seen him.

"Is that you, Ieuan?"

He made no reply.

"Ieuan. It's me, Frank."

Again he refused to answer.

Frank approached. "Good heavens, boy, what are you doing here? Aren't you going home tonight?" He smiled in the darkness. "Come, come, lad," he said brightly. "Don't take things to heart so. Tomorrow's another day, you know." The moulder linked his arm in Ieuan's and drew him gently away.

The timekeeper stood in the doorway of the inner office, smoking a pipe. His overcoat was buttoned, and he was ready to leave. He grumbled inaudibly as they pegged out, then proceeded to change the tapes on the clock for the next morning.

When they reached Tony Marasiano's shop, Frank halted.

"Like a cup of tea?" he suggested. "It'll warm you up, and help a lot."

Ieuan shook his head. "No thanks, Frank. I haven't far to go — I'll be home soon."

For a while there was a silence between them, selfconscious and embarrassing, as if each were afraid of expressing his thoughts. Frank blew into his hands and shuddered. A keen wind cut across from the Station Square. The tall hoardings facing the railway booking office swayed. A tram clanged by with the last load of workers, leaving the road empty and deserted. The lights in Tony's shop were switched off.

"What's on your mind, Ieuan? Tell me." Frank's voice was low and persuasive. "Still worrying over what happened today?"

Ieuan hesitated. "Yes, Frank," he said at last. "I hate the foundry. I—I can't stand it. I'll never be able to work there. Bull Jackson, Reg Bowen — all of them — they're cowards — bullies and cowards. I don't want to go back, Frank. I can't ... I can't."

Frank took his arm again. "I'll walk with you as far as the Square. There's a lot I have to say to you, my boy, and maybe it will help you to feel that life is not quite as terrible as you want to picture it. You've been in the foundry one day, Ieuan — one day only — and now at the end of it you feel everything is lost. You imagine that Bull and the others have a grudge against you, and you alone, and that they are determined to make things unbearable for you in the foundry. We all go through that phase, Ieuan — each and every one of us, and we all feel that the end of the world has come. But it's all selfpity, my boy. You must snap out of it, face up to life, to the foundry, and all it holds. You are intelligent, Ieuan. Some day you'll be able to break away from this background, but until that day comes you'll have to fight and prove to the boys that you're strong. The harder you fight, the more respect they'll have for you, and, believe me, this persecution you've suffered on your first day here will die a natural death. Show yourself a weakling and they'll look upon you as someone to despise and ridicule."

They beat their way through the swirling wind, on past the tram terminus and the station entrance, each absorbed with his own thoughts. Presently, Frank paused to light a cigarette, turning his back to the wind as he cupped his hands over the flame. He pulled hard and deep, and exhaled the smoke loudly and with satisfaction.

He placed a hand on Ieuan's shoulder, and the boy warmed to the touch, feeling proud and honoured to be spoken to with such kindliness and confidence.

Frank sighed. "I wish I could explain it simpler, Ieuan. Anyway, some day — maybe soon, maybe late — you'll find out these things for yourself — from books, from your meeting with men whose knowledge is far greater than mine, and most of all from the fight you have to put up yourself. But you'll find out, Ieuan — you'll find out."

They reached Station Square.

"Well, boy, this is where I leave you. Chin up, now. And don't forget what I've told you. You've got at least one friend you can rely on in the foundry, and in time you'll have plenty more. You just listen to old philosopher Frank. So-long, lad."

"So-long, Frank. And … thanks."

"Half a mo' — I just thought of something." Frank stroked his chin. "Listen, Ieuan, what about coming over to the house Sunday afternoon?"

"House … ?"

"My house. Just for a cup of tea and a little chat. I've got such a lot to tell you, really. I'll let the missus know. Now, what time can you come along?"

"But I —" Ieuan stammered.

"Three o'clock," Frank said, with a finality that waived aside any objections Ieuan might hold. "We'll expect you at three." He chuckled. "It's been a long time since Doris and I had any guests, so this'll give her a chance to make one of her famous trifles and custards. Doris is a darn good cook. Your visit'll be an excellent excuse to keep her hand in. So that's settled. You'll be over at three, Ieuan. Number six Prospect Place, first turning right after Vauxhall Bridge. Don't forget, now."

Ieuan watched him as he turned into the main street. Frank was a real friend, a good man, and the kindest he had ever known. But the advice he had given — was there any truth in it? Would he become friends with those who had tormented him? Was life going to be easier in the foundry, now that the first humiliating day was over? He had fought, but he had gained no respect. Would he always have to fight them?

The thoughts depressed him. Thrusting his hands deep into his pockets, his head bowed to the wind, he shuffled homewards along the dimly lighted streets.

* * *

He opened the back-lane door and trudged up the uneven, stone-flagged garden path. The light from the kitchen window splashed on to the grimy, whitewashed wall of the ad joining house. The bare branches of the lilac tree creaked and sighed in the wind, as though in melancholy welcome.

He stopped near the window. From within came the sound of quarrelling. His heart beat violently. Once again he began to tremble with fear and apprehension. He pressed himself against the wall. The shrill voice of his mother was raised in anger.

"When he came home to dinner, nothing but cheek he gave me. A fine way for a boy to be talking to his mother. And after all I've done for him."

"But, Millie," his father's voice was weak in protest, "he didn't mean anything. He was just frightened. It was a big strain on him, that first morning in the foundry. Everything was new to him. He had no friends. No one he knew worked in the foundry. It was a frightening experience, Millie — frightening. And you know what a nervous and sensitive boy he is."

"Rubbish to all that talk. I've heard it till I'm sick. Sensitive, indeed! Too cheeky and self-willed he is, if you ask me. He wasn't going back to the foundry, oh no — that's what he said. Fancy telling me that, after all the trouble I went to getting new things for him. A lot of money I've spent on Ieuan, I can tell you. Then what did I get for traipsing down to meet him in the pouring

150

rain? More cheek, that's what. A fine thing for a mother to expect from her own son, isn't it? Is that the way you bring him up — to speak to his mother like she was a nobody?"

Ieuan clenched his fists. Was there no end to mam's nagging? She was a tyrant whose tongue was sharper than a sword blade. Each word she uttered stabbed into his heart and made him wince. But dad — why did he accept her nagging, her insinuations and threats? Wasn't he man enough to stand up to her and fight?

Fight. That was the word Frank had used so often. And he had said that one must show courage. The harder one fights the more respect one gains. Where was this courage of his father's? Fight! Fight — that's what dad should do. But it was so easy to talk. Was he prepared to fight in the foundry for the rest of his life, or become a coward, despised and rejected by all who worked with him?

He hated the foundry. Dreaded it even as he did when he passed out through the gateway half an hour ago; even after Frank had left him.

"You'll have to give him a good talking-to, Dick."

His mother's voice cut in on his thoughts.

"You're his father and he sticks closer to you than he does to me, though why, I can't for the life of me make out. I'm the one who's fed and clothed him and sacrificed myself to bring him up decent. But what do I get for it? What do I get for it?"

Despondent, a deep gnawing ache at the pit of his stomach, Ieuan entered the kitchen. The quarrelling ceased. His mother, tight-lipped, busied herself about the gas stove, casting an angry glance at her husband as he greeted Ieuan with a feigned show of good humour.

"Hallo, Ieuan *bach,* how did it go at the foundry? I bet you showed them the stuff you were made of, eh?" Dick Morgan got up from his chair near the fire. "Sit here, boy — you'll soon be the new man of the house. You wait till you get your first pay." He smiled. "That will be the day, eh, Millie?"

"Yes, that will be the day." Mrs. Morgan pushed a hot plate on

151

to the table. "Get yourself washed, Ieuan. And don't be too long. Your dinner's ready. Not many mothers would have done this for you after the way you —"

"Millie!" Ieuan heard his father's curt interruption. He waited, hoping that he would say something further. But it was "Millie!" and nothing more, for a harsh look from the mother silenced him.

CHAPTER SEVEN

THE first week dragged by, and to Ieuan it seemed an eternity. The persecution at the foundry continued. He suffered the indignities in silence. His talk with Frank had made him realize that any attempt to resist only forced his tormentors to become more aggressive in their attitude towards him. And yet, even though he strove to control his temper, they still inflicted their boisterous and sometimes humiliating jokes upon him.

Abraham had long since resigned himself to the daily interruptions. His threats to report the occurrences to Lu were never regarded as serious, for Bull and his cronies knew that the charge-hand, like many of the older men, was sick and tired of his job, and looked forward only to the day when he could retire.

There was no pension on retirement after years' service, but a gold watch was too valuable a gift to cast aside. And Abraham had always wanted that symbol of pride. The absence of security meant little. The gold watch meant everything.

Ieuan learnt much of his trade in the hours he was left to work unmolested, but his heart was not in it, and he welcomed the loud screech of the hooter at the end of the day. Frank had slipped into the coreshop often to pass an odd minute or two with him, and the more Ieuan saw of the young moulder the more attached to him he became.

He looked forward eagerly to the Sunday visit to the house. Somehow he felt that Frank would prove to be a trusted friend, giving him that intimacy he had never yet found with his father. With Frank he knew he could be unselfconscious and free from his inhibitions and fears. His face had a certain nobility of character, and he possessed a dignity of manner that made him stand apart from the rougher element in the foundry.

153

Frank was intelligent and considerate, tolerant of others' weaknesses, yet ready to fight against the persistent bullying of the older improvers.

* * *

Sunday afternoon was chill and raw. A colourless sun hung in the sky. Ieuan dressed in his best suit, his first suit of "longs," stepping into the trousers as he stood on a chair in his bedroom, mindful of the crease. His mother glanced casually at him as he came down into the kitchen.

"And where are you off to?" she asked.

"I've been invited out to tea, Mam."

His father, seated in the armchair, smiled. "Not a young lady, I hope?"

Gweneira and Phyllis looked up from their knitting as they curled up on the sofa and giggled selfconsciously.

"Our Ieuan's too young to go courting, Daddy," Phyllis chirped.

"Danny Derrick's got a sweetheart, I've seen them together in the back lane," Gweneira ventured.

"That's enough!" their mother warned. "Sweetheart, indeed! Dick, what's the matter with you? Such silly talk. That's the kind of nonsense that puts ideas into young boys' heads. Next you'll have him wasting his time parading up and down the High Street of a Sunday night."

The father turned in his chair. "Oh, snap out of it, Millie. A joke's a joke, girl, and it's nice to have a bit of fun in the house now and again. Honestly, this place is getting to be more like a funeral parlour every day. Smile, Millie girl. A lovely smile you had when I knew you first, and a treat it was to see it. A really pretty creature you were, too. Oh, ay."

Mrs. Morgan tossed her head. A trace of a smile appeared on her lips, but when she caught Ieuan's eye on her, she instantly became straight-faced again.

"And who's asked you out to tea?" she demanded.

"Frank Jones, he's a moulder at the foundry," Ieuan replied. "He and Mrs. Jones are expecting me."

His mother began to show interest.

"Well, that's very kind of him, very kind indeed. I'm glad you've found somebody, Ieuan. It bears out what I said about your soon making friends in the foundry, doesn't it? This moulder, Frank — you did say his name was Frank? — where does he live?"

"Prospect Place."

"And what time are you supposed to be there?"

"Three o'clock, Mam."

She looked at the clock. "Well, it's gone half past two, Ieuan, and you've got a good step to walk. You'd better hurry, my boy. Here, let Gweneira brush your suit down for you, so that you can be nice and tidy. I wouldn't like them to think nobody's looking after you. Gweneira! Come now, girl, do as I say. You can go on with your knitting again."

At last Ieuan was ready to leave.

"I expect you won't be very late coming home," his mother hinted as he stepped up the passageway. "But have a good time and enjoy yourself."

Then, as he opened the front door he heard her say to his, father: "See what I told you, Dick! I knew he'd meet someone tidy in the foundry. That old talk he gave us about being afraid was all a lot of childish rubbish. Why, everybody's got to start work some time, and if we all made such a fuss where would the world be, I ask you? On stop, a proper full stop, too. Listen to Ieuan and people'd think the foundry was like a jail. But I'm glad he's made a friend with someone, Dick, right glad. The boy will feel more settled now, and p'raps it will put an end to those silly notions he's got about books and studying. Schooling is all right in its place, but one can get too much of that. However, it seems I was right from the very start — about the foundry, I mean. I knew he'd soon find his feet. Not quite as dull as all that is Millie Morgan — a little bit of sense, she's got."

155

"Indeed. Plenty of sense," Ieuan heard his father reply. "You're a good mother to the children, and I've got no complaints to make, no complaints at all."

Ieuan slammed the door.

* * *

The High Street was crowded with young people who walked aimlessly up and down, whispering and gesticulating. Boys and girls ogled each other, inviting an approach.

Here, the privilege of hunting was not left solely to the male, and the chase, which led from the Town Hall on the south end of the street to Brady's Emporium on the north, provided an excitement that was not to be found within the sober confines of the Sunday School buildings.

Ieuan hurried on. The Town Hall clock boomed a quarter to the hour as he crossed into Vauxhall Street. The iron bridge, named after the street, spanned a river swollen from the recent rains — a river that was yellowed by the fumes and acid from the tinworks which sprawled along its banks on the outskirts of the town.

This rushing current was normally a shallow stream into which the housewives of the slum streets emptied their garbage. A river which in summertime made passers-by hold their breath for fear of contamination. At that time of year the townsfolk made use of it as a disposal ground for unwanted cats and dogs. It was not unusual to see a swollen, putrefying carcase being carried slowly downstream under the bridge to find a deeper grave in the yellow estuary to which the river flowed, or to find a mysterious, foul-smelling bundle wrapped in a rotting sack wedged between the slime-covered stones, rusty cans and bits of junk that were tossed into the water.

So evil of reputation was the river that even though the town had been built around it, no one felt honoured to name it as Abermor's river. No one claimed it with civic pride, save perhaps

156

the beady-eyed, bold, black rats who scurried under the bridge where they fattened on the refuse, the offal from the butchers' stalls in the nearby market and the grain blowing from the corn merchants' warehouses.

The first turning to the right at the end of the street brought Ieuan into Prospect Place, a row of workers' houses whose only prospect was a narrow road, pot-holed and bellying, which terminated at an open stretch of land made bare by the countless feet of playing children.

The houses were drab-walled, neglected and shabby. On the corner stood a tall, derelict building. Splotches of faded blue and yellow paint covered the pine end wall which once advertised the merits of Colman's Starch and Monkey Brand Powder.

The house next door bore a sign over the doorway, "Fish and Chips," and as Ieuan passed he caught a glimpse of the elaborately enamelled frying machine in the front parlour, the Latin phrase *"Senatus Que Populus Romanus"* transcribed to "Small Profits Quick Returns."

Farther along the street another front parlour had been converted into a business premises. The small, curtainless window was crammed with second-hand Army boots. Five and six a pair. Boots caked with mud. Some crinkled and shapeless.

Ieuan stopped. He looked into the window, attracted by the unusual display. Boots. Nothing else. Four shelves, along which they had been neatly arranged, toes outwards and facing the prospective customers. But the lower half of the window was piled high with them, as though the good shopkeeper had been suddenly overwhelmed with his goods and had tossed them there haphazardly.

"Boots, boots, boots, boots,
Marching up and down again ..."

Ieuan's imagination began to play. These boots had marched. Marched in mud. The mud of Flanders? The Somme,

Paschendaele, Verdun, Vimy Ridge. He had heard many stirring tales of the war from Captain Jim Llewellyn when the leather-faced, unsmiling officer came home on his drunken leaves, and the names of the various battlefields came easy to his mind.

"Up to our eyes in mud, Ieuan boy. Living in it, sleeping in it. Ay, and even eating in it. I've seen men die in the mud ... wounded foot-sloggers, youngsters some of 'em not even started shaving. And I've seen some of my men falling into it, wounded, to be suffocated. And not a damn one of us could do anything to save 'em."

Were there boots in the window that had once marched under Captain Jim's command? The boots of a V.C. perhaps — that pair in the corner, their leather tongues curled and stiffened?

And the men who once fought valiantly in the mud — where were they now?

If he were still at school he would have written a composition, "The Story of a Pair of Boots." He had once read a book by Talbot Baines Reed, *The Story of a Three Guinea Watch*. A pair of boots, especially one that had tramped the battlefields of France and Belgium, would make a wonderful subject for a composition.

The young recruit's first pair of Army boots .... How he tingled with pride when he drew them on.... How they echoed along the sunny country roads of England .... Tramped in the rain, the snow ... and then the Flanders mud where the young hero died.... And afterwards, the boots were stolen from the corpse — stolen as it lay half-buried in the foul mud, a red splash of blood staining the uniform so proudly worn in life.

Soldiers robbed the dead, he had been told. But who would rob a hero of his boots? And how would the mudcaked boots of a dead soldier come to rest in a window of a parlour shop in a little Welsh town? It would be a story of laughter and tears. Of death in the springtime of life. Of men's courage and cowardice. Of cannon's roar and bullet's whine .... Yes, if he were still at school he would write a composition.

School! Ieuan stood staring into the window, his forehead cold against the shining pane. It was no use thinking of school now. He had told his mother that he would speak again to Mr. Griffiths, the headmaster, but a week had passed and he had forgotten.

So much had happened at the foundry to occupy his mind. He was tired, physically and mentally. Maybe he would see Mr. Griffiths later and ask his advice. He'd attend evening classes at the Higher Grade School in the winter months that lay ahead. And study hard. Then he'd show them in the foundry what he was really made of. He was not going to waste his life and energy in the foundry. Five years to learn a trade — and what then? Low wages, unemployment, a body sick with fatigue. Nothing to look forward to but the daily, monotonous round of core-making, moulding, casting. No real freedom. No leisure, except for a few brief hours — for the morning hooters would bring him sleepy-eyed from his bed, and the weary trudge to the foundry would begin again. Was the struggle worth while? No, he would never remain there five years. Think of the knowledge he would gain in one year alone. Sufficient to enable him to seek another and more favourable job away from the foundry.

He would take up English literature. Specialize in it. There were many opportunities. He could become a teacher, a lecturer, or a writer. He loved to write, and Mr. Griffiths had often complimented him on the excellence of his essays and compositions, taking them from classroom to classroom to show to the other pupils and emphasizing that talent was the fruit of industry.

"Talent, the fruit of industry?" Surely that was a strange statement for Mr. Griffiths to make? How could industry —

A door opened lower down the street.

"Hallo there! Fancy anything in the window?"

Ieuan startled. He looked round to see Frank standing in the doorway in the distance. He stepped away from the little shop and hurried to meet his friend.

Frank leaned against the door, a door painted with a brilliant red, with the heavy knocker enamelled with black. Ieuan could not take his eyes off it.

Frank grinned. "That's what I would call unorthodox, others would say unconventional. But don't let it scare you. It's nice to have a spot of colour around here. Sort of growing a flower in the wilderness. It was Doris's idea, anyway." He took in a view of the street. "And I can't say I blame her."

"Well," Frank invited Ieuan inside, "I thought you'd got lost, or changed your mind. Say, you didn't think of buying a pair of boots, did you? I think you'd have had a bit of a job persuading old Mathias to sell you a pair. He's grown attached to them. I've never yet seen him sell any, or known of anyone who has fancied a pair. But come on, don't let me keep you from your tea. You must be starving, boy."

The casualness of the joke and the twinkle in Frank's eyes put Ieuan immediately at ease. It was with no little trace of embarrassment, however, that he stepped into the front parlour to meet Mrs. Jones. She was a dark-haired, pretty and rather buxom young woman, with a smile as engaging as her husband's.

"Hallo, Ieuan," she greeted, taking his cap. "Frank's been talking a lot about you lately, and it seems as if I've known you quite a long time."

Ieuan sat down nervously on the edge of a chair, taking care not to lean against the lace chair-back. The parlour was a holy place, and one should behave most circumspectly when invited into it. Never even speak above a whisper. He had been taught to believe this, but when Frank and his wife began to crack jokes with him and he heard himself laugh out aloud, the belief soon became an illusion.

"Well, draw up your chair and come and have a meal. Doris is right anxious to hear what you have to say about her Sunday trifles." Frank sat at the table. "There's just Doris and me, and she's happy as Judy to have me bring a friend along now and again. But it's just to see what impression her trifles make. I told you that before, remember? Anyway, make yourself at home, Ieuan. Nothing very grand about us, as you see." He swept a hand across the room.

"I—I think it's a very nice house," Ieuan ventured, not knowing what to say, and anxious to be well-mannered.

"Thank you, that's very nice of you." Mrs. Jones reached for the teapot. "But please don't take Frank too seriously — not on Sundays, anyway. Do you know, he wanted me to make tea in the middle-room today! Tea in the middle-room when we have visitors, indeed! What will he suggest next?"

"Well, Doris, the parlour's only to be used for weddings and funerals, my girl. Every Welsh man and woman and boy and girl knows that. However, I can see you looking very wild at me, so I'd better keep quiet, eh?"

"You'd better. And do talk a little sense today, Frank. You're making Ieuan feel as if he's stepped into a mad-house, I'm sure."

The tea-time passed pleasantly, and Ieuan felt happy and relaxed in his new-found companionship. They were nice and friendly people, and they had made him feel comfortable from the very start. But why, he wondered, why had Frank taken the trouble to invite him to the house? He was just a boy. Did Frank pity him? Or was he genuinely fond of him?

And Mrs. Jones, who possessed the same likeable qualities he had found in Frank, why had she gone to the extent of arranging the table as though she were preparing a meal for someone of importance? The thinly sliced bread, brown and white, the tasty round cuts of meat, the decorative trifles in slender-stemmed glass goblets. And she had used her best china and silver, not to mention the shining white tablecloth, lace-edged and scalloped.

They had treated him as they would treat a best friend, and he felt honoured and glad. This was the first real kindness ever shown him, and gradually he began to sense an inward relief from all the pain and frustration he had suffered since the knowledge came to him of his mother's plan to apprentice him in the foundry.

"Now we'll adjourn to the middle-room — I beg your pardon, the drawing-room." Frank got up. "Shall I help you with the

161

dishes, madam, or shall we leave them to Mary?" He clicked his tongue. "Dear, dear, how absentminded of me. It's Mary's night out, isn't it, Mrs. Jones?"

"Indeed, Mr. Jones."

Ieuan smiled happily at the banter between them.

"Indeed, it is Mary's night out. And I believe James, the butler, is off duty, too. So if it's not presuming too much, I suggest that you wash the dishes."

"But, Mrs. Jones ...." Frank heaved a tremendous sigh.

"Later," said Mrs. Jones. "After our guest has left us. And now, shall we go into the drawing room?"

Frank sighed again with comic relief.

"After you, madam."

* * *

"Like to have some music, Ieuan?" Mrs. Jones opened the pedestal gramophone which stood in a corner of the room. Frank relaxed in an easy chair.

"Give us the overture from *The Barber of Seville,* Doris. Ieuan will like that, I'm sure. Then we can have a little chat together, just him and me," he said.

So that was the purpose of the invitation, Ieuan thought. Frank wanted to talk to him again. But of what? The foundry? There was nothing else, surely?

The gramophone played. He listened, captivated with the gay music, stirring to the staccato rhythm of the violins and the loud, crashing climax. And as he rested back on the settee, his eyes half-closed, he saw Frank reach for a book from a narrow shelf above his head.

"So it's to be a chat on books, is it?" he heard Mrs. Jones say with mock despair. "Well, if that's the case I'd better be going." She paused. "I wonder if this is a trick to get me to wash those dishes?"

Frank tapped her playfully as she bent over to close the gramophone lid, and Ieuan blushed at the gesture of familiarity.

162

"Mrs. Jones, you may have the pleasure of washing the dishes if you like. I grant you the privilege."

"And I accept — on condition."

"And what is that condition, Mrs. Jones?"

"That you'll not keep the boy too late."

"Granted."

Frank suddenly leaned forward in his chair.

"Ieuan, do you like poetry?" he asked.

Taken aback for the moment, Ieuan hesitated. "Why, yes, Frank. Yes, I do."

"That means you're going to hear a recitation," Mrs. Jones smiled.

"Correct, Mrs. Jones. And what shall I recite?"

"The only poem you know." Mrs. Jones winked at Ieuan. She closed her eyes.

"Let me live in a house by the side of the road," she began.

Frank slapped the book on his knee.

"Silence, Missus!" he commanded.

Ieuan laughed heartily at her pretended display of fear.

"I shall recite. It is my poem, and therefore my privilege to speak it."

"Your poem, except for the fact that you didn't write it."

"Silence, Mrs. Jones."

Frank sat back. "No, all jokes aside, Ieuan, this is a wonderful poem, and I'm very fond of it ... and so was another man. A very great man, I must say."

"Yes," Mrs. Jones now became serious, "it is a lovely verse, Frank. Come on, let Ieuan and me hear you."

Presently, Frank began to recite in a quiet, low-pitched voice, his right knee raised, his fingers clasped around it.

"Let me live in a house by the side of the road,
Where the race of men goes by,
The men who are good, and the men who are bad,
As good and as bad as I.

163

I would not sit in the scorner's seat,
Nor hurl the cynic's ban.
Let me live in a house by the side of the road,
And be a friend to man."

He shook his head solemnly. "What a philosophy, Ieuan. And what a man I would be if I could carry it out. A fine poem, don't you think?"

"Yes," Ieuan replied thoughtfully. The poem — its simplicity, the rhythm and, above all, the message it conveyed, had moved him deeply. He felt like crying. Not motivated by any self-pity, but by a deep and sudden affection for this young couple who had shown such interest in him.

Frank, in spite of his wish to live up to the sentiments the poem contained, fulfilled its ideals. He was a friend to man. He had brought sympathy and kindness to one who had known so little of these virtues. His house was by the side of the road, and he had stood outside the door to welcome in a stranger to whom he had given solace and comfort.

"Penny for your thoughts!"

Ieuan came to with a start, conscious of Frank's warming smile.

"Well, lad, could you write a poem like that? I hear you're a literary scholar. Is that right?"

"I—I like literature. It was my favourite subject at school — if that's what you mean, Frank."

"Then what are you going to do about it?"

Ieuan paused. Mrs. Jones made some excuse — there were dishes to be cleared, a room to be swept. He heard her close the door behind her.

I don't know, Frank. Sometimes I feel I'd like to be a writer. "A writer!" Frank's forehead creased. "But kind of a writer, Ieuan? What do you want to write about?"

"That's a question I've never asked myself," Ieuan replied thoughtfully. "I-well, I just love books, and ...."

"Yes?"

164

"Well, I suppose I'd like to be able to write a book some day."

"It's not impossible, Ieuan. Not by any means. The education you've had will help a lot, but education from books isn't everything. There are many writers who have never been to school — not school as you and I know it. I should think the most important thing of all is to have experience behind you. Without experience of some sort how can one ever hope to write a book?"

"What would you advise me to do, Frank? It's not — not too big an ambition, is it?"

"Of course not. Why shouldn't you aim at being a writer if that's the way you feel. Everyone has an ambition of some sort. The trouble is that we're not all fortunate enough to be able to see our ambitions realized. But I'd better not dwell too long on that or you'll have me expounding my theories again."

Frank got up from the chair. He beckoned to Ieuan.

"Have a look at this book, my boy."

Ieuan glanced at the spine. "*The Iron Heel* — Jack London," he read.

"He was a writer, and by that I mean a *real* writer," Frank said with admiration. "To me, Jack London is one of the greatest men who ever lived. Hero-worship you can call it, if you like. But there, most of us have some little god of our own. Some go crazy over footballers, tennis players, Olympic champions, film stars. Others pay homage to people who have contributed something more substantial to life and progress. I count Jack London as my hero, because he had all the qualities I would like to possess. That poem I quoted — it was his favourite verse, and, by heavens! it expressed the man himself. Have you read any of his works, Ieuan ?"

Ieuan hesitated to reply. He had not read anything by the American author. He had heard of him, yes, but all he knew of him was that he had written books dealing with the Alaskan gold rush. And was there not a novel about a dog, which was regarded as a classic? *White Fang*. Yes, that was it!

"I don't know much about Jack London — that is, I only know he wrote *White Fang*."

"A grand book, Ieuan. And so is *The Call of the Wild*. Jack London can give you all the adventure you need. But first and foremost you must remember that he was a fighter. A champion of the oppressed. Come here, I'll show you something."

Ieuan crossed to the bookshelf. He cast his eyes along the row of books Frank pointed out to him. He noted the titles: *The Abysmal Brute, People of the Abyss, The Road, Before Adam, Revolution, The Sea Wolf, John Barleycorn, Strength of the Strong*.

"Those are a few of the many he wrote," Frank went on. "I'm not concerned with his technique. The finer points of story telling are lost to me. What I'm concerned with is truth. And here," he flicked the row of books with the tips of his fingers, "here it is. Raw, naked, sometimes hideous and cruel — but truth just the same. Jack London wrote of life, and he didn't camouflage what he knew of it or had to say about it with pretty words and fine phrases. Life is a perpetual struggle, Ieuan, a struggle in which the fittest survive. That was his belief. But for all that, he was a fine and courageous personality, and if I was half the man he was, I would indeed be proud of myself."

Frank's praises of the writer continued, and Ieuan listened attentively, feeling warmed and gladdened by his companion's complete indifference to the fact that he was speaking to one many years his junior on a topic which many a man would feel disinclined to discuss with a boy.

Here was no question of superiority. He was being treated as an equal, and his intelligence was acknowledged and respected.

"Ieuan, all that I've spoken of to you in these last few minutes is just a preliminary to the more important things I have to say. And they concern you and the foundry. That's why I asked you to come here today."

"Yes, I know — now," Ieuan nodded. He looked at Frank with affection. A firm hand patted him on the shoulder.

"Good for you, lad. But don't be annoyed with me if I sound preachy. My grandfather was a Baptist minister with a reputation for keeping his congregation in their seats for hours on end once he got started on his sermons, so I suppose it's in the blood. However, this is what I have to tell you, Ieuan. I've been through all you've experienced during this week, Ieuan, and I daresay I felt the same as you did. I had my ambitions when I was a boy, but they came to nothing. And why?"

Frank shrugged. "I was too hot-headed and, unfortunately, too lazy. I could have got out of the foundry if I'd tried hard enough. But the effort was too much — I preferred to let myself slip into the routine of the work, content with being a moulder and getting the rate. Now I'm sorry, but it's too late. You've got to avoid that mistake, Ieuan. You've got talent, and in the foundry it will be wasted. You've got to get away from the foundry, Ieuan. Not now, this instant. You are young, there are many more years in front of you. Make full use of them. Study, if you want to study. Go to night school if you think that will help. Become a writer, if that is your ambition. But while you're in the foundry don't let it break your spirit. Don't let Bull Jackson, Reg Bowen and the rest of them feel they've broken you in."

Frank spoke softly, each word measured carefully. There was no anger, no reproach.

"You think of Bull and his pals as cowards and bullies. Yes, I would call them bullies, too. But really it's a kind of self-defence, a bravado they show to the rest of the men. They want to appear tough and be able to take things on the chin. But they're not cowards, Ieuan. Not really. They seem unjust and cruel because conditions have made them appear so. Remember this, my boy, all the men in the foundry have been through the same as you. They suffered, even as you have. They protested and fought, just as you fought. But they kept on fighting, and that's what you must do. Not with your fists, but with that inner courage which I know you have. Don't hate your fellow-workers, Ieuan. In time you'll see that Bull and those you hate now will grow up to realize the injustices that they, too, have suffered. And they'll band together to fight these wrongs. Oh yes, they'll fight all right. I have faith in them. It's a long fight, Ieuan, and there's no room in it for anyone who pities himself. It's a fight against injustice everywhere, in the foundries, in the steel mills, the coal mines and the factories. A fight which is eventually carried on outside in the battle of life, which means a fight against war and all oppression. And in this fight, Ieuan, great heroes are made. They wear no medals, and there's no waving of banners, no drums beating, no brass band to lead them in a fine procession. Not even a crowd to cheer them on their way."

Frank took the book from Ieuan's hands. "Jack London was one of those heroes," he said quietly as he replaced it in the shelf. "And that's the basis of my admiration for him. He was always ready to reach out to help his fellow-man. And he did it not only through the enlightenment he gave to the countless thousands who read his books, but by practical means as well. Read about him, Ieuan, and you'll come to respect him even as I have .... As for the foundry, don't let it beat you. You have ambitions, and," Frank smiled, "well, Rome wasn't built in a day, you know."

A clatter of dishes from the other room brought an end to the conversation. Frank stepped to the door.

Mrs. Jones, her arms laden with cups and saucers and plates, glanced ruefully at him.

"Well, did you have your little chat?" She let Frank take some of the dishes from her, and as she glanced over his shoulder Ieuan saw the twinkle in her eyes which belied her seeming annoyance.

"I bet you had to listen to a long-winded speech, Ieuan. Frank invited you here to tea, and what happens? You have to hear his philosophy of life, and, what's more, he doesn't even let you sit down to listen to it."

She hurried forward with the dishes and placed them on the table. "But there, had you sat down he probably would have sent you off to sleep. Frank's voice is very soothing, I think. Sometimes I wonder why he never became a doctor. With such a voice he would be a great comfort to his patients."

Frank's eyebrows raised. "H'm! That's an idea."

She regarded him with a smile. "Indeed, Frank — but now, if you'll just look at the time …. "

Frank looked. "Good heavens! Ieuan, what will your mother think? It's nearly eight. We've kept you here for five hours."

"You've kept him," Mrs. Jones emphasized. "That long, long speech."

"Gee, I'm sorry. Honest, Doris, I had no idea time had passed so quickly."

Ieuan hastened to assure them. "It's been a lovely afternoon, and I've enjoyed myself grand, Frank — and Mrs. Jones," he said shyly.

"Then you must come again."

Frank and his wife walked with him to the door.

"Next Sunday," Mrs. Jones invited.

Frank nudged her. "What about Thursday night, Doris?"

Ieuan saw her smile.

"Next Thursday, next Sunday, any day. You're welcome any time you feel like calling, Ieuan. Our house is always open."

"How right you are, Mrs. Jones." Frank drew his arm around her and hugged her playfully. " 'Let me live in a house …'" he began to quote.

"That's enough! Let the boy go home in peace. Good night, Ieuan."

"Good night, my boy. See you tomorrow morning at seven."

"Good night, Frank. Good night, Mrs. Jones. And — thank you. Thank you very much."

"Good night!"

* * *

The visits to Frank's house continued, and Ieuan became a regular weekly caller. The young couple grew very fond of him, and treated him as though he were a son. Frank lent him the Jack London books, a gesture which Mrs. Jones assured he would show only to his most intimate friend, for he regarded them as his most valued possessions.

These Ieuan read avidly until he became as enamoured of the writer as Frank. Jack London's tales of hoboing South in The Road, his stories of life and adventure in the South Seas and the frozen vastnesses of the Yukon thrilled him. But thrills a'nd adventure were not enough. He read the essays on revolution, and the prophetic *Iron Heel* awakened him to the class struggle of which Frank had spoken to him often in the quiet evenings at the fireside in Prospect Place.

Here was a writer who had struggled against adversity, through and, by sheer grit and determination, had won through to a position of eminence in the American world of literature. All his life had been devoted to the finest cause of the liberation of mankind.

Ieuan joined the public library. The first volumes he brought home from the bookshelves were two heavily bound biographies of Jack London, by his wife Charmain, and these gave him a glimpse of the writer as a man, a human personality distinct from the artist. And he came to love him as though he were a brother, moved to deep compassion and pity when he came to the closing chapters describing Jack London's tragic death. He realized then how Frank must have felt, and the author's countless admirers. The loss of such a virile, lovable and courageous man was a tremendous blow to progressively thinking people all over the world.

Influenced by Frank, he began to interest himself in politics. The desire to study and learn consumed him. The young moulder had made him aware of the intensity of the class struggle, and spoke to him of the injustices and inequalities existing in the prevailing system. And Ieuan, his perceptions sharpened, looked around him with open eyes. He saw for himself the truth of Frank's observations.

Even in his own district there was stark poverty. Davie Dan's mother and father, the Derricks, and the Williamses, who lived in a rat-infested house at the bottom of Bythaway's Lane — a house where in wintertime the floods invaded every room on the ground floor, driving the family and their pathetic bits of furniture into the bare, cheerless and draughty bedrooms.

Then there was the Evans family who lived next door but three. So poor that once, when they were surprised by the unexpected visit of an uncle from Cardiff, they were forced to borrow a bed from Mrs. Thompson next door, in order to put him up for the night. They owned not a sofa or a couch, and what furniture they had was fashioned from plywood tea-chests which the father bought for a few coppers from the grocers' up town.

The Evans family's poverty gave cause for humour. But it was ironic that the jokes concerning them were made by people who were not many degrees better off.

Shon Davies, the crippled pensioner who lost his right arm in a tinworks' shear when a boy, would repeat his favourite anecdote about the Evanses so often that finally he was nicknamed Shon Repeat.

"So many children Jack Evans and his missus got," Shon would chuckle, stroking his stubbly chin, "that in the night he just rocks 'em to sleep in his lap and then stands 'em up in a corner. Breed like rabbits, do Jack and Flo. But there, making children's the only bit o' pleasure they get out o' life, strikes me."

Yes, even Shon made fun of his own neighbour's poverty. Shon, whose wife was as incapacitated by her rheumatism as he was by the loss of his right arm, and who was forced to take in washing, brew ginger-beer, trudge to the cinder-tips in search of fuel, and stand on the corner of Hickman Street every Thursday, summer and winter, selling the weekly *Mercury*.

She did all the housework as well, sometimes for other people who would pay her a few shillings. She had tried all ways and means of earning money, even to the extent of gathering willow twigs and decorating them with buds of coloured modelling clay. These she sold to neighbours who stuck them in flower vases in their front parlours. And often she would work industriously

171

with scraps of silver wrappings from chocolates and sweets, fashioning them into miniature dolls for the children. Shon would offer encouragement and advice from his seat on the biscuit tin, while he counted and hoarded the hundreds of cigarette ends he had collected from the gutters in the main streets.

The more Ieuan read, the more he became convinced of the inequalities that existed around him. In the Pleasant Row neighbourhood, as in all the other workingclass districts in the town, lived hypocritical landlords who attended chapel faithfully. Landlords who battened on excessive rents paid for hovels which were not fit to house cattle.

Children in many families were under-nourished. They had to wear clothes handed down from one to the other. Some had no boots to their feet.

He began to question himself. To reason. Why should men be forced to work for a wage that was barely sufficient to keep body and soul together? Why should there be rich and poor? Were not all men born equal? Then why the distinction? Why should a man, by reason of his investments, enjoy every luxury, while the worker who produced received but a pittance which afforded him no luxury other than a cheap seat at the cinema, a pint or two of beer, or an occasional football excursion to Swansea or Cardiff?

Why should people starve when there was an abundance of food in the world? Why were the miners' wages so meagre when coal cost human lives? Why the class distinction even in the educational system?

His mind became confused with the questions that required an answer. He wanted to discover the reasons for these injustices, and why they had existed throughout the centuries. Were the workers to blame? Was it their submission to oppression and exploitation that had given a world of plenty in which people starved to death or lived in dire poverty?

Frank tried to explain that man was a victim of his environment. Jack London wrote of the survival of the fittest. In primeval days

172

the strongest conquered the weakest and wrested from the latter that which he owned, be it a sheep, a plot of land, or a wife. That survival of the fittest had existed ever since creation.

Man forced those whom he had conquered to work for him, and profited from their labour for his own benefit. The struggle continued. The conquered revolted; the rebellions were crushed and the ringleaders tortured and killed. Throughout history, men of noble character and high ideals had risen from the ranks of the exploited to lead them away from the paths of slavery. Yet the true emancipation of man was still to come.

Filled with conflicting doubts and fears, Ieuan tried to find the solution in religion. Why did God allow those whom He had made in His own image to suffer the degradation of slavery and exploitation? If He was a merciful God, where, then, was His mercy shown?

The long discussions with Frank enlightened Ieuan considerably, but there was a great deal yet to learn. His mind had not matured sufficiently to grasp the full implications of the class struggle. The conceptions and theories of Socialism were still vague to him. Many problems remained unsolved, and his outlook was blurred.

His mother resented his deep interest in his books, and disapproved of his visits to Frank's house. "I thought he was going to be a good friend to you, Ieuan," she grumbled. "Instead of that, I find he's only filling your mind with old Socialist nonsense like what they spout from their soapboxes on the Town Hall Square on Sunday nights. The world is all right if people would let it alone. But some folks want a heaven here as well as after they've left the old earth."

Mrs. Morgan had imagined, now that Ieuan had been introduced to the foundry and got over the first humiliating week, that his ideas for self-advancement would have been forgotten. But the boy was stubborn: his head full of dreams. Silly notions about being a writer or some such daft job. Dreams were all right. But who could earn money by writing? Only people like

Ethel M. Dell and that woman who wrote a story about a sheik, whose name was Rudolph Valentino. Ieuan a writer! What next!

"If you was to put aside them books and have your mind on your work in the foundry, you'd get along much better, I'm telling you," she railed at him one night. "Abraham Jenkins's wife said to me that her husband don't think you have the makings of a moulder, and he can't see no shape in you getting the rate. No real interest you've got in your work, she said. Abraham's been speaking a lot to her about you. Now, he's a first-class tradesman. Been in the foundry all his life, and he knows what he's talking about."

Ieuan took it all in, determined not to argue. But she went on. "What will happen to us if you was to lose your job? It's only a few shillings, I know, but even a couple of coppers are helpful these days. And every year you will get a raise, not much. Nothing to sneeze at all the same. Yes indeed, it would be tidy if you lost your job, after all the expense and trouble I've gone through with you. But there, I suppose you still want to get out of the foundry. No matter about your poor mother."

Ieuan continued to listen in silence, and his reluctance to speak fanned her discontent. She appealed to her husband, who hadn't ventured an opinion or said anything in Ieuan's defence.

"You say nothing, Dick, but just sit there reading your paper like a dummy. Two deaf and dumbs I got on my hands now, seems to me. Why don't you talk to him, not let me do all the worrying."

Ieuan closed the book he was reading. Gweneira and Phyllis had gone to bed an hour ago. That's the place for me, he thought, the only place where I can get a little peace and quiet.

He tucked the book under his arm, and began to make his way along the passage. It was no use mam bringing dad into the argument. It would serve no purpose, for nothing would be said. Nothing that would calm his mother down.

"Ieuan!" Her shrill voice echoed along the passage. He stopped. His nerves jarred. He clenched his teeth.

"Yes, Mam."

"And where are you off to?"

"To bed."

"What about your supper?"

"I don't want any, Mam, thanks."

He heard her snort. Then she spun round to her husband again. "There I see, Dick, tantrums now. Pouting as if he was a little boy being packed off to bed. What am I to do with him?"

Dick continued with his reading. Incensed by his demeanour, she threw up her hands in a gesture of wild despair and sank dramatically into a chair.

"I'm shutting up!" she cried. "Shutting up, d'you hear?" Then suddenly she burst into a fit of weeping. "Nobody cares what happens to me," she wailed, her sobs shaking her whole body. "Nobody in the world. Why, oh why did I ever get married — to bring ungrateful children into the world?"

Ieuan waited at the foot of the stairs. He felt a surge of pity sweep over him. He felt sorry for hjs mother. He wanted to rush back into the kitchen and throw his arms around her. Say he was sorry. That he wouldn't give her cause to worry again. And he might kiss her. Kiss her? The thought seemed repulsive to him at the moment.

What was he made of? What strange complex did he suffer, that the thought of kissing his own mother disconcerted him? He never remembered kissing her, and her show of affection for him was so little that he scarcely could recall any occasion when she had caressed him.

To put his arms around her would embarrass him. That he knew. It would reveal his weakness, and once he showed that he was sorry for her and ready to forgive, she would regard it as a triumph. Then her domination of him would increase.

He must not feel sorry for her. He must not give in. Let dad comfort her.

He peered into the kitchen.

His father put down his paper.

"Now, now, Millie, you're overtired," he said, with no trace of compassion in his voice. "If I were you I'd get a little bit of supper and go off to bed. You'll feel better in the morning."

Mrs. Morgan glanced sharply at him through her tears. She hastily dried her eyes on her apron.

"Yes, go to bed? That's it, bed! Anywhere out of the way," she shouted.

"Now, Millie-please ...the children!"

"Fat lot they care, fat lot anybody cares. So long as I'm able to cook, and mend, and darn — that's all my worth is to them."

Ieuan gripped the banister rail. The beginning of another quarrel, he mused bitterly. It would go on until they went to bed. And in the night hours it would still continue until sleep claimed them both.

But he was glad. Relieved that he had not given way to the momentary compassion he had felt for his mother. For it would have brought nothing but self-recrimination and pain. He wanted to love her. He ached for the love which she had never shown him. But his heart was closed, and she would never be able to open the door.

Slowly, he walked up the narrow staircase to his room. He heard his sisters call to him, but tonight he did not even wish to speak with them.

CHAPTER EIGHT

GRADUALLY, as the winter months passed, Ieuan's impressions of the foundry grew clearer. The tall, grim and forbidding buildings that had first frightened him as they lay shrouded in the darkness of early morning, became as familiar to him as his own home. He came to know every corner intimately. There was no longer any mystery. But the dread remained.

Day after day he trudged through the rain, the snow and the slush, greeting by name the many men he had come to know as he stood in the queue at the time office, or picked his way across the darkened yard.

Stumbling along between the curving rails that shimmered in the reddened glow of the steel furnace. A heavy mist drifting in from the estuary. Dull, leaden clouds tumbling across the sky. The air filled with the tang of salt from the leaping bay, and penetrating fumes of sulphur from the furnace landing.

Somewhere far away the plaintive whistle of a locomotive.

Along the scrap-littered path, and through the sackcovered entrance of the fettling shop. Then into the steel foundry. A place silent, weird; another world of sleep, of things inanimate. The dim, greenish-white buttons of light sewn along the roof. Shadows stilled across the dry, dusty floor. Mounds of brown, clayey moulding sand.

Shovels, their well-worn handles sticking up like fence posts, their silvery blades embedded in the brown soil; tall, iron rammers; rusty, dented buckets; moulding boxes red with rust, blackened with soot.

These greeted him every morning of his waking life. All were there to welcome him into his miserable world.

Grey, indistinct forms huddled together in the dark corners

near the mould-drying stoves, or crouched over a slowly burning brazier of coke.

These were his companions, his fellows; moulders, improvers, labourers, gantrymen, clad in greasy dungarees, darned and patched. Their faces hideous in the green light.

The hooter has blown. A shrill whistle sounds. The figures startle into activity. They disperse to the many untenanted moulds scattered along the foundry floor.

From other corners men seep out of the shadows. Buckets of water are thrown over the dry banks, shovels grasped, the sand turned over, chopped and mixed.

The gantrymen climb, hand over hand, up the iron ladders, monkeys clambering to their cages.

Palms are spat into. Ice-cold, steel pneumatic rammers grasped. Wrists flicked.

Rat-atat-tat … rat-atat-tat … rat-atat-tat.

Another working day has begun.

* * *

Bull and his cronies, for no apparent reason other than their antipathy towards Ieuan's soft-spoken manner and the better education he had received, continued to rag him whenever opportunity came their way.

One evening Titus had seen him coming from the public library with two books under his arm. This caused much mirth among his companions.

"Two books," Titus emphasized as they sat on the wooden seat near the coreshop stove the next morning. "Iron reads two at a time."

Bull sniffed with disgust. "Bloody swank," he commented, spitting a gob of phlegm into the dust.

"Bet he hasn't never read Aristotle, though," Titus sniggered. "He don't know nothing about girls."

"Harris Dottle?" Bull was perplexed. "Who the hell's he?"

178

"It's a book, not a man," Titus explained. "About babies and things." He nudged the elder youth.

"You know," he said suggestively. "Pictures in it, too."

"Not French pictures?"

"Oh, no. But they're photos you can't show to everybody."

"You got one of them, Tight-arse? Wouldn't mind having a penn'orth."

Titus lowered his voice. "There's one in the house," he confessed. "But —"

"But what?"

"Well, 'tisn't mine. It's my father's. I found it under the mattress."

"Then bring it over. Let's have a decko, us lads. Don't keep a good thing from us. You can sneak it out when your old man's looking the other way."

The conversation among the apprentices and improvers turned to sex as easily as water turned on from a tap. No encouragement was needed. They were preoccupied with it, and spoke of their various shabby little conquests over factory girls and "skivvies" not with any sense of shame, but boastfully and arrogantly.

Their masculinity was measured by the number they had seduced, or attempted to seduce, in the dark, furtive alleys of the town, the more remote glades of Dinas Wood, or in the sheltered paths leading to Lovers' Lane. And they described their feminine companions as "pieces of skirt," "janes," "molls," "tits," "tarts," "pushers," "shove-arounds" and "bits of fluff."

Their lives revolved around sex and sport. To read books other than the twopenny thrillers or the weekly sports journals was regarded as "sissy," and Ieuan's interest in literature was fiercely resented.

"Bloody snob," "Bernard Shaw," "Professor Know-all" and "Bill Shakespeare" were the appellations hurled at him, but he took them with all the good grace he could muster, which only tended to aggravate them further and goaded them to a fury resulting in physical violence. Only by physical strength alone could they

179

claim victory over him, and this Ieuan knew. Consequently, he did his utmost to avoid antagonizing them. But it was useless. They were determined to make life untenable for him in the foundry.

Abraham interfered when he felt inclined to do so, but his concern was not for Ieuan's discomfiture or persecution, but for the work in the coreshop for which he was responsible. A delay in getting cores ready for the moulds meant a row with Lu. This, Abraham could not stand. His sense of pride suffered. He was a competent tradesman, and failure to produce the necessary cores was a reflection on his ability to take charge of a department.

Once he gave Bull a stinging blow across the face with a heavy hempen swab when the apprentice tossed Ieuan's corebox into the water bosh.

"What's the idea?" he shouted, threatening Bull with a second blow. "D'you think I get paid for to see coreboxes being messed up? It's not to Lu I'll report you, but to Mr. Bevan himself, and then you'll find yourself in a fine pickle. Out through the gate you'll go on your neck, and a damn good riddance, I say. A damn good riddance. No second chance you'll get from Mr. Bevan. He's not so soft as I am with the lot of you. Get on with your work, that's what you're paid for."

Abraham need not have worried unduly over the production side of the coreshop, for towards the end of April a noticeable slump hit the foundry. A trade depression had caught the whole town in its grip. The tinstamping, the chemical works and the smaller factories were on part time.

The only industries that maintained their normal level were the steel-rolling mills and the tinworks, for Abermor was essentially a tinplate and steel town.

Bevan's Foundry, dependent on the trade orders received from the tinstamping and the other factories; was the first foundry in the town to feel the effects of the depression.

Rumours of a "week-in, week-out" system of working were prevalent in the steel shop, fettling shop and all the other departments. It became the chief topic of discussion in the latrine. Within a week the rumours were substantiated as fact when the fettling shop closed down indefinitely. Another fortnight, and the pattern makers were on the dole, and the fitting shop maintained by half its usual complement of men.

The fear of insecurity gripped the older men and those who had dependants. The dole meant twenty-four shillings for a man and wife. The prospect was demoralizing.

Shop meetings were held to discuss the problem, and to see if some other arrangement could be made to prevent the total closing down of the foundry. The management was approached. The moulders' main argument was that the steel foundry was the most important section in the group, the fettlers, pattern makers, fitters, roll-turners all being dependent on the output of castings from the foundry.

Why, in face of this, should the moulders be put on the dole? Could they not arrange a shorter working week? Eliminate the Saturday morning shift, or start work at nine in the mornings instead of at seven. Cut down the number of weekly casts to a minimum, so that the orders they had in hand could be prolonged.

The men's case seemed valid enough, and the directors agreed to their propositions. They were prepared to give them a trial, anyway. And so the work continued. But there was little to do to keep the moulders fully occupied. Jobs which usually took a few hours to complete during the normal period were made to last as much as an entire day.

Men took advantage of the slump. They sneaked out often from the foundry to the various hide-outs in the "bughouse," the watchman's shanty and the furnace landing. Hours were spent in the latrine. The improvers had discovered that the flat roof of the pattern stores made an excellent sun trap, and here they sunbathed in the afternoons, stripped to the waist.

They played cards in the canteen, or held an impromptu cricket match in an open space sheltered by the walls of the fitting shop and pattern shop. When in the foundry they made country jobs.

And Lu, the foreman, closed his eyes to it all. He appeared to enjoy the breathing space the slump had afforded him. His responsibilities were lessened now that there was not much work to be done, and instead of arriving at the foundry in the early morning he never came before nine.

The coreshop became a rest-house. What cores Abraham gave his employees to make were all for stock. The standing orders that remained had been completed within the first week after the men's meeting with the directors.

The charge-hand occupied his time in forging new tools. Old Isaiah had found a corner under the furnace arch where he would content himself for hours, smoking his pipe. In the steel shop the men took a busman's holiday, casting tools for their own use at the trade, or hammer-heads, bakestones, door-knockers, which they carried out under their coats when the day was over.

The improvers found much to divert them from the daily routine they had been used to. One morning Ieuan saw a crowd of men and boys gathered round a small culvert behind the pattern shop. It had been raining heavily the previous night, and the culvert had overflowed into the yard.

Drawn there by curiosity, he discovered the object of their interest. Charlie, the improver, was on his knees over the culvert, his arms elbow-deep in the dank water.

"Is he still there?" someone asked.

"Yes-yes, I think I've got him now."

The crowd edged nearer. All at once Charlie withdrew his arms. In his cupped hands he held a large, brown-backed frog.

Pushing through the ring, he raced towards the coreshop, with Bull and the other improvers following excitedly.

"What's happening?" Ieuan inquired.

"Charlie's going to make a lead frog," Thomas said.

"A lead frog!"

"Sure — it's easy."

"But I don't understand."

Thomas threw him a knowing look. "Ever heard of gypsies

182

eating hedgehogs?" And before Ieuan could reply, he went on: "Well, first of all they catch 'em. But then they have to cook 'em. And it's just like that we make lead frogs. I've made plenty," he boasted.

"But —" Ieuan began.

"Oh, hell, don't be stupid, Ieuan mun. Look here, first of all, gypsies get hold of a hedgehog. Then they kill it and cover it all over with clay and bake it." Thomas shrugged. "Let's go over and watch Charlie. You'll see for yourself what I'm trying to explain."

When they drew near the stove outside the coreshop they found the same crowd gathered round. The frog, its eyes dilated, its throat moving spasmodically, was held firmly in the improver's hand.

"Hurry up, Tightarse!" he called into the coreshop. The onlookers grinned.

Presently, Titus came running, a mess of soft, yellow clay in his hands. Without hesitation, Charlie plastered the clay over the frog. The creature struggled. Its legs kicked, but soon the soggy mixture had stopped all movement.

Charlie added more clay, dabbing it quickly and rolling it over in his hands until it resembled a small yellow football.

Ieuan looked on, horrified and repelled. The stove door was pulled open and the ball of clay tossed on to the redhot coals. Then followed a wild activity. Bull had been chosen to play his part in the experiment. He darted into the coreshop and brought out a long-handled crucible.

Charlie's hands were now occupied in cutting a length of lead piping on the anvil. The crowd still waited.

"Think it's cooked now?"

Titus scooped out the clay ball, now baked stone-hard. Holding it down on the floor with a strip of iron, he pricked a half-inch hole through the centre of the ball. The crucible was filled with lead and thrust into the fire. In the meantime, the clay ball had cooled. Titus blew sharply into the hole. A small cloud of blue ash rose into the air, the incinerated remains of the once-living creature.

"O.K., boys, ready for up-ladle?"

Molten lead was poured rapidly into the hole, and hardly had it filled when Titus shattered the clay ball with the strip of iron.

A dull-red casting glowed, which suddenly changed to a pale grey. And on the floor, crouched as if ready to leap, was a perfect replica of the brown-backed frog, every vein and muscle in relief.

Ieuan turned away. The thought that they should have roasted the creature alive was inconceivable. But they had done it, and he had felt sickened, yet compelled to watch them. Now the fascination had worn off. His instincts revolted.

Thomas looked at him. "What's up?" he asked. "Nothing to be upset about. All us chaps have made lead frogs. There's no wrong in that. It's an easy death — I mean, the frogs don't feel no pain."

Ieuan said nothing.

"By crikey, you're a queer chap," Thomas grumbled. "Too bloody sensitive, that's what's the matter with you."

Charlie, beaming with success, showed the lead casting to the admiring crowd. He held it up for Ieuan's inspection.

"Have a decko, Iron. Masterpiece, eh?"

Ieuan ignored the invitation and gave no sign of approval.

"Aw Christ, don't be a bloody softie," Titus mocked.

"What's a frog got to lose? I bet you've killed worms and pulled spiders' legs off before today, and if you say you haven't, then you're a flaming liar. Don't try and come the goody-goody, Iron, we all got you taped. You ought to come and see us when we catch rats. They sizzle like hell when they're cooked."

* * *

In the last week of July the foundry closed down. A second deputation to the manager's office had met with a definite refusal to keep the men in employment any longer.

184

The directors considered they had acted charitably in conceding to their demands on the first occasion. The foundry was losing money steadily. If no orders came soon the firm would be faced with bankruptcy. The position was precarious. Salvation lay only in amalgamation with one of the other foundries in the town.

The matter was to be discussed at the next directors' meeting. Meanwhile, the men would have to go on the dole. Was there an alternative? Could the men suggest a solution to the crisis?

The directors sat back in their chairs. "Our cards are on the table. What have you to say? We are as badly hit as you. We have money invested in the firm. Our losses are heavy — very heavy, and we will suffer. Still, we shall do our best for you. As soon as prospects become rosier we'll notify you. Bevan's have never yet let an employee down. We're a firm with a reputation for honesty and loyalty."

The depression had arrived in earnest. Out of the town's population of forty thousand, a third were already unemployed. The Employment Exchange clerks worked overtime to cope with the ever-increasing queues that formed from early morning till late afternoon.

But to one person at least, the closing down of Bevan's Foundry had come as a relief. Ieuan welcomed it, as a boy welcomes a holiday from school. No more waking before dawn. No more the dismal journey to the coreshop. No more greasy dungarees, the clangour, the shouting and the cursing. No more hiding in furtive corners, waiting for the hooter to release him from his prison.

The tenseness had gone. He felt free at last. Now he would devote himself to his books. The days were his to do with as he liked. Let the foundry remain closed. He did not care.

Was it a selfish thought? What of the men whose lives, whose very existence depended on the foundry? Did they look forward to the prospect of weeks, perhaps months, of unemployment, not knowing when they would be able to earn a week's wages again?

He was just a boy. No responsibilities. But now he was happy, for freedom was his. A freedom he had known only in his schooldays. The release from the foundry had been welcomed. He looked forward to the respite, and the fact that he might be out of work for many months did not worry him.

Ieuan's visits to the library became so frequent that the chief librarian and his assistants soon came to know him by name. They advised him on the latest additions to the bookshelves, reserved volumes for him, and did their utmost to help him in every way possible. It was not often that the librarian met so young a boy with such a thirst for knowledge. He encouraged Ieuan to read books on elementary psychology and economics, loaned him special editions on art and literature, and promised to obtain for him any volumes he needed from the Central Library in Cardiff.

And Ieuan read everything that was put before him. All was knowledge to be gained, and he garnered it like corn at harvest time. While he read, and became impervious to life around him, the depression swept through the town. Factory after factory emptied its workers into the long, straggling queues at the Employment Exchange. Even the three other foundries, which had been working on a part-time basis, finally pasted up "Closed" notices on the main gates.

In mid-August, Dick Morgan found himself without a job. Abermor became a derelict town.

Still Ieuan read. He formed a plan of study but it was unsatisfying, so one night he sought advice from his old headmaster.

Mr. Griffiths, grey-haired, bespectacled, welcomed him effusively.

"Come in, come in, Ieuan. It's good to see you again." He showed him into the front room and made him comfortable. "Well, my boy, how is life treating you these days? And the foundry — how do you like it there?"

The headmaster regarded him gravely. "H'm! Never mind the latter inquiry, my boy. I can see you haven't — er — shall we say, you haven't yet adapted yourself to the foundry. We'll change the subject, shall we? Now, what brought you here tonight — anything troubling you, Ieuan?"

Ieuan explained his reasons for calling.

"You should try and win a scholarship to the university," was the headmaster's counsel. "A bright boy like you should find no difficulty. After all, you don't want to spend your life in the foundry. To be quite frank, though it's none of my business really — I can't for the life of me understand what possessed your mother to take you out of school in the first place."

"But the university, Mr. Griffiths; how can I enter? I mean, what should I do about applying for a scholarship?"

"Well, first you must matriculate, Ieuan. Afterwards, there are many opportunities. And there's plenty of time. You're young. You can afford to wait a few more years. But in the meantime you must study. I'll mark out a course for you, if you like. The subjects you should specialize in. Literature, for example. You're still interested in literature, Ieuan?"

Then Mr. Griffiths went on to explain the educational opportunities provided by various trade unions. Some contributed to working men's colleges, and educational grants were allowed to members who wished to make use of them.

"You could take a year's course at Harlech," the headmaster suggested. "What about it? Or perhaps you'd like to go to Ruskin College, Oxford. Does your trade union allow any grants for education?"

"I don't know, Mr. Griffiths," Ieuan confessed. "I didn't even know that trade unions could help one."

"Oh, yes they do, I assure you. You must find out about your particular union, Ieuan. Ask your secretary, or speak to the shop steward. They'll be able to help you."

It depended entirely on Ieuan himself, the headmaster explained. He could decide on a course of action, and then adhere to it. There were difficulties — oh, yes. A routine of study was easily arranged, but to follow it out meant hard work. It needed determination. The summer months lay ahead. There were many

187

distractions. A boy need never feel lonely, with practically all the men and youths in the town out of work.

The cinemas, the playing fields, swimming in the dock — oh, yes indeed, there were many items to distract a student, Mr. Griffiths emphasized. But, of course, it was up to Ieuan. No one else could decide for him.

If he wished to find a career for himself other than the foundry, he would have to apply himself in earnest to the task. Things never came easily to one in this world. One had to fight, and fight hard, if the battle must be won. And it meant sacrificing many things.

"You have an ambition to become a writer, Ieuan?" Mr. Griffiths asked him one evening later in the week. He looked at him wisely. "Rather young to think of that, eh? It's a hard task. But it can be accomplished. Will mean many years of practice, Ieuan, you realize that? And success will not fall into your lap. But as I said the other night, there's plenty of time, my boy. You'll have to gain much more experience of life before you become a writer. At the moment you are far too young to contemplate writing books. Why, even a journalist has to devote years to his trade. He has to be apprenticed to it, even as you have to be apprenticed to your trade as a moulder. But there," the headmaster smiled kindly, "the only way to become what you want to be is to write. That's simple, isn't it? In theory, anyway. And you must practise. Start writing now. You'll at least gain proficiency in expressing yourself on paper, and that, added to the experience which is yours to come, will help you attain your ambition. It's a lofty ambition, Ieuan, but I admire your determination to see it through."

Before he left, Ieuan was given a book. "Here, my boy, take this," the headmaster said as he handed it to him. "I think it will help you a great deal." He stroked his chin pensively. "You might find it a little difficult to grasp at first. Still, it will give you a basis on which to work. Read the section on the histories of phases of civilization, and the other on the histories of fine arts and literature."

Ieuan weighed the book in his hands. It was *Courses of Study,* by J. M. Robertson.

"Thank you, Mr. Griffiths. I'll take great care of it, and I'll bring it back as soon as I've finished with it."

"You needn't concern yourself about returning it, my boy — not for a while," Mr. Griffiths remarked. His eyes smiled, behind their glasses. "Not for quite a long time, I should have said. You'll be fully occupied, believe me."

* * *

The headmaster's advice was fuel to the fire of Ieuan's determination to study. The days found him in a quiet corner of the Town Hall grounds, or lying on his stomach on a grassy patch in the little park near the Royalty Theatre — the little park called "Loafer's Rest," where came men of the town too old to work, and the younger men who had no inclination for it.

His books beside him, notebook and pencil in hand, he wrote busily. The old men looked at him and envied him his youth and industry, while the others cursed him for being a fool to waste his energy reading and scribbling.

At home in the evenings he retired to the parlour and, if disturbed, took to the privacy of his bedroom. His preoccupation with books and writing had become almost an obsession. It seemed as though he had but a few months in which to accomplish all that he had set out to do. He had formulated his plan.

First, he would cram as much general knowledge as possible. Then in the winter he would arrange to attend the evening classes at the Higher Grade. Next summer, matriculation. At eighteen, he hoped to carry out the advice given him by Mr. Griffiths and strive to win a scholarship to the university.

What if he failed? The possibility was there. Well, he'd apply for a year's course at Harlech, or find someone to sponsor his application for a stay at Ruskin. No doors were closed against him now. It was up to himself, as the headmaster had said. And

189

he would see to it that nothing would prevent him reaching his goal.

Before long, however — sooner than he had ever anticipated — Ieuan tasted the bitterness of disillusionment once again. He had begun to write short pieces of fiction and essays, which he submitted to the local newspapers. They were speedily returned. This did not discourage him. He had never expected to see his efforts in print. To find any contribution of his published would have been so great a surprise that he would not have been able to acknowledge it.

The source of his early despair of his writing was his father's attitude towards it. One night he stepped into the parlour.

"Ieuan, what's wrong with you lately?" he asked, and his voice was pregnant with anger. "You're most unsociable. Not a word from you. Your mother's on to me about you and your reading and writing. But what can I do about it? God knows, I've got plenty on my mind, things being as they are — no job, and trying to live on the little we get from the dole. Look here, Ieuan, what are you doing? What's all this writing about?"

"Practice," Ieuan said cheerfully, his enthusiasm burning. "Some day I'm going to he a writer, Dad."

"Writer! Nonsense! What's got into you? Writer, my eye. Why, you haven't seen anything of life yet. What have you got to write about? Besides, how can you hope to earn a living at that sort of thing?"

Ieuan flared with resentment. "Perhaps you'd rather see me sticking in the foundry, Dad? That's mam's ambition."

"Leave your mother out of this, Ieuan. I'm talking to you now, and I don't see no sense in your scribbling on bits of paper. It's a waste of time, boy. You'll gain nothing out of it. Chuck it, Ieuan — chuck it now, before you get any more false ideas into your head. Writers are born, my boy, not made. And whatever purpose you were born for, you certainly weren't born to be a writer. Get out into the sun, Ieuan, and get some air into your lungs. We're fair worried about you — your mother and me."

190

Let them worry, Ieuan thought. Nothing was going to stop him now. What did they care, so long as he was able to struggle on at the foundry for a few paltry shillings. Frank, Mr. Griffiths, they encouraged and advised him. They recognized his ambition. They wanted to help him and went out of their way to do so.

Mam's only concern was for the money he was able to earn now, at the immediate moment. She had no eye for the future, no imagination. And now dad was sharing her views.

From dad he had expected sympathy, but it was evident that mam had nagged him into his present state of mind. She gave no one any peace of mind. Just nagged, nagged, nagged. If dad wanted to be rid of his anger, then let him quarrel with her. Shout at her for a change, and prove himself a man, not vent his spleen on him.

He wanted to be a writer. Why couldn't dad encourage him like the others, who were strangers? But he would continue to write. Yes, in spite of their disapproval. He had made up his mind, and nothing would force him to change it.

"Ieuan!" His mother's voice called from the kitchen.

"You'd better come," said his father, "or there'll be ructions."

Ieuan pushed his papers and books aside. He seethed with anger and impatience, and the enthusiasm he had entertained a few minutes ago flickered and died. What was the use of trying to better oneself? What advantages could he hope to gain from his books and his studies when he was given no peace of mind, no solitude for concentration. Of what use the plan for the future?

"Ieuan!"

"All right, Mam. I'm coming." His tone was harsh, and his father regarded him with a frown.

"There's no need to raise your voice, Ieuan. After all, you should show some respect to your mother. She's going through a hard time just now. If you gave up this daft idea you have about being a writer, we'd have a little peace in the house. I don't want you to stay in the foundry, boy. There are other jobs you can get into later — though I can't see why you shouldn't be satisfied with the foundry. It's a steady job — I mean, you'll get a fixed rate of wages in time, and you won't be pushed around from pillar to post like a labourer. Look at me. Can I claim the wage a moulder would get? Two pounds ten, Ieuan, that's my rate. Now, wouldn't you rather be a tradesman? Can't you show a little appreciation for what we've done for you?"

In the kitchen, another tirade awaited Ieuan. His mother was preparing the supper. Gweneira and Phyllis sat at the table, and watched him furtively as he drew up a chair beside them.

Phyllis put a finger to her lips to warn him of the impending storm. The mother saw the gesture.

"That's enough, Phyllis! I don't want you making motions behind my back," she snapped. She turned to Ieuan. "I hope your father's given you a talking-to for once. It's time someone should, for it's daunted I am — long ago."

Ieuan squirmed. He wanted to scream. Was there ever any peace for him? Did mam have to shout and rave all the time? What was wrong with her?

"Listen, Mam," he said, returning her stare, determined to stand up to the petty bullying she had so consistently imposed on him, "what have I done to make you feel so angry with me?"

He saw her lips tighten. For the moment she was confused. Her self-assurance wavered. She opened her mouth, but no words came.

"Your mother's not angry with you," he heard his father say. "You've got the wrong end of the stick, boy. Come now, eat your supper. Don't take things to heart so much."

"I'm not taking things to heart, Dad," Ieuan returned. "Mam's always finding something to grumble about. I—I'm not being disrespectful, but, after all, I've got a right to try to educate myself. I'm not going to stick in the foundry all my life, dad, and neither you nor mam's going to force me to."

A silence hung over the small kitchen. Gweneira and Phyllis fidgeted in their chairs. They glanced nervously at their mother, as though afraid that they, too, would soon be involved in the argument which they sensed would surely develop from Ieuan's boldness.

Then the mother spoke, and this time her voice was cold and dispassionate. Her eyes betrayed her contempt.

"You'd better hold your tongue, Ieuan Morgan. The sooner the better you learn to respect your elders. Don't it teach you that in your books? I'll not force you to stay in the foundry, indeed! Since when do I have to be dictated to by a boy, I'd like to know?"

"I'm not dictating," Ieuan protested.

"Keep quiet! Your opinions I'll ask for when I want them. While you're in this house you'll do as I say, my lad. Oh, yes, don't start getting fine ideas about how important you are. Twelve shillings — that's what you brought into this house when you were working. And now it's ten. Ten shillings a week — not enough to keep you on bread. But are you starving? No. And for why? Because I — yes, I — feed you. And what do I get? Nothing — nothing but cheek and impudence."

Ieuan bristled. "You don't know what you're saying, Mam."

"Shut up! None of your cheek, I tell you. Here you are, wasting your time with books and a lot of nonsense, when you could be earning something to keep the home going. How much longer d'you think I can manage to feed and clothe you on ten shillings?"

Ieuan looked at her strangely. What new development was this, he wondered. What had eaten its way into her mind now? First, his books, his writing had annoyed her. Now she had switched over to something entirely different.

He was soon to find out.

"There's work in plenty for you at the tinworks," she said icily. "They're on full time. Don't know what it is to be unemployed, them tinworks men."

"Millie!" His father leapt into the argument. "Millie, you don't know what you're saying, girl. Tinworks, indeed!"

"And why not?"

193

"But — but it's ridiculous. Whatever made you think of such a thing? Ieuan is apprenticed in the foundry."

"He can be taken out, can't he?"

"That's daft talk, Millie — absolutely daft. What's come over you, girl? Another thing, what do you know about trade union agreements and all that sort of thing? You just can't push a boy into a trade one minute and take him out the next."

"There's no money coming into this house. Is it daft for me to make suggestions that the boy should look for something to do?" came the sharp reply. "Or is it better to let him sit around on his backside reading a lot of books?"

"But, Millie, I tell you, you don't know what you're talking about. Heavens alive, girl, give the boy a chance. You wanted to put him in the foundry, and here you are wanting him to go look for another job the first couple of weeks he's out of work. Perhaps it's just a hint to me, eh? P'raps you think I should look for another job? Well, you're making a big mistake, Millie — a hell of a mistake."

Ieuan pushed his chair away. Gweneira and Phyllis, apprehensive of the quarrel that was rapidly approaching, disappeared up the passageway. They tip-toed upstairs to their bedroom without so much as a word uttered.

The mother sniffed. "If that's how you feel, Dick, then you'd better go out for a walk and cool off. I've got no time for a man who swears in front of his children."

"Swearing, by damn! You're enough to make any man swear. Why, if I ...."

The quarrel continued. Upstairs, the children slept, huddled closely in each other's arms. And Ieuan waited, until anger and despair drove him to his room.

* * *

The trade depression worsened. Eventually the steel mills and tinworks closed. Men who had never experienced a day's

194

unemployment lined up for the dole. Abermor, no longer a thriving Welsh industrial town, became a subject for debate in the Commons. It was discussed in synonymity with the hard-hit towns in the mining valleys of the Rhondda.

The main thoroughfares were crowded daily with men who wandered aimlessly up and down, or stood in groups at the street corners only to be moved on by the police, whose vigilance became the object of anger and derision.

Unemployment. September, October, November, December ... month after month dragged by. There was a restlessness in the air. An undercurrent of dissatisfaction. The first weeks of summer had provided many diversions which kept the men's minds away from the spectre of insecurity that had come to haunt them.

Bowling greens, country walks, angling for mullet in the old dock, cricket matches on Potter's Park. It was a brief holiday. Soon they would be back at work again. This could not go on indefinitely. Abermor had never suffered an industrial depression.

Cheer up, lads. This'll be over before we know it. Make the most of the holiday, for holiday it is. And, by crikey, we're getting paid for it, too. Not much, but pay it is just the same. Enough to spare for a weekly packet of Woodbines, a pint of beer, or perhaps a seat — a fourpenny one — at the cinema on Wednesday afternoons, if one was careful.

Unemployment. Then came demoralization. Apathy. The men had no inclination to do anything. Energy and will were sapped. Life became one long monotonous round.

On Monday and Wednesday mornings, at the specific times arranged for signing, Ieuan would meet his fellow employees at the Exchange. Leaning up against the wall in the yard, the younger moulders and improvers would discuss their plans for the day. How best to occupy the hours that lay ahead.

A suggestion. "What about a walk to Carmarthen, boys?"

"Carmarthen! Hell, it's twenty miles."

"We got plenty of time, haven't we?"

195

On other days they would amble to the Town Hall Grounds, or to "Loafers' Rest," there to sit on the greenpainted seats, staring at the grass. Or walk together in groups through Dinas Wood, discussing every subject save the foundry.

When it rained they splashed their way to the market, crowding round the cheap-jacks' stalls; gazing at the glittering array of tawdry jewellery, watches, penknives, perfumes, soaps, combs; listening to the cheap-jacks' sales talk. And not a man with a penny in his pocket — the price of a razor blade.

Hours in the silent court room of the Town Hall; sauntering around the counters of Messrs. Woolworth, and Marks and Spencer; a furtive joke with the pretty salesgirls, the bloom of whose skin was more wondrous than the film stars' gazed at from the Wednesday afternoon "fourpennies."

And in the front parlour at night, Ieuan would write of what he had seen. Of the bitterness, frustration, anger, despair; of the little joys, the ironic humour.

He wrote what he felt, a sullen hatred within him, a fierce resentment against a system that had made outcasts of men. He wrote of surly clerks at the Exchange, trim in their black suits and starched white collars, who treated with contempt the men who had come to claim their meagre benefit. The arrogance and uncivility they displayed towards those who were less fortunate — the human flotsam and jetsam of the industrial tide.

And he wrote of others, his own fellow-workers. Of the anger he felt when, summoned to the supervisor's office, they entered, cap in hand, knees shaking, as though called to the presence of the Almighty for judgment on their sins.

His impressions of the long-continued slump were jotted down in his notebooks. All his passion and his anger.

Shuffle, shuffle. Drag your soleless boots along the shining, polished floor. Lean against the counter and stare with tired eyes at the printed notices: "Box 5," "No Smoking."

Answer with tired tongue the dreary question: "No work?"

Touch your cap, you snivelling underdog. Look around you and

*see the empty faces devoid of all human hope and love, staring...
staring... staring.*

Oh, you fool. Get away from it all!

*But where? Around the corner where Despair sits, brooding and
melancholy, his dark, shadowy frame deeper than the shadows
that encompass him?*

*No, not there! Look at the green fields, the trees, the blue sky
above. The radiance which is nature's smiles around you, but you
see it not. You see only the dusty pavements parched with summer
thirst, and the living dead who walk beside you; the mean, dirty
streets, unclean as a leper's hideous sores; the pillared building,
EMPLOYMENT EXCHANGE, where the bodies and souls of men
are for sale.*

*Get away from it all! Sit you down, my boy. There, on a seat in
the park. Listen to the beggar as he passes, ragged pants, down-at-
heel.*

> *"Oh Da-a-a-an-ny bhoy*
> *The pipes, the pipes are caw-aw-lin'*
> *From glen to glen, an' down the mountainside ...."*

*You look in your pockets, but you have nothing to give to your
poor, unfortunate brother — nothing. And you remember,
suddenly, a night when winter snows lay crisp and white along
the silent streets. You saw, then, a man and woman. They were
both young in years, but aged in body — maybe in mind, too. He
was dressed in coat and trousers. He had no vest or shirt, and
the night was cold.*

*She was dressed in a long, ragged coat; a thin coat, with no
lining. They had canvas slippers on their feet, and the man was
pushing a heavy, dilapidated pram filled with odds and ends, their
worldly possessions, and covered with tarpaulin.*

*They stopped to talk to a policeman. You saw him in uniform
pointing up the road, and up the road was the workhouse.*

The woman was swollen with a life unborn. God, what a world!

A new life to be born to parents with no clothes to their backs, and no place to go. And yet so many have so much. It made you mad, remember? You felt like saying to the wretched couple: "Come with me, and I'll give you everything I've got."

But you couldn't do that because you had your own troubles to consider. When you weighed up everything, you were not much better off yourself. You had nothing to give. Some day you might be pushing a pram around and looking for a place to sleep, and asking a policeman the way to the workhouse.

Remember how once you planned a holiday? Things we're going well then. But did you really plan a holiday? What plans could you make? Could you say: "I'm going for a month's vacation to Blackpool"? Oh, yes, you did say so. Well, there's no harm in just saying it. You could even say, and prove at the same time, that you had twenty-five pounds saved in the Post Office ready for the holiday.

But wait, brother! What if you were taken ill? What if the foundry closed down and you became unemployed? What if you were sacked? What if your wife fell ill, or your child?

You weren't married? Well then, if your mother, or father, or sister, or brother became ill, and depended on you for help? What of your twenty-five pounds then, and your lovely dreamed-of holiday on golden sands, with music, laughter and silken girls?

"Oh, you mustn't think of things like that," you say. "It's too depressing."

You said it, brother. Your whole existence is depressing. You have no security. You have no right to plan a vacation: Now, if you were one of the privileged few you would, and could, arrange your future in a more methodical and certain manner. Then you could say: "I'm going to Blackpool for six months," or you could choose Madeira — "— that's where they go to chase the sun and pretty ladies. You could even say: "I'm going to reserve a suite" — a suite, mind you, not a single room in a cheap boarding house, two-and-sixpence bed and breakfast.

You could have someone to arrange the details for you, and

what's more, you could tell yourself — if you felt like it — that you would have a gay time with the ladies.

Oh yes, and you needn't worry about unemployment, and being ill, and such things. You needn't even take the trouble of packing your bags, writing for rooms, booking your fare. No — that would be done for you by someone who would not be in a much better position than you are in at the moment. And you would go to Blackpool or Madeira, sleep in the best bed in the best room, eat the best food, drink the best wine, enjoy the best music, make love to the best dressed or undressed ladies.

Ah, you'd have a grand time. All you'd have to worry about to prevent you going would be something mighty serious, like death.

But never mind all this, brother. Don't worry, for there's a good time coming, if you live long enough to see it. The good time that is to come; the silver lining in the big black cloud; the rainbow of good, good fortune ... all elusive as the Bluebird of Happiness.

Far away you hear the sound of a fiddle:

> *"The merry love the fiddle,*
> *And the merry love the dance . ...."*

Sit down, you poor, blind fool! You are but something in boots — boots that are no longer boots.

Ah, so you wish you were dead? Remember, brother, life is sweet after all.

Isn't life wonderful? Yes, a thousand times, a million times. But wait, you deluded, crawling wretched atom of humanity! Don't you, can't you, realize that you yes, YOU ... are DEAD?

* * *

Ieuan had welcomed the freedom from the foundry. He had been relieved of all that had made him bitter, sullen and morose. Relieved of his fears and his persecutions.

But now, with the passing of the months, the endless routine of monotony palled him. He had his books, his studies, but they did not occupy every moment of his time. What he saw around him filled him with hatred against the powers in authority who had condemned men to inactivity and given them no sustenance.

Living in Abermor had become a problem. There was no money. The smaller shops were thrown out of business. In January the coal shortage had become so acute that the army of unemployed was forced to search for fuel in the slag banks and coal tips of the disused collieries on the outskirts of the town.

To break away from the monotony, Ieuan and his father joined in these daily excursions to the coal tips. They chose the five-mile tramp to the Waun colliery. A weird pilgrimage. Hundreds of men and youths trundling wheelbarrows, handcarts, broken-down prams, boneshaker bicycles, and grocers' two-wheeled trolleys along a single-track railway, tearing a way through a wilderness of gorse bushes and tangled undergrowth, climbing an endlessly winding country lane until at last Mecca was reached.

A series of huge slag tips reared up from a countryside which was green and fertile. Cattle moved in the fields below the tips. A whitewashed farm building stood clear and bright in the winter sun. A wooded copse encircled the foot of the tallest of the grey-blue pyramids, and beyond it came the murmur of a stream.

Deep into the crusted slag the army dug with pick and shovel, the more experienced diggers propping the holes with timber, the amateurs risking life and limb as they burrowed far into the blue depths.

Sacks were filled with lumps of dull slag which bore not the slightest resemblance to coal. But it helped to keep the fires burning, and that sufficed.

Then came the long trek home. The weary procession, a Dürer etching come to life, plodded down the steep hill, heels braked against the cobbled road. Shoulders bent under the weight of heavy sacks. Muscles tensed.

Knees quivered. Hands were blistered from the strain of pulling the laden carts. Ribs ached from the steel frames that dug into them as the boneshakers were trundled downhill at an angle of sixty degrees. Hands and faces were blackened with coal dust, fingernails torn, feet blistered. Yet, for all the misery, there was laughter to be heard, and a smile seen on the grimy, perspiring faces.

They were brothers in distress. A community of down-at-heels. Misfortune was common to each, and pride was banished.

"Don't know where the hell I'm going to dump this lot — bloody coal-house is full already. Been up here ten times."

"Shouldn't worry over that, Kim. There's plenty o' chaps here'd be glad to get rid of it for you."

"Jesus! Who'd like to be a collier?"

"Not me, you bet your life. Give me the mills every time."

"This load's for Marged Ann Matthews, the Bungalow. One-an'-a-tanner a sack she's offered me. One-an'-a-tanner ! Two pints and three packets o' Woodbines — a bloody fortune!"

CHAPTER NINE

AT last the long era of unemployment came to an end. It happened as suddenly as it began. Once more the factory chimneys belched their black fumes over the town. The deep holes in the Waun slag tips became covered with weeds and grass, or shored in to give no clue that an army of tatterdemalions had once invaded the bleak slopes. The street corners and the parks were deserted. In the hours before dawn the clip-clop of the tinworkers' clogs was heard again.

Prosperity had returned to Abermor, such prosperity that only came to the workers in a weekly wage packet on Friday afternoons.

It was April when Bevan's opened its gates and Ieuan found himself back with his companions of the coreshop and steel foundry. His plan to attend night school in the winter months had not materialized. Attendance there had been affected by the mass unemployment. There had been no incentive for study. The younger men had been in no mood for it. Consequently, the classes were abandoned.

Ieuan's distaste for the foundry still remained, and his ambition alone gave him strength to face it once more. The nine months he had been unemployed had added to his knowledge, a knowledge acquired not from books alone, but from his own observations of life around him, and he valued his experience, brief though it was.

This summer he would matriculate. That was his intention. He was now seventeen. Another year, and he hoped to be free of the foundry.

He wrote in his notebooks, conveying his impressions rapidly, filing them away into a small cupboard in his bedroom. Occasionally, he would take them out, glance through the pages, re-reading what he had written. Pausing to alter a phrase here and there. Trying to acquire form, a style of his own.

Frank had seen very little of him during the time they had been out of work, but now that the foundry had restarted he would call in at the coreshop whenever he had an opportunity.

"Met your old headmaster, Ellis Griffiths, the other night," he remarked one afternoon during a break between the casts. "Doris and I were beginning to wonder what had happened to you, Ieuan, but Ellis told me you were concentrating on your studies. Your nose deep in books. What's your intention, Ieuan? Going in for some exam?"

Ieuan told him of his hopes, and felt heartened when Frank complimented him.

"You'll be out of this place sooner than you know it, boy. Stick to your books. Don't be a darn fool to let yourself get into a rut, as I did. And good luck to you, Ieuan. All the same, don't overdo it. Get out sometimes. Have a little enjoyment. All work and no play — well, you know the old saying. Drop over to see Doris and me sometime. Any time you feel like it. She'd like to see you again. Kind of empty house, without someone to call around for a chat now and again."

Bull Jackson, bored by the long period of inactivity, appeared glad to be back at work again, and for the first few weeks concentrated on his job at the bench, much to Abraham's amazement and relief.

The charge-hand's relief was shared by Isaiah and Dicky, but Thomas, with a characteristic shrug, commented: "Bull won't be bloody quiet for long — just you wait. A couple o' week's pay and then he'll start his shenanagins again."

A system of piecework introduced into the foundry gave Bull and his cronies further cause to provoke and intimidate Ieuan. Piecework prices were fixed on various jobs, and the men had to calculate their earnings on each job and submit the list to Lu every week. The majority of them found it intricate and difficult. Others had not the time or the inclination to worry over mathematics. But knowing of Ieuan's capabilities, they came to him for help.

"Look here, lad. The old brain's a bit rusty, but seeing as you're fresh from school ... well, it's like this. Fifteen pounds ten we're getting for this job, and there's five of us working on it. We reckon piecework rate's about one-and-sevenpence-farthing an hour .... How long d'you count we should take on the job for to make it pay?"

He worked out the figures on scraps of paper. The men thanked him. Soon, his name was mentioned to other moulders who were confused by percentages, flat rates, piecework rates, jobs-and-finish, waiting time, and so on. They came to him often, yellow timesheets in their hands.

"Work this one out for me, there's a good chap."

The improvers resented his sudden popularity, and Bull was among the first to show his antagonism.

"Bloody stuck-up snob, is our Iron getting to be, since fellers who don't know how to add two and two keep coming to him. Guess we ought to bring him down a peg." And the same odious jokes were played on Ieuan, tarring of tools, deliberate breaking of cores that were needed in a hurry. Anything to embarrass him was their aim, and the coreshop once again became the scene of violent quarrels between Abraham and the rowdy element from the steel shop.

At home, life was not much pleasanter. Mrs. Morgan, still resentful of the manner in which Ieuan had stood up to her nagging, treated him as though he were a stranger. She spoke to him only when she found it necessary to do so, reserving her judgment of him for the ears of her husband in the evenings when the children were in bed and Ieuan in the front parlour with his books.

"Maybe I should have left him in school," she would grumble, "then by this time he'd have got fed up with it. Some boys don't know when they're well off. Selfish, that's what he is. No respect at all for his elders. Talking to me like as if I was an old tramp woman on the roads. Him and his old books. Just you wait, Dick — one day he'll be glad I sacrificed myself for to put him in the foundry. You wait till he gets the rate. But I suppose when he gets to earning decent money he'll meet with some girl or something, and before we know it he'll be off and married to her. That's just the sort of thing he would do, I'm thinking. No thought for his mother who's struggled all her life. That's our Ieuan all over. And if he's what you call a scholar — then thank God I've never been one. Not selfish I am, that's one thing no one can say about Millie Morgan."

As she spoke, her husband would nod and say nothing, except to interject with an occasional "But, Millie — ," which was all he was allowed to say before she renewed her attack on whatever phase of Ieuan's behaviour happened to annoy her at that particular moment.

One evening in May, Dick, desperate in his desire for peace and solitude, and distracted from his attempt to settle down to the evening paper, shuffled up the passageway and into the front room.

He was nervy and irritable. Millie's constant tirades were getting him down. He wanted seclusion. Quiet.

In the parlour he found Ieuan writing. This annoyed him, for the boy's absorption in his studies had inflamed the mother's temper again.

"Listen to me, Ieuan," he began. "Why don't you fling those books of yours away for a while? God! This house is fair driving me daft. What with your mother's rampagings, and you with your head buried in books all the time...This is a fine place to come home to after a day's work."

"But, Dad, I'm not worrying anyone," Ieuan protested.

"Oh, close them books, boy. Get out into the street. You're becoming a real hermit. There's no sense in it, a young boy like you staying in the house night after night. I thought you'd have had enough of studying after that long stretch when we were out of work. You were at it then till all hours, boy. It'll get you down.

There's a limit to everything, and it's not natural for a growing lad to be spending all his time in a stuffy old parlour when there's plenty to occupy his time and mind outside."

Ieuan closed his books. "All right, Dad, if that's how you feel I'll go out. I'm sorry."

"That's no way to speak, Ieuan. I think it's me who should say I'm sorry. But it's getting worse in the house every day, honest it is. Things were bad enough when we both were out of a job. Now, I thought your mother'd brighten up a bit. She had a rotten time when there was no money coming into the house, but now …well, it beats me, Ieuan. I give up."

Ieuan walked to the door. "Sit down, Dad. Don't let mam upset you like this. Honestly, sometimes I feel like shouting at her, and when I look at the foundry I start wondering whether I'm happier there than I am at home. At least, I do get a bit of peace there sometimes."

"Peace, Ieuan … at the foundry! Why shouldn't you get a bit of peace there? Don't tell me you're still getting your leg pulled. I thought that nonsense had stopped after the first week."

"'ve been there over a year, Dad, and it's still the same. I hate the place," Ieuan said, bitterly. "Hate the fellows like Bull Jackson and his gang. I can stand up to them all right. With my fists, too, if it comes to the point. But I'll stick it for a while longer, and then I'm handing in my notice, whether mam likes it or not. She's satisfied so long as I bring in a bit of money every week. And if mam's satisfied — well, I suppose that's all that really matters in this house."

His father looked hard at him. "Ieuan *bach,* don't get to feeling that way about your mother," he said, pained. "After all, if she hadn't put you into the foundry we'd be in a mighty bad way right now. You're helping us out a lot with your wages every week. Twelve-and-three for the first year wasn't much, I know, but now you're earning twenty-five shillings. That's a big help, Ieuan, and if you don't realize it, your mother and I do. And let me tell you again, my boy — there are far worse jobs than being

206

an apprentice moulder. Take those young lads in the tinworks, for example. A pretty tough life they get, and they earn their money — every penny of it. You take things too seriously, Ieuan. This talk about exams and matriculating .... I know it's a good idea. But working in the foundry is enough, boy. You need all your energy for that. So don't let it worry you like it does. You want to go out and enjoy yourself. Make the most of what little time off you get, or you'll end up in a corner. And then who'll want you? Nobody — you take it from me. Look here, the fair is on tonight. Why don't you take a walk up there and have a good time?"

Ieuan pursed his lips. What was the use of building up hopes, cherishing dreams of a future that would bring him happiness and a richer benefit to his parents? Even his father, from whom he had expected so much, had no encouragement to offer him. Was dad blind? Could he still not realize that he wanted desperately to be out of the foundry?

Dad once had an ambition, but nothing came of it. Was he now, in some subtle, stubborn way, determined to stifle whatever hopes he had for his future? If Frank and Mr. Griffiths were prepared to interest themselves in him and to offer encouragement, then surely his own parents could help?

But it was evident that all they were concerned with was his earning capacity. All this arguing, quarrelling, the vague excuses — just because he felt that he could never adjust himself to the foundry. Because he wanted to break away from it into a career where he would be better fitted to play his part.

Sometimes his pity for dad changed to bitter scornfulness. The way he gave in to mam, always seeking to pacify her, caring nothing for anyone else's discomfort but his own.

Why torment himself with such thoughts? Dad wanted him to go out. All right, he would get out. To the streets. Or to the fair. Anywhere.

* * *

The fairground was thronged with people, pushing, jostling, swaying. Crowds of careless, high-spirited boys and girls screamed and giggled, their shrill voices echoing above the pulsating dynamos, the blare of roundabouts, high above the sharp crack of bullets at the miniature rifle ranges and the stentorian cries of the sideshow barkers.

Ieuan shouldered his way along the crowded avenues between the gaudy hoop-la stalls, coconut shies, and merry-go-rounds, his eyes taking in the scene. The May fair had come to Abermor. King Carnival reigned.

The steady, monotonous chug-chug of the dynamos drummed in his ears. Their bright brass bearings gleamed, reflecting the rows of coloured lights swinging above the canvas booths.

Fairground in May. The glow of flares in the darkness. Coconut stalls: "Try your luck, sir .... Three balls a penny .... Come on, guv'nor, show the young lady what you can do."

Swings. Up and down. Into the darkness, and back again into the light. Screaming girls. Skirts pulled tightly over knees. A glimpse of a satin underskirt, and a blush hidden in the dark.

Fortune-telling slot machines. "See your future husband. The man of your dreams." An isolated canvas booth. "Your fortune revealed. The original Gipsy Rose Lee."

A twelve-pound wooden mallet and a bell that rang in the heavens. "Try your strength, sir. Ring the bell and get your money back."

French nougat, and French ladies in lingerie. Merry-go-rounds. Hoop-la stalls. Lean-faced boxers, arms folded, muscles rippling under the naphtha flares.

"Five pounds to any man what stands up to four rounds with young Tommy Driscoll. Five pounds! Come on, who'll have a go? Tommy Driscoll, here on my right. Nine stone six. Who says 'no' to a fiver?"

A hand waving in the gloom. A pair of boxing gloves tossed over the crowd. A pat on the back. "Good for you, boyo!" And the crowd surge into the darkened booth.

208

The Fat Lady, The Thin Man, The Wild Man from Borneo, Cow with Six Legs, Lady with Two Heads, The Smallest Elephant in Captivity, The Tattooed Lady, The Hairy Man.

"Roll up, roll up! Come and see the Hairy Man. Guaranteed genuine. More hair on his arms than a monkey's got on his … Run away there, boys, run away and play."

Monstro, The Ugliest Man in the World. "Only sixpence. Step up, step up, ladies an' gents. The Hunchback of Notre Dame is a fairy prince compared with Monstro. 'Lon Chaney,' did I hear someone say? Brother, you ain't seen nothing yet."

Human oddities on exhibition. Sixpence adults, three-pence children. A sight for old eyes, young eyes, bright eyes and tired eyes. A sight for all but the blind. Vice and ugliness on parade.

Ieuan pushed on through the crowd. Familiar faces smiled at him. A slap on the back in greeting from a worker in the foundry. Elwyn and Danny from the tinworks, a tinsel flower buttonhole, coconut under one arm, a flashily dressed, loud-voiced girl linked in the other. Girls smelling of cheap scent, nursing kewpie dolls.

Two old men striving vainly to recapture their youth. Paper top hats on grizzled heads. Waving coloured streamers. Cracked voices sing, "Oh, won't you come home, Bill Bailey?"

And the merry-go-rounds went round, travelling constantly in the same small circle. Music blaring, the unseen orchestra conducted by a marionette figure in satin brocade. Round and round, going nowhere.

Without the music, how foolish the merry-go-rounders would look. So Ieuan thought. But this is not the place to think, not in a fairground in May. Capture the spirit of gaiety. Live and laugh. Forget the cares of the day.

"Step up and get the thrill of your life. Mademoiselle Yvonne …. Direct from the Folies Bergere …. See her do the Dance of the Seven Veils…. A sight to make the old men wish they were young again, and the young men …. Step up, step up …. This way, ladies and gentlemen…Your money back if not satisfied."

And Ieuan still wandered from stall to stall, booth to booth.

Presently, he stood on the fringe of the crowd. Nearby, a housey-housey stall with its circle of prospective clients. He could hear the attendant's raucous call: "Last two tickets, now .... Who'll take the last two? ... The very last two .... I say, sir ... What about you an' the young lady? ... Try your luck, sir .... The very last two."

All eyes turned, and the young man bought one ticket. The attendant muttered to himself. He caught Ieuan's eye. "You, over there .... Come on, young fellow .... Be a sport .... Have a go! ... Last ticket. ... The very last one."

Ieuan took the ticket.

"Good for you, young sport.... Now, ladies and gentlemen, we're all set to go.... Choose any number you like on the board, and throw your darts .... All ready, now ....Go!"

Ieuan scanned the small, numbered board in his hand. He leaned over the encircling rail, and took aim with his dart. Suddenly, he was conscious of someone staring at him. He threw his dart, and missed the number he had chosen.

Once again he became selfconscious, uneasy. He looked across the stall. On the opposite side, her hands resting on the wooden rail, stood a young girl. Neatly dressed in a light blue costume and white silk blouse. Her dark hair gathered into a pale blue ribbon.

She averted her gaze as Ieuan looked at her.

"Six .... Seventeen .... Thirty-two," the attendant's voice called. The players watched their boards.

"Housey! I've got it!" A young flapper waved her board, and giggled with delight.

Ieuan glanced across the stall. The girl's eyes were on him again. He straightened his tie, and coughed nervously. Then he saw her smile. He looked over his shoulder. Her smile widened. He returned it, bashfully.

She was smiling at him! By golly, she was a pretty girl, too. Not that he had ever taken much notice of girls. But this one looked very attractive. Maybe he should go over and talk to her.

Or perhaps it would be wiser not to. The fairground was a place to "click." Like the Monkey Parade on Sunday nights.

Was she trying to "click" with him? Maybe she just wanted someone to treat her. That's what most girls wanted at the fair, anyway.

Should he approach her and see what she had to say? Perhaps she wasn't one of those flighty pieces, the type of girls that Bull Jackson, Titus, and Reg Bowen chased after. She seemed a refined girl. There was something about her that made him think so. The way she smiled. How she seemed to blush when he smiled back. And she wasn't gaudily dressed and brazen like the tinworks' girls.

He edged his way through the crowd, and as he drew near the girl, she lowered her eyes.

"Faint heart never won fair lady. Or am I making a fool of myself?" he thought. "What has made me behave like this? Girls have meant nothing to me before. Then, why ... ?"

But it would be nice to walk out with a girl. He was seventeen. Almost all boys of his age were walking out. He needed company. He had come to the fair, so why not enjoy himself?

"Good evening...." He touched his cap. The girl smiled shyly and moved away from the rail. He caught her lightly by the arm. "May — may I see you home?" he asked, his confidence wavering.

She looked into his face. She gave a nervous little laugh.

"I—I don't know, really."

"But there's no harm in that — I mean, just seeing you home."

"No, I—I suppose not."

"Then won't you please let me walk with you?"

She did not reply.

"You are very shy." Ieuan cleared his throat, and swallowed. "Almost as shy as I am."

"You don't seem to be shy," she said.

"Well, believe me, I am," he assured. "I—I don't go round fairgrounds trying to pick up girls."

He saw a hurt look in her eyes. "Oh, please don't misunderstand me," he hastened to say. "I didn't mean to say that you were—"

"That's all right. It's my fault, really."

"Your fault?"

"Yes-I smiled at you, and ... well, I shouldn't."

"You've got a very nice smile, too," Ieuan tried to be the gallant. "And you're a very pretty girl."

He waited nervously. "May I see you home?" he asked again.

"All right, then, if you like. But I haven't far to go."

"Where do you live — if that's not too cheeky of me?"

"It's not cheeky to ask me where I live if you want to take me home. How could you walk home with me if I didn't tell you where I lived?" She laughed, and Ieuan felt that never had he heard such a sweet sound. "Oh, dear — what am I trying to say?"

He escorted her through the crowd. They stood on the bank of the river which trickled along the borders of the fairground. The lights shone down on the greasy yellow water. A rat scuttled away among the stones. The music, the laughter, and the low murmur of voices from the fair, died.

They crossed the road over a small footbridge. Ieuan held her arm lightly. He helped her over the kerbstone and let her walk on the inside of the pavement.

"How far do you live?" he ventured.

She hesitated. "Crooked Row," she said in a whisper, as though ashamed.

"Oh, I know Crooked Row well," said Ieuan, hoping that his nonchalance had put her at ease.

What a place to live in, he thought. He did know it well. Too well. Tumbledown houses huddled together as if each depended on the other for support. Whitewashed walls peeling with age. Windows stuffed with strips of sacking. Noisy, unwashed children. A narrow lane, crooked as the line of sagging roofs. Abermor's slum area.

He glanced at the girl by his side. He noticed how clean she was, how neat. Her trim figure. Surely she did not live in that bleak, poverty-ridden area? The way she smiled at him. She seemed happy, well cared for.

212

But as they came into the brighter light of the High Street he saw that, in spite of her neat appearance, her clothes were cheap. Her costume was well worn, the cloth at, the wrists threadbare. Now he had a better opportunity to judge her.

As she turned her face to speak to him he was startled by the pallor of her complexion. She was very beautiful. Her eyes were large and expressive, yet there was a lack of lustre in them, as though she were tired or strained.

He felt a sudden surge of pity for her. He tried to think of something to say, but could not.

"You're very quiet?"

"I—I'm sorry," he stammered. "I—I was just thinking." She coughed, a hollow-throated cough, and clutched his arm.

"Gee, that's a bad cough." Ieuan had found a subject for conversation. "Sounds as if you've got a cold."

"It's nothing really," she said. "Just a frog in the throat."

"It's an awfully big frog," he said, glad that he had found his tongue again. "But, seriously though, you ought to see the doctor. Have you been to him?"

"No."

"Well, you ought to, you know."

"Oh, it's nothing, I tell you. I've always had a cough, ever since I can remember. Maybe it's the house, mam is always complaining about the dampness."

"Yes, Crooked Row is a very unhealthy spot. The council should have pulled the houses down years ago. There's no sense in people having to live in them."

"It's an awful place," she said. "Sometimes I'm ashamed of telling people that I live there. I wish we could move somewhere else, but mam and dad's tried until they're daunted. I'd never live there if I was married."

Embarrassed, Ieuan said nothing for a while. They continued to the end of the High Street, then walked through a winding lane that took them into a quieter area. Crooked Row stood ten minutes away.

Ieuan drew up in the shadow of a doorway.

"Shall we stay here a minute?"

"I don't mind," she said. "But I mustn't be late."

"There's — there's something I'd like to say to you before you go."

"Yes?"

Ieuan toyed with a button on his coat. "You — you don't think I'm a masher?" he asked suddenly. "I mean, I didn't try to click with you at the fair."

She laughed. "Of course not. I know you're not like the Monkey Parade crowd. Why, you haven't even asked me my name yet."

"Your name! Gee, of course I haven't. Well ... ?"

"Sally," she said. "My name's Sally Marvin."

"Marvin! You — you're not Welsh?"

"Well, yes — and no. Mam's Welsh. She was born here, but dad comes from Devon."

"I—I thought it was an odd name. My name's—"

"Morgan," she said. "Ieuan Morgan."

Ieuan looked at her with surprise. "You know my name! But how ...?"

He saw her blush as she stammered a reply. "I—I was at school the same time as you, and — well, boys and girls come to know each other's names sometimes. I've heard other boys speak about you. You were a good scholar, weren't you?"

"A bit. But you were at the County, too?"

"Yes."

"Are you still in school?"

She laughed. "Goodness me, no. I'm working now. At Simpson's the Dyers. I'm seventeen."

"And I'm working, too," Ieuan smiled.

"In Bevan's Foundry."

"Gee whizz, you know that, too? You must be a detective."

"One thing I know ...."

"Yes, what's that?"

"That you shouldn't have left school. I heard Mr. Griffiths, the

214

County headmaster, speak about you to my father one night. He said you were the most promising pupil he had ever taught. Dad was trying to get a job for me, and Mr. Griffiths was doing his best to persuade him to keep me at school. He said what a shame it was that parents wouldn't realize how important education was these days. Then he mentioned your mother, and—"

"We-we'll talk about that some other time ... Sally. There will be another time? I—I mean, you'll let me see you again?"

"If you want to, Ieuan."

"You — you'd be my girl?"

"Yes, if you like me enough."

"I—I think you're a very nice girl. I'd be glad to go walking with you, glad and happy, too."

"All right then, Ieuan ... I'll see you some other time."

"When?"

"Sunday night."

"Gee!"

"To meet you ... where will I meet you?" Ieuan pondered. Too excited to think clearly. "What about Howard's Park? Seven o'clock. Is that too early. I mean — do you go to church or chapel?"

"Not next Sunday," she said softly. Suddenly, she began to cough again.

"Heck, you'd better look after yourself." Ieuan became solicitous. "That's an awful cough. I'd go to the doctor's if I were you."

"I will," she smiled.

"That's a promise?"

"Cross my heart."

"And I — I'll see you Sunday night?"

"Yes, at seven o'clock."

"By the park gate. You — you won't forget?"

"A promise is a promise."

"Good, Sally. I'll be there." Ieuan glanced at her shyly. He touched his cap. "Good night ... until Sunday."

215

"Good night … Ieuan."

Turning, he made his way back towards the High Street. His heart sang, and for the moment he knew no sorrow, no pain.

* * *

Ieuan's meeting with Sally had given him new hope. He began to find joy where before he knew only bitterness and grief. The foundry still rankled him, but the anticipation of the pleasure he would find in the girl's companionship gave him solace. It was something to look forward to. He had a girl. A pretty girl. One who was intelligent. Who would share his tastes. And he liked her — so much that she occupied his every thought.

He kept his secret to himself. He dared not tell even Thomas, for he knew what the other's reaction might be. Thomas might let it slip out in conversation. He might even poke fun of his meeting with Sally. And if Bull and his cronies were to hear of it there would be no peace. They had always jeered at his preoccupation with his books and regarded his disinterest in girls as a mere pose.

But why worry over Thomas, Bull and the whole crowd of them? He now had Sally's company to look forward to. There was happiness ahead. Happiness, and a love which only he knew and felt.

At home, his mother noted with some satisfaction that his absorption in his studies had suddenly ceased. For four nights now he hadn't been near the front parlour. She commented to her husband on the Saturday night after Ieuan's introduction to Sally:

"Something funny must have happened to our Ieuan lately, Dick. He's a lot brighter. Listen to him laughing up there now, with Phyllis and Gweneira. Can't make it out at all. D'you think he's settling down to the foundry at last?"

There was a note of hope in her voice, but it was soon dispelled when her husband answered:

216

"No, Millie — frankly I don't think he's settling down at all. He hates the foundry just as much as ever he did. He told me so the other night. But don't ask me what's happening to him. The boy is getting older. He's changing, like all boys do at his age."

"Changing! What d'you mean?"

"Well, just that — changing. He's at an awkward age, Millie. He's getting to be a man now. Can't expect him to stop at sixteen, can you?"

"You — you don't mean he — he's taken up with some girl?"

"I don't know so much. He's just the age for that sort of thing. Anyway, as you say, he seems chirpy enough these last couple of days. Much more pleased with himself since I made him go out and enjoy himself at the fair. To tell you the truth, Millie, I wouldn't be surprised to hear that he's made a hit with some little girl at the fairground. Ieuan's a good-looking lad. Carries himself well, and he's got brains, too."

Mrs. Morgan winced.

"That's fine talk coming from you, Dick Morgan," she said sharply. "Girls, indeed! I hope he's old enough to have more sense. Two and sixpence in his pocket — he's rich to be finding himself a girl's company, isn't he?"

"I didn't have much more in my pocket when I met you, Millie."

"Nonsense! Half a crown meant something in them days, Dick. But where does it take you today? Besides, you was earning a man's wages when you went courting me — not twenty-five shillings."

"Was it much more, Millie? Come, girl — don't work yourself into a state of nerves about the boy. Let him enjoy himself. Give him a bit of a fling. You've been on to him plenty since he went into that blasted foundry. Last couple of weeks you've hardly said 'boo' to him."

Mrs. Morgan snorted. She jammed her fists into her ribs.

"What I should be asking is not what's got into our Ieuan, but what's got into you, Dick Morgan. Sharp is your tongue, and I can tell you I don't like it, d'you hear? I've been on to the boy, indeed! Good job somebody got his interests at heart, or God help him. Would you like to see him spending his time and money on a girl? And what if he got her into trouble or something? Such things do happen, you know. Look at all them flibbertigibbets parading up and down the High Street every night. Painted and powdered like Jezebels, the lot of 'em. Silk stockings and scented handkerchiefs. Only out to 'tice young boys. What if Ieuan got in with one of them sort? A fine thing, indeed! A fine thing for a boy from a respectable family to be knocking around with a painted doll who's got no gumption how to even dress decently. Oh, yes, our Ieuan could get some girl into trouble all right. You say he's not a boy any more — well, all the more reason why you should have a talk with him and find out what's happening."

"Millie, Millie girl, you're letting your imagination run away with you," Dick expostulated. "The boy get a girl into trouble, my eye! Come, come — you mustn't excite yourself like this, over nothing at all. Maybe the boy hasn't a bit of interest in girls. I was only joking, Millie. You can take a joke now and again, eh?"

"A very strange way you have of telling jokes, Dick Morgan," came the sardonic reply. "But I tell you this — if our Ieuan is messing around with some girl I'll soon put a stop to it. I got ways of finding out these things. I'm not stupid."

"Did I say you were?"

"No, but it makes me wonder what's going on in that mind of yours sometimes."

"Oh, hush, Millie."

"Don't 'hush' me. I'm not a child."

"All right, then. I'll say nothing."

"Yes, that's just you all over, Dick Morgan. Say nothing — but let the house go to pieces, let the children go where they like and do what they like. So long as you get your cigarettes and your paper and your glass of beer, nothing else matters. Leave the worrying to me."

The quarrel continued the following morning, and when Ieuan and his sisters sat down to their Sunday dinner their mother said hardly a word to them. Her fury had been exhausted, and she sat in stony silence, attending to their various needs at the table.

That evening, however, as she prepared the two girls for chapel, she turned her attention to Ieuan. Dressed in his best suit, he stood before the kitchen mirror, combing his hair.

"Making plenty of fuss over yourself tonight," she said. Then, suspiciously: "You are going to chapel, I hope?"

He bit his lip. The question had taken him unawares. He had never expected it. Chapel-going on Sunday evening had become a routine. It was accepted that he would attend the evening service.

What was the reason for mam's sudden query? Had she found out about Sally?

"I asked you, Ieuan, are you going to chapel?"

"Well ... y-yes," he lied. "Why?"

"Oh, I was just thinking that p'raps you had something else on your mind. Some other place to go. Your father was telling me the other night that—"

"Millie!" His father looked up from the armchair.

"Yes, what is it, Dick Morgan?"

"Leave the boy alone. If he doesn't feel like going to chapel — well, what's wrong with that? You don't go, I don't go. So what?"

Out of the house, Ieuan felt relaxed. He glanced at his reflection in a shop window at the street corner. His best suit fitted him well. Perfectly. He flicked a speck of fluff from his lapel, drew out his tie a little, and patted the corner of the white handkerchief he wore in his breast pocket.

Sally had not seen him in his best suit. She would be pleased to find him looking so tidy. Just as pleased as he would be to see her. He wondered if she would be dressed in the blue costume she had on that night when he met her. She looked pretty in it. The colour suited her complexion and her dark hair. Would she wear the blue ribbon in her hair?

He liked to see a girl with a ribbon in her hair. Maybe tonight Sally would wear a hat? It was Sunday, and girls never walked out on Sundays without a hat on their heads. Why shouldn't they? he thought. He fastened on to the problem, seeking anything to ease the nervousness he felt. But he had not found the answer as he climbed the steep hill from the High Street to Howard's Park.

It was almost seven o'clock when he came to the tall iron gateway leading into the park. The road near the entrance was thick with people who had just come out from the Presbyterian church nearby.

Members of the congregation stood in groups in the middle of the road and on the pavement, discussing the sermon, the weather and other topics with a genteel air so becoming to the Sabbath. The minister, surrounded by his deacons, held court a little distance away, and smiled benignly on the members of his flock who acknowledged him with a word or a hand raised.

The younger people had already dispersed, the girls pairing off and tripping along the pavement towards the hill and the High Street, the boys grouped some distance away from the chapel, smoking and chatting. Later, they strolled down the hill, or crossed to the park entrance, there to mingle with the many hundreds who had come to spend their Sunday evening in the open air.

Ieuan waited anxiously at the gate. The Town Hall clock chimed the hour. Seven o'clock! Would Sally come? He looked down the hill. There was no sign of her.

"Hallo, Ieuan!"

He turned quickly around, gladdened by the sound of her voice.

"Sally! I—I thought you'd forgotten."

"A promise is a promise," she reminded him. She smiled and his heart lifted.

"I'm so glad you turned up," he said. "And you're right on time, too." He returned her smile.

"Shall — shall we go round the park?" he suggested.

"All right, Ieuan. I'd love to. It's a lovely night for a walk."

He took her arm in his. They walked slowly side by side through the gateway.

"Do you like my new hat?"

Ieuan, momentarily taken off his balance, looked quickly into her face. She was dressed in the same blue costume and white silk blouse, but on her head she wore a small, tight-fitting blue hat.

"Why, I—I think it looks very nice," he said awkwardly. Then, anxious to please, he added: "I like your new handbag, too."

She held up the cheap leather handbag for his inspection.

"Oh, I've had this a long time, Ieuan. I bought it at the Bon Marche. It's a cheap little thing, really." She smiled, grateful for his compliment. "You look very smart tonight. A real dasher, Ieuan."

He was about to reply when an elderly couple passed by and smiled at him.

"Hallo, Ieuan! So you've started courting, eh?"

The remark made him blush. He cleared his throat, and quickly withdrew his arm.

"I—I'm sorry, Sally," he said later, as the old couple turned into the rose garden.

"Sorry about what, Ieuan?"

"I took my arm away ...."

She laughed. "I hadn't noticed it. Gee, you are shy."

The conversation suddenly ceased. A crescendo of drums and brass shattered the evening air. The Town Band, resplendent in their blue-and-red uniforms, had begun the usual Sunday night concert.

The young couple continued their leisurely walk.

"Doesn't seem like Sunday, does it?" Ieuan said presently in an effort to renew the conversation.

Sally smiled to herself. "It's nice to see people enjoying themselves," she said.

"Yes-yes, of course .... Oh, Sally, what's the matter with me? I'm acting like a kid." Ieuan took her arm again, firmly. "Come on, let's go and sit by the pond for a while."

They found a secluded corner near the lily pond at the extreme

221

end of the park, and sat down on the edge of the grass. The air was pungent with the smell of earth and the early spring flowers. The white blossom of cherry trees glistened in the sun. Nearby, the pollen from a yew tree hung like a transparent blue cloud in the air.

Ieuan breathed deeply. He glanced shyly at his companion. His arm stole around her waist. Nervously, he awaited her reaction. but she made no effort to dissuade him.

From the distance came a confused hum of voices. A girl's shrill laugh echoed above the blare of the brass band. Somewhere, a baby cried.

The park was as crowded as on a bank holiday. People of all ages swarmed round the bandstand. Some, with a complete disregard of the printed notices warning them to keep off the grass, sat on the lawn to listen to the music. Others leaned against the heavy bronze chains encircling the flower beds. The green-painted seats around the bandstand were all occupied.

It seemed as though a holiday feeling was in the air. Women in gay spring dresses, whose vivid colours emphasized the green of grass and trees, sat or reclined on the lawns, many with their shoes off. Others, clad in fashions that appeared to outrage the feelings of the elderly, sober-minded chapel people, sauntered along the paths bordering the park, showing off their freakish hats to the multitude, and silently enjoying the sensation they caused.

A dull thud of a rubber ball made Ieuan turn his head. Nearby, on the children's playing field, a group of young men chased after a tennis ball, kicking it with the precision of professional footballers. They pranced and posed, taking their game in all seriousness, as though the small audience that had gathered to watch them at their play had paid for the privilege.

In the farthest corner of the park, away from the clamour of the music and shrill-voiced children, sat the old men and women whose legs could carry them just to the park and back. They sat on the curved iron seats, the women with hands crossed over laps, the old men leaning forward on their sticks, watching in quiet meditation the colour and pageantry that moved before them.

"Ieuan!"

"Yes?" His face brushed her hair as he turned to speak to her. He felt a warm tingling in his blood.

"What made you go to work at Bevan's?"

His face clouded for a moment.

"Why do you ask that, Sally?"

She nipped a blade of grass and played with it between her fingers.

"Well ... I should think it's no place for you. You should have gone into something better — an office, or — "

"An office!" He smiled. "No, not that, Sally. But there are other things I would like to do. You don't think I relish being at the foundry?"

"Then why don't you leave it, Ieuan?"

"I intend to. I hate the foundry and everything to do with it."

"Then you — you have something else in mind?"

"Yes, Sally. I'm getting out from Bevan's as soon as I've had a chance to sit my exam — you bet I am. I'm not going to be a moulder for the rest of my life. Mam can do what she likes about it. I'm old enough now, anyway, and I've had eighteen months at the foundry — eighteen months too long."

Sally was silent for a while.

"Penny for your thoughts," Ieuan pressed her gently.

She laughed. "They're worth more than that, Ieuan."

"Then tell me, and I'll give you twopence."

She brushed the blade of grass from her lap.

"I was thinking what a waste of schooling it was to put a clever boy like you into a job where there's no chance of getting on. What made your mother do such a thing?"

"Oh, there's plenty of chances to get on in the foundry, Sally. One can become a charge-hand or a foreman," he teased.

"I don't mean that, Ieuan. It's—it's so wrong to have had a good education, and then to throw it away."

"But I'm not throwing it away, Sally. I tell you, I'll be out of the foundry before this year's gone — that is, if I'm lucky."

"Mr. Griffiths told me you were hoping to matriculate, and then trying to get a scholarship. You'll pass, Ieuan. I know you will. All the boys at the County used to talk about you, how clever you were."

He drew his arm away from her waist and supported himself on the grass.

"What about yourself, Sally? Seems to me that Mr. Griffiths had a lot to say about you. He was on to your mam and dad for taking you away from school, so you told me. And you were at the County, too."

"But I've got a nice job, Ieuan. I'm quite happy in it."

"Happy! In Simpson's the Dyers?"

"Yes. But then, I'm a girl. I won't always be working — that is, I hope I shan't be stuck behind a counter all my life."

"You want to marry a millionaire, eh?" He smiled. "Well, if you marry me, you won't have a—"

A spasm of coughing shook her. She held a handkerchief to her mouth.

"Sally!" Ieuan caught her hand. "Sally, why don't you see a doctor about that cough?" he implored. He rose and helped her to her feet. "And here we are, sitting on the grass," he said, alarmed. "It's daft, honestly it is. The ground is damp this time of year. I ought to have had more sense."

Her coughing continued and he waited anxiously until it ceased. He looked into her face.

"Do you feel better now?" he asked earnestly. "Shall I take you home?"

"No, no, don't let's go home yet. I'm all right, Ieuan."

"Sure?"

"Yes."

"Would you like to go for a little walk?"

"Yes, Ieuan."

They followed the path back to the middle of the park.

The bandsmen finished their piece, and sat down to wipe their perspiring faces. The audience clapped. Hands dipped into pockets as the collecting boxes were passed round.

Flushed, eager-eyed boys and girls ogled each other. Children, unable to remain quiet for more than a few minutes, chased noisily round the bandstand, heedless of harassed parents' warnings and remonstrances.

The bandsmen rose again. The strains of the National Anthem swelled out over the park, and slowly the people began to make their way towards the exits.

Dusk settled over the playing field, the bowling green and the wide lawns. A chill breeze stirred with a short, sweeping rhythm through the trees.

Ieuan shuddered slightly. Sally looked up.

"Cold?"

"Yes," he confessed. "Feel a bit chilly. I should have brought my coat with me." He paused. "Wonder what time it is?"

"Nearly nine, must be. The park closes at nine, I know."

They stood outside the gate. He felt reluctant to leave her.

"It's a bit too early to go home, what do you say, Sally?" he ventured. "Would you like to go somewhere else? That is, if you feel all right."

"I don't mind, Ieuan. But I must be in by ten."

"Then what about...." He hesitated. "Listen, Sally, would you care to go round Lovers' Lane for a walk? We shan't stay there," he added quickly.

"All right ... but remember, I mustn't be late."

The first turning on the right a hundred yards up the main road took them into Lovers' Lane, a narrow path flanked by tall hedges that wound for a mile or so into the countryside.

Darkness had fallen as they climbed slowly up the hill, arm in arm. From the shelter of the hedges came furtive whispers. Someone struck a match, and the narrow lane, suddenly illuminated, revealed young couples leaning against the hedges in rapturous embrace.

Embarrassed, Ieuan quickened his pace. The match died, and he sighed with relief as they walked in the darkness again. When they reached the top of the hill and began their slow walk homewards, Sally had another spasm of coughing.

Ieuan drew her into the side of the lane. They leaned against a broken gate leading into a field.

"You'll have to do something about that cough," he said worriedly. "Sally, it scares me — honestly. You must see a doctor."

She did not answer him. He sensed that something was wrong.

"Oh, Sally girl, please listen to me," he begged. "I don't mean to be fussy .... You sound ill. When I met you tonight I noticed how pale you were. Oh, why don't you go to the doctor?"

He put his arms around her. He wanted to protect her. She was his girl, his first girl, and nothing else in the world mattered. And he would protect her. And fight for her. He would be to her as Sir Lancelot was to Elaine, Sir Geraint to his Enid. As all the chivalrous knights of Arthur's court.

Oh, Sally, I love you, he thought. You are the only one I shall ever love. You are my girl, my sweetheart. I will do anything for you. Anything.

Then he felt abashed. Foolish. He was seventeen, and dared to think of love. A boy and a girl together in the darkness. Romance in a country lane.

But he did love her I What was this feeling for her that consumed him? He wanted to hold her tightly to him. To kiss her. To feel his body at one with hers. There was a throbbing in his veins. A hard rock in his throat. He wanted to cry. To laugh. And as he looked at her standing there before him a great wave of pity and love overwhelmed him.

"Sally!"

He embraced her with all his strength. He pressed her backwards against the gate. He felt her trembling under him.

"Ieuan!" she breathed. "Oh, Ieuan!"

A couple passed by. He heard a familiar voice, but he did not try to recall where he had heard it before. His thoughts were of Sally alone.

Her knees were tight against his. He could hear her heart beating. His hands caressed her young breasts. The thin silk fabric of her blouse clung to his fingers and crackled in the dark.

Her nipples hardened as his fingers lovingly stroked the warm flesh. Then a sudden intensity of passion seized him as her young body burned beneath his touch. He felt the blood rush maddeningly in a flood through his veins, and he trembled.

He pressed his mouth to hers in a long kiss that drained all strength from his body. She relaxed, limp in his arms, her head thrown back. He kissed her cheeks, her hair, her throat, and again his hands wandered over the silken roundness of her breasts.

He whispered her name, joyfully, then fiercely. Her legs opened wide. Suddenly she threw her arms around his waist and drew him wildly towards her. She pressed her body into his. Her fingers dug into his flesh. Their thighs mingled. She kissed him passionately, a long-drawn-out sigh from her lips passing through his whole body, making him shiver with ecstasy. And he held her tightly, pressing her to him with all the fervour he was capable of.

Then, with the sudden slamming of a gate in the distance, came an awareness, a realization of what they had done.

She drew herself away.

"Oh, Ieuan .... Please .... We mustn't."

She began to weep. He stood there, awkwardly, not knowing what to do or say. The tumult was over. He was troubled with a deep sense of guilt. What would she think of him? He had said he was decent — that he never ran after girls. But now this had happened, and he had done nothing to prevent it. He had wanted it to happen.

And yet he could not have resisted. She had awakened a part of him that had never been alive. He had wanted to be in one with her. To cling to her. Never, never to let her go.

And now retribution. He wanted to take her in his arms. To kiss her again, tenderly. To tell her he was sorry.

"Sally!"

She looked at him through her tears.

"I—I'm sorry, Ieuan," she sobbed, choking with emotion. "I didn't know what I was doing. This — this has never happened to me before."

"It's — it's all right, Sally," he whispered. He took her arm. "I'm the one that is to blame, and I'm sorry — terribly sorry."

He led her away from the gate. They walked down the hill in silence. "Please don't think I'm a rotter," he pleaded, tormented by his thoughts. His voice was low and restrained. "But I do ... love you, Sally."

She dried her tears. "I like you, too, Ieuan ... only I wish — I wish that hadn't happened. We shouldn't behave like — like married people. It's wrong, Ieuan — wrong."

"But, Sally, nothing's happened. Nothing that we should be ashamed of. We were — well, I was carried away. I promise you it'll never happen again — never."

He gripped her arm tightly.

"Sally, there will be another time? I mean — you'll promise to see me again?"

The anxiety in his tone was apparent to her. She clasped his hand.

"Ieuan ...."

"Yes, Sally?" he asked, breathless.

"I—I'm very fond of you," she said softly.

A sinking feeling came over him.

"Fond of me! Is — is that all?"

She lowered her eyes. He sensed her confusion.

"Well, I ..." she began.

"Yes, Sally, go on. Say it!"

"I—I love you, Ieuan."

"Oh, Sally." He kissed her fondly. She nestled once more in his arms, and they stood there in silence.

A ship's siren sounded out in the bay, and then, like an answering echo, came the low, plaintive hoot of the harbour pilot's tug. The

Town Hall clock struck, its chimes reverberating loudly over and beyond the houses, the factories, and the silent countryside.

Sally started. She broke away from their embrace.

"Ieuan ...it's late!"

He smiled, and reassured her. Time — what did it matter? He was in love. She loved him. She had said so. Nothing mattered, nothing but the moment of living. Now, this very moment when life had given him the greatest joy. Her words had made him happy, delirious. He was light as air, free as the birds that nestled in the trees above him.

"It's late. We must hurry, Ieuan."

"Late! How late?" he asked, abstractedly. She drew him back to earth with an anxious: "It's after eleven ... and we've got half an hour's walk yet. Oh, please let's hurry, Ieuan. I don't know what mam will say ...."

* * *

The High Street was deserted save for a solitary policeman who strode slowly from shop to shop, flashing his torch into the darkened doorways.

Breathless with anxiety, Sally hurried through the side streets. Ieuan kept pace with her, trusting hard that she would not be upbraided too harshly for her homecoming at such a late hour.

Abermor was Nonconformist in the extreme. The people in the main were narrow-minded and sectarian in their attitude. A girl of seventeen out after half past ten at night was looked upon as loose and immoral. And if it were known that she had been in company with a boy in Lovers' Lane at that hour, she would be doomed to suffer a torrent of abuse from her more severe elders.

Ieuan and Sally paused in the shadows at the end of Crooked Row. They glanced furtively up the street. Midway stood a tall woman, her head thrust out from a doorway. She took a quick survey up and down the street, then withdrew.

229

"It's mam," Sally whispered nervously. She bit her lip. "Oh, Ieuan, I must go."

"When — when shall I see you again?" he asked urgently.

"Tuesday, if you like. Same time. Good night, Ieuan."

He squeezed her hand. "Good night, Sally. I—I hope you won't have a row."

He watched her hurry up the street. Suddenly he remembered. "Sally!"

She half-turned, apprehensive.

"Where?" he whispered. "Where shall I see you?"

The woman's head appeared in the doorway again.

Sally called softly. "Near the park — same place." Then she ran towards the house.

Ieuan saw the woman step out of the doorway to let her pass. He heard her sharp reprimand. The door slammed, and there was silence.

* * *

"Where have you been, Ieuan?

His father was half-undressed and ready for bed when he entered the kitchen. He appeared anxious and worn.

"A fine time we've had here, wondering what had become of you. D'you know what time it is? Nearly twelve!"

"I'm sorry, Dad."

The door in the passageway opened, and his mother appeared, clad in a nightdress, a shawl over her shoulders. She frowned at him.

"I heard you come in," she said sharply. "A fine time for a young boy to be out, and on a Sunday night, too! What the neighbours will think, I don't know."

She drew the shawl about her. "Your father's been on the doorstep since half past ten. Worried stiff, we've been, thinking you'd had an accident or something. Asked Jamesie Harries if he'd seen you. But nobody round here seems to know where you'd hopped it to. And your father had to leave the front door open for you. Where've you been?"

Ieuan sat down on the sofa. He began to unlace his boots.

"I asked you where've you been," his mother insisted.

He took no notice of her.

"Your mother asked you a question, Ieuan," his father said.

He looked up. "I've been ... well, I've just been out, that's all.''

"Out! That's pretty obvious, isn't it? But where, boy? That's what your mother wants to know."

"Yes, where?" his mother demanded. "'Out' is no answer to my question."

"If you want to know, Mam, I've been to the park."

"The park closes at nine," she reminded him.

He flung his boots under the sofa.

"Now then, there's no need to go off in a huff! After all, we've got a right to know where you've been. Who were you with?"

"No one. I—I just went for a walk on my own."

"H'm! A fine cock-and-bull story! On your own, indeed. I'll soon find out if you were by yourself. If you was up the park, then there's plenty of people must ha' seen you there. I'll find out. Oh, yes."

"All right, Mam. Find out if you like. I'm tired."

"Indeed you are. And so am I — not to mention your father."

"Millie, please ...." His father motioned her back to the bedroom. "The boy's been out for a walk. Leave it at that. He's home now, that's all that matters. Come on, let's go to bed."

He ruffled Ieuan's hair. "Good night, boy. Don't be too long. You've got to get up early tomorrow."

"Good night, Dad."

He stood up and faced his mother.

"I'm sorry, Mam. I didn't mean to keep you up. I'd have come home earlier if I'd known."

His father smiled. "We'll have to buy you a watch, Ieuan. Time you had one, especially—"

"That's enough, Dick." Mrs. Morgan ushered him before her.

231

Over her shoulder she called: "Your supper's in the oven. Don't blame me if it's cold."

* * *

Disquiet settled on Ieuan that night. His mother's attitude angered him. Why should she still persist in treating him as though he were a child? Her threat to find out whom he had been with was spiteful and petty. He was seventeen, and old enough to take care of himself. Did she have the right to decide what company he should keep?

Sally was a good girl. She was not to be compared with the rowdy, strident-voiced girls who habitually paraded the main streets in their flashy clothes and tawdry jewellery.

She was quiet, refined. Would he have chosen anyone less gentle than she?

What if mam did discover that he had been with her at the park? What if someone told her they had been seen together in the lane? He would tell her truthfully and without fear that he liked Sally. Yes — and that he intended keeping company with her. What right had mam to interfere, anyway? He was not a little boy any more.

Steeped in this mood he met Frank on the way in to the foundry.

"Morning, Ieuan!" came Frank's cheerful greeting. "Where've you been keeping lately?"

Ieuan sank his hands into his pockets.

"Hallo, Frank."

"Hey, hey-come on, snap out of it, boy. Down in the dumps, I see. What's up?"

"It's nothing, Frank. Nothing to worry about."

"Seems to me you've got plenty on your mind, Ieuan. Listen, boy, when are you coming over to see us? Doris is still waiting for you to call, you know."

"I'll drop in some night, Frank. Honest I will. I'm sorry to let you and Mrs. Jones down after promising to call."

232

Frank grinned. "Cheer up, Ieuan. You sound as if you've got the weight of the whole world on your shoulders. Look up — look at the sun shining. It's a grand day, a beautiful day." He spread out his arms and breathed deeply. "Just the day for a lazy lie on the sands, or a nice quiet picnic in Dinas Wood."

His words failed to raise even a smile from Ieuan. After they had walked past the pattern shop, he stopped.

"What's on your mind, Ieuan?" he asked, frowning. "Are your studies getting you down? Overdoing it, I suppose? I warned you about that, remember? You should slow down a bit. Go out more, especially now that the fine weather is with us."

"I took your advice, Frank. I have been out."

"So it's something else that's biting you, eh? No — no trouble at home, is there?"

Ieuan shook his head. He regarded Frank earnestly.

"I'll tell you what it is, Frank. I — I've met a girl. And I'm very fond of her."

"Good! That's good! Well, I shouldn't worry if I were you. It's time you made company with someone. I bet she got you away from your books all right, and that's just what you need for a while."

"That's just the trouble, Frank. I can't think of anything else but her. My studies …I don't seem to be attracted to them any more. And the exam — well, I'm not so enthusiastic."

Frank looked at him quizzically.

"How long have you known your — your girl?" he asked with a smile.

"Only a few days."

"A few days! Ieuan, my boy, you've been bitten hard. Calf love's what we call this stage in your development. Oh, come now, don't look hurt. I didn't mean to poke fun at you. Hell, I had it just as bad as you. When I first met Doris I was a kid of fifteen — that makes my sickness two years older than yours. As for your studies — you just can't give them up now, Ieuan. Not after the effort you've made. Take things easy for a while, and

233

you'll settle back smoothly into the old routine. Take your girl out walking. Enjoy yourself. But don't let your pleasure ruin everything you've set out to do ...Ieuan!"

"Yes?"

"I bet she's a nice little girl."

"She's fine, Frank."

"Then stick to her."

Cheered by Frank's kind words, Ieuan tried to absorb himself in the work that awaited him on the bench. But thoughts of Sally and his mother's reaction when she found out about their association still returned to trouble him, and he maintained a deep silence from the moment he took his place at the bench.

Thomas shrugged when Abraham queried: "What's got into him today?" Ieuan's silence irritated the chargehand.

He was in a bitter mood. Lu had approached him earlier in the morning and warned him that a rush order for some casting had come in. The extra cores would have to be made that day. He reminded Abraham that he would tolerate no delay. The castings were needed urgently.

"'Work on till seven tonight' — that's Lu's orders," he grumbled to Isaiah. "Ought to give me plenty of time to get ten big cores ready, he says. What's he think I am — a machine?"

His displeasure increased when he discovered that Bull had clocked in after half past seven, which meant that the apprentice would not be allowed to do any work until nine. The thought that Bull might now be sleeping in some corner of the foundry incensed him, yet he knew he could do nothing about it.

But Abraham was mistaken. Bull was very much awake. Taking advantage of his hour's freedom, he strode into the coreshop just after eight o'clock and immediately approached Ieuan. He tapped him on the shoulder.

"Iron, I got something to say to you."

Abraham watched him closely.

"Any trouble from you," he warned, "and I'll have Lu to say a word or two. We got ten extra cores to make today. If you've anything to say to Ieuan tell it to him breakfast time."

Bull gave him an angry look. "Who's talking to you? I'm my own boss now. You nor Lu nor nobody else can tell me what to do, so dry up!"

He tapped Ieuan again on the shoulder.

"Iron — you heard me. I got something to say to you."

Ieuan ignored the remark, and continued with his work.

"O.K., if that's how you feel. But I got something to say about a certain chap — I could spit on him, he's not so far away — and a certain jane...mooning in Lovers' Lane last night..."

A trowel clattered to the floor. Ieuan's lips quivered. He spun round to face Bull.

"What's on your mind?" he shouted.

"O.K., O.K., Iron — take it easy." Bull smirked. He turned to Thomas. "I said I saw a certain chap and a jane mooning in Lovers' Lane last night. Want to know all about it?"

CHAPTER TEN

THERE was an awkward silence. Then Thomas spoke.

"Aw, get out an' chase yourself. I've got no time to listen — I'm busy."

"That's right." Abraham scowled at the cocksure Bull. "Go out the yard or somewhere, not come in here disturbing everyone. Far better if you was to get up earlier in the mornings and try to help me out when there's extra work to do. Go on, clear off. I'll see you at nine, and give you plenty to occupy your time for the rest of the day. And you'll be here till seven tonight, let me tell you."

"If you don't want to listen," Bull continued, addressing Thomas, "maybe the chaps in the foundry would like to have a earful?"

"Oh, no you don't." Ieuan caught him by the wrist. "What have you got to say about—"

"Sally." Bull grinned. "That's her name. I heard the chappie call her ... and, by Christ, was she hot! You ought t'have been there, Tommy. Why, she—"

"You — you bloody swine!" Ieuan aimed wildly at Bull's face, but his blow fell harmlessly as the apprentice side-stepped.

Abraham rushed between them, waving his arms. "Now then, what's the idea," he shouted. "Stop it — stop it! Where d'you think you are — in a fairground? Ieuan, back to your work. You, Jackson," he jerked a thumb towards the door, "get out while you're still in one piece. Clear off, before I do something I'll be sorry for."

Ieuan stood by, his face a deathly white.

"Sally! Oh, my Sally!" Bull mimicked. He puckered his lips and embraced an imaginary girl. "I saw you, Iron — and hell, could she take it!"

236

"Shut up!" Abraham bawled. He drew a hand back over his shoulder. "Shut your mouth, or I'll flatten you."

Bull gave a leering smile.

"Didn't know Iron was a skirt-chaser," he taunted. "Always thought he was a little virgin."

Ieuan made a rush at him, but Abraham intervened again. The charge-hand appealed to Thomas and Isaiah to help him, but they made no attempt to interfere.

Then Bull laughed. In that moment Ieuan felt the blood rush in a flood to the region of his heart. His legs trembled, every muscle in his body twitched. His speech became confused. Without being conscious of it, he began to shout at his tormentor, loudly, hysterically.

He wanted to reach out and grip him by the throat. To plunge his fingers deep into his flesh. Bull's inane grinning goaded him into maddening fury. His fists closed. He felt his nails digging into his palms. He swung back his right arm.

With a loud, frenzied cry, he hurled himself at the apprentice, and before the other had a chance to defend himself, he hit him savagely in the eye.

Bull staggered backwards, his hand clapped over the injured eye. He stumbled against an iron core box and hurt his thigh.

Abraham tried to stop the fight. Ieuan pushed him forcibly aside, and threw himself again at Bull. He was insane with fury. He swung back his arm and hit him with all his strength in the other eye.

Bull began to yell. He was completely blinded.

"Stop him! For Christ's sake, stop him!" he shouted at the top of his voice. He groped along an iron shelf behind him. His fingers closed over a heavy core.

Ieuan anticipated the move. He raised his foot and kicked him hard on the wrist. The core shattered in fragments to the floor.

Bull screamed with pain. He began to whimper. But Ieuan knew no mercy. He pummelled him with both fists, raining blow after blow on his face and arms.

Bull's cries brought a crowd racing in from the steel shop. They stood by to watch the fight, while Abraham, distracted by the uproar, tried vainly to persuade one of them to interfere.

Bull crouched against the iron shelf. He covered his face with both hands, but there was no relief from the wild attack. Ieuan struck him again and again. The bully's face was streaked with blood and tears. He cried like a child, imploring to be spared from the savage onslaught.

No one stepped forward to help him. Reg and Charlie once made a half-hearted attempt to step in, but Ieuan swung round on them, his eyes blazing. He gripped a heavy iron rammer.

"Keep back!" he shouted. "Keep back, or I'll brain you!"

His whole body trembled violently. He jumped at Bull and grasped him by the collar.

"Say you're sorry!" he shouted. "Sorry! D'you hear me ...you dirty-minded ... blackguard."

Bull stumbled blindly through the crowd. He groped for the water bosh and thrust his bloody face into it. Sobbing loudly, his head buried in his arms, he lumbered into the compo shed.

Ieuan waited until he had disappeared. Still trembling, he turned to face the crowd. No one spoke a word. There was a heavy silence. Then Abraham slid open the stove door.

"A fine how-de-do," he mumbled. "A fight first thing in the morning. Haven't I got enough to worry about already, without this — this quarrelling and fighting? That Bull Jackson deserves a packet. He's asked for it plenty, and now he's had it."

He beckoned the crowd to move away. He looked at Ieuan.

"Better go wash your hands," he said.

Ieuan stepped across to the wall and took his coat off the nail. His anger was gone. He felt sorry for what had happened. Sorry for Bull. The blood seemed to flow easier through his veins. But within him burned the same desperate, savage hatred of the foundry.

He drew the coat over his shoulders and made towards the

coreshop door. Abraham threw him a wondering look, but he had no need to question him.

"I'm going home," he said wearily.

* * *

The timekeeper regarded him with the same puzzled look as he punched his number on the way out.

"Ill?" the old man queried.

The clock bell rang, and that was his only answer.

"What's eating him?" the timekeeper grunted as he turned again to his ledgers. "Young folk today got no manners — not the same as when I was a boy."

The works' hooters blew for the first break in the day when Ieuan turned the corner into Pleasant Row. At the top of the street he saw a woman kneeling on the pavement, a bucket of water beside her. She was his mother. He began to feel apprehensive of meeting her. Not that he was afraid of her anger, but the constant anticipation of her senseless nagging when he was in her presence made him tremble inwardly.

What would she have to say when he told her of the fight, and of his clocking out before half past eight in the morning? he thought. There would be another rumpus, an undignified and needless bout of anger. Was there no end to it?

She looked up from her scrubbing of the doorstep when he drew near. She wrung the damp cloth in her hands. The dirty water streamed into the bucket.

Her mouth opened with surprise.

"W—what's wrong?" she gasped. She rose clumsily and wiped her hands on her apron. "Are you — are you feeling sick or something?"

"No," he replied, nervously.

"Then what's the matter? Why are you home so early?"

"Nothing ... I just don't feel like working today, that's all."

"You don't feel like working? Nonsense! Everybody's got to

239

work, whether they feel like it or not... What if I started to think that I—" She stopped. Her eyes fell on his hands. His knuckles were bruised and swollen. Pieces of skin were broken and the blood showed through.

"You're in trouble, Ieuan." She eyed him suspiciously. "Have you been fighting?"

"Yes," He admitted.

"Huh! And a fine mess you've got yourself into, I can see. Fighting, indeed — and me thinking you were ill." She glanced quickly up and down the street. "Go into the house," she said sharply. "I don't want the neighbours to be poking their noses into my business. If they see you in that state, there'll be plenty of questions asked. And I got no time for nosey parkers."

He passed over the scrubbed doorstep and polished brass rod. She followed him into the passageway, her canvas slippers flapping loosely on the bare linoleum.

"Well, and what is it all about?" she demanded as they reached the kitchen.

Ieuan sat down near the fireplace. He nursed his swollen hands.

"I had a fight with Bull Jackson."

"And over what, may I ask?"

"Nothing, Mam — nothing that would interest you."

She waited a moment, then put the kettle on the stove. "You weren't fighting over some girl, were you?"

The question caught him completely off guard. He tried to stammer a reply, but she cut him short.

"I've got eyes in my head," she said, "and I think I can see farther than people give me credit for. You have been fighting over a girl, haven't you? That girl you had with you in the park the other night."

"Girl! I—I .... " Ieuan rose and stepped awkwardly to the sink. He turned on the tap.

"Don't try and push any more of your lies on to me," his mother's voice rasped. "I told you I'd got ways of finding out things. You were with a girl, and don't deny it."

He refused to answer.

"I said you had a girl with you on Sunday night — isn't that true? Or would you like to call old Mr. and Mrs. Nathaniel a couple of liars, eh? They saw you — oh, yes. Arm in arm with her, like as if you were a grown-up man and woman. Now, come on. Stop your nonsense, and turn off that tap. Who is she?"

Ieuan sank into a chair. "She's a nice girl, Mam," he began. "She's decent, and—"

"I asked you who she is. What's her name? Where's she from?"

"Marvin, Sally Marvin, that's her name," he replied, hesitantly. "She lives in Crooked Row ... but she's a good girl, Mam."

His mother silenced him with a quick, angry look.

"Marvin! Never heard of that name. Is she one of those English people from up the north? One of them Lancashire families that came to work in the tinstamping?"

"No, Mam, she's Welsh, just like me."

"H'm! Funny name for a Welsh girl. She can't be up to much."

Ieuan jumped up. "Mam!" he cried angrily. "You've got no right to say such a thing."

"If she lives in Crooked Row, that's enough for me," she challenged. "A fine place to live in. Full of drunken sots. Children running all over the place like as if they was rabbits. What decent family lives there, tell me? Why, there's not a house that has a decent bit o' furniture in it. Too poor to buy even a piano."

"Poor! Can people help if they're poor?" Ieuan said, roused by her taunts. "Are we millionaires, that you can talk like that about other people who are no worse off than we are? And Sally comes from a respectable family. She's decent and clean, I tell you. Decent — d'you hear?"

"Now then!" His mother's voice rose to a shriek. "Don't you dare shout at me, you young bully! You're not in the foundry, and I won't stand for it.... Oh! Oh!" She clutched her apron and held it to her face. "A fine way for a boy to talk to his mother," she wept. "Here am I, working and slaving day in, day out, to

241

bring you up decent and respectable, and you answer me back, and shout at me like — like..."

Ieuan sighed. He clenched his teeth.

"I'm not shouting at you, Mam," he said, striving to control the flood of temper that seethed inside him. "I've told you the truth — I was with a girl. I've told you her name, where she lives... and I've told you she's good, clean and decent. What more can I say? D'you think I'd want to make friends with those girls who parade town every night? If I picked up one of them you'd have something to say. I'll be eighteen this year, and surely I can walk out with a girl if I want to. I'm not a baby any more, Mam, and you — you're making a fuss over nothing."

"Oh-h! Listen to him — listen to him," his mother wept. "There's ungratitude for you .... Oh! Oh!" She rocked her body sideways and sobbed loudly into the folds of her apron.

Ieuan held her arms. "Mam, listen to me," he pleaded. "I don't want to speak like this to you, but you were wrong — wrong about everything. If you want me to go back to the foundry today, I'll go. But please, please don't say any more about ... Sally. I like her, Mam. She's a fine girl, and ...."

He dropped his hands. Her sobbing suddenly ceased. Without saying another word, he turned and walked out of the house.

* * *

Sally's name was not mentioned in the house again, not in his hearing, but Ieuan sensed that his father had been told. He still met her in the week and on Sunday nights, and their companionship and love ripened with every meeting.

The fight in the foundry had reached Lu's ears, and the foreman promptly arranged to transfer Bull into the steel shop to work with the improvers. Abraham was warned to stop him entering the coreshop unless it was on urgent business. But the animosity between Bull and Ieuan grew. The other improvers supported Bull, and treated Ieuan with contempt. They kept out of his way as much as possible, but never failed to cast some sneering remark at him whenever occasion drew them together in the course of their work.

The summer months slipped by. It was September, when, one Saturday afternoon, Sally and Ieuan arranged to go on a picnic in Dinas Wood. They walked arm in arm along a deep-rutted lane leading from the main path into the depth of the woods, Ieuan carrying a cloth-covered basket to which they had contributed their portion of food and drink.

For the past months, ever since he met Sally, he had neglected his studies. He could not concentrate. He did not wish to. Everything was excluded from his mind. He had no thoughts for anyone or anything save her. His studies would come later. There was plenty of time. He was young. There was no necessity for him to matriculate. There were many other opportunities open to him. He would take a course at Harlech. Or inquire about a scholarship to Ruskin.

Plenty of time. He was happy with Sally. And happiness was such a rare joy. Let his books and studies wait.

His attitude, this sudden show of disinterest in the ambition that had fired him, troubled Frank a great deal. He had spoken to Ieuan concerning it one night, when, after a prolonged absence, he called at the house in Prospect Place.

"You'd be a fool to give up, now," he said with conviction. "Think of the chances you are throwing away. Why, many a young chap would give his right hand to be in your shoes. Don't be rash, Ieuan. You've got brains, so use them! Do I have to tell you all over again of the mistake I made when I was your age? I thought you wanted to be a writer. By God, Ieuan, sometimes I feel I could kick you — honest, I do. How can you expect to get anywhere if you're not prepared to sacrifice? Stay in the foundry for the rest of your life, like me — and then you'll curse yourself for not making the most of your opportunities when you had the chance."

Frank had spoken vehemently, and he had been angered by Ieuan's excuses. And now, Sally was equally alarmed.

They walked up the path until they came to an open glade. It was a clear, bright day. A day when the sky seemed so close to the earth that Ieuan felt he could reach up and touch it with his fingertips.

The air was fresh and sweet. Near by a small stream trickled musically into a brown pool. Pink stone islands from which green reeds sprouted, peered above the water.

"Shall we sit here, Ieuan?"

Sally took the basket and sat down to prepare the picnic. Ieuan lay on his back and shaded his eyes from the strong rays of sunshine that pierced the tree tops. He listened to the stream as it sang on its way into the pool.

He was happy. Happy as the sun glittering on the waters of the stream like the laughter of a child.

Then Sally spoke.

"Ieuan — I'm worried over you."

He raised his head and laughed.

"Worried! Go on with you." He pushed her playfully. "Get the dinner ready, girl. I'm as hungry as a wolf."

"I'm serious, Ieuan." She leaned over him and stroked his hair. Her eyes clouded. "And somebody ought to tell you ...."

"Tell me what, girl?" He caught her hand. "Sally," he said, "you are like Olwen." He pressed a finger to her lips. "Do you want to hear about her?"

"No," she answered, brushing his finger away. "I want to speak to you."

"She was the fairest lady in the Mabinogion," he went on. He closed his eyes and lay back on the grass. "'The maiden was clothed in a robe of flame-coloured silk, and about her neck was a collar of ruddy gold, on which were precious emeralds and rubies. More yellow was her head than the flower of the broom, and her skin was whiter than the foam of the wave, and fairer were her hands and fingers than the blossoms of the wood anemone amidst the spray of the meadow fountain. The eye of the trained hawk, the glance of the three-mewed falcon was not

244

brighter than hers. Her bosom was more snowy than the breast of the white swan, her cheek was redder than the reddest roses. Who so beheld her was filled with her love. Four white trefoils sprung up wherever she trod. And therefore was she called Olwen...'"

He sighed deeply and opened his eyes.

"Now, do you believe me, Sally?"

She smiled. "Nonsense, Ieuan. To begin with, my hair is dark."

" 'More yellow was her head than the flower of the broom ... .'"

" ... And I'm no beauty. You — you're just making fun of me."

"No — oh no, Sally. No," he said quickly. He sat up. "You are just as beautiful ... to me you are the most beautiful girl in the world."

He put his arm about her and drew her to him. "And now, after paying you such a compliment, are you going to worry any more? Another thing — one day we'll be married, then you'll have cause to worry. Especially when you find me locked up in a room night after night, scribbling away by candlelight. Turning out books, and selling them just as fast as I write them."

"That's just what I want to talk to you about, Ieuan," Sally said. She arranged the food on the outspread cloth.

"Oh, come on, Sally girl — I was only teasing you."

"But I am serious," she maintained. "It's your studies, Ieuan. You've done nothing about them ever since we met. Why have you daunted so soon?" she asked, sadly.

He rested his head on her shoulder. A shaft of sunlight fell on his face and made him frown. He shielded his eyes. "I've not given anything up, Sally," he said. "There's plenty of time yet. You can't expect me to have my head stuck in books when I've got you, and ..." he swept his arm around him, "and this lovely weather. Next winter I'll work really hard, I promise you."

"You were going to sit your exam this summer," she reminded him with a hint of reproach in her voice, "and now summer's gone. It's too late."

"Never too late for me, Sally," he said flippantly.

She lowered her head.

"I'm sorry, I didn't mean that," he smiled, turning her face to his. "Next winter — it's a promise. I'll study like an old professor, and then by the end of next year I'll be out of the foundry for good. See?"

No reply came.

"Oh, Sally, listen to me," he pleaded. "I've told you the truth. You wouldn't like me to stop meeting you, so that I could spend my time in the parlour with my books?"

"If I knew I was interfering with your work, Ieuan, I wouldn't see you again," she whispered. "You've got brains. Oh, why don't you use them?"

He paused. Her words brought Frank back to his mind. He had used the very same phrase. But why — why let the thought distress him? He had time enough in which to accomplish his task. There were months ahead of him yet. The winter frosts and snow would keep him in at nights. There would be no incentive to go out, except when he had Sally's company to look forward to.

He pushed the thought aside, and made himself comfortable on his knees before the impromptu table. But Sally persisted in her efforts to make him listen to her reasoning. He refused to accept her words.

Some other time, perhaps? he suggested. When the sun wasn't shining. When there were no blue skies, no picnic in the woods, no silver stream and brown pool. Some other time, but not now. This day was theirs. Let them make the most of it.

She gave in with a sigh.

"All right, Ieuan, but I won't give you any peace after today, not until you—"

His kiss prevented her saying more.

* * *

The long walk home along the country lanes was exhausting, and as they came to the outskirts of the town Sally suddenly drew up at the roadside.

She began to cough. A violent retching seized her, and she grew pale and distraught.

"Oh, Ieuan," she cried, clutching his arm in fear.

He looked at her wildly.

"Sally! Sally — what's wrong?"

She leaned back against the hedge.

"I'm ill, Ieuan," she breathed. "I — I feel faint."

He stroked her forehead. It felt cold and clammy.

Beads of perspiration glistened on her cheeks and temples.

"I'll get you a glass of water," he said urgently. He ran to a nearby house and hammered on the door. The woman of the house answered him. She came presently with a glass of water.

"Come into the house for a while, my girl," she said kindly, "and have a little rest." She took Sally's arm. "Perhaps it would be best to send for a doctor?" she suggested.

"No — no thanks," Sally whispered. She smiled feebly. "I — I'm all right, now. Indeed, I am — thank you."

"Are you sure, my girl?"

"Yes, quite sure. I — I think it would be better if I went home."

Ieuan, torn with anxiety, helped her along the road a little way. A passing bus stopped to his signal, and they boarded it together.

"Sally," he breathed as they rode homewards. "You must see the doctor. You've got to, d'you understand?

She nodded. "All right, Ieuan — I'll go."

"Good!" He squeezed her hand affectionately. "And to make sure, I'll come with you … tonight."

* * *

When they got to the surgery that night they just managed to find two vacant places. The cold, bare room was filled to capacity. The patients sat on the hard wooden benches lined against the walls, the latecomers stepping in timidly as if they were entering some sacred precinct. A red-haired lady dispenser, a tyrant in tweed skirts, woollen stockings and heavy brogues, handed out the record cards from her files with an air of complete indifference and boredom.

Ieuan looked around. A few well-thumbed, illustrated magazines lay in a tumbled pile on a table. An elaborate marble grate stood in the far corner near the dispensary, but although the night was raw and chilly, no fire burned.

Some of the patients sat staring at a rectangular glass case high on the wall, in which five red discs had been fixed, each bearing a doctor's name. Others played nervously with their record cards, glancing surreptitiously at the clinical notes and diagnoses.

All at once a bell would ring, a disc quiver — and the doctor was ready for his next patient. Sometimes, two or more bells would ring simultaneously, and a whispered quarrel would ensue when one patient challenged the other for priority.

"Excuse me, I'm before you."

"Oh, no you're not."

"Oh, yes I am. I've been here since half past five." An appeal to the seated audience: "Aren't I first?"

Then the dispenser would thrust her beaked nose beyond the portals of her sanctum and freeze the offenders into silence with a piercing glare.

"What she wants is a man to chase her into bed at night," Ieuan heard one old man mutter toothlessly to his neighbour. Both glared balefully at the lady dispenser.

The old man's neighbour, senile and rheumy-eyed, shuddered.

"Might as well go to bed with a frozen lump o' meat," he mumbled. "Though there's a lot to be thankful for the dark, mind you ... if you know what I mean?"

A worried-looking mother with a child wrapped in a thick Welsh shawl complained to the woman next to her.

"If you get a stomach operation they'll take out your appendix same time, to save trouble later on. That's gospel for you .... No matter if your appendix is happy as Punch."

248

A young man, his face lined with pain, sat near Ieuan. An acquaintance nodded to him from the other side of the room, then stepped across to speak to him.

"How do you feel tonight, Jack?"

"Rotten, Bill ... rotten." The young man tapped his chest. "The other day I coughed up some blood. Doctor James said 'chronic bronchitis.' ... Gave me some medicine.... All right for a couple of months. Then same thing happened again .... Came back here, but Doctor James was away .... His assistant, an Austrian chap ... very clever boy, too.... Said he could give me more medicine ... but he wants to give me a good overhaul... Sounds like an X-ray ...."

Time dragged by. The bells rang shrilly, and the procession of patients dwindled. Then Sally's turn came.

She smiled nervously. "I—I hope it's nothing serious, Ieuan."

"Don't be silly," he tried to joke. "A bottle of medicine and you'll be right as rain in no time."

He waited anxiously. The woman with the baby in the shawl was engaged in bitter argument with the dispenser.

"You must bring your own bottle," the dispenser reprimanded. "The notice says so, plainly."

The woman was almost in tears. "But I didn't know, Miss Barratt," she pleaded. "I—I'll pay you for it."

"I'm sorry ... but rules are rules," the dispenser insisted. "Besides, I have no bottles to spare. You'd better come back tomorrow morning." With that, she slammed the door, and the woman tearfully made her way out from the surgery.

Ieuan revolted inwardly. How dare they treat patients in this manner, he thought. Like so many cattle. Poor patients in search of comfort, solace, and ease from pain. Did they deserve anger and derision? To be treated with contempt?

"Bring your own Bottle" ... "No Smoking" ... "Please refrain from Talking Loudly."

Why not more notices? "Please do not Laugh". "Please do not Smile" ..."Please do not Cough". "Please do not BREATHE."

249

What kind of a place was this so-called sanctuary for the sick in mind and body? A cold, bare room where the living dead sat and waited as they would wait for the resurrection morn, their life record cards in their hands. And the dispenser in her trim white smock. Fierce-eyed, ungraceful of manner and carriage. Her white smock, symbol of authority. "Give a man a uniform, and he ceases to be a man."

The surgery slowly emptied. It seemed an interminable time before Sally appeared.

On the roadway he asked her: "Well, what's the verdict?"

She showed him two slips of paper.

"Prescription," she said, "and a medical certificate." Ieuan took the certificate.

"But what did he tell you?"

"My lungs are affected," she said. "I must take things easy. He told me to rest in bed for a while. But it's not serious, Ieuan, and I'm glad."

"I see." Ieuan's face was strained. He glanced at the certificate. "Chronic bronchitis," he read, and then he remembered the pale young man who had sat next to him.

The young man suffered the same complaint. He needed a thorough overhaul, so the doctor had told him. He would be X-rayed. But why the X-ray, if the doctor had already diagnosed chronic bronchitis? The disease was of a more serious nature ... Tuberculosis perhaps? Did Sally have tuberculosis? He dared not think of it.

But her constant bouts of coughing, her deathly pallor.

Were these not symptoms of the dread disease? Fear gripped him. He saw in his mind's eye, the drab, barren lane where she lived. The cheerless houses. And then he recalled her words: "I've always had a cough, ever since I can remember. Maybe it's the house, mam is always complaining about the dampness."

No, it couldn't be true, he thought. The doctor would have told her. If he had held the slightest suspicion of tuberculosis he would have sent her to the clinic. Yes, of course he would. Of course.

But the young man in the surgery?

"Ieuan! What are you doing?"

He pulled himself together.

"Look," Sally pointed to the slip of paper she had given him. It was screwed into a tiny ball.

He laughed nervously. "Crikey! Your certificate — I'd forgotten all about it." He unfolded it and handed it back.

"What's the matter, Ieuan?" she asked. "You've gone quite pale."

"Matter! Why, nothing," he answered, leading her towards the High Street.

"But you're white as a sheet!"

He laughed it off. "Just wanted a little fresh air, I suppose. It was very stuffy in there just now, wasn't it?"

"I thought it was very cold."

He paused.

"Sally — did the doctor examine you?" he queried.

"Why, yes."

"And how long did he say you were to stay in bed?"

She looked at him, perplexed. "He didn't say exactly how long, but just that I should rest for a while."

"And he didn't mention anything about ... well, I mean did he advise you not to go out at all?"

"No .... But why do you ask me all these questions, Ieuan?"

"You'll have to take his advice, Sally, and rest. Maybe I shan't be able to see you for some time."

"Of course you will, Ieuan. I'll be better soon."

"Yes, you must get better, Sally. But gee! I'll miss you."

"Not if you come and see me," she said, as they crossed into the crowded High Street.

Ieuan did not know what to say for the moment. He glanced appealingly at her. "But your mam and dad, Sally — I've never met them."

She smiled. "All right, if you're nervous, I'll come and see you. We'll meet at the park as we always do."

251

"Oh no," he said firmly. "Not until you're better."

"And some night I'll take you home to supper," she went on. "You ought to meet mam and dad now. We've been going together for a long time, and I've told them about you. But don't be nervous over it. Some day very soon you'll be chatting away to them as if you've known them all your life." She touched his arm lightly.

"I—I'm so happy to have known you, Ieuan."

"So am I," he said earnestly. "Some day we'll get married, Sally. Just you wait till I get going, there'll be no stopping me."

"I'll wait, Ieuan, no matter how long .... You're so good and kind to me. There's no one else I'd ever marry. "I'm so happy with you, and I know we'll always be happy. Always."

Her words kept recurring in his mind as he walked home that night. In the brief hours he had shared her companionship he had known much happiness. And he would know more. Sally would get well. She must get well. Yes, happiness was his, great happiness. And nothing must ever happen to mar the bigger joys they were yet to share together, Sally and he.

CHAPTER ELEVEN

FOR three weeks Ieuan and Sally did not meet. He thought of her constantly. The uncertainty drove him into a state of abysmal gloom, and he began to imagine the worst. His studies and his promises were forgotten.

He became listless and dispirited, and the complete indifference he showed towards his work at the coreshop made Abraham fume with indignation.

The charge-hand approached him one afternoon.

"You've been here for two years, now — two years this month," he said, disgruntled. "I've been talking to Lu about you, and he's arranging for you to go out with the improvers next week."

Ieuan's heart sank.

"I wouldn't like to be transferred to the steel shop," he said. "Listen, Abraham — couldn't you let me stay here? Isn't there any way you could persuade Lu to change his mind?"

"It isn't a question whether you like it or not," Abraham returned with a frown. "If Lu says it's time you had a move — well, that's that. Don't ask me to try and make him change his mind. It's out of my hands. Besides, I don't feel like talking to him just now, not with Lu in the mood he's in. He's like a bear with a sore head, these days."

Ieuan made another appeal. He turned to Thomas for support.

"It's no good you looking to Thomas," said Abraham. "He can't help you."

"But he's been here before me. Why should I be sent out first? I don't understand."

"There's no need to understand anything," Abraham remarked drily. "I'm in charge of this place, and I'll give orders here. Thomas stays in the coreshop. I want him. I made that agreement with Lu last year. Thomas is experienced — more experienced than you are for this class of work, and one of you's got to go. There's a new boy starting here next month." He sighed. "God help me."

Disconsolate, Ieuan went in search of Frank to ask his advice. He was the only person he could think of who might be able to help and try to persuade Abraham to alter his decision. Abraham had no right to send him to work in the steel shop. Not while there was another and older apprentice in the coreshop. Neither did the foreman have the power to make this arrangement. It was a violation of a trade union ruling on the question of seniority right.

But was the matter worthy of discussion? Let them send him to the steel shop if they liked. He would not be destined to remain there for long.

He smiled bitterly. What a thought! Had he done anything to facilitate his leaving? He was to become a writer. It was funny! Too funny for words!

Where was his ambition, now? Everything had gone wrong. Since Sally's illness his whole world had tumbled around him. He felt no inclination to do the slightest task in the foundry, and he knew that at home he would find no solace in his moods.

When Frank was told of Abraham's decision, he shook his head.

"Nothing we can do about it, Ieuan," he said. "There's nothing unconstitutional in Lu wanting to take you out of the coreshop. You've been there two years. But why worry over that? It's a small matter, considering that you hope to be out of the foundry completely before very long. That is, if you're still interested that way?" he hinted.

"Oh yes, Frank," Ieuan assured. "I'll be out of this place soon. I'm determined."

"Good! Then you're back with your learning again?"

Ieuan hesitated. "Well, not exactly, Frank, but I mean to. Just let this month pass and then I'll set about it in earnest."

"You'd better," Frank advised, "because once you're out here good and proper you'll get into the same rut we all find ourselves in. You won't have the time nor the will to do anything much after your 'day's work's done. You'll just sit around waiting for tomorrow—counting the days until Saturday comes along. I know it, Ieuan, I've been through the same thing myself. Be wise to yourself, boy. Don't be a fool to keep on postponing all the time. You've set yourself an ambition — well, go on, do something about it. You can't expect to sit back and wait for things to fall nice and quietly into your lap. If I were you, I'd ...."

He stopped. "O.K., that's all for now, Ieuan. Lu's got his eye on us. I'm behind on the job, so I'd better get cracking."

They looked down the foundry. The foreman stood on a wooden plank bridging the deep castings pit. He motioned Ieuan curtly back to the coreshop.

"You two holding a council meeting?" he shouted.

Frank grinned.

"Don't let the old world and its troubles get you down, Lu. I'll make up for lost time," he called cheerfully.

Then to Ieuan, he said: "I've got a spindle to close ready for the afternoon's cast. Pop down and see me if you have a chance, and we'll continue where we left off, eh?"

Ieuan nodded. "I'll be there, Frank."

* * *

Half an hour later, when the furnace was almost ready to be tapped, Ieuan returned to the steel shop. Lu, his arms folded, still stood on the plank covering the pit.

He peered at the men from under the peak of his cap as they bustled around in the casting bay getting the moulds ready.

"Get a move on!" he rasped. "It's up-ladle at three. You've got ten minutes left. Hey, you — Dick Rees!" he called. "Don't stand there like an ornament. Give Frank a hand with that spindle." He pointed to a mould, its top and bottom halves contained in two steel boxes approximately seven feet long by three wide and three deep.

"Make sure the joints match," he muttered. "We've had a hell of a lot of complaints from the main office, and I don't want any more. The castings have been a damned disgrace lately."

Ieuan leaned against a water bosh, out of the foreman's sight. Lu certainly was in a bad mood, he thought. He hesitated whether to see Frank or not. Perhaps it would be wiser to wait until five o'clock, then he could meet him on the way out and have a talk.

He watched the men as they worked. A long line of moulds had been assembled ready for the day's cast. The moulders and their helpers worked rapidly, testing the heavy steel cramps that secured the top and bottom halves of the mould boxes. They cursed and muttered under their breaths as Lu repeatedly kept warning them that the furnace was waiting.

Frank and his partner finished their work on the spindle. The top half of the mould had been lowered, the joints sealed with soft, yellow loam, and the flanges secured by a row of steel cramps wedged with triangular pieces of scrap iron.

The spindle was then raised to an upright position and placed on a bed of dry sand. Two piles of boxes placed on each side supported a wooden plank for the teemer to stand upon.

"Up-ladle!"

The loud cry echoed through the foundry. The big crane rumbled along the girders. The control levers clicked. Brakes groaned. Slowly, the ladle was raised to the mouth of the furnace trough.

Ieuan drew Frank's attention and prepared to go forward to meet him.

"See you later," Frank called softly. He jerked his head in the direction of the foreman who stood a few paces away. "Stay where you are. I'll come over as soon as we've cast."

A team of furnacemen appeared on the landing. The furnace was tapped. A river of white hot metal raced madly down the clay-lined trough.

Ieuan stepped back and shielded his eyes. He felt his cheeks burning with the fierce heat. The first burst of liquid steel plunged into the ladle with a loud, ominous thud that shook the girders. A white sheet of flame shot into the air and flashed out over the ladle rim. An umbrella of dancing sparks twinkled and showered to the floor, spitting viciously as they fell upon the row of cold steel boxes ranged along the casting bay.

The ladle filled almost to the brim. Tiny red and blue flames darted from the air-holes in the riveted sides, hungrily licking the soot-covered plates. Around the lip a circle of yellow-tipped tongues curled and weaved.

Ieuan looked on, fascinated. A new world had suddenly been revealed; a fairyland of coloured lights, of shooting stars and flickering shadows. The men waited in the casting bay. Taking advantage of the short lull, they sat on their haunches or leaned against the moulds. Their green faces were tinged momentarily with a ruddy glow, then kissed by the shadows that danced across the foundry.

"O.K., take her away!" Lu hurried into the casting bay. "Over to the spindle first!" he shouted to the craneman.

The teemer, an elderly, grey-haired man scrambled up the pile of boxes facing the spindle. He sank to his knees on the wooden staging and reached for the nozzle lever.

"Swing her over an inch to furnace, Dai!" Lu shouted to the craneman.

The girders trembled.

"That's got it! Let her go!"

The teemer pulled downwards. The white-hot steel rushed in a circular stream from beneath the ladle and dropped into the spindle with an angry, muffled roar. Slowly the gurgling, boiling metal rose to the rim of the mould.

Frank climbed up over the boxes. As the ladle swayed along to the next mould, he tilted a bucket of powdered blacking on to the bubbling steel and prodded the thick crust with a long iron rod.

He looked across to the water bosh. Ieuan saw him raise a hand in acknowledgment, and returned his cheery grin. Then Frank climbed down to lend a hand to the other moulders in the bay.

The men jumped quickly to their work, following the ladle as it traversed the row of moulds, checking a run-out from a faulty joint, throwing shovelfuls of dry sand over the open necks as the moulds filled. Lu had returned to his vantage point on the pit from where he issued his orders to the cranemen and the teemer, his voice sounding high above the din.

The air was filled with clouds of dust and the tang of sulphur fumes. Dust seeped into the men's nostrils, their hair, and ears. It settled on their caps and jackets, clung to their perspiring faces, and made them appear as if they had been dipped in a fine, grey powder.

Then the clamour ceased as suddenly as it had begun. The cast was over and the empty ladle was swung back to its bed beneath the furnace landing.

Shoulders drooped, head bowed, the perspiring teemer shuffled to the water bosh. Ieuan stood aside and watched him as he thrust the soles of his wooden clogs into the water to cool.

The teemer glanced sideways at him.

"Nice work, isn't it?" He dipped his arms elbow-deep into the bosh. "By Christ! A pint'd go down well now." Ieuan gave him a forced smile, not knowing what to say. The teemer walked back towards the empty ladle. All at once he wheeled sharply around, his eyes wild with fear. He rushed to the bosh and grasped Ieuan's shoulder. "Look, boy, the spindle. It's—its running out! Call the men, quickly! Frank's down there — trapped like a bloody rabbit."

A wild, piercing scream cleaved the air. A moulder ran out from the casting bay.

"Help! For God's sake, help!" he shouted frantically. "Give us a hand, quick. The spindle's burst!"

The moulders left their jobs and came rushing down the shop. Ieuan did not wait for them. Pushing the agitated teemer aside, he raced over the pit.

He stumbled into the casting bay. Suddenly, he stopped.

Before him, his eyes dilated with terror, stood Frank on one foot, precariously balanced on a single brick near the centre of a rapidly filling pool of white-hot metal. Momentarily the foot slipped from the brick, and he screamed:

"Doris! Doris! Oh, Jesus Christ! Christ! Christ! Doris! Doris!"

Frank's agonizing cries shrieked above the thunder of the cranes as they jerked to a standstill on the quivering girders.

A pungent smell of roasted flesh hung in the sulphur-laden air. The yellow flames bit into his hands and face.

Paralysed with fear and pain, he shrieked continuously, loudly and terrifyingly.

"Do something, one of you!" Lu yelled to the horrorstricken moulders in the bay. He caught one by the arm. "Phone the doctor! Hurry, for God's sake!"

Without further hesitation he threw a board over the space, tore off his jacket and darted forward. Throwing it around the tortured Frank's body, he grasped him in his arms and dragged him to safety.

Gently he laid him on the ground. The crowd of men, whispering and gesticulating, closed in around the prostrate figure.

"Give him air!" Lu snapped fiercely. He threw out his arms and braced his shoulders against the crowd. He glanced apprehensively around. "Where's Dick? Has the doctor come?"

"Make way there!" someone shouted authoritatively. Pritchard, the timekeeper, followed by two others carrying a stretcher pushed his way to the front.

From a small box he took out a bottle of greenish liquid, pads of cotton-wool and rolls of bandage. He called the stretcher bearers to his side.

"Easy now."

One of the men placed his hands under Frank's legs. A charred boot crumbled at his touch, pieces of brown, roasted flesh adhering to it. The man retched. His face turned a sickly green.

His hands slipped down Frank's trousers and came in contact with the raw, shining heel bone.

Frank whimpered with pain. His fingers clawed wildly at Lu's shoulders. The skin of his closed eyelids was blistered, the eyelids singed. His face, a dirty yellow, drawn and haggard, glistened with cold sweat. Now and again he shivered convulsively.

Lu tenderly raised him to a sitting position.

"Frank, Frankie," he choked. "Jesus, God, why did I send you on that, that job." He looked into the timekeeper's face.

"It's too late," he sobbed. "Nothing can be done."

Frank stared at him vacantly. His fingers and lips moved. He coughed weakly.

"A fag," he whispered. "A — fag."

A cigarette was placed between his lips; it fell from his mouth and rolled to the ground.

Lu pillowed Frank's head on his knees and stared wildeyed at the gaping crowd.

"He's dead! Dead."

Ieuan moved in with the crowd. His face blanched. He swayed on his feet and grasped a box for support. The scene swam before his eyes. He felt as though he were going to collapse. His heart seemed to stop beating. A violent retching seized him. He closed his eyes.

Someone gripped him by the shoulders.

"Steady on, son."

He opened his eyes. The crowd dispersed slowly. They stood in groups under the furnace landing, their eyes intent on the prostrate figure lying in the dust.

Then the doctor came.

* * *

There was no more work done that afternoon. A grim silence fell across the foundry. The men spoke in whispers. The heavy cranes were deserted, and there was no relief from the tension until the hooter blew.

260

Ieuan waited until the coreshop emptied. Heartbroken, he made his way down the silent yard.

Frank was dead. Dead. His friend was dead. Vainly he tried to accept the truth of the tragedy. But the accident and its consequences were too horrible to visualize.

It had been a dream, a nightmare. It was impossible to conceive that Frank was dead. Gone. Blotted out from existence as suddenly as the fusing of a light.

Yet it was true. He would never see him again. Never. His voice was silenced, even as the limbs that once pulsated with life and vigour were stiffened and cold.

The cheery grin he would see no more. The friendly words would never again be spoken. Death had come. Final and irrevocable. The foundry had killed him. Taken him in the prime of his young manhood. The Frank he had known was no more.

The streets were deserted as he walked wearily homewards, and the only sound he heard was the dragging of his heavy boots along the pavement.

Frank's terrifying screams shrilled in his ears. Try as he would to rid himself of them, their echoes still persisted. He lived over and over again the catastrophic moment of that afternoon, and the present seemed an eternity of agony.

Blindly he walked on, his mind obsessed by the tragedy. At the corner of the street where he lived a figure waited, vague in the dim light that shone down from the lamppost.

He drew near. The figure turned.

"Ieuan!"

"Sally — it's you !" He looked at her, distraught. "You're ill, Sally. Why — why are you out?"

"Oh, Ieuan, I heard the awful news, and I—I just had to come and see you."

"But you shouldn't be out. Please, please go back."

"I'm better now, Ieuan — truly I am. Much better, and I felt I must see you."

He grasped her hand tightly.

261

"That was lovely of you, Sally, but you shouldn't ...."

Suddenly a wild paroxysm of grief seized him. He began to sob unrestrainedly.

"Please, please, Ieuan." Her voice was eloquent with pity. Her eyes filled with tears. "I—I'm so sorry, Ieuan. So sorry for him. It was horrible, horrible."

Ieuan looked into her face.

"He was a fine man, Sally," he choked. "He was the only pal I had."

He brushed away his tears, roughly. His eyes glinted with anger. "The foundry did it, Sally — the foundry killed him. I saw it happen — he had no chance. I hate it, hate it."

"Yes, Ieuan, the foundry did it, I know. Everybody knows," she answered low. "That's why I came to see you tonight. You must get away from it now, Ieuan. You must. Ever since it happened I've been thinking about you, and they were terrible thoughts. Oh, promise me you will, Ieuan. Promise me."

A woman passed by. She paused and glanced at them as if in search of someone, then hurried on. A cold wind blew up the deserted street. The rain began to fall.

Ieuan drew her into a doorway.

"I promise," he whispered. "Honest. But, Sally" — he placed a hand under her chin and raised her face — "please go home now. Please. It's been wonderful to see you, and you'll never know how glad I am that you came."

She smiled wistfully.

"I am better, Ieuan," she emphasized. "Really I am.

"I—I'll see you Saturday night, shall I?"

"No, no, you mustn't, Sally."

"But I'm better, Ieuan," she insisted softly. "That's why I came out tonight."

"You — you're just telling me that to make me think you are well again."

"No, Ieuan. I've told you the truth. I've been out of bed three days now. I will see you Saturday night?"

262

He stood a while before giving his answer.

"Please, Ieuan."

"All right, then. I'll meet you, Sally. But if you're not fit you mustn't come out."

"No," she said. "If I feel ill I shan't come." She kissed him lightly on the cheek. "At the park, Ieuan. I'll meet you there at six. And please, please, don't worry about well, you know."

* * *

There was an awkward silence in the house that evening when he entered. His mother and father sat at the table. A place had been prepared for him. But he wanted nothing. He felt no hunger. A deep, aching pain gripped him in the pit of his stomach.

His father looked up.

"You had bad news at the foundry, Ieuan. I'm sorry."

"Yes, it was a shock, indeed," said his mother. "Terrible accident. The poor chap didn't have a chance, so I was told. Burned to a cinder, and they say he was screaming something awful, Dick."

"He was your friend, Ieuan," the father said gravely. "I just can't say how bad I feel about it all."

Ieuan sat down. He rested his head on his arms.

"The foundry killed him, Dad. I—I just can't stick it any more."

His mother's lips pursed. "Come now, Ieuan — don't talk like that, boy. I'm sorry for the poor chap — very sorry. But you must remember that's how life is. No one knows what's in front of him, and we must thank God for such a mercy. You shouldn't let yourself get upset like this, Ieuan. You'll only make yourself ill."

"I saw him, Mam. I saw him lying there on the ground. He called on Christ and—"

"Of course, of course. The poor fellow must ha' suffered agonies. But you must pull yourself together, stop worrying about the foundry. It's an awful thing to say, but what is to be, will be.

263

Leave yourself go to pieces, Ieuan, and where will it get you? Life is short enough, and you can't afford to be making yourself ill like this. Go and have a wash, now. You'll feel better then, and after you've had something to eat."

She filled a pan with hot water from the kettle and got a towel ready for him.

"Today the poor fellow died," she said, half to herself. "That means his funeral will be on Friday afternoon. You'll have to have a new hat, Ieuan — a bowler. It's a bit of an expense, but I think I'll be able to manage somehow.

Ieuan stared fixedly in front of him.

"Don't worry, Mam. Frank wouldn't mind if I wore a hat or not," he said bitterly.

"That's nice talk, isn't it?" she flared. "No respect for the dead, and the poor chap not even in his grave. I said I'd buy you a hat. I have to think of expense. Things like that come naturally to my mind, me being a mother with all the responsibilities for to look after. You mustn't be so touchy, Ieuan. After all, it isn't my fault the accident happened."

"Millie, for God's sake stop it!" her husband shouted. "Can't you see the boy needs sympathy? Don't you know what he's been through? I'm shocked at you. Hats, hats — what have hats to do with it?"

"Plenty," she snapped, "and don't you go interfering, Dick Morgan. I come from a respectable family and I've brought my children up decent. Would you like the boy to be seen in a funeral without a hat on his head? P'raps you wouldn't mind if he didn't wear his black suit and went to the funeral in a pair of grey trousers like that old ruffian, Mostyn Probert, always does. Grey trousers in a funeral — no wonder people do talk about him. If a man can't give proper respect to the dead, then how can he expect people who are alive to show respect to him? All this fuss now again — just because I mentioned buying a hat. Things like that have got to be mentioned when someone dies. And I—"

"Yes, yes, Millie, but another time, girl. Not now," the father interrupted. "I'm sorry I lost my temper."

He relapsed into a silence which only goaded her to nag him further. And Ieuan sat in the kitchen, past caring. Hearing nothing, seeing nothing, thinking only of Frank and the tragic events that had fallen so swiftly on that bleak November afternoon.

Gone was a prince among men.

* * *

To Ieuan the sense of loss he sustained by Frank's death was more acute on the Saturday after the funeral than at any other time since the accident. The lowering of the coffin into the grave was the final and complete severance with life.

"From ashes to ashes, dust to dust..."

He recalled the funeral. The slow, winding procession up the hill. Frank's coffin swaying on its last journey. His wife, grief-stricken, wide-eyed and pale in her distress. And from the hill he had looked away from the open grave. Anywhere. Across the wide, lonely bay where white-crested. waves raced eagerly, proudly to the shore. To the town below, sprawled beneath a canopy of whirling smoke from the tall chimneys of the steel works.

Then his eyes had been drawn back again to the grave.

The little band of mourners watched the coffin as it slowly disappeared into the sodden earth, pathetic in their grief. The minister's white surplice fluttered around his waist.

"Man that is born of a woman is of few days, and full of trouble. He cometh forth like a flower, and is cut down; he fleeth also as a shadow, and continueth not. And dost thou open thine eyes upon such a one, and bringest me into judgment with thee?

" ... His sons come to honour, and he knoweth it not; and they are brought low, but he perceiveth it not of them. But his flesh upon him hath pain, and his soul within him mourneth."

Every corner of the foundry now held a memory, and it weighed upon his mind, dragging him down relentlessly into the same bitter moods of frustration, anger and intolerance.

The work resumed its normal course, and in the foundry Frank was forgotten. The funeral was over. The body lay in the dark womb of earth from which it had sprung. Frank had lived. He had breathed, loved, hated. He had known joy and happiness, and he had tasted pain and sorrow. Now he was gone. The mourning had ceased. No more tears were shed, for there was work to be done and bellies to feed.

The present alone mattered. Frank had worked in the foundry. They had known him only for the hours he had spent there with them. There were no strong personal ties, and therefore the tragedy had affected them only at the moment of its occurrence. There was no grief, no deep personal grief felt now that Frank had been buried.

Bull and the improvers were concerned with the coming of the new apprentice. Here was further opportunity for them to practise their various jokes, another outlet for their sadistic inhibitions.

Ieuan's hatred and contempt for them had become an obsession, but they still kept aloof from him, deliberate and malicious in their cunning as they sought by this measure to ostracize him from all who worked in the foundry.

He was happy only when he thought of Sally and their future together. She was the only one he had left, now. The only one who would give him comfort, who would stand by him.

Tonight he would tell her of his plans; of his determination to make the next year his final year at the foundry, come what may. Nothing would prevent him reaching his goal. Nothing.

* * *

He stood outside the park gate. The night was cold. A sharp wind blew fitfully along the darkened street. The trees in the park stirred, and bare branches creaked. People hurried by on the pavement, muffled in heavy clothing.

Ieuan waited. The Town Hall clock struck six, and Sally had not come. Fifteen minutes passed. A half-hour. And still Ieuan waited.

Fear began to assail him. She was ill again! Why had she disregarded the doctor's orders and come out to meet him on the night of Frank's death? If only she had listened!

She said she was better, and he had believed her. But tonight — where was she? What had happened to her?

He saw a young girl approach in the darkness on the other side of the road. He hurried forward eagerly.

"Sally!"

The girl drew up under the light.

"I beg your pardon?"

"I—I'm sorry," Ieuan flustered. "My mistake."

She tossed her head. "Masher!" Then walked on.

A quarter to seven, and Sally was not there. Nor was there any sign of her coming. She must be ill. How could he find out? What could he do?

Anxiety drove him to pace slowly up and down the road, and his mind was torn with indecision. Should he call at her home and inquire? Should he wait another five minutes? Perhaps she had been delayed somewhere? Her mother was ill?

But she would have let him know, somehow? Should he go to her home? If he left the gate, she might come, and they'd miss each other. And what if he called at the house and she was not there?

Finally, he made his decision. He would call at the house.

"Is—is Sally in?" he asked nervously.

The man who had opened the door to him nodded.

"Just a minute," he said. He walked down the passageway.

The kitchen door opened. Ieuan saw him speak to a woman. She came to the door where he stood waiting, a tall, frail woman with a lined face.

"You have come to see Sally?" Her voice was low and strained. "Come in. Jim shouldn't have left you out therein the cold."

An oil lamp hung from the ceiling in the passageway and shone down on a narrow, rickety stairway.

"She's in bed," said the woman. She looked at him, a wan smile on her face. "You are Ieuan?"

He nodded.

"Sally has told me a lot about you," she said. "She's very fond of you, poor little thing. Would you like to see her?"

"Yes, Mrs. Marvin."

He followed her up the narrow stairs. His heart beat violently. A heaviness pervaded his whole being and, try as he would, he failed to rid himself of it. It seemed to cling within him, gripping his heart and body with sharp fingers which searched through every part of him.

The mother showed him into a small bedroom. A lamp burned on a table at the bedside.

"I'll leave you here for a while." She stepped across to the bed and drew up a chair for him.

Sally lay back on the pillows. Her pale face turned to the light. Her eyes smiled at him.

"Ieuan, I'm sorry about tonight," she whispered. "I would have come, but I just—"

"That's all right, Sally." He patted her hand resting on the coverlet. "I guessed you were ill, that's why I came."

"I tried to get someone to let you know, Ieuan. But there was no one. I'm so glad you've come."

He forced a smile to his lips. "Now, Sally, you mustn't worry. That's what you always tell me." He drew his chair closer.

"What happened, Sally? That night when you waited for me — you caught a chill?"

She turned her head away from him.

"No, it's — it's worse than that, Ieuan," he heard her say, and her voice seemed as though it came from far away. "I've got T.B. Doctor says I've got to go away. How long, I don't know — six months, perhaps."

His heart pounded. There was a tightness in his throat. "No, Sally, don't say that," he pleaded. "There may be some mistake. They — they're not always right."

His words, his manner were unconvincing, and he knew it. And yet, the doctor could be wrong! It was a hope, and he clung to it, refusing to accept the fact that she was seriously ill. Did he not diagnose "chronic bronchitis?" Why had he changed his opinion so soon? If Sally was tubercular, surely he would have discovered so when he examined her? Or he would have sent her to the Tuberculosis Clinic?

"Sally, how did the doctor come to think that?" he asked hesitantly. "He may be wrong, you know."

"No, Ieuan, there's no mistake. I've got T.B."

"You mustn't think of it, Sally."

"Last night, Ieuan...." Her voice was muffled. She began to cough.

"Sally, please don't say anything." He reached for a glass of water on the small table. "You must rest. You'll get better, and you'll be out of bed again before you know where you are. And we'll go for a picnic again. Remember the picnic, Sally — that day in the woods? It was lovely. We'll go lots of places together, you and me. You must get well soon."

"I shall get well, Ieuan." She took the glass from his hand. "But it will be a long, long time. Last night," she paused, "I had a haemorrhage. It — it was terrible. I thought I was dying ... and then the doctor came. It's no use pretending, Ieuan, I'm very ill this time. But I shall get better, I promise you. It will be a long time, and I shan't see you again — I'm going away. But I'll come back, and then we'll have our picnics again, Ieuan. It will be summer time. We'll go lots of places together, as you say. Oh, we'll have a happy time, Ieuan, to make up for all this."

"Where — where are they taking you, Sally?" His lips quivered. His eyes were misty with tears.

"To Calon y Nos. Tomorrow morning the ambulance will be here. Oh, Ieuan!" She buried her face in the pillows. Her shoulders shook with her sobbing.

He leaned over the bed and grasped her gently.

"Please, Sally ...." He kissed her forehead. "Please ...."

But words failed him. He walked to the door. "I—I'll come and see you … soon," he promised. "At Calon y Nos."

Downstairs, Mrs. Marvin waited for him.

"She's very ill, my boy."

"Yes, I know. But I never thought it was so serious."

"It is serious," she said. "Tomorrow they are taking her away, taking my baby away from me. The doctor told me that she'll be there, at Calon y Nos, for a long time. "

"How — how long, Mrs. Marvin?"

Her thin shoulders drooped. She held out her hands.

"Two years … three years. Who knows?"

"Two years!" Ieuan gripped the banister rail. "Surely there's — there's a mistake?"

"She had a haemorrhage last night. It was awful, awful. I—I thought my darling was going to die."

Two years! There was a drumming in his ears, a numbness in his brain. He felt sick. His vision swayed.

"I—I'll call again," he managed to blurt. "Good night, Mrs. Marvin."

Outside, he leaned against the wall. His knees weakened beneath him. His heart palpitated wildly. He felt he was going to collapse, to die. A string had been drawn tight across his temples. The tension was unbearable. He pressed his fists against his forehead. He wanted to scream.

Sally was going away. Away. Two years … three years. Perhaps a lifetime. He might never see her again. It was impossible! It couldn't be true. There was some mistake. There must be a mistake. But the doctor had been called … the haemorrhage … tomorrow, Calon y Nos … and she would be gone.

Sally! Scenes flashed through his mind, each bringing a spasm of pain that clutched his heart as if in a vice. The tears burned on his cheeks. In his throat there was a hardness that he could not swallow.

Sally! He saw himself at the fairground.

"May I see you home?"

He remembered her smile, her nervous little laugh.

"I—I don't know, really."

Then the first walk in the park. The silence in the darkness of Lovers' Lane where he had held her in his arms.

"I love you, Ieuan."

Her words brought a fresh spasm of pain to his heart.

The love and happiness they had known — What of it now? What was there left to live for? Nothing — nothing!

The only two who had given him joy had been taken away from him. Frank to his grave on the lonely hill, Sally to the grey, forbidding sanatorium whose very name made people shudder with fear.

He walked aimlessly home along the dimly lighted streets, his mind overwhelmed with the tragedy. At the corner of the lane a neighbour hailed him, but he gave no answer. The back-lane door dragged open on its hinges. He stumbled up the stone-flagged garden path, overwrought, and anxious only to reach the privacy of his bedroom.

As he drew near the kitchen he heard his father and mother quarrelling. He stopped, his body rigid with apprehension.

"It's that girl, Dick. Spending far too much of his time he is with her. He's out with her tonight again. As sure as my name's Millie Morgan, he'll be having her in trouble one of these days."

His mother's voice shrilled in his ears. He clenched his teeth. God! would it never end, this ceaseless nagging?

"When I spoke to him about her, what did he say? You know, Dick-you-know what he said. I'll never forget that day, not as long as I live."

"Yes, yes, I know what he said, Millie." The father's voice replied impatiently. "I've heard all that before. The girl is a decent sort, Millie, or Ieuan wouldn't go with her. After all, he's getting to be a young man now. You take things too seriously, Millie, worrying yourself over a slip of a girl. Who knows that Ieuan won't forget her? She's the first girl he's ever met, and I don't suppose anything will ever come of it. He'll meet plenty more before he's through."

"Forget her?"

"Well yes, Millie. You know how young fellows are — first girl they meet and they think there's no one else in the world for them. Romantic ideas, books, the cinemas — look what they do to young people."

"He'd better forget her," came the sharp rejoinder. "And the sooner the better. She can't be up to much, as I've said before. Crooked Row, that's enough for me! A lot of poverty-stricken people. What goodness can come out of such a slum, tell me?"

Ieuan turned. He could stand it no longer. With fist jammed against his mouth, he raced down the path and out into the lane.

He heard the kitchen door open. His father called urgently:

"Ieuan! Ieuan!"

But he did not stop. Consumed with fear, he ran blindly along the streets and the deserted lanes. Ran until exhaustion brought him panting for breath outside the school gates on the hill he had climbed so often as a child. He tested against the low stone wall. His temples throbbed. His hands and face were cold and clammy. A great weight seemed to press upon his scalp. Every nerve in his body ached. He felt he was losing his sanity.

With eyes closed, he leaned heavily against the wall. Slowly, his breath returned again to his aching lungs.

He looked vaguely around, not knowing where his feet had brought him. And then he saw the familiar outlines of the school buildings.

He stepped through the wooden gate, and then slowly up the worn steps.

A sense of loneliness, an indefinable loneliness overwhelmed him. He was once again in the land of memories.

The walls, the asphalt playground, the iron railings — all reminded him of those days so far away. The atmosphere breathed a sense of quietude. Ghost-like, the school reared before him.

He peered in through the windows. A small light burned, and in the far corner of the room a woman knelt scrubbing the floor.

There was a heavy silence, broken only by the faint sound of the cleaner at her work. But as he listened, he seemed to hear again the happy laughter, the shrill whisperings of those companions whom he once knew and loved in schooldays.

Nothing had changed in this world of memory. In front of the class, his heavy, cumbersome frame seated on the desk, was Jackson, the assistant headmaster. He could hear again his voice as he took him back along the faraway road; away from the world he then knew around him, to the glittering, sunbleached shores of Ballantyne's coral islands.

He felt the rock in his throat; his eyes were tear-brimmed as the voice chanted weirdly the tales that had stirred him so in his childhood. A feeling of nostalgia swept over him as the bitter-sweet memories of the past raced lightly, lovingly through his mind.

And in the distance, as if to add to the painful sweetness of it all, a gramophone played the soft, sorrowful music of Mascagni's Intermezzo.

The oaken desks, polished, mute, gleamed at him. Their surfaces were carved with many names: names of friends, enemies — friends and enemies when all was young within school walls, and all without was old. A world where armoured knights rode on white, plumed steeds, their flashing lances tilted at the foes of virtue.

* * *

Beyond the gate, fenced in by a broken railing, stood the old stone quarry. He walked towards it through the wet grass, his mind almost bereft of conscious reason. He stared down into the deep pit. A stone dislodged and hurtled to the bottom. The wind whistled through the grass. It drove against him, threatening to push him over the quarry brink into the engulfing space below.

Perhaps it would be simpler if he offered no resistance, he thought. Let the wind hurl him over on to the sharp rocks below, there to lie dead and bleeding.

273

What was there left in life? Frank and Sally had been taken from him. At home there was no love, no peace, no rest. There was no purpose in living. No hope in life. The past had given him happiness, a brief happiness he had known in childhood, and then had shared with two who were now gone from him. The future offered nothing — nothing but pain and grief.

Here in the quarry he would kill himself. Life was not worth living. Just one step, and then eternity. It was so simple. And yet...

In the far distance a railway engine puffed. A yellow trail of sparks spat from the funnel. The engine gathered speed and chugged into the nowhere of darkness. Beyond, the waves in the estuary roared shorewards. The sea moaned and tossed like an awakened conscience.

A furnace door in the steelworks on the bank of the estuary was raised. The glow cut a red hole in the night.

Ieuan watched it all, his mind assailed with conflict. He stared down into the black depths once more. He knew this spot of earth so well. Here in the deep quarry he had played with the eagerness and abandon of childhood.

It was a place of happy memories. Here he had galloped on the proud white stallion his imagination had given him, when he and his companions, in those carefree days of sunshine, were heroes all.

Sliding down "Hill 60" on toboggans of zinc sheets; climbing the rock face; fishing in the green pool; exploring the dark caves; singing, laughing, shouting with the zest that lived only in childhood.

Remembrances of yellow noons in yellow days of childhood when all was fair and lovely. The air shimmered and danced, and the little houses in the winding streets laughed to the sun. In those days, when he was but a tiny spot on the surface of his native earth, his heart leapt into his throat with the joy of living. He loved, then, the earth, the trees, the grass, the flowers, the sky, the sun, the rain and the wind, and every living bird and beast and man and woman that walked with him in the fair days of the summer world.

The world smiled around him in the sunlight and in the warm shadows. And in that smile he had basked, a child living and breathing the breath of innocence and love. Malice, greed, envy and bitterness were unborn to his soul, and all the living people were his friends as he laughed and danced on his journey through the untroubled days.

"Man that is born of a woman is of few days, and full of trouble ...."

He moved closer to the edge. He felt the wet clay move under his feet.

"Do you expect things to fall into your lap? .... You must fight ... the stronger we fight, the firmer we become ...."

"Oh, Ieuan ... your studies .... Why have you daunted so soon ...? You've got brains, Ieuan.... You must get away from the foundry...."

He saw Frank and Sally. Their words crashed into his inner consciousness. Did they give up the struggle? Sally had cause to throw away her life. But did she ...?

"I'll get well again, Ieuan ... I know I will."

And Frank had fought for survival to the last second of his breathing; struggled to live in spite of his pain and agony.

With a cry of fear, he leapt back into safety. He heard the wet clay hurtle into the depths.

God! what had come over him? To throw away his life — was that the solution to his pain and sadness? He was young. Life was a precious gift. To end his own grief would bring only further grief to others. It was cruel, selfish.

He must face up to life, face up to its problems. He had talent given him, it was his duty to make use of it.

Sally ... Frank ....

Their images persisted. Their words hammered in his brain. He must live. To end life was cowardly. They would never forgive him — never.

And yet to die was hard. He was young, and life was precious. In that awful moment, the urge to live was strongest, for he had someone else to live for. Sally — she was his. She would always be his. He would wait for her. She would get well and strong again. He loved her, and to her he would give all that was his. On her he would shower the gifts of his hands and his brains. Give her everything that was in him. Everything that was possible to give. The song of the lark, the silver raindrop from an April shower, the gold from a butterfly's wing. All the beauty in the world he would reach for, and give to her.

A great weight seemed to have lifted from him. Suddenly he felt as though his limbs were imbued with new strength — a strength which gave him conviction that courage was the one virtue he must develop within himself. He must have courage. He must face up to life.

The foundry, grey and despairing, would always be so if he surrendered to it. But it had to be changed, and it would be changed. Everything changed — the sea, the land, the sky, the rain, the wind, the sun, the moon, and the stars. Life was always changing. And he, too, would change.

Let fears of Sally's illness consume him no longer. She would get well, and they would know happiness again. He must have faith and courage. He must.

Nor let the fear of the foundry plunge him again into sorrow and despair. Some day he would get away from it. He had the weapons in his own heart and brain. He would use them. He would study hard and diligently. No more the idle dreaming, the procrastinations. Then one day he would be free. Free from the foundry. Free to write of it as he would want to write. To show the world how the men there lived and worked. Write of their hopes, their sufferings; but, above all, reveal the true spirit of men like Frank. Men of strong faith and courage.

With this new resolution burning within him, he ran down the hill. No longer was he afraid. A new hope had been born to him. A new life had been given him.

276

Along the road he raced, riding the same proud white stallion of his childhood. His body felt suddenly freed of all ache and pain. His mind was eased of fear and sorrow. Not even the chill blast of the wailing November wind did he feel as he turned into the street where he lived and knocked loudly on the door.

John Bowen (1914–2006) was born and educated in Llanelli. On leaving school he won a scholarship to Llanelli School of Art and in 1939 was appointed art master at Llanelli Boy's Grammar School, where he stayed until his retirement from teaching in 1979. He served for five years in the R.A.F. during World War II. Although his work was very much rooted in his home town, he exhibited widely across Wales and later in his career began to paint extensively during his travels in southern Europe, particularly Spain. The artist and critic Mervyn Levy referred to John Bowen as a "master of design". He was deeply serious about painting but was happy to remain out of the limelight. Many examples of his work can be viewed at Parc Howard Museum and Art Gallery in Llanelli.

Huw Lawrence was born in Llanelli, and trained as a teacher in Swansea before resuming his education at Manchester and Cornell Universities. He is a three-time winner of prizes in the Rhys Davies Short Story Competition, a Bridport prize and a runner-up position in the 2009 Tom Gallon Trust Competition. His debut collection of short stories, *Always the Love of Someone*, was published in 2010. He lives in Aberystwyth.

LIBRARY of WALES

The Library of Wales is a Welsh Government project designed to ensure that all of the rich and extensive literature of Wales which has been written in English will now be made available to readers in and beyond Wales. Sustaining this wider literary heritage is understood by the Welsh Government to be a key component in creating and disseminating an ongoing sense of modern Welsh culture and history for the future Wales which is now emerging from contemporary society. Through these texts, until now unavailable or out-of-print or merely forgotten, the Library of Wales will bring back into play the voices and actions of the human experience that has made us, in all our complexity, a Welsh people.

The Library of Wales will include prose as well as poetry, essays as well as fiction, anthologies as well as memoirs, drama as well as journalism. It will complement the names and texts that are already in the public domain and seek to include the best of Welsh writing in English, as well as to showcase what has been unjustly neglected. No boundaries will limit the ambition of the Library of Wales to open up the borders that have denied some of our best writers a presence in a future Wales. The Library of Wales has been created with that Wales in mind: a young country not afraid to remember what it might yet become.

Dai Smith

LIBRARY of WALES
FUNDED BY

Noddir gan
Lywodraeth Cymru
Sponsored by
Welsh Government

CYNGOR LLYFRAU CYMRU
WELSH BOOKS COUNCIL

A CARNIVAL OF VOICES
WWW. PARTHIANBOOKS.COM

WWW.THELIBRARYOFWALES.COM